Judith reached for her. Both women knew just what they felt and what they wanted, and each had made love to the other in her mind. They held each other tightly, savoring the feel of it, and then their lips touched. It was a long, soft, tender kiss.

Judith ran her fingers slowly, sensually, along Drew's back then over the contours of her hips. "I'm tingling all over."

Rising to one elbow, Drew brought her head down slowly until she covered Judith's mouth with her own. Her tongue explored Judith's lips and the hot inner lining of her cheeks, and then she slid her tongue along Judith's neck and downward until she reached cloth. She undid the first button of the skimpy top, smiling into Judith's eyes as she did, then let her tongue go further down. She undid the second button and then the rest, spreading the fabric wide. . . .

## WORKS BY CAMARIN GRAE

# PAZ

## CAMARIN GRAE

## the NAIAD PRESS inc.

1986

Printed in the United States of America

First Naiad Press Edition 1986

PAZ was first published in 1984 by Blazon Books

ISBN 0-930044-89-4

## ACKNOWLEDGMENTS

My thanks to Kathe McCleave and Dan Eierdam for their editorial comments and to Marie for her flying typist fingers.

Two leaves, floating separately, gradually moved closer and closer together until they met and overlapped and remained wedded as the current carried them downstream and out of Drew's sight. "I wish they weren't coming," she said.

Judith, too, had been watching the leaves. "The guys, you mean?"

"Mm-hm."

The two women sat side by side on the hill by the river, their tanned bare legs almost touching. Drew spun a lavender wildflower slowly around in her fingers, handed it to Judith, then picked another.

"I can't say I've really missed Vic," Judith said, slipping the flower through the hair above her ear.

"David's going to insist on building all the fires." Drew laughed scornfully. "His boy scout training, you know. Only he can do it right." She tossed the flower into her motorcycle helmet. There were four flowers in the helmet now, two lavenders and two pinks. "We had great fires, didn't we, Judith?"

"The best," Judith said. Judith Brodie was the prettier of the two, with her creamy smooth skin, straight narrow nose and large deep brown eyes. Drew McAllister had larger, less refined features and was more muscular.

They were quiet a while, watching the river. Even when relaxed as she was now, there was a hint of tension about Drew, and sadness. "The time went too fast," she said. Her eyes met Judith's. "This has been a great vacation."

They looked warmly at each other for a long time, then Drew looked away. She was feeling something she could not precisely identify. Lying back on the grass, she cradled her head with her arm and took several deep breaths. "I can't remember when I've felt this good." She stretched out her other hand letting it brush against Judith's.

"I know what you mean, it's been a perfect week." Judith wrapped her arms around her knees feeling the breeze brush over the skin of her cheeks and neck. There was a touch of cold in the wind. Over the tree tops, clouds pushed across the sky. Judith's eyes followed them. "Storm's coming," she said.

Drew sat up again. "That was sure sudden."

The wind pulled a strand of sand-colored hair across Judith's face, dislodging the little flower which dropped to the ground and blew away.

"We better get back. Maybe we can beat the rain." Two rapid slits of lightning gashed the sky.

They sped along the county road on their red mopeds as the wind grew stronger. Several large drops of rain splatted on their helmets.

"I'll stop to check on the kids," Drew said.

In the play area of the campground, Becka Tremaine-McAllister climbed the metal stairs, oblivious to the drops of rain falling on her curly hair and thin arms and legs. She scooted down the slide with an eight year old's nonchalant confidence, then climbed again, Jenny at her heels.

"Becka!"

Becka waved. "Watch this, mom!" Hair flying, she plunged downward, swishing to a graceful landing.

"Into the lodge," Drew shouted from her bike. "You're going to get soaked. You, too, Jenny."

"Aw, it's not raining hard."

The sky, close to black, suddenly glowed eye-pinching bright with lightning, then dark again. Galvanized by the thunder that followed, the children ran, without a word or looking back, to the shelter of the lodge.

At their campsite, Drew helped Judith cover the logs with tarp and move the box of groceries, the canvas chairs, the lantern and other supplies into the van. The wind had stopped. No more rain fell. Judith picked up a towel that had blown off the picnic table and tossed it into the front seat. Stillness had settled over the campground.

It was two in the afternoon but as dark as night as the two women began the quarter mile walk from their campsite to the lodge. Drew, who was large-boned, quick-moving and lithe, had a long stride and walked several yards ahead of Judith, who, two inches shorter and smaller-framed, hurried to keep up. They appeared to be about the same age, though Drew, recently turned thirty, was three years older than her friend.

The jukebox in the lodge gameroom drowned out the radio warning of the tornado on its way. Becka shoved the air hockey puck to Jenny who missed and giggled. Blue-jeaned boys danced with blue-jeaned girls while plaid shirts hunched over pinging video games. Beer was being drunk, and several people, older ones, stared uneasily through the window at the blackness.

They were now half way to the lodge. At first Drew thought it was a jet she heard, flying low, much too low. Then it sounded more like a giant train, roaring madly through the field on the very path they walked. The sound grew louder and louder, beyond loud; it was pounding, deafening, overloading her ears, straining the tympanic membrane, and even vibrating her teeth.

The angry wind pushed back against their movements. Scraps of paper flew past them, followed by a cardboard carton. As they approached the washroom area, a garbage drum rolled thundering over the ground passing inches from Judith's legs. Large branches tore from trees and crashed on either side of the pair as they pushed their bodies forward, leaning against the force of the violent wind.

They could barely breathe, the air too rough to pull into their lungs. It tore at their clothes and stung their faces and arms and legs with little particles of debris. A flying chunk of wood caught Judith's shoulder spinning her off balance and to the ground. Drew, yelling soundlessly, pulled her to her feet and the two stumbled forward, bent double.

The lodge was less than fifty yards ahead, visible now through the flailing tree branches, but Drew never reached it.

It was a slim sliver of glass that stopped her, a needle fragment from a broken mirror, fired by the wind through space like a bullet. The mirror arrow pierced the thin skin of Drew's temple, penetrated the hard bone of her skull, and stopped at last, its point embedded in the vulnerable tissue of her brain. She dropped immediately. She did not know that a flying piece of car fender then

3

gashed her arm and cracked the bone beneath her limp biceps. She did not know that the tornado finally finished its destructive sweep and moved on, nor that an ambulance came and took her to the hospital where the splinter was removed from her brain and the broken arm set and the bleeding lacerations stitched and taped.

## 2.

The motel was on the edge of town, near the hospital. Judith rested her foot on the balcony rail and stared at traffic while David talked.

"Brain tissue damage," he said again. "That could mean anything, you know. Paralysis maybe, or blindness. Maybe she won't be able to talk, or..."

"There's no way of knowing," Judith interrupted. She detested his morbid speculations. Her own worry and dread were eating a hole in her stomach. "Not until she regains consciousness."

"*If* she regains consciousness." David's voice faded and they both remained silent. TV sounds drifted to the balcony from inside the motel room where Becka and Jenny, pajama clad, sat on pillow piles watching a sitcom.

"Where did Vic go?" David asked.

"For beer." Judith stared at the semi tailgating a VW bug. Her face was lined with worry and fatigue. For once, she looked her age.

David looked at his watch. "It's been almost forty-eight hours," he said. He began pacing across the balcony again, the frown unbecoming on his face. David Furmanek was a classically handsome man, though his features were undistinctive, almost too balanced and correct to be interesting. "If nothing happens before nine tonight, I'm going to have to head back to the city. I've got a lecture at eight in the morning. What about you? What are you going to do?"

"I'll stay," Judith said.

David sat again on the plastic chair, his elbows resting on his knees. "I still think we should have her moved to a decent hospital."

"David, why don't you go for a walk or something."

The two were silent for several minutes.

"Poor Drew," David said after a while. He shook his head. "Maybe she'd be better off if she doesn't come out of the coma." He went to the balcony railing and looked toward town. Through tear-blurred eyes, he could see one corner of the yellow-brick, five story hospital building.

Drew was on the second floor. She was alone in a silent room of tubes and bottles, monitors and whiteness, lying pale and motionless, except for her eyes which moved in darts. She had been conscious for five minutes and was thinking about life and death and trying to identify what felt so different. She had already assessed her injuries, was aware of the cast on her arm, the bandage on her head, and the achiness everywhere. She remembered there was a storm and assumed it had caused her injuries. What troubled her now and kept her mind occupied was that odd sense of shift she felt. Things looked strange somehow, the fabric on the drapes, her own hand, the frame around the doorway. But it was more than that. She *felt* different, inside, not in a way she could pinpoint, but strangely, undeniably different.

The door moved inward. "Well, hello." It was a smooth voice, like a caress. "How are you feeling?"

Drew nodded her head slowly. Her lips were dry and her voice cracked when she spoke. "I'm here, I guess."

"Yes," the nurse said warmly. "Welcome back." She checked the monitors. "Let me get the doctor."

"My daughter...?"

"She's fine, and the other little girl. Your friend, too. None of them were injured."

Drew McAllister had much time to think as she mended. The medics were pleased with her progress, maybe even amazed, although they would not say that. She passed all the tests; there were no neurological signs, no loss of function. She answered their questions and submitted to their x-rays and probings, gave up bodily fluids for their test tubes and waited while she healed. She thought about many things, about Judith, whose relief at Drew's recovery and whose caring was so clear, about her future, about Becka and David and about that fleeting feeling of disappointment she'd had when she realized she was alive.

Becka sounded happy on the phone and, yes, she was getting along with her daddy and his new family and missed her mom and couldn't wait until Saturday when Judith would bring her for a visit. David came and was sweet and loving and complained about the

5

traffic making the three hour drive from Chicago take nearly four. Wiley Cavenar visited on Wednesday. The two had a long talk in the sunroom, a good talk. Wiley's a rock, Drew thought. She had told her about the subtle shifts she felt and Wiley, who was a clinical psychologist as well as a good friend, talked about stress and depersonalization and reassured Drew.

Drew continued to heal. The aches were gone, the headaches were lessening, no longer did she jump at loud noises, the frightening dreams had stopped. She spent her convalescing time reading, watching TV, and visiting with other patients. Occasionally, she played a game of chess with Allen Lamont, a freckled, auburn-haired eighteen-year-old from Spring Green, Wisconsin. Allen was clearly troubled and depressed. Once in a while he would talk about it with Drew, but mostly he was closed deep within himself. Drew knew he'd had a car accident. He was driving with his girlfriend on the highway, tried to pass a car, but didn't make it in time. He and his girlfriend, Susan, were injured in the accident, as was the man in the other car, though all would recover. Allen had told Drew this. He also said he could not see his girlfriend anymore because he did not deserve to, and that he should have died. He would berate himself for his negligence, confessing repeatedly how his filthy mind had been more on Susan than his driving, then he'd grow silent. Mostly they'd play chess without speaking.

One afternoon as Drew and Allen were sitting quietly together looking out the window, Allen began to cry and express more feelings of hopelessness and self-contempt. "I should have died. I feel dead. I have no life..." His pain and some of his words reminded Drew of the futility of her own periods of depression. Unlike Allen, her dejection was never set off by a single event, but was more diffuse and global. The self-doubts and fears would take over sometimes and the vague dissatisfactions grow to consuming self-condemnation.

"Allen, listen to me!" she said impulsively. Her voice was firm. He turned to face her.

"You're not a bad person, for God's sake. What you did doesn't make you a villain. You made a mistake. You can learn from it, but you have to quit torturing yourself with this guilt."

Allen stared at Drew, not blinking. He did not try to speak, nor turn away. He appeared dazed as he listened to her words, though fully absorbed by what she said.

"Now let go of it," she ordered with finality. "You're OK, understand? Let go. You have a lot of living to do, kiddo."

Allen continued staring at her eyes, his own wide and glazed,

6

his jaw slack. Then he raised himself a few inches in his wheelchair, no longer slumping. For the first time since she'd met him, Drew saw Allen smile. He had a very nice smile, wide and bright.

"You know," he said. There was a spark of energy in his voice. "I...I don't know...I had this thought." He was still smiling. "I think I want to go be with Susan. She asks for me every day." His face glowed then. "She's my girlfriend. She's up on three. I'm going to go see her. Excuse me, will you, Drew, I'm going to go see my girlfriend. I'll catch you later."

Amazed by his sudden transformation, Drew watched Allen maneuver his chair around tables and out the doorway. Alfredo, an orderly, sauntered into the sunroom at that moment, interrupting Drew's thoughts. He waved to her, flashing a distracted smile, then went to the opposite corner of the room and sank loosely into a chair. Soon he was joined by a young woman and, though Drew preferred not to hear, their conversation was unavoidably audible.

"I don't care if he *is* a so-called friend of the family," she heard Alfredo say in a loud angry voice, "I said you're not going." There was a short pause. "So help me, Rose, if you try to sneak...if I find out you saw that bastard, I swear you'll end up on Orthopedics with a broken goddamn nose."

Drew felt her stomach turn.

"You are so jealous all the time, Alfredo." The woman's voice was creamy.

"Hey, babe, look, I love you, remember? You're my girl. You belong with me, all right? Come on, let's get outta here. I'll buy you some coffee."

Revulsion settled in a clump somewhere between Drew's stomach and her heart. It had been more subtle with Steve, she thought, his brand of sexist overlording, but just as toxic. Suddenly, she felt tremendously tired. She made her way along the shiny corridor to her room with the flowers from Wiley and the cards and the wonderful drawings Becka had made, one of a mean black sky looking down over a little girl in a tent. Drew pulled the sheet way up almost covering her face and was just beginning to slip into sleep when a voice pulled her back. Jennifer, the day shift nurse, spoke pleasantly as she wrapped the blood pressure cuff around Drew's right arm and began squeezing air into it. Drew was fully awake now and irritated.

"...only take a couple minutes."

She wanted to say something, express her annoyance, but could not bring herself to speak. Do it, chicken-shit. "Jennifer."

"Mm-hm."

"I was sleeping."

"Good," Jennifer said cheerfully. "You need to rest."

Drew liked Jennifer and was tempted to abandon this silly confrontation, but something made her persist. "You woke me."

"Oh, you can go back to sleep. I have to get the reading. It will just take a sec'." The young nurse positioned the stethoscope in her ears.

Drew waited until she finished. "I've got something I want to say to you," she said. "Come over here, will you?" It's probably not her fault. Maybe I should just forget it. It's not that important, anyway.

Jennifer moved to the side of Drew's bed. "Yes, what's on your mind?" She seemed clean and fresh and innocent.

Drew forced herself to look firm and serious. "You know," she began, "it's really not necessary to wake me up just to take my blood pressure." She paused for a reaction. Jennifer was looking at Drew attentively. Encouraged, Drew went on. "Or my temperature or to do any of those routine things. You know that's true."

Jennifer continued to look deeply into Drew's eyes, listening. She did not move. She seemed barely to be breathing.

"It's not always in the best interest of the patients to disturb them like this," Drew continued. She was feeling more courageous now. "Your routines need to be more flexible. It's more sensible to go by people's medical needs, not a rigid timetable." Drew was surprised at herself, almost amused at the fact that she was actually delivering this little lecture.

The nurse hadn't moved since Drew began her speech. She remained rigidly attentive for several seconds after Drew stopped talking, almost imperceptibly nodding her head, then she blinked her eyes and began to gather her equipment. "Sorry about the interruption," she said. "These rigid timetables for taking vitals don't make much sense."

Drew leaned back into the pillow. She was delighted that she'd made such an impact, and that she had not offended the nurse. "I'm glad you agree with my arguments," she said.

Jennifer looked puzzled. "What do you mean? What arguments?" She switched off the light.

"About flexibility," Drew responded.

"Hey, you're still half asleep, aren't you? Well, let the other half catch up. I'll leave you in peace now."

Drew slipped down between the sheets, but she did not feel at peace. Over and over, she reviewed each element of the inter-change, each time seeing especially vividly the look in Jennifer's eyes. It was a long time before she slept.

The next day, Judith came again, a surprise visit. She said she happened to be in the neighborhood and Drew laughed and felt grateful for the company, but more than that, she felt a wish to touch Judith, to hold her and... Instead they talked and laughed and made plans for Drew's return to Chicago which would be in three or four days if all went well.

On Thursday morning, Alfredo wheeled her rapidly down hallways making cracks about the shapely legs he saw and "nice pairs". Drew tried to tune him out. In the elevator, his eyes roved her body.

"When you get those bandages off, I bet you're not a bad-looking chick," he commented. His mouth curled into a suggestive smile. "I come into Chicago for weekends once in a while. We should get together sometime." He brushed the back of his hand along Drew's cheek.

The rage of innumerable similar scenes rose up Drew's spine and tightened in her chest. She wanted to tell him he was a pig. She wanted to spit on that presumptuous violating hand and smack the leering grin from his disgusting, ignorance-spewing mouth. She felt her heart beating fear at her audacious thoughts and outrage at his audacious behavior.

Impulsively grabbing his wrist, Drew held it firmly. "Listen, Alfredo, stop the macho shit, huh? It's a real pain." Her tone was surprisingly calm. The rage transformed to impatient annoyance as she held his eyes and he did not move. "Deep down in your chauvinistic heart, you know that the way you treat women is stupid." He stayed staring at her, his mouth hanging open, nodding his head just enough for Drew to feel urged on. "Women aren't things, you know, nor are we your inferiors. All that crap you believe about us is bullshit. Women are complete human beings, not objects. We are fully as competent as males. You can stop treating us the way you do, then maybe you'll deserve our company."

The elevator had stopped but Alfredo did not move to push the wheelchair. He stood, gazing intently at Drew, then rubbed his face and eyes. Still not saying a word, he gripped the handles of the chair and wheeled her silently along the corridor. At the X-ray Department, he sat between Drew and a gray-faced woman with a wracking cough. When he finally spoke, his voice had a decidedly different quality.

9

"Have you ever noticed," he began, "how most of the nurses around here are women and the doctors men?" The woman on the cart next to him emitted a protracted, productive cough.

"I've noticed," Drew said.

"That's dumb. It ain't right."

Drew nodded, her heart pounding again, but not with anger. What the hell is going on, she thought.

"It's not because of ability, you know. Women are just as...just as competent as...It's prejudice, that's what it is. It's a bunch of bullshit the way women are treated around here. I could tell you stories..." His voice faded. He shook his head. "They aren't getting a fair shake." His jaw was tight with indignation. "Guys are always pushing them around, making them feel like they're...It stinks! The whole damn setup stinks."

Drew's head buzzed. What she heard amazed and frightened her; but she had to hear more. She took a deep breath. "I'm surprised to hear that coming from you, Alfredo. For some reason, I had the impression you kind of like pushing women around."

"Hey, bullshit," Alfredo replied angrily. "I hate that kind of thing." He paused. "Well, actually I have been known to treat my women...to treat women...well, I used to think...God, I don't know..." He shook his head vigorously from side to side. "I got a lot of figuring to do about this whole...thing..." His voice trailed off and he remained silent.

Drew watched him, his brow furrowed, his mind obviously filled with serious, disturbing thoughts. And so was hers. How can this be? The X-ray technician came then and Drew was wheeled away.

Both Judith and Wiley came to the hospital to take Drew home. The bandages were off her head, the puncture wound at her left temple healing well, and her left arm was supported by a sling. Allen came to say goodbye. He was light-hearted and energetic as he'd been all week, since the day he'd decided to see Susan. He chattered about the university he'd be attending in the fall and the baseball games he'd soon be playing. He thanked Drew for the chess sessions, wished her well, and left with a vigorous handshake that turned into a warm hug.

Judith helped Drew gather the rest of her things and put them in the knapsack. In the hall, the nurse, Jennifer, was telling Wiley her feelings about the nursing profession and about hospital policy and procedures. Wiley always gets people talking, Drew thought.

"I feel real good about it," Jennifer was saying. "I always used to accept things like that even if I didn't agree with them. I thought you couldn't fight city hall, you know, but not any more." She stood

10

very straight and, though Wiley was four or five inches taller than she, looked her right in the eye. "Hospitals have to center more on patient needs, not just staff convenience. I'm serious about it, and I think I'm getting through to them. It's going to be discussed at the board meeting this month."

Judith forbade Drew to carry anything but the gift she had brought her, a small bouquet of lavender wildflowers. She held Drew's arm protectively as they walked toward the exit. Drew did not object.

As they waited for the elevator, Wiley noticed a large hand-printed sign on the bulletin board. "Rights of Female Hospital Employees," she read aloud. "All staff invited. How about that! Feminism in the boonies." She read some more. "On second thought, it may mean nothing. It's being organized by a man, Alfredo something."

Drew stared at the bulletin, smiling uneasily, feeling slightly dizzy. "It means something," she said softly.

---

## 3.

"I'll buy it!" Becka screeched, bouncing on her chair.

"You always get Boardwalk." Drew fake pouted and Becka laughed, counting out $450 in Monopoly money.

David had come last night, soon after Drew's arrival home, and insisted on taking them out to dinner. Drew would have preferred not to go. She wasn't sure why. It wasn't the injuries; she felt fine physically. He wanted to stop by again today but Drew had put him off. She and Becka had big plans for the day, both of them needing and wanting to be together, just them for a while. *I know he was hurt*, Drew thought, and considered calling him. She rolled the dice, landed on *Chance* and was ordered directly to jail. *No, I don't want to be with David now.* She and Becka had made cardboard geodesic ornaments and painted them in bright colors and baked a pile of chocolate chips which were still cooling on the plate. A whole day with her eight year old dynamite super kid was a treat, especially after the separation. Becka visited her mom in jail and

Drew rolled again landing on a railroad which she bought, of course.

No matter how she tried to keep them from her mind, thoughts of her conversations at the hospital kept returning. Allen, how had he gotten over his depression so suddenly? It doesn't work that way. Jennifer, fighting for changes in hospital policy, denying our conversation. Why? What does it mean? And Alfredo, that's the real miracle. She kept seeing their eyes.

"Your turn, mom. Are you daydreaming again?"

"What, me daydream?" Drew looked appalled. "I'm plotting strategy," she said, "trying to figure out how I'm going to make sure you don't get Park Place." She rolled the dice.

And last night, when she had gone for dinner with David and Becka, it had happened again. They were about to back into the parking space when a sneaky little sportscar shot into it. Big man David bounded over to the usurper and the two exchanged words. David handled it poorly, Drew thought, rudely, and the sportscar driver was smug and stubborn. "That's the breaks, man," he had said. David stormed back into the car, cursing, but Drew was not ready to give up. Despite her experiences to the contrary, she still believed that fairness and respect for others' rights were part of everyone and would ultimately triumph. Shy of confrontations, she had to dig for courage, but she went, over David's objections, and approached the man herself. He was locking his car to leave.

"You know we were waiting for this space," she began pleasantly. She felt acute discomfort.

The man, dressed in casual expensive clothes, looked at Drew in a detached way.

"Listen," she said, more firmly, "we both know this is a congested area, right?"

The man's cool, unbending look suddenly shifted to one of intense concentration, his eyes held by Drew's.

"The fair and appropriate thing for you to do is give us this space," she continued. "We were waiting for it before you came. It's rightfully ours."

The man was still staring unblinking into Drew's eyes when David approached and took Drew's arm to pull her away.

The man spoke then, directing his words to David. "I'll tell you what," he said. "I know just how you feel. Same thing's happened to me a dozen times. It's not fair, man. Yeah, I know how you feel." He unlocked his car and got back inside. "It's all yours, buddy," he said, starting the engine.

Why? Drew wondered, moving the tin thimble down the board

and landing on Connecticut Avenue. Why had he changed his mind? It wasn't simply that he saw the unfairness. There was something else. Why did he get that look when I was talking and then suddenly do exactly what I wanted? It's almost like I hypnotized him or something.

"I own it. Let's see, your owe me...." Becka looked at the card. "Six dollars."

"Six dollars. Big deal."

"It adds up."

Drew laughed and placed the Monopoly money onto her daughter's neatly stacked money piles. "Capitalist pig," she said.

"What's that mean?" Becka patted the wad of fives.

"It means you've got the right attitude for this game, sweetie pie."

Later in the afternoon, mother and daughter walked to the butcher's. Drew shopped there occasionally, hoping that the meat really was better, that maybe the chickens weren't injected with chemicals or the beef cancerous, or was it vice versa?

"Look at that filet mignon," she said to Becka. "Don't you think we deserve a good steak?"

"Mm, yeah. Let's get two big ones."

"All right, we won't even think about the price."

"Is it expensive?"

Drew laughed. She looked at the butcher. "Did you hear that?" She thought again about the parking incident of the night before and boldly decided to test her theory. "I'd like to talk with you about your prices," she said.

The butcher said nothing, looking impatient, perhaps bored.

"Your filet mignon is overpriced, you know. It's far too expensive."

She spoke calmly with a low voice.

The butcher's face changed as Drew spoke. He now gave her his full attention.

"You know you'd really like to sell me two of those steaks for half-price. Two of them, one for me and one for my hungry daughter."

Drew waited for the magic to take effect. Becka looked quizzically at her mother then walked along the counter, brushing her fingers across the glass. Drew waited, watching the butcher's eyes. Was it her imagination that they had the same glazed look she'd seen in the others? It frightened her. She was half hoping he'd tell her she was nuts. But he did not.

"Say, I've got an idea," he said instead, lifting up his glasses and rubbing his eyes. "I've got a special offer for you and your little girl there. You pick out the meat you want and I'll give you a fifty percent reduction on it."

Drew felt her heartrate jump. "That's very generous," she said, trying to sound light. "What got into you? Why would you want to do that?"

The man thought a moment. "An advertising program," he said. "Yes, every week ten customers get all their meat half-price. I'm just beginning to develop the idea. It'll be a raffle system." He withdrew two large filets from the case. "I still gotta work out the details. You're my trial customer. How do you like the idea?"

"Interesting," Drew said, barely audibly.

"Would you like anything else?"

"No, that's...that's quite enough." Her heart did not slow down. She felt excited and frightened as she paid for the meat, and also a little guilty.

## 4.

On Monday Drew went back to work. She was an administrative assistant at the University of Illinois-Chicago, a job she'd held for five years. The work was tolerable, mostly routine, occasionally challenging. The pay was moderate. Her arm cast would certainly be a hindrance, but unfortunately, Drew decided, not enough to justify staying home. The broken arm had gotten her some special treatment from Becka who was eager to help her poor handicapped mom, carrying things for her, opening doors, helping her put her socks on. That had lasted the first hour or so. Drew figured the same thing would happen in the office. Touching the spot above her left ear, she thought how fortunate she was that there were absolutely no effects from the brain puncture.

Drew's co-workers, solicitous and curious, welcomed her back. They had seen the TV footage of the tornado's work—the torn up campground, Winnebagos on their sides, tents strewn helter-skelter across the countryside. Drew told them of her experiences at the campground and in the hospital, but did not mention the odd results of her conversations with Allen or Jennifer or Alfredo at the hospital or with the sportscar driver or the butcher. Though she did not speak of these, she could not stop thinking of them. After the butcher, Drew had decided not to test it again, not yet, not until she spoke about it with someone, probably Wiley.

The next evening, she and Wiley sat in the dimly lit living room. A pleasant night breeze came through the window. Becka had just gone to bed after singing four or five TV commercials for Wiley who sang along on a couple of them. Sarah, the college student who'd been boarding with Drew and Becka for the past year, was in her room. The best cook in the house by far, Sarah had made them Chinese food that night, and after dinner, gone back to her books.

Drew had been waiting for this moment, for the opportunity to talk with Wiley alone, but now that it was here, she felt reluctant to speak of the bizarre incidents. Wiley, as always, sensed Drew's mood.

"Something's on your mind."

Drew hesitated. She knew Wiley wouldn't push if she chose not to speak. She looked around the room, at the plants, the soft comfortable furniture, Becka's dirty tennis shoes. Everything seemed so normal. "Something weird's been going on," she said.

"Those feelings you talked about before?" Wiley asked. Her almost black eyes grew even darker and more serious. She was part Iroquois Indian and, at times, that heritage showed clearly on her face. "The sense of differentness. Has it come back?" She looked at Drew with obvious concern. Though she leaned forward as she spoke, her long, angular body remained solidly rooted on the sofa. She wore bluejeans and a t-shirt and vest.

"No," Drew said. "No, it's not that." She hesitated again. "It has to do with people—me and other people."

"Oh?" Still leaning slightly forward, her back arrow-straight, Wiley waited for Drew to go on.

"At first I thought it was just coincidence." Her fingers played with the tweed fabric of the sofa. "But then it kept happening, even when I tested it intentionally." She looked at her friend, at the downturned edges of Wiley's very serious mouth. "It works every time."

"What's that, Drew? What keeps happening?"

Drew adjusted her arm in the sling. "My ability to influence others," she answered. She paused, her eyes averted.

"What do you mean?"

Drew took a deep breath. "I know this is going to sound weird, Wiley," she said, "but...well, lately, when I...when I tell people

15

things, certain things, they believe them. They act on them. Things that...that are very different from what they originally thought."

"I'm not sure I know what you're saying, Drew." The triangle of a frown deepened between Wiley's thick black eyebrows. "You find you're influencing people somehow, getting them to believe things and do things. What do you mean? Tell me more." Her voice remained soft and concerned.

Drew emptied her coffee cup in a long tense swig, then lit a cigarette. Leaning back against the paisely pillow she had gotten from her mother, she told her friend exactly what had happened. Beginning with Allen, she recounted each event up to the filet mignon. Wiley listened closely, nodding and asking a question here and there.

When Drew finished, Wiley looked at her for several seconds, frowning in that way that Drew thought made her look so professorial, and then she spoke. "Drew, I'm going to be honest with you." She looked very earnest. "What you say concerns me. You went through something pretty damn traumatic. The stress may have..."

"I was afraid you'd think I'm losing it," Drew said sharply.

"Wait now, hold on." Wiley placed her hand on Drew's. "Let me finish. I'd like to help you figure out what's going on. Does that sound OK? I want to ask you some questions, all right?"

"All right."

"And I want to be straight with you about what I'm thinking, OK?"

Drew nodded.

"OK, first let me give you my reaction."

Drew pulled her jogging jacket around her shoulder. She suddenly felt cold. She watched Wiley's mouth as she spoke, her own very sensuous one almost in a pout.

"From what you've said, several hypotheses occur to me," Wiley began. She looked across the room, squinting her eyes. "One— that you're putting me on, intentionally bullshitting." She turned her head and caught Drew's eye. "I doubt that, but it's possible."

Drew started to speak but Wiley went on.

"Two—that what you say is true, that it's true in all the details and implications, that is, that you do have a strange and powerful influence on others, something much beyond the ordinary." Wiley did not pause. "Three—that what you report is basically true, but less dramatic, and that it's explainable as a form of hypnotic suggestion."

"I thought of that," Drew interjected. "Do you think that's what

16

it is, and if so, how...?"

"Hold on, hon, let me finish, OK?" Wiley spoke more rapidly now. "My next hypothesis is that you're distorting your experience, not intentionally, that you believe what you told me really happened, but that it didn't. I've got to deal with that one first, Drew."

Drew leaned back, crossing her arms. "You think I'm crazy."

"Tell me what *you* think is going on, Drew. If you do have this power you describe, how do *you* explain it?"

"I don't know. That's just it, I can't..."

"Any theories?"

Drew shook her head.

"Even way out theories? Anything?"

"No, it's too weird. I can't imagine..."

"Have you been having any other unusual experiences?"

"Like what?"

"Anything."

"No, nothing that I'd call unusual."

"Unusual thoughts? Ideas about things?"

"No."

"Hearing voices?"

"Wiley!"

"Are you, Drew?"

"No, I'm not hearing voices. And I don't believe I'm being controlled by Martians or that the CIA is after me, or that I'm God or the Goddess."

"All right, Drew, I don't mean to upset you. The questions are important."

Drew nodded.

"Have you been taking any drugs?"

"The pill. Aspirin once in a while."

"No other drugs?"

"No."

"How are things at work?"

"OK."

"Normal? Nothing unusual?"

"Same boring shit."

They talked a while longer. Wiley asked more questions and Drew answered them honestly and, for the most part, seriously, although the interview was annoying her.

Finally, Wiley said, "You seen pretty intact to me."

"So, I'm not nuts?"

"You don't seem nuts to me."

"But I could be?"

17

Wiley laughed. "Well, you've always been a bit nutty," she said, "but who isn't?" She looked pensive then. "From what you describe about these events, it doesn't really sound like hypnosis, although similar in ways. Your subjects seem to have the focal concentration typical of trance, but there's no aura, no set or expectation they have when you're talking to them. Your induction doesn't seem to involve any enhancement techniques; you don't talk about heavy eyelids, for example." She seemed to be thinking aloud then. "They do end up staring at you, but you don't focus on this or imply that you're causing it. They certainly do seem to enter a trance state." She looked at Drew again. "You know, it *is* possible to induce trance through fear and coercion." She shook her head. "But the circumstances you describe just don't fit. Frankly, Drew, I'm having trouble believing this. At least, the way you're describing it."

"Wiley."

"Yeah."

"You know what I think."

"What?"

Drew fixed her gaze intently on her friend. "I think you have a taste for an icecream soda."

Looking puzzled, Wiley began to reply, but Drew went on, speaking calmly and intently. "Listen to me, Wiley. You are becoming aware of a very irresistible urge to get some icecream. Yes, right now, there's nothing you want more than to taste the creamy coldness of a sweet delicious icecream soda."

Wiley did not speak. She stared at Drew without moving or blinking her eyes.

"You can't get it out of your mind," Drew continued. "You have to have an icecream soda now, as soon as possible."

Wiley continued to sit immobilely for several moments, then blinked and moved her tongue across her lips. "Drew, we need a break," she said, stretching her legs. "Let's go get some icecream someplace and then think some more about all this. What do you say?"

"Do you know why you want icecream now?" Drew asked, her voice rising excitedly.

"We could use a change of pace," Wiley said calmly, reaching over and placing her hand on Drew's shoulder.

"You never eat icecream!"

"That's true," Wiley said, her calm voice contrasting with Drew's frantic one. "I rarely do, but it sounds good to me right now. How about you, would you like some?"

"Wiley, I just put that thought into your head. I told you you wanted icecream and you stared at me just like everybody else, and now you want icecream."

Wiley looked very serious and somewhat sad. "Drew, I'm worried. I don't understand it, but something strange is going on with you. You're imagining things that..."

Drew jumped up. "OK, let me prove it to you," she said. She ran to the buffet in the dining room, got a piece of paper from the drawer and wrote something on it. She folded the paper, sealed it in an envelope and brought it to Wiley who had been watching her closely all the while. "This is the next idea I'm going to zap you with," she said. "Hold onto it." Drew felt excited...and powerful.

"All right, Drew." Wiley tucked the envelope into the back pocket of her jeans. "Is there a place that sells icecream around here?"

"Down the street," Drew said, smiling. "Let me make sure Sarah's going to be around for Becka."

Minutes later, the two of them walked into the balmy evening, past the cleaners and bookstore and several other shops.

"Look at that," Drew said, pointing across the street.

"What?"

"The butcher shop—look at the sign. 'Fifty percent reduction on your meat purchase for lucky number customers'. He's done it. I started that when I zapped him the other day."

"Drew," Wiley said solicitously. "Isn't it possible that it was that sign that gave you the idea...that made you think..."

"Shit!" Drew said. "This is frustrating." Then she smiled. "But you won't be skeptical much longer, Wiley."

Drew had a cup of coffee while Wiley hungrily downed her soda. She enjoyed watching Wiley enjoy it, relishing every bite and slurpy sip. Wiley, who never cared much for icecream.

They talked of various things—a workshop Wiley was developing; her satisfaction with her decision, made nearly a year ago now, to quit her job at the Mental Health Clinic and expand her private practice; Becka's latest adventures at daycamp; Drew's growing dissatisfaction with her relationship with David; the status of the Women's Movement. There was a brief period when Drew spoke to Wiley in a calm forceful way and Wiley stared silently at her with glazed but focused eyes. They remained at the table talking long after the soda was gone. Finally Wiley picked up the check and signalled the waiter. Drew watched her, waiting. When the waiter came, Wiley declared indignantly that the soda had been awful.

"The icecream was grainy; it tasted like sandy paste. I must say, I feel insulted that you actually intend to charge me for it."

The waiter pulled back a few inches. "You managed to eat it all," she said sarcastically.

That's irrelevant," Wiley retorted. "It was atrocious and I have no intention of paying for it."

The waiter argued, then the manager came and she too argued with Wiley but Wiley remained firm, saying they could call the police if they liked, but she would not pay. Drew finally intervened. She persuaded Wiley to wait outside while she calmed the people and paid the bill.

"What a dive," Wiley said when Drew joined her. They began to walk toward Drew's apartment.

"Open the envelope," Drew said.

"Now? I thought..."

"Open it."

They stood beneath a street light as Wiley read aloud: "You will refuse to pay for your icecream." Her voice tapered off at the end, so the last words were barely audible. She looked at Drew, her face full of a mix of emotions. She ran her fingers through her thick black hair and, shaking her head, read the note again. She was chewing on her bottom lip and breathing loud enough for Drew to hear.

She looked at Drew then and took Drew's hand and held it, squeezed it tightly in her own for a long time. "This is scarey," she said at last. "Let's go home and talk."

Wiley kept Drew up well into the night, her questions and fascination endless. Drew's relief at having her experience confirmed was so great that she was more than willing to answer all Wiley's questions and repeat her stories in full detail.

As the evening progressed, Drew realized Wiley was becoming more protective than usual and even somewhat authoritarian. She kept referring to the need to be careful, not to tell anyone yet, and admonished Drew not to use the power again until they learned more about it. She said they had to formulate some plans, that they needed to test the extent and limits of the power. Repeatedly, Wiley speculated about what could be causing it, talking some about hypnosis, but then about energy fields and the unknowns of the mind. At one point, she told Drew it reminded her of a movie she had seen.

"The government gives some people an experimental drug and, as a result, one of them acquires a power over people, kind of like yours. He can make them think and do what he wants. 'People-pushing power', they called it. His nose would bleed every time he did it."

They were in the kitchen. As she listened, Drew poured some grains of salt on the table and, absentmindedly, tried to balance the salt shaker on them. "You know, a short time ago," she said, "I would have thought something like that was ridiculous." The salt shaker fell. "You don't think they gave me any weird drugs while I was in the hospital, do you, Wiley?"

Wiley shook her head. "I think that's very unlikely." She went to the sink for her third glass of water. The icecream had made her thirsty. "I think it might be from the brain injury," she said.

Drew touched her temple. "You do? How could that be?"

"I have no idea."

Drew continued rubbing her temple. "So what happened to the guy in the movie?" she asked after a while.

"Well," Wiley said, "mainly the story was about his daughter. She had the power to start fires at will. The government went after them, kept them prisoners for a while. They wanted to use the girl as a weapon or something."

"But what about the guy? What did he do with his power?" Drew asked.

"Let's see." Wiley took a large drink from the water glass. "He used it a number of times. He used it to try to escape from the government guys. Oh, yeah, and he blinded a couple of them with it."

Drew turned up her nose.

Wiley patted her arm. "This isn't the movies, hon. We're going to proceed real cautiously with this."

They continued talking well into the night. As Wiley speculated about the potential of the power, its possible uses, she got more and more excited and animated. Drew listened more than she spoke. When the two women finally parted, both were drained. Wiley's reactions so riled Drew that she lay awake for hours that night, thinking very interesting thoughts.

Reality was no longer what she thought it was. Suddenly, the world was less understandable to Wiley Cavenar, less predictable and controllable than she had always believed. She barely slept that night. Her mind would not stop. Ordinarily, there was nothing Wiley loved more than to grapple with a new idea, ponder on it, dissect it, and ultimately digest it, and integrate it neatly into her understanding of the whole. But this was different. Drew's revelations shook the very foundation of Wiley's concept of reality, and would not let her rest.

Boundless, the ramifications are boundless, she thought, tossing on her bed. If it is what it seems, we...Drew, has the potential of altering the course of history, changing the whole direction of civilization. Wiley shuddered, feeling the terror of it, and the lip-licking excitement. She rested her head on her arm, eyes wide in the darkness. What does it mean about the mind, she wondered, sighing. How little we really know. And why Drew? Why now? She was sure such questions had no answers, and yet, she no longer felt so sure about what she was sure about. No reason, she thought, no reason beyond chance. That shaft of mirror striking in just the right place. A lesion affecting the neurons in just the right way to tap an aspect of human power never before... She bunched the pillow up under her head. Lying flat on her back now, she stared toward the edge of light coming from the window. Over and over she reviewed what she knew so far. Her mind took her further into the fantasies, the projections, of what Drew could do, of what the future could be. Drew McAllister's life will never never be the same, she thought, filling her lungs deeply. Nor will my own.

Despite her lack of sleep, Wiley felt no fatigue the next day. In her comfortable Loop office, with the lamp she'd brought from home and the oriental throw rug, she became absorbed, as always, in her clients' worlds and their struggles; but in the in-between spaces, in the pauses in their talk, in the time between appointments, Wiley's head filled with Drew McCallister and Drew's power and how they'd explore it and how it could be used.

Drew was full of ideas of her own. The impact of her gift, the potential of it, was becoming clearer and bigger. She recalled the childhood fantasies... "If I were magic..." She knew she would quit her job soon. There were much more interesting ways to spend her time. She closed her eyes and saw herself a child again, on the threshhold of puberty, sitting eagerly astride her new year-ling, ready to give rein and fly. From somewhere Wiley's voice came, calling her, saying in her calm and grown-up way: "Go slow-ly, Drew, rein in. Test it first." But Drew did not want to hear this. For the first time, she was feeling completely free, unconstrained, and unafraid. She wanted to go at a gallop, to feel the wind buzz past her ears with her hair blowing wildly as she tore up hills, leaped crevices, flying faster and faster.

"I'm sorry, Miss, I'm afraid I can*not* arrange an appointment for you. Mrs. Pendleton does not receive all callers." The stiffly coiffed receptionist turned away, dismissing Drew with her gestures and tone.

"Excuse me," Drew said, in a low compelling voice. Her self-confidence was not an act this time.

The receptionist looked up.

"Listen," Drew said, "there's something important I have to say."

The woman was captivated immediately, staring intently at Drew. Her hand, holding a pen, remained suspended in the air.

"You want me to have an appointment with your boss. You want to arrange it, to set it up with the appointment secretary for as soon as possible."

It was another ten seconds before the woman slowly lowered her hand, letting it rest on the desk. Her eyes cleared. She looked at the pen she held. "Miss...what was it, oh yes, McAllister. Miss McAllister, before you leave, give me a number where I can reach you. I sense that your mission is important, so I will do what I can to arrange a meeting. I'll call you when that's accomplished."

"Thank you," Drew said. She gave the woman her office number and left, smiling.

I *am* magic, she thought, whistling, as the elevator whisked her down 38 floors in seconds. I can get anything I want. In a gold-coast storefront window, she watched her reflection jubilantly walking along Michigan Avenue. Anything I want. She sucked in her breath, feeling overwhelmed, then quickly turned her thoughts to Althea Pendleton and how to conduct herself when she sat face-to-face with the reactionary, multimillionaire, philanthropic snob.

Ordinarily, Drew would feel cowed at the prospect, very nervous and ill-at-ease, but she was surprisingly calm when, the following day, she was ushered into the richly adorned inner office of the very rich and somewhat famous Mrs. Althea Pendleton. When she walked out, Drew had a check for $4000 and an agreement that a similar amount would arrive each month. A smiling Mrs.

Pendleton accompanied Drew to the door, her arm around Drew's shoulder, telling her how lucky she felt to have found such a worthy cause and excellent tax write-off.

At home that night, Drew stared at the check. Twinges of guilt mixed with her elation. They all buy it, she thought, all of them. Whatever I tell them to believe, they believe. She slung her shoeless feet up onto the coffee table and leaned back in the big soft easy chair, picturing Althea Pendleton. After her eyes cleared, the older woman had listened to Drew, nodding and smiling, then thanked Drew for the opportunity and wrote the check.

It's uncanny, Drew thought. I love it! I love it! The elation was clearly winning, but then the guilt slipped in again. It shouldn't be. No one should have that kind of power. A frown creased her forehead. It could be terribly misused. The frown intensified. Am I misusing it? She recalled what she knew of Althea Pendleton: an ultraconservative bigot who had inherited the accumulated wealth of a long line of ruthless capitalists. The Pendletons, Drew knew, had fought tenaciously against unionization or workers' rights of any kind. Their factories were among the last to acknowledge that workers were humans, and they only made reforms because they were forced to. No, I don't feel guilty about swindling money from such as she. Drew twisted uneasily. Robin Hood came to her mind. This is just a beginning, she thought, to ease herself. There's so much I can do. She fantasized the pleasure she would feel giving her notice at work and thought about the next steps she would take in her plan. The phone interrupted her. It's probably Wiley again, she thought, tempted to let it ring.

"Mommie, the phone's ringing."

Wiley had been calling Drew frequently since the icecream soda evening. Drew's revelations haunted her, she said, driving her to spend every free moment reading, researching, looking for reports of similar cases and thinking about the possibilities. Late at night, she told Drew, when everything was quiet, she worked on the design for the research to test the hypotheses she'd come up with. Several times she made vague allusions to ways the power could be used, once mentioning the possibility of arranging meetings with world leaders. Drew expressed her uneasiness with this and so Wiley said no more about it. "Before we do anything," she cautioned repeatedly, "we must know precisely what the parameters of the power are." Invariably, she would also inquire about Drew's state of mind, how she was handling it, thoughts and feelings she was having. Though always concerned about Drew's well-being, her interest now was greater than ever.

"Hello...Oh, hi, David...Mm-hm...No, I don't think that's so. I've been busy, that's all...What do you mean? How am I different?...Maybe. I do have a lot on my mind...Just things...Not now, we'll talk later, David...No, I haven't been avoiding you, I just..." Drew drummed her fingers on the table, wishing she had let the phone go unanswered. "I can't tonight, I told you I'm meeting Judith for a drink tonight...All right...Yes...Sure, I want to see you, too...OK, Friday then...'Bye."

David was beginning to get on her nerves. Since her divorce four years ago, Drew had dated quite a few men, and had let herself begin to get deeply involved with several of them. Each time, though, she had pulled away. Something was missing for her. Something seemed wrong with the dynamics in each relationship. Usually, Drew blamed herself.

She checked her watch. Another hour until Becka's bedtime and her meeting with Judith. She looked forward to seeing Judith with an excitement rarely there for David.

Drew was wondering about this when a crash sounded in the hall. She jumped to her feet and ran in the direction of the sound, her mind filling with horrifying images of her daughter lying hurt, bleeding. Then Becka, too, ran into the hall.

"What was that, mom? It's not a tornado, is it?"

"No, hon, no. Something fell in the apartment, that's all." She put her arm around Becka. "It must be in Sarah's room."

Drew knocked on Sarah's door. There was no response but she could hear crying. She pushed the door open. Sarah was bent over the desk, head down on her arms, her back rising and falling with her sobs. Books were strewn all around the floor. Drew went to her. "Sarah, what is it?"

Sarah turned. "Oh..." She sat up. "Oh, I'm sorry," she said. She tried to stop the crying. "I made a lot of noise, I guess." She wiped at her face with the palms of her hand.

"What's wrong, Sarah? What happened?" Drew's hand was on the younger woman's shoulder.

Sarah turned further in her chair to face Drew. She looked miserable, her face red and tear-streaked, mascara smudges beneath her eyes. She threw her arms around Drew's waist and cried some more. Becka backed up and stood near the door, watching with fascination.

"It's this fucking exam," Sarah said. "I just can't do it." Her breath came in gasps. "I don't have what it takes, Drew. I don't. I know I'm going to flunk."

Drew rocked her and rubbed her back. "Wow, you've got

yourself in quite a state," she said.

"I can't concentrate. My mind goes blank."

Drew stroked her hair. "I didn't know you were having such a time. The biology course?"

Sarah nodded. "My mind keeps getting off the track." She looked around for a tissue. Drew handed her one from the box on the bookshelf. "I can't study. All I can think about is that I'm going to fail this course and blow my average and my chance for graduate school and my whole career and..." She blew her nose.

"Don't you understand the material?" Drew asked. She was sitting on the stool now, next to Sarah, who often reminded her of herself. She gave her another tissue.

"I do. When it's not exam time and I'm relaxed, I understand it. I even like it." She shook her head. "But, I just can't concentrate any more." More tears came, wetting again the olive skin. Strands of dark hair stuck to her face. "I've forgotten everything I already learned. I re-read things I knew just last week and they're meaningless. Then the words blur and...God, it's so frustrating." She looked at Becka who continued to watch the scene with undisguised fascination. "I sorta threw my books around," she said. "Did I scare you, Becka?"

Becka nodded. "A little, but that's OK. One time I had a hard arithmetic test and I cried, didn't I, mom?"

"Yes," Drew said. "But just one tear, remember? And then we sat and talked."

"Yeah, and then mom helped me learn to do it. Long division. It's hard, but mom helped me and I got a 95 because then I felt better and just did it."

Sarah smiled. "Good for you, champ," she said. Her large teeth shone white against her deep-toned skin. Sarah Morena was pretty and funny and Becka liked her very much. She was from Cuba and sometimes told Becka how to say things in Spanish and often made her laugh.

"Sarah, listen to me," Drew said firmly.

Sarah looked at her.

"You don't need to panic yourself." Drew's voice was low and adamant.

Sarah stared.

"You can relax and let yourself focus on the material you need to study. You don't have to worry yourself about flunking. You know that if you just put your energy into studying, it will come. You know you're able to understand it. You can relax now and let yourself do what you know you're capable of. It's OK to stop worrying. You know that. You can free yourself from it and focus on your studying."

Sarah did not move as she listened to Drew's words. Becka continued to watch, moving in closer now. Drew waited.

"You know," Sarah said after several seconds, "I think I just needed to cry and talk a little. I feel much better now." She waved her fingers at Becka, who giggled and waved back. "It's really dumb to be so worried and tense about this, Drew. I know I'll do fine." Becka was standing right next to her now. "I think I'll even have time to read a bedtime story to you, if you want, Señorita Beckita." She looked at Drew again. "Thanks for listening," she said. "I really do feel much better. Sorry about the noise."

Drew was smiling with satisfaction.

"I'm going to study for a while now," Sarah said. "You tell me when you're ready for the story, Becka. Which one do you want to hear?"

"Maybe *Alladin and the Magic Lamp*," Becka said.

"You love magic."

"Runs in the family," Drew said softly.

## 6.

Judith Brodie was sitting in a rear booth when Drew arrived. She caught Drew's eye. You are a very beautiful person, Drew thought, approaching her, returning the smile. She slid onto the bench. The glow of the table candle sparkled amber on Judith's face reminding Drew of their campfire nights. "Let's go camping," she said.

Judith laughed in her robust, *I appreciate you* way. "Bravado queen," she said. She cocked her head, the sand brown hair falling softly on her shoulder. "You're supposed to be scared of campgrounds now."

"Oh." Drew lit a cigarette. She felt very close to Judith. Their friendship had developed slowly, growing finally to the point where it would be very hard to imagine life without her. "You ordered my Sangria."

"Mm-hm."

Drew took a sip. "How do you know I didn't want a beer?"

"Intuition. I figured you for wine this evening. Am I wrong?"

"You're not wrong."

The bar was quiet tonight. On weekends folksingers came and people who liked folksingers. "You look like you have a secret," Judith said.

Drew could tell Judith just about anything, even about her scared and sad parts, and about her fantasies. Right now, more than anything, she wanted to tell her about Althea Pendleton. She smiled mysteriously. "I'm magic."

Judith nodded. "You're magic," she repeated. "OK." She waited.

The temptation was almost irresistible. Drew wanted them to be excited together and *ooh* and *ahh* about her amazing magical zapping power. Judith would love the part about her new found source of income. They had a mutual disdain for people like Althea Pendleton. She wanted to tell Judith everything so they could marvel at it together, but Wiley's warnings stopped her. Instead, she spoke of other things and listened and joked and they enjoyed the comfortable intimacy, until they were interrupted.

"Hi, girls," the man said. "Can I buy you a drink?" He leaned over them, hands on their table. "What would you like?" He wore a thin black jacket; his hair was nearly as black.

"No, thanks," Judith said. "We're fine. Thanks, anyhow."

"Oh come on, honey, don't be unfriendly." He sat down next to Drew. "Let me guess...you're both private eyes, discussing a case, right?" He withdrew a pack of cigarettes from his jacket pocket and offered one to Drew. She ignored it.

"We really don't want company," Drew said. "We're talking, all right?"

"Sure, I like to talk. What are you talking about? What happened to your arm? You get in a fight with your boyfriend?"

Judith rolled her eyes. "It doesn't change," she said to Drew.

Drew shook her head. "The 'fair-game syndrome'." She turned to the intruder. "We really would like to continue our conversation," she said sharply. "Privately. Do you mind?"

The man sneered. "Snobs," he muttered, rising from the booth. "I don't get it, I really don't. Don't you like men, or what?" He left without waiting for a response.

Drew laughed. "You know, sometimes I really don't," she said.

They had another drink and talked some more. Judith was in her pensive, sardonic mood, which Drew especially liked, and both women were having a very good time. It was quite late when they left the pub.

Drew's car was parked a block away, around the corner. The night was very quiet, the streets deserted. A few doors down from the bar, a man stood concealed in a doorway, barely visible in his black jacket. Drew and Judith walked his way.

"Well, well, look who's here."

Drew gasped and pulled back.

"The two bitches."

She grabbed Judith's arm, ushering her swiftly on. The man followed. They quickened their pace even more. The car was just ahead, but he overtook them as they were turning the corner and stood in front of them blocking their way.

"What's your hurry, girls?"

They tried to move around him.

"You know what cunts like you deserve?" he said.

"Hey, leave us alone, huh?" Judith said. Her heart was pounding. "We didn't do anything to you."

He smiled a wet malicious hate-grin. "I'm going to do something to *you*, sweetie." He grabbed Judith's wrist, twisted it, and with his other hand pulled out a knife and held it against her side.

"Oh God!"

"In there, both of you. In that hallway."

His voice was guttural and hoarse. He pushed the blade against Judith's ribs, pricking her skin. She winced and let out a sharp cry. He moved her toward the door.

"You too, cunt," he hissed at Drew, "or I'll cut your little girlfriend open."

It was dark inside the hallway, the entrance to an apartment building. Just one dim light bulb burned. Keeping the knife against Judith's ribs, the attacker ordered Drew to take off her pants. "If you're too crippled to do it, bitch, I'd be happy to cut 'em off for you," he said. "Maybe I'll just cut 'em off anyway." He moved toward her, nudging Judith too, the knife blade still cold against her back.

Drew looked him fiercely in the eyes, praying there was enough light. "There's a problem," she said. "Listen, there's something you have to hear." Her voice was firm and steady.

The man seemed uncertain for a moment.

"It's your arms," Drew said. She kept talking with the same low voice and he did not move as he listened, nor take his eyes from hers.

"You cannot move them. Your arms are paralyzed. It's true,

you know it is. They're totally paralyzed!''

Slowly, the stunned man's grip loosened on Judith's arm. She moved away instantly, both women then tearing out the door. The man remained immobile. The knife slipped from his useless hand and clinked onto the tile floor.

They heard him groaning in the night, behind them, panic searing his throat, his arms hanging limply from his shoulders.

## 7.

"So I had to tell her," Drew said.

"Of course you did. Don't worry about it."

"It freaked her out. That, on top of the rape attempt. Look at me, I'm still shaking.''

Wiley took Drew's hand. It was trembling. She stroked it comfortingly and listened as Drew talked some more about what had happened.

"I thought he was going to kill us. I saw that knife and...'' A tremor shook her body.

Wiley removed her robe and wrapped it around Drew.

"When I took Judith home, we sat in her living room for hours. She was...she was a mess, really freaked. I stayed with her until finally she was so exhausted...I thought *I* was fine.''

Wiley stroked Drew's neck, rubbing softly across her shoulders. She pulled the edge of the warm robe so it covered Drew's leg.

"She has a mark where the knife was. Just a scratch, but...and then the stuff about my power, my 'zapping' power. It was too much for her. I never saw her like that. For a while she got real quiet. That really scared me. But then she started talking again. I don't know what shook her up more, Wiley, that creep or the stuff about me.'' Drew had been sitting near the edge of Wiley's sofa. She leaned back now. I hope she'll be OK.''

"I'll give her a call tomorrow."

"I guess I held myself together so I could be there for her," Drew continued, "but as soon as I left her place, I started shaking. I could hardly drive. I hope you don't mind my coming here at this hour.''

She looked at her watch. "Oh God, it's three o'clock. I'm sorry, Wiley."

Wiley sat in a t-shirt and pajama bottoms, her hand now resting on Drew's knee. "It's been quite a night for both of you," she said in her gentle caring way. "How does a glass of wine sound?"

Drew nodded and when Wiley returned, sipped the wine and talked some more. Gradually she began to feel calmer, safer. And then the anger came. "That son of a bitch." Her lower lip, trembling earlier, was drawn taut now. "If it weren't for my freak accident, Wiley ..." She touched her temple. "...he would have..."

"That was quick thinking, Drew, to use the 'zap' the way you did."

"You should have seen it. His arms just went dead. They hung there like two heavy logs."

"Serves the bastard right," Wiley said.

Drew moved her own arm around, the one not in the cast, flexing the wrist, rotating it at the shoulder joint, as if testing it. I wonder how long he'll stay paralyzed."

"Who knows." Wiley frowned. "That's one of the things we have to find out, how long the effects last. I bet he'll think twice before he tries to rape again."

"He may never be able to grab *anyone* again—ever," Drew said. "I should have paralyzed his prick, too." She threw her head back and laughed hollowly. "Say, I've got an idea, Wiley. We form this brigade of rapist-finders, see, and they bring the rapists to me and I have a little talk with each of them." She laughed again, a bitter angry laugh.

Wiley narrowed her eyes and drew the edges of her mouth down, as she often did when dealing with some serious thought. "Maybe someday we'll actually do something like that, Drew. Seriously. But we need to plan it well, plan how you're going to use your power. Systematically, not randomly."

Drew's eyelids began to droop.

"Come on, Miss, you need to be in bed. Here, give me your hand. You can stay in the guest room."

"No, no I can't stay, Wiley. Sarah has an early class tomorrow. I have to be there for Becka."

"OK, I'll drive you home, then," Wiley said, helping Drew to her feet. "Don't go to work tomorrow."

Drew did not go to work the next day, nor did Judith. They spent most of the time together. Judith was doing fine. She had talked by phone to Wiley, which helped a lot, she said, and to Vic, though for him, she minimized what had happened. "Some guy tried to mug us," she told him. "No, I don't want to deal with the police. We're OK. It was frightening, though." He told her she shouldn't go out alone at night.

Every once in a while, as she and Drew sat on Drew's porch, talking, Judith would look askance at Drew and shake her head. "Astounding," she'd say, or,"Far out," and then they'd talk some more about zapping and the brain and indulge in another round of mystical speculations.

That night, Wiley came over as planned to discuss with Drew her hypotheses and ideas for investigating Drew's power. Even though she was obviously excited about the project, she showed no impatience to begin their discussion, encouraging Drew, instead, to talk some more about the night before, sensitive to her friend, and caring. Drew did not have much more to say about it.

"It's over, really. I'm done with it."

"You seem OK," Wiley said. "We'll see how you do in the next few days."

Drew nodded and pushed herself back into the sofa. "I'm ready to hear what your fertile mind has come up with, professor." She looked at Wiley's briefcase. "Lay it on me."

Wiley withdrew a file from the case and set it on the table in front of Drew.

"Mom, the TV's fucked up," Becka said, poking her head around the corner.

"Just a second, hon. Say, Wiley, do you think there's something wrong with Becka? She loves to say things like that."

Drew left to tend to her daughter without waiting for an answer. When she returned, Wiley handed her some sheets of paper. "We'll proceed with the experiment in phases," she said. "Read this over and let me know if any of it is unclear; and keep in mind that the hypotheses are just that. They all have to be tested."

Drew leafed through the stack. "You've been busy," she said. She put her feet up on the coffee table and began to read, skimming quickly over the introductory section, then slowing down when she came to the hypotheses.

1. *That D.M. is able, by stating to a person that he or she believes X, to implant in the person (recipient) the belief that X is true even though, prior to the implantation, the person did not believe X.*

2. *That any belief can be implanted whether or not it is accurate (truthful), realistic, or consistent with the recipient's previous beliefs, values or perceptions.*

3. *That the implanted belief is permanent.*

*4. That after implantation, the recipient believes the implanted belief came from her/himself.*

*5. That a belief can be implanted only via face-to-face, oral communication....*

There were twenty hypotheses in all. Wiley watched Drew expectantly as she read, following her eyes. The moment Drew finished, Wiley spoke. "Well, what do you think?"

Drew grimaced. "Do you really want to know?"

"Yes, of course."

"I think you have a boring way of saying fascinating things." She smiled sweetly.

"All right," Wiley said, a little impatiently. "What else?"

"I have a question."

"Yes?"

"Who's D.M.?"

"You shit."

"And I have an opinion."

"What?" Wiley asked, more skeptically now.

"It's really a diagnosis."

"A diagnosis? What do you...?"

"It is my clinical opinion," Drew said teasingly, "that you are obsessive-repulsive."

Wiley laughed. "I know," she admitted .

"Maybe I could help," Drew offered, "zap you into hanging a little looser, perhaps. Just look into my eyes."

"Drew!" Wiley looked irritated, maybe frightened. "Dammit, you can't just play with it."

Drew's mood changed immediately. "I can do what I want!" she snapped.

Wiley moved back several inches. "Oh, oh," she said. "It's getting to you, isn't it, Drew. The power, I mean. It has to change your life, inevitably, change *you*. It's beginning to happen, isn't it?"

Drew did not respond, but looked stonily across the room.

"Tell me what's going on, Drew," Wiley said kindly. "Do you feel I'm pushing you too hard?"

Drew shrugged her shoulders. "I don't know." She looked toward the window, then back at her friend. "I'm scared, Wiley," she said softly. She was leaning forward now. "I could zap you into being a blubbering idiot, do you know that? Or make you my slave. I could..."

"Yes. I see what you mean." Wiley looked empathically at Drew. "It must be an overwhelming feeling, to suddenly...to transcend..." Wiley's eyes had a dreamy cast.

"I'm afraid of it," Drew said, "of how I'll use it." Her playfulness was totally gone now. "I don't want to control people, Wiley, not really. But in a way I do, maybe...but not my friends." She looked beseechingly at Wiley. "I want normal relationships. I don't want to use this power to..."

"Do you think it would help if you and I made an agreement," Wiley interrupted, "a contract of sorts, an agreement that you won't implant any beliefs in me without my consent."

Drew tilted her head. "I might cheat," she said, the glint returning to her eyes a bit.

Wiley saw through the humor. "You really don't trust yourself, do you, Drew?"

Drew thought about this. "I don't know," she said after a time. "I think I'm OK with it. I think I won't let the power take over, but there's a lot to think about, so many possibilities..."

"Right, that's why, for your sake, and maybe humanity's, we've got to explore it, Drew, test it, then plan how you want to use it."

"Maybe I shouldn't use it."

Wiley's eyes widened with alarm, but she covered her reaction immediately. "Not in ways that feel wrong to you," she said calmly.

"I've been doing a lot of thinking about right and wrong, lately."

"I'll bet you have."

"I'll never use it on you, Wiley."

"Probably not, Drew, not to hurt me, at least."

"I don't want to use it on you at all."

"OK. Don't."

"But, what if..."

"You have the capacity to choose, to decide. It's a very conscious thing, isn't it?"

"Yes. Do you trust me, Wiley?"

"Yes."

"Then why did you want us to make an agreement?"

"For you."

"OK, I agree."

"Agree to what?"

"Not to zap you, unless you want me to some time."

"I do want you to. If you can bring yourself to read the rest of this, the design for the experiment, you'll see that I'm the main guinea pig for the first phase." She paused. "I've been thinking of revising it, though, of using Judith instead, now that she knows, if she'd be willing."

"Maybe I could zap you into believing I couldn't zap you."

Wiley raised her eyebrows. "That's a thought," she said. "Actually it's included in one of the hypotheses, number twelve, I think, the one about whether subsequent implantations can supercede earlier ones."

"Zap-reversing zaps," Drew said.

"Right."

"Let's test it now."

Wiley looked at her papers, neatly spelling out, step by step, the experimental procedure to be followed. "That would be deviating from the design."

"Let's deviate."

Wiley tilted her head, in the way that Drew found so appealing. "OK," she said, laughing conspiratorially. "Something benign, please." She hesitated, then added. "I wonder if the recipients have any ill effects from the zaps. I wonder if it messes with the neural connections or anything."

"Do you think it might?"

"It's possible, but I doubt it." Wiley scratched at her head. "But, it's possible." She paused. "But I doubt it."

"Maybe we shouldn't try," Drew said.

"Let's try."

"It's *your* brain."

"Don't you care about my brain?"

"It's full of ruminations about variables and subject factors and all this other shit. Your brain's a mess already."

"So what's to lose then. Anyway, I seemed to have survived the icecream zap."

"So far."

"Cut that out. Now, think of a zap."

"OK." Drew placed her thumb in the middle of her forehead and closed her eyes.

"What are you doing?"

"Thinking of a zap."

"Oh."

"This is how you think of zaps."

"Oh."

Twenty seconds later: "I got one. You ready?"

"Ready."

Eyes holding eyes, D.M. told Wiley that she felt a strong desire to hear some rock music, right now, that she wanted to listen to rock music for the next half hour. When Wiley's eyes cleared, she went directly to the radio and turned on a rock station.

Becka and Jenny appeared almost immediately. They began

dancing around the room. Wiley watched them, snapping her fingers.

"You're lucky, Becka. My mom hates this music," Jenny said.

"It's kind of loud," Drew said. "Maybe we can find another station."

"Leave it," Wiley insisted, "for a while. The kids are enjoying it."

"How about you, Wiley? Do you like it?"

"It's not my favorite," Wiley answered thoughtfully, "but I think it's important to be aware of youth culture."

Drew laughed. "Yeah, right." She watched Wiley swaying with the music.

This went on for five or ten minutes until the children tired of it and left. Wiley remained engrossed in the raucous sounds, ignoring Drew, but Drew got her attention, and held it firmly while she zapped her into believing she wanted to hear Latino music now. Wiley turned the radio dial and eventually found the right station. She listened contentedly until Drew removed the suggestion. Wiley then switched off the radio declaring that their break was over and Drew should think of a zap.

"I already did. It works."

"What?"

"I can remove zaps."

"How do you know?"

"Think about it, Wiley."

Wiley thought about it. "The music?"

Drew nodded.

"You zapped me?"

Drew nodded.

"I really don't care for rock," Wiley said.

"So, now we know I *can't* zap you to be zap-resistent."

"Now Latino music is another story. Some of that, I can really get into. Olé! Hey, what did you say? You can't zap me to be zap-resistent? I'm confused." She looked confused. "Why don't you try a direct approach, Drew. Try implanting the belief that I'll be zap-resistent."

Drew did, and afterwards, when Wiley became animated again, she said, "Listen carefully, Wiley, I have something important to say to you." She paused. "You feel very warm, uncomfortably warm. You need to take your shoes off, and then you'll feel cool again."

A minute later, Wiley sat barefooted, smiling in relief. "Ah, that's much better."

36

"That was a zap," Drew said, pointing to Wiley's feet.

Wiley nodded. "You told me I'd be zap-resistent?"

"Yes."

"And then you told me I'd take my shoes off?"

"Yes."

Wiley was still nodding. "So, then, it's up to you, Drew. Apparently, you can't zap someone into immunity. Subsequent zaps can override previous ones. I guess you'll have to rely on your own will power."

"You know what I've been thinking about," Drew said.

"Oh, let's see. The meaning of life?"

"I've been thinking about filmmaking."

"Oh, yeah?"

"Mm-hm, learning more about it."

"Taking a course, you mean? You already seem pretty accomplished to me. That last one with Becka and Judith's dog was wonderful."

"I mean serious filmmaking. Sixteen millimeter. I'm thinking of becoming Art Trevor's apprentice."

Wiley laughed. "Good luck, kid. You'll be the 5000th in line. Remember, he's the one who gets turnaway crowds when he gives a guest lecture at Columbia."

"I know. I told you that."

"I know. You told me that."

"He's going to teach me everything he knows about film."

"Is that so?"

Drew nodded.

Wiley frowned. "Drew, I don't think you should do it."

"I figured you wouldn't like the idea."

"I told you before, if anyone...if certain people find out about this power you have, you could be in real danger."

"I suppose. Life is risk, you know." She had the playful glint in her eye again.

"You *are* thinking about life."

Drew laughed. "I'll pay him for his time."

Wiley was silent.

"Don't worry. They get amnesia, remember?"

Wiley still did not respond.

"I'm quitting my job."

"Drew!"

"I've found a benefactor."

"Drew!"

"I zapped Althea Pendleton to support me while I 'develop my creative potential'. Am I bad?'' Drew asked sheepishly.

Wiley shook her head. "Well, you chose the right person to rip off, at least. No, I don't think you're bad. You're human, you..."

"I want to play with it, Wiley, make my dreams come true."

Wiley laughed. "I guess no one could blame you, but...there are so many possibilities, and...it scares me, Drew. We know so little about it, and if the wrong people find out...Be careful, will you?''

Drew nodded.

Sarah came into the dining room then. "Hi, people. What's happening?''

"The scholar emerges," Wiley said. "How's the studying going?''

"Real well." Sarah poured herself a cup of coffee from the pot Drew always seemed to have warming on the buffet. "I'm going to ace that exam. I'm just breezing through the material. You know, I feel like I could even teach it now." She dumped three teaspoons of sugar into her cup. "I can't believe I'm actually enjoying studying for an exam." Grabbing a cupcake from the plate on the table, she took a large bite, then immediately made a face. "Say...this, uh...cupcake, it tastes icky." She pushed the remainder aside.

"Sh-h," Drew admonished. "Becka's first attempt."

"Drew's rewarding successive approximations," Wiley said, "to gradually shape Becka into taking over the cooking."

"Well, good luck," Sarah responded, carrying her coffee into the living room. She looked at the stack of papers on the table. "What are you two up to?''

"Re-designing the world," Wiley replied, gathering up the papers and slipping them back into the file.

"Oh, I see." Sarah looked at Wiley. "Psychologists are weird," she said smiling. "Don't take that personally." She sat down on the floor at the end of the coffee table.

"I've got to get going," Wiley said. "Read the rest of this, will you, Drew?" She tapped her finger on the manila file. "At some point, we've got to discuss the bigger picture. My ideas are all in there. Let me know what you think." She looked at her watch. "I'm late. Good night, Sarah. Try not to eat all the cupcakes."

Sarah grimaced.

"And good luck on your exam."

"Oh, yeah, thanks. Good night, Wiley." Sarah was looking at the file, trying to make sense of the doodle on the cover.

Drew walked Wiley to the door. "Don't forget to keep in touch," she said.

Wiley laughed. "You clown."

Drew blew her a kiss.

"Mom, can you come here and help me and Jenny with this fucking fliptop box?" Becka yelled from her room.

Drew went down the hall. Sarah remained in the living room with her coffee, idly leafing through the file Wiley had left.

## 8.

Drew rested on her elbow in David's bed. She wore only her arm cast.

"How was it for you?"

"Fine, David."

"Hm-m, you don't sound very enthusiastic." He put a pillow at the headboard and leaned against it, his very handsome face looking troubled. "What's happening, Drew?" he asked. "Ever since your accident, you've been...I don't know...distant."

Drew had thought she'd be the one to bring it up. "It started before that," she said, pulling on the tangled chocolate plaid sheet until she was covered up to her waist.

"What started before that?"

She looked at him sadly. "Changes...changes in my feelings, David." She pulled the sheet up a little higher, covering her breasts now. "About us...towards you."

"Hey, no, don't talk like that." He reached for her hand. "I love you, Drew." He bent and kissed her lips. "I want you. You're part of my life."

"I don't know, David. I just feel..."

"Is it something I've done? Tell me. Look, I'm open to change, you know that. I'm willing to compromise." David shifted positions, the cast was gouging his ribs.

Drew felt the heavy sadness like a weight.

"Is it that I'm still too controlling or 'macho', like you said before. Is that it?" David became defensive then. "Look, I can't help my conditioning, you know. I didn't make things the way they are, Drew. Besides, I've bent over backwards for you. I listen to your feminist raps, don't I? I even read that book you gave me...some of it, at least. You'll never catch me opening a door for you. I can't

39

help it if I'm controlling or condescending or whatever it is you complain about." He shrugged his broad shoulders. "It comes with the Y chromosome." His hand tenderly stroked her knee. "Be flexible, will you, Drew?"

Drew only half listened. She had heard it all before and not only from David. If only... Suddenly she sat up, straight-backed, her legs crossed in front of her. She smiled broadly. "David, I have something important to say to you." Her sadness was gone, her voice light but firm.

David waited, looking at her.

She spoke slowly at first, pausing after each phrase. "You can let yourself experience the pleasure and freedom of realizing, David, of acknowledging that you and I...that we are equally capable people. Yes, that we're both capable of...of things, of leading sometimes and of following, of being active and passive, of giving and receiving from each other, of caring and being cared for." The rate of her speech picked up now. "You can be tender and vulnerable and open with me. You truly respect me, David. You value me as a full human being. You do not have to outdo me to feel good about yourself. You do not need to dominate me, even in subtle ways, or use me." Drew's eyes were shining. "You realize that it does not make you less to acknowledge that I am not less than you. You want me as your equal partner, not your complement; to share with you, not to complete you. We're each whole in ourselves. You know this now. You respect me."

Drew stopped talking then and waited until David's beautiful thicklashed eyes began to move, and he spoke.

"If you do decide to give up on me, I'll understand," he said. His voice did not have the usual arrogant edge. There was no sarcasm or condescension. "I hope you don't, though. It's scarey for me...threatening maybe, to acknowledge what I know...and feel, to act on it. I've always had this 'attitude' about women, but I do feel differently about you, Drew. I suppose that's hard to believe."

"I believe it, David," Drew said, for she knew it was true.

They spent the next two hours talking, and the hour after that making love again. It was different this time, the lovemaking, in subtle ways that Drew had trouble identifying, but she felt filled and content and cared about. This made it easy to care about David, and the nagging dissatisfaction that had been gnawing at her was not there.

When it was time for Drew to return home, David did not protest. He'd often seemed to resent Becka, how much of Drew's time and energy she required, but tonight he was supportive of Drew as she readied herself to leave. He even empathized with the burden part of her responsibility of parenting and said how she must treasure the relationship she has with her daughter.

He got dressed and walked her to her car. This is something he used to do when they'd first begun their relationship nine months ago. Drew felt herself falling in love as he touched her hair and she stroked his face and they tenderly said goodnight.

## 9.

It was a sunny August Sunday. Drew had slept late and her first cup of coffee was just beginning to bring her to life when Judith and Sandy stopped by. They invited Drew and the "squirt" to join them for a bike ride along the lake shore. This was one of Becka's favorite things to do; she was outside mounted up and waiting to go before Drew had time to grab her Super-8 and find her sunglasses.

There was only moderate traffic on the bike path as they made their way through Lincoln Park toward the lake. Drew went slowly, her cast-covered arm challenging but not daunting her. After a while, they stopped for cokes at a refreshment stand and sat to talk and rest and watch the water. Becka was not ready to rest and rode up and down as the women sat.

"So, what's been happening, Sandy?" Drew asked. "I haven't seen you in ages." Sandy was more Judith's friend than Drew's, though Drew sometimes enjoyed the younger woman's company. She was lively and energetic, and amused Drew.

"Nothing quite as dramatic as your adventure," Sandy replied. "But, I did have a strange experience."

Drew rolled her eyes, knowing what was coming.

"I used to go with this guy named Frank, two, almost three years ago. He left Chicago and that was it. Went to New Mexico. I hadn't talked with him for all that time and I'm sure he never even crossed my mind for over a year. Until last week."

Drew nodded and found her eyes drifting out over the lake, watching the sailboats float silently by.

"I was sitting in the bathroom, you know, and he just flashed into my mind. Frank Abbott. I wonder what ever became of him."

"And then there he was, in the bathtub," Drew said.

"No, but not ten minutes later the phone rang."

"No!"

"Yes. It was Frank. He said he'd been thinking about me and wondering how I was doing."

"I'll be damned!"

Judith poked Drew in the ribs.

"Did I ever tell you about the time I had this feeling that I shouldn't take the bus," Sandy continued, "the one downstate, to Urbana. It was last winter. I was at the bus station. Had my ticket and everything. But, I got this feeling. So I cashed in my ticket and I took the train instead. What do you think happened to that bus?"

"It was captured by extraterrestrials."

"No, seriously. It went into a ditch. The people were stranded for hours. They nearly froze."

"M-m," Drew said. "Was it snowing that day?"

"Yes, almost a blizzard."

"So, you made a good deduction based on the information you had."

Judith left them at that point and went to walk along the beach.

"What do you mean?" Sandy asked.

"You inferred that the bus might have trouble on the road."

"No, it wasn't an inference; it was a premonition, Drew. You'd have to experience it to know what I mean. Things like that happen to me all the time."

"Sandy."

"Yes."

"You really know better than that. Listen to me."

Sandy did. She listened to every word that Drew said, never moving her eyes from Drew's.

"It's not possible to see into the future," Drew began. "The mystical-type experiences you've had are coincidences. You've made many other low-probability predictions that have not come true, but you tend to forget them. In fact, there is no such thing as psychic experiences. Everything can be explained by natural cause and effect. Some events are very unusual and intriguing and it's tempting to look for explanations beyond the reality that we can sense and infer, but if enough information were available, all those events could be explained reasonably based on the reality of physical facts and human psychology. To look for mystical explanations is a lazy, magical cop out."

Becka and Judith were throwing stones into the lake, and when Sandy's eyes cleared, she turned her head and watched them for a long time.

Drew wanted to know the effect of the zap. "What other things like that have happened to you?" she asked.

"What do you mean?"

"Experiences like the bus and the phone call from Frank."

Sandy didn't answer right away. She seemed deep in thought, her face more serious than Drew had ever seen it. Actually, she looked miserable.

"To tell the truth," Sandy said at last, "it's always fascinated me, Drew, the possibilities of other dimensions. Energy fields. Psychic things. But..." She shook her head sadly. "...I don't really believe it. It's just fun to speculate about. Actually, there's no real evidence for any of that stuff. You know, this really is all there is, Drew. God, it's boring." Her shoulders slumped; she looked indescribably sad. "Everything's so mundane and dull. Do you ever feel that way? Like there's nothing exciting, nothing to look forward to. Just routine. Day after day." She stared out at the lake, apparently no longer aware of Drew.

"Did you rest long enough?" Becka asked, running up to them.

The four bicyclers continued their ride, eventually ending up at Sandy's studio apartment, near the zoo. Sandy brought out snacks and drinks, but was not talkative.

"You OK?" Judith asked her. "You seem kind of down, Sandy."

"Oh, I don't know," Sandy said. "I've just been thinking."

Becka was lying on the floor looking at a book she'd found. "What's pa-si phenima?" she asked.

"Psi phenomena," Sandy replied. "It's nothing, Becka, just nonsense. I have a book on insects. Would you like to look at that?"

"Did she say 'nonsense'?" Judith said to Drew. "I can't believe it. I wonder what's going on with her."

Drew looked unhappy and did not reply.

"Judith, do you think I can get my money back on that course I started?" Sandy asked. "I only went to two sessions."

"The Parapsychology one? You want to drop it?"

"Yeah. That garbage is a waste of time and money. Cost me 150 bucks. I hope they don't give me a hassle about the money. Oh well, it doesn't really matter anyway."

Drew felt sick. A wave of nausea swept her stomach; her head and face were hot. Excusing herself, she went to the john and stayed there a long time. *Fools rush in, fools rush in*, kept going through her mind. I've got to be more careful. Wiley's right. Damn.

43

She sunk her face into the basin of cold water. I shouldn't tamper that way. I've got to zap Sandy again, erase it before she goes into a real depression.

Drew called Sandy to the john. She asked her about the unusual abstract oil painting on the wall and then she zapped her, saying that Sandy wished to disregard the earlier zap and return to her previous beliefs. The light was back in Sandy's eyes when they joined Judith and Becka. She began talking happily about what she was learning in her new course and how fascinating it was.

Judith looked puzzled; Drew, relieved.

## 10.

Monday Drew gave her two-week notice. She'd miss some of the people, but that was minor. She was looking forward now; the possibilities were limitless. The next morning, at the breakfast table with her coffee, she was thinking about that, about the future, and realized something was holding her back. She hadn't contacted Art Trevor yet, to arrange for her filmmaking training, though she had planned to do so yesterday. She wondered why. Was she having second thoughts about zapping people after what happened with Sandy? She thought of Alfredo, the hospital orderly, and wondered what effects her zap was having on him at this point. Was he miserable? Torn apart inside by the clash of beliefs? Certainly what she'd done to him would have to alter his life radically. Had she made a psychological cripple out of him, a man at war with himself?

Drew helped Becka find her swimsuit (it was under the potato chips box in the pantry) and walked outside with her to wait for the camp bus.

"Are there camps for grownups, mom?"

"You mean like yours? Day camps?

Becka nodded.

"No, not really. Not that I know of. There's Club Med." Drew chuckled to herself. "There are day hospitals for people who are mentally ill, and programs for the elderly. Why do you ask?"

"Well," Becka said, scratching at her button of a nose, "I thought that maybe when you stopped going to your job like you said, you might be lonely or can't think of anything to do. Camps are fun for doing stuff."

Drew laughed. "I'll be OK, sweetie. I'll have plenty to do."

"Bake cakes and things?"

"No."

"Karen's mom's always baking."

"Maybe she enjoys it."

"You don't."

"No."

"Well, that's OK. You do what you like, mom."

"Thanks, Beck. You see that yellow thing?"

"The bus, you mean?"

"You got your lunch?"

"Yep, 'bye, mom."

In her office, Drew called the hospital in Wisconsin. Alfredo didn't come on duty until eleven. No, they could not give out his home phone. Drew finally reached him late in the afternoon at the nursing station during his lunch break.

Yes, he said, of course he remembered her, and, yes, she said, she was coping with one-armed living satisfactorily.

"I imagine you're surprised to hear from me, Alfredo." She groped for a cigarette, but couldn't manage it with one hand. "Hold on just a second." She got the cigarette lit. "The reason I called is that I was curious about you, about your project, that is. It impressed me when I heard about it, you know, that you were getting something going for the women employees at the hospital, so I was wondering how it's going."

Alfredo seemed neither displeased nor suspicious about Drew's call. In fact, he seemed very glad to have the chance to talk about the project and about his own life. "I been reading everything I can get my hands on," he said, and proceeded, quite articulately, to discuss feminist theory with Drew, and to talk about his attempts to start a men's consciousness-raising group. "It's frustrating, but I think we're gonna pull it off." His girlfriend, Rose, was having some trouble adjusting to the changes in him, although she liked them, he said, and he had come to appreciate her in totally new ways. "We both got a lot to learn yet. We're working on it together. I like that." Alfredo went on and on, talking almost non-stop. He was happier than he'd ever been, he declared, though angry about much that he'd been learning about women's oppression. "A lot of my old buddies and I don't get along so good anymore, but that's the way it goes." He talked about the new friends he was making, partially through his efforts to start the men's rap group. Alfredo talked for nearly an hour, obviously pleased to have an interested listener. He had no idea why he'd changed, he said, but interpreted it as a gift of insight that had added a lot to his life. "So, good luck with your arm and all," he said when Drew finally told him she had to get back to work, "and keep in touch, huh?"

After they hung up, Drew sat at her desk, smiling with satisfaction. She thought about Art Trevor and how she'd contact him and how she'd word the zap. She thought about David. Everything's going to work out real well; she was sure of it.

## 11.

David brought a folder full of his photos. Drew looked them over, nodding, saying little. He watched her expectantly.

"I'm surprised you're showing these to me. It's been so long." She continued going through the stack as she spoke. "In fact, I don't think I've seen any of your work since that class we took together at Hull House."

"Black and White Photography II. I almost didn't ask you out."

"You didn't," Drew said. "I asked you." She held up a silhouette shot of a tree and squinted as she looked at it. "To a party, remember? It was the first time I'd ever asked a man out." She smiled. "It was hard to do, so I remember it well. But, what do you mean? Had you thought about asking me out before that, but decided not to?"

David laughed. "I was attracted to you from the first day in class, Drew." He averted his beautiful eyes, eyes that inspired poetry in some of his female students. "But when I realized what a good photographer you were, I felt...I don't know, intimidated, I guess."

Drew looked at him, tilting her head. "I didn't know that."

"You were so good and you were relatively new at it. I'd been doing photography for years, and you just...it seemed to come naturally to you. I had to work my ass off. I resented you for it. I think that's one of the reasons I've always looked for ways to put you down." He bent and took Drew's fingers, the ones that pro-

46

truded beyond the cast, and kissed them. "I feel awful about it, Drew, about a lot of things. I never told you what I thought of your work. Not honestly. But, I want you to know now. I think you're extremely talented. You have a photographer's eye. I really...respect you."

Until the last phrase passed David's lips, Drew had found herself immensely pleased. She was enjoying the praise, but especially David's honesty, his willingness to reveal himself this way and to compliment her genuinely. But when he mentioned "respecting" her, Drew felt the sinking drop in her stomach. She recalled the words she'd used last week when she zapped him. Does he really mean this, she wondered or...Well, of course he means it. He has to. I made him. But it's meaningless. He "respects" me now, but not because of genuine...or is it genuine? Did my zap just free him...or is it all bullshit?

"I'd like to hear your critique of my work," David said. "I mean, I'd appreciate it, if you're willing. I know I can learn a lot from you."

Drew didn't say anything. She stared at his photographs, not seeing them, feeling angry. "So what changed you?" she challenged. "Why are you telling me this now?"

David thought about her questions. He was sitting on the leather footstool leaning forward, his arms resting on his legs. "I've been trying to figure it out myself," he said. "Saturday night when we talked, when you seemed so far away for a while...I guess I got scared. I saw the proverbial writing on the wall. You were thinking about ending it, I know. Maybe that jolted me, made me realize how much you mean to me. You've been on my mind constantly since then. You're not like other women, Drew. I feel very fortunate. You're the best of both worlds, a terrifically warm, soft, sweetheart who's also...who I respect and value. I don't feel competitive with you, or superior to you or scared of you."

They were in the living room, David's photos spread out on the coffee table. Drew couldn't remember ever seeing him look so sincere. He reached over and put his hand on her leg, neither with possessiveness, nor condescension, smiling expressively. It was a gesture of deep caring and regard, and Drew felt the light, filling sense of being deeply loved.

"With men," David continued, "I feel like I'm in a race, jockeying for position, you know, the 'mine's bigger than yours' crap. With women, I've always felt it was a given that I was on top. They were soft and emotional and vulnerable. Good need-fillers for me. With you, though, I don't feel either of those ways, Drew. It's like

47

you've got it all, both sides, so there's no tug of war, nothing to prove, nothing to use. Am I making sense?"

Drew swallowed and nodded.

"You're a special person to me... a whole person, an end in yourself, not a means to something..." David smiled. His eyes were glistening with tears. "I feel clumsy," he said. "Like I'm not able to get it across right, to tell you what's going on in me...how I feel about you."

Despite herself, Drew responded. She felt more love for David at that moment than she'd ever known, and the feeling took over. She wrapped her good arm around him and pressed her cheek to his, sensing in the contact and warmth of their skin, a closeness that seemed to close the gap and fill up the empty spaces.

They talked about his photographs and David listened to Drew in a way he never had before, attentively, openly, hearing her non-defensively. Later, they went for a walk, hand in hand, and laughed, even giggled together, and they sat on the porch steps talking softly until Becka came from her friend's and sat with them, the three telling stories, beneath the moon, on a summer's evening.

He rarely left her mind. In her office, Drew went through her files, organizing them for whoever would take her place; she handled her correspondence and phone calls and sat through the meetings, but somewhere, alternating between foreground and background, David was always there. The memory of his touches. The way he looked at her. What he said. How he said it. His openness. Never a biting remark. No more of those little jolts or "clicks". He was delightful to be with and, over the next few days, he and Drew spent every moment they could together, and connected by phone when they had to be apart. Friday night they went to Judith's to have dinner with her and Vic.

Judith had always found the four of them a compatible, congenial group. They had spent many enjoyable evenings together. Tonight, though, from the moment Drew and David arrived, Judith felt edgy. Something was different. At first, she couldn't quite identify what it was, but eventually she realized that, tonight, it was with David, rather than herself, that Drew was exchanging meaningful looks. It was with David, she realized, that Drew traded quick, coded comments. Judith condemned herself for the jealous feelings that bit at the edges of her skin. They've obviously cemented their relationship tighter than it used to be, she thought. So that's good. Good for them. I wish them well. But Judith's resentment grew as the evening wore on. When she found herself withdrawing, she resented it even more and pushed herself, forcing joviality she did not feel, then becoming uncharacteristically boisterous and argumentative.

"It's another excuse to harass people," she almost shouted at one point. "Granted, there are a lot of illegal aliens here, but that in no way justifies what those creeps in the Immigration Service have been doing." Her face was twisted in anger. "They drag people from their homes onto the streets, for Christ's sake, intimidating the hell out of them, pushing them around, degrading them. They're pigs. They don't even pretend to have probable cause. They completely disregard these people's rights. Fascist pigs!"

"All right, Judith, we hear you," David said patronizingly. "We know how you feel about the poor, miserable, unwanted, downtrodden. But your emotions blur your thinking, dear." He smiled condescendingly at her. "I know you'd like us to throw wide the doors, let them all come and suck generous America's bountiful breasts. But use your head, Jude." He chuckled. "Sometimes you remind me of my students. Full of feeling but short on data and logic."

Vic laughed. "Let me quote from Professor David Furmanek," he said pompously. "Most of the girls in my classes have their brains in their tits. End quote."

"Now, that's not exactly how I put it," David defended. "I believe I said that while they may not be able to string together a set of words to make a complete thought, they can sure swing their asses and jumble up everyone else's thoughts."

The two men laughed. Drew felt the sickening jolt, a "click", an unwelcome *deja vu*. She and Judith caught eyes.

"There's one in my Intro class," David went on, directing his words to Vic. "Dumb blond type. She stares at me with her big, vacuous eyes like I was Robert Redford." David laughed and poured himself some more wine. "Ten to one she won't get through Freshman year before she starts turning out babies."

"Or turning tricks," Vic added. "So, have you scored with any of these hot coeds?" he asked, smiling teasingly at Drew.

"Only lustful thoughts," David said, chuckling. "Drew's more than enough for me. Most of those girls are juicy empty packages; nicely decorated, but hollow. Drew, on the other hand..." He reached toward her. Drew reflexively pulled away. "Hey, hon, you know I'm just kidding."

Drew looked away from him, staring across the room.

"I've said repeatedly many of my brightest students are women. There are numerous exceptions."

"Exceptions?" Drew and Judith exclaimed simultaneously.

49

"That's right. Shit, I'm not saying it's their fault. It's conditioning. They're trained to be what they are, socialized into it. Fortunately, fortunately for me..." He looked at Drew lovingly. "...there *are* exceptions."

But it could not be regenerated. It was as if the loving feelings that had grown in Drew over the past few days were suddenly coated with a festering mold, suffocated beneath the stench of deeply ingrained rotting, rotten attitudes.

Drew said something about coffee and went to the kitchen. Judith followed. For Judith, the sunshine had returned. She and Drew spoke together in low tones, angrily at first, about what had just gone on; then they moved past it, reaffirming their female bond and unity.

"I've got a confession to make," Drew said. She could hear David pontificating to Vic in the next room. "I did it to David last Saturday. Implanted a belief in him. That he respected me and valued me, things like that." She shook her head in disgust.

"So, that's why..."

Drew nodded. "He's been wonderful. My Pygmalion. I fell in love with my own creation, Judith. I made him into what I wanted and then fell in love."

"You didn't do a very complete job."

"I know."

Judith got up from the kitchen chair and began scraping garbage from their plates. "So, now what?" she asked. "More zaps? Make the transformation complete?"

"I could."

"I know. Do you want to?"

"Female version of the Stepford Wives," Drew said, playing absentmindedly with some crumbs on the table.

Judith laughed. "Oh, right, I remember," she said. "That's the book where the men made their wives into robots, isn't it? Robots who served their husbands joyfully."

"Yeah," Drew responded. "Domestic and sexual service with perfect contentment." She put her cigarette out on a potato peel. "It sucks."

"You could do it."

Drew shook her head. "Sure. I could zap David into being the ideal mix of everything I like. Tailor-made perfection, guaranteed to have no rough edges, unless I choose to put them there for a little challenge."

"Are you tempted?" Judith asked, fairly certain what Drew would say, but anxious nonetheless.

50

"The prospect makes me sick."

Judith breathed her relief.

"There's something eerie and ugly about it. Something obscene even. It would be like having a perfectly programmed toy. But not a relationship. It wouldn't be real. I'd know that. I've felt it several times already with David, since I zapped him, but I pushed it away. You know," she said, standing up and joining Judith at the sink, "I'm glad this happened tonight. I'm glad I didn't zap him any more than I did, do a complete job as you said. If I had, I may never have realized..." She hugged Judith. "There are people who've come by it naturally," she said, "or honestly, at least."

"Hey, you need any help out there?" a male voice called.

Both women, looking into each other's eyes, shook their heads.

"No," Drew said. "We're doing fine without you."

"Just get you feet from off our necks," Judith added, laughing.

On the drive home that night, Drew restored David to the self he seemed destined to be. The change was sudden, though subtle. He did not pull her by the hair to grovel at his feet, nor order her to serve, nor discount her every word. He returned to the very civilized, sophisticated, carefully polished sexist pig he'd always been and Drew thought about just how she'd say goodbye. She wondered if his pride and need would make his response mainly anger or mainly hurt. She felt sad and knew it didn't really matter. It was his problem.

_____ **12.**

"You're not serious."

"I'd never kid you, Wiley. Be happy for me."

"I'm nervous for you."

"I don't need that."

"But, Drew, Europe! Now? I mean that's great, a trip to Europe. Fine, fun, ordinarily, but shit, you're not an ordinary person. You can't just do ordinary things."

"Yes I can, Wiley."

Wiley took a deep breath, and let it out very slowly. "I know you can, Drew. That's not what I mean. I mean, you have to be careful.

51

Where in Europe?''

"You worried about the Russians?''

"Don't laugh.''

"You're paranoid.''

"You're a world resource. If what you have were known, every nation on earth would be after you.''

"So far you have me to yourself,'' Drew said, feeling something akin to suspicion. "I trust you won't tell,'' she added rapidly, keeping it light, pushing away the other feelings.

"It's the temptation *you're* dealing with, the temptation to use the power. That's what creates the danger, the possibility of someone finding out.''

"Do you want to come along? Chaperone me?''

Wiley paused. Yes, I definitely want to go along, she thought. "No, that's not the solution. You're leaving in a week?''

"A week from tomorrow. In three more days, I'm getting this dirty piece of plaster removed.'' Drew tapped the cast with her knuckles.

"Are you taking Becka?''

"No, she'll be with her father. Their summer vacation time together. I'll get back before school starts.''

"Just you and Judith?''

"Right. Relax, Wiley. Nothing's going to happen.''

I doubt that, Wiley thought uneasily. "I had hoped we could begin the formal part of the study soon,'' she said. "We'll have to postpone.''

"Yes, but I did find a storefront for us,'' Drew offered quickly. It felt awful to let Wiley down. She watched her trusted friend's face bend into a smile. "I thought that would please you. It's on Lincoln Avenue. Good location. Rent's a little high, but affordable. And I'm getting the cards made up—Drew McAllister, Portrait Photographer. So, you can start recruiting subjects.''

"Excellent. I'd like to check the place out. Help get it set up.''

They talked about the studio and the experiment and then there was a pause.

"It's really over with you and David?'' Wiley asked.

"Done.''

"You didn't tell him anything, did you? About the zapping power?''

"Wiley, is that all you can think about?'' Drew brought her cast down on the arm of the chair with an angry clunk.

Wiley didn't answer right away. "Sorry, Drew,'' she said finally. "You can understand, can't you?''

"I guess, but I don't like it." Drew shifted positions on the chair. "Actually, I'm not sure I do understand."

They were sitting in Wiley's sprawling back yard. Drawn by the sun, they had dragged her two worn and frayed lawn chairs from the old shed in the rear of the house to Wiley's favorite spot, about ten feet from the water. Wiley had owned the roomy old house on the banks of the Chicago River for nearly ten years. The yard was wildly overrun with flowers, flowers she had planted in a burst of spring and barely attended since.

"What do you mean, Drew?"

"How this is affecting you. What your stakes are in it...in me."

Wiley flinched, barely perceptibly, but she drew back a fraction of an inch. How much does Drew suspect, she wondered.

Drew felt guilty now. Guilty and angry. The tornado had twisted her life all around. Here she was, suspicious of one of her closest, most trustworthy friends.

Wiley looked at the river. She could see something floating by. Maybe it was a tree branch, or maybe some rotten piece of human garbage. It collided with a rock and split into two, the chunks now moving separately, getting further and further apart. "Do you want me to back off?" she asked. "Leave you alone? Stay out of it? Forget about...about the experiment and the plan?" She looked serious and pained.

Is she, Drew wondered. Would she back off if that's what I wanted? Good lord, what's wrong with me? Why am I so suspicious? Wiley's a rock; the most reliable, unselfish, responsible person I've ever known. Drew's face was dark and drawn. At least, I always thought she was.

She looked at her friend. Although Wiley knew she was being scrutinized, she kept her gaze to the river. She's so serious, Drew thought. Always thinking, figuring things out, figuring people out, weighing things, making plans; always talking about what's needed to make a better world. She hardly ever talks about her own needs.

Drew thought back over the five years she'd known Wiley, of the endless conversations they'd had, how caringly Wiley always listened to her. She thought of Wiley's contemplative nature, her sincerity, her fairness, her concern for social justice. She's such an idealist. She wants so much to change things, to change the way people are, to change social structures. I guess she *does* talk about her own needs, Drew realized.

They'd first met at a planning meeting of the E.R.A. Task Force. Although there were only eight women there, Drew had barely

53

noticed Wiley until near the end of the meeting. It was then that Wiley spoke, that is, spoke about her own perspective. Prior to that, she had intervened only occasionally during the discussion. When someone was getting off the track, she nudged her back. When conflicting views began to distract them into argumentativeness, she smoothed feathers and got things moving again. She seemed to be the lubricant for the group, not a gear, until near the end of the meeting. Drew remembered that clearly. As the meeting was nearing a close, Wiley had concisely summarized the main points of what had transpired so far, integrating some additional relevant information into her overview. Then she made a clear proposal as to the steps they could take. The others listened attentively, nodding, asked a few questions, then agreed to her suggestions without major modifications. They divided up the tasks and adjourned.

After the meeting, Drew and Wiley had gone for coffee. Drew couldn't remember how that had come about, who suggested it, but she remembered much of their conversation. Wiley seemed very interested in her and Drew found herself discussing details of her past and present that she rarely disclosed to anyone. She talked at length about her marriage, but without the usual glossing over of her discontent. She told Wiley how it had been when she and Steve first met in college. That was in 1972 at the University of Wisconsin in Madison. Drew had been on the fringes of the civil rights/war-protesting/hippie culture spawned in the sixties, and Steve Tremaine pulled her closer to its center. His radicalism peaked during his undergraduate years. He spoke at rallies and marched and hailed the coming of the revolution, and he liked Drew at his side with her long wild hair and devotion to him and her own budding radicalism which he could foster and guide. When they moved in together, to the fourth floor walkup, her role gradually stabilized. She was present during the many strategy sessions and even, occasionally, contributed a comment or two, though mostly she listened. At first she felt honored, fully enjoying the back-up role she played, along with the other women of the left. They edited the men's speeches. They made sure that everyone ate and had a place to sleep. They were available to their men, careful not to be uptight or *bourgeois* sexually. Even Drew, on occasion, found herself beneath a pumping revolutionary prick other than that of Steve whose bed she shared most nights and who called her his old lady.

Drew told Wiley that night in the coffee shop that all of this would have been OK for her, she thought, if she had moved on then, learning from it, if she had just passed through. Instead, she married

54

Steve. She always thought the idea occurred to him only after discovering that liberated sexuality was fine for everyone except "his woman".

Somewhere deep down Drew knew even then, even at the wedding ceremony in the woods with the poetry and guitar music, that this was not for her, that Steve was stifling her and did not want her free. But they married. Steve went to dental school, his second choice when no medical school accepted him. He rationalized that dentistry for the people was noble, too, but "the people" soon faded as the establishment took him in and his hair grew short. Becka was born and most of Drew's growing feminist awareness came from books then, for there was little time for meetings and consciousness-raising groups. Drew had her B.A. in Sociology, and so she typed and answered phones and diapered and mothered and watched Steve change. She cooked for him and lay beneath him and would have been very unhappy except for Becka whom she loved instantly and fully.

Drew told all this to Wiley that day five years ago in the coffee shop after the meeting of the E.R.A. Task Force. She told her all this and more and much more after that as their friendship grew, and Wiley talked a lot too. Only her talk was different. She talked ideas. Philosophy, psychology, feminism, social justice, politics. She often grew angry in those conversations, expressing her frustration at the "system", at inequities and injustice and at her own limits. Although she was certainly highly adept at persuading people, gradually getting them to see things her way, she'd often said, Drew recalled, that this was not enough.

What did she really want, Drew wondered. Why, over all these years, has her personal life remained so indistinct and blurry-edged?

The setting sun illuminated the left side of Wiley's head, casting shadows over the contours of her broad, almost-handsome face. I don't really know you, Drew thought, even though I know you well. "Would you back off if I want you to?" Drew asked.

Wiley looked upwards, at the orange sky, and then at Drew. "It would be hard," she replied. "I'd worry."

"Why else would it be hard?"

"Because it fascinates me, the power you have, the potential of it. Because I want to know what happens with it, with you, and be a part of it."

"You've been an unbelievably loyal friend, Wiley. You're always there for me. You don't seem to ask for much back for yourself. What about *your* needs? I tell you mine, all of them, and I rarely ever hear of yours. I'd even come to think that's all there is to you, but that can't be. I have the sense that you keep part of yourself hidden from me."

Wiley nodded. She looked at her friend, the waving leaves from the overhanging trees casting rippling shadows on Drew's face and arms and legs. Wiley felt weighted and old, and perhaps somewhat afraid. "And now," she said quietly, "because of the zapping power and because of my involvement in it, you need to know more. You need to know if you can fully trust me."

"Yes," Drew answered, feeling almost ashamed.

"I've let you in as close as I thought you'd want to come."

"I don't understand," Drew said softly.

A bee buzzed near Wiley's feet. She watched it without fear, knowing that if she did not provoke it, it would go away and find some juicy flowers, far more suited to its nature than her toe. "Are you afraid I'll take advantage of you somehow, of your power, try to use it for myself?"

"No," Drew replied immediately, her guilt and shame bludgeoning her. "Well," she amended, "it has crossed my mind." She began to cry, just a few drops, at first, then, feeling them on her cheeks, a flood followed, and she sobbed and asked, almost pleaded, for Wiley to help her, to take her doubt and fear away.

"I can't do that," Wiley said, leaning towards her friend, but not touching her, feeling her tears, but not trying to wipe them away. "But, you need a friend in this; *I* know I can be that friend. *You're* not sure. If you think it would help for me to tell you more of who I am, I can do that."

Drew reached for Wiley, grasping her hand, and held it tightly. "Am I being awful?" she asked, more tears coming. "Unfair to you? I don't know, Wiley. I don't know what to think."

"You're dealing with something that probably no one else has had to cope with, Drew. I don't know if I can allay your fears about me or set your mind at ease, but for both our sakes, I'm willing to try in whatever way you think will help."

Drew removed her hand from Wiley's and wiped her face. She sat back in her chair. "What did you mean when you said you've let me as close to you as you thought I wanted to be?" she asked. For some reason, she felt entitled to the information. Her guilt receded as she waited for Wiley to respond.

"That I *have* kept part of myself from you." Wiley rubbed her tense fingers over the dented aluminum arm of her chair. She'd spent many hours in this chair, sat out here with many friends. Drew was in Elena's chair. "Because I thought you wouldn't want to know. Probably because I feared you'd run or, at least, drift away. I guess I feared your rejection."

"What is it?" Drew asked, surprised to see Wiley vulnerable, concerned about her, but determined to hear more. "What did you think I'd reject you for?"

"Maybe now is the time. Maybe it would help if I told you..." Drew waited.

"Besides my mother," Wiley said, "you're the only person I love who I've hidden important parts of my identity from."

Drew continued to wait, sensing what it was Wiley would reveal, but dismissing the thought almost before it formed.

"When I met you, I was at the low point of my life. I was throwing myself into my career, the Task Force, writing." The lines of strain around Wiley's mouth grew deeper; there was a very slight tremor on her lips. "I had just ended a seven year relationship, Drew. A love...lover...relationship. My lover was an alcoholic. A wonderful person, but hopelessly addicted. I couldn't help and I couldn't stand the destructiveness of it."

Drew listened, her heart pounding, rapt attention and caring focused on her friend. Why had she never spoken of this? I could have been a support, listened to her, maybe even consoled her in some way. So that's what happened; how hard it must have been. And she must have totally given up on romance after that.

"Her name is Elena Weldon. She lives in Oregon now. We write occasionally."

"A woman!" Drew didn't know if she was really shocked or even surprised. She repeated the words, "a woman", softly this time, simply stating what was now an obvious fact.

"Before that, and since, I've had other lovers, other women lovers."

Drew nodded, making connections, thinking "of course", feeling numb.

"As you know, I also have many straight friends. Most of those who are close to me know of my sexuality. I knew you would know, too, one day. I just didn't know when."

Drew knew she had to speak. She had to give something back now, but she was confused. It makes no difference, of course, she thought. But was that true? Did it make a difference? She'd met other gay women, mostly through the women's groups she'd been in, but none were friends. She wasn't sure why. There had been one, Lisa Gold, at college. They had almost become friends, but for some reason, she and Drew had drifted apart. I've always believed it was a viable option, totally acceptable, Drew thought.

But, Wiley! My friend. We've slept together in the same tent, showered together at the pool, been naked in the same room untold times. Did she ever think of me that way, Drew wondered.

"I feel attracted to Judith," Drew said. She did not know she would say this until the words came out. "I don't think it's a sexual attraction, but one time I was sitting with my legs over a chair and Judith passed by. Her fingertips brushed against my legs. I got a reaction I couldn't believe. I felt all liquidy and...It was a rush, Wiley. Mostly I pushed the thoughts away, and the feelings. I'm attracted to her, in a way. Women, some women, are..." Drew felt very flustered. This is not what she wanted to be saying. This was not relevant. She thought of David and the times when she had felt an almost overwhelming love for him and how her body responded. And of other men she'd known. No, it was just a close friendship bond with Judith, just a warm, close friendship. Nothing more.

"Women can be very lovable," Wiley said. "I went through a fairly typical adolescence, dating and all that. My coming out was very slow."

"Are you OK with it?" Drew asked, not knowing quite how to phrase the question.

"Yes. And have been for years. But I'm cautious, discreet. I don't fool myself about the biases most people have, the myths they believe."

"I'm sure I'm not free of them," Drew said. "Deep down, I mean. They taught us in psychology, the Psychology of Adjustment, that homosexuality is a psychosexual fixation. Later, I decided that was bullshit, but it's hard to..."

"I know."

"I really don't think it makes a difference to me, Wiley, about you."

"It makes a difference," Wiley said, "but maybe not a negative one. We'll see."

"I'm OK with it."

"Give yourself time."

"Yeah." They watched the river for a while. The sun was disappearing. "It must have been hard. About Elena, I mean."

"Yes, it was. Like so many couples, we thought our commitment was forever."

"She's still drinking?"

"As far as I know."

"I had a crush on the dorm director when I was a Freshman at U.W.," Drew said. "Miss Palmer. I used to get goosebumps whenever I'd see her, and become tongue-tied. She must have thought I was weird."

"My first was the playground director at my grammar school. I've thought of her since. I'm sure she's a lesbian."

Drew looked uncomfortable.

"Are you feeling uneasy with me now?" Wiley asked.

Drew thought a moment. "No," she said. "No, I don't think so. You're Wiley, my cerebral, obsessive, loving, lesbian friend."

Wiley smiled. Her hands rested loosely on the arms of the chair. She seemed much more relaxed now.

They didn't speak of Drew's trip again.

They didn't say much at all for a while.

Each woman was full of her own thoughts.

"The mosquitos are out."

They watched the river silently, although they could barely see it any more.

"Did you come on your moped?"

"Mm-hm. Sarah took Becka to a play, the 'Witches Switch' or 'Which Witch' or something like that. They have the car." Drew laughed. "I think Sarah gets as much of a kick out of those kids' plays as Becka."

It grew darker and still they sat, slapping at mosquitos and rubbing their arms from the coolness of the evening.

"Wiley."

"Mm-hm."

"I think it *is* a sexual attraction. With Judith. I have fantasies about her."

"Oh, hm. What are you doing with it?"

"Mostly nothing. Putting it all away, convincing myself that I simply feel affection for a close friend."

"Mm-hm."

"It's different, though."

"Yes."

"I keep imagining what it would be like to kiss her, to *really* kiss her. I find myself touching her a lot, and getting those rushes when I do." Drew lit a cigarette and stared at the match until the flame disappeared. "What do you think it means?" she asked.

Wiley paused. "What do you think, Drew?"

"I don't know. That I'm sick of dealing with men, maybe; or that because Judith is so dear to me, I'm confusing that love with something else, another kind."

"I don't know," Wiley said.

"Will you answer me honestly if I ask you something?" Drew

asked, thankful for the darkness that covered them now.

"Yes," Wiley said, "or tell you I don't want to answer at all."

"You've been...attracted to...you've been a lesbian for years..."

"Yes."

"I know you have straight friends."

"Yes."

"But, *our* friendship, yours and mine...You seemed to really...I don't know...you seemed to like me, from the start. A lot. You called me, invited me places..."

"Yes."

"Well..." Drew kept moving her head around and squirming on her chair. "Here comes the question."

"OK."

"Wiley, did you pick up something about me? Did you think... or maybe...Did you think *I* was attracted to women, or that I could be, that...Is that why I was interesting to you?"

"That might have been part of it," Wiley said. She, too, seemed unable to sit still. "Of course, I knew right from the start you were married. It was pretty clear that you weren't aware of any feelings... feelings towards women, that you were fully identified as heterosexual. But, yes, I picked up something, I don't know exactly what."

Drew was silent for a long time, going over memories, looking for signs in herself, wondering how one knows. I didn't know about Wiley, she thought, for all those years. "You never let on," Drew said at last.

"Hm?"

"All those years and you never said anything. You listened to me talk about my romances, all my miseries and frustrations and periods when I thought I was in love. You were my closest confidant. You listened to all that and you never once talked about your own...It never occurred to me..." She leaned a few inches closer to Wiley. "But you know, I think it was easier to have it that way, for me I mean, to see you as somehow self-contained, not struggling with anything, not subject to...I mean, you know, not emotionally vulnerable or needy, not dealing with anything... other than the stuff you did talk about." Drew smiled, then added, "What you thought I was ready for." Sighing, she pulled her knees up to her chin and encircled them with her good arm. Wiley seems more real now, she was thinking, more human, filled out. "What's it been like for you, Wiley? You said you've had lovers since Elena. Anything serious?"

"I was with Carolyn for awhile. Carolyn Greene. You met her

a few times.''

Drew nodded, picturing Carolyn Green, attractive, bright, an artist with two children.

"It was good. Now, we're just friends. I'm not with anyone right now, but I may partner again. I'm open. I'm patient.''

Another wordless stretch of time passed. Drew's thoughts jumped from one thing to another, all connected with their conversation. Was it Wiley's secretiveness that had made me suspicious, she wondered. Do I trust her more now? "There's so much to digest,'' Drew said at last. "I think I may have reached overload.''

"I'm not surprised.''

Her moped took her home. Drew had no memory of the route she took nor what she passed. Becka was waiting for her, to tell her each scene and frightening moment of the play and how she screamed when they turned the lights out. "Sarah got kind of scared,'' Becka said, "but she felt better when I told her that they were just actors on the stage.''

_____ *13.*

Over the next week, Drew and Judith planned their trip, starting with which country or countries they'd include. They decided on Greece. A couple of years earlier, they had taken a trip to Colombia, and the planning had gone on for months. Both enjoyed the fact that this one was happening so quickly. Getting the plane tickets turned out to be no problem, nor was the financing. They spoke often of Mrs. Pendleton's generosity. Since the conversation with Wiley, and Drew's own naming of what she thought might be, she was much more tuned into her reactions to Judith. The feelings of attraction were clearly there and seemed to be growing more intense. She struggled with them and at one panicky moment, almost called David, but she didn't, nor did she push away the feelings.

On Wednesday, Wiley had a small dinner party. Drew came early to help with the food preparations since Wiley's cooking skills were limited to dishes that could be prepared in fifteen minutes or less, preferably in the microwave. Brenda and Sam Epstein were there. Brenda was a dentist, Wiley's dentist, in fact. She bragged about the two crowns she'd recently completed on Wiley's lower bicuspids and Wiley had to show them off for the other guests to admire. Brenda's husband, Sam, was an assistant front page editor of the Chicago Tribune whose sense of humor Drew loved. Teresa Corolla was at the dinner; she was a typesetter and a frequent companion of Wiley's. The other guest was Bill Iyodyne, a psychologist friend of Wiley's. The evening was pleasant. Bill had to leave early to get somewhere by 9:00 and Teresa left a half hour later. It was at that point that Wiley brought out her new purchase, a video camera. Drew was surprised. It didn't seem the sort of toy Wiley would be interested in. They played around with it, Drew giving Wiley some pointers on its operation, and filmed each other playing charades, which was Sam's idea. At one point, Wiley took Drew aside, into her big old-fashioned kitchen where the ancient sink stood next to the food processor and microwave oven.

"I've got an idea."

"Not another one."

"How would you feel about doing a zap or two on the dynamic duo out there, and I'll video tape it."

Drew made a face. "What for?"

"I'd like to."

Drew had had a bit of wine and was in a very good mood. "I'll zap Sam to believe he's the dentist and Brenda the editor." She giggled.

"How about zapping Brenda to believe she's a singer."

"Oh, that's great! She has an awful voice." Drew giggled again. "She hates to sing."

"I know, and tell Sam..."

"I know, I'll tell Sam he believes Israel should be given back to the Arabs."

"That's nasty."

"A good test of his debating skills."

"OK, let's go. Hey, wait, don't forget to zap them to forget they witnessed each other's zapping."

"All right. You really want to do this?"

Wiley nodded.

It went smoothly and was very funny. Brenda insisted they all sing together and her voice stood out unforgettably until Drew mercifully removed the zap. They listened to Sam's pro-Arab arguments awhile, Brenda incensed at his absurd turnabout; and when the argument between the couple grew hot Drew erased

Sam's belief and their memory of the discussion. Wiley got it all on tape. They had a final cup of coffee, then the Epstein's left and Drew stayed a while longer cleaning up.

"What are you going to do with the tape?"

"Save.it."

"For what?"

"You never know, it might come in handy sometime. Demonstration. Proof. Who knows?"

Drew looked at her friend, her eyes slightly narrowed. Wiley seemed not to notice. She got a chair and put the video tape on the top pantry shelf behind the dusty pressure cooker.

On Friday, Drew's co-workers had a goodbye lunch for her at the Greek restaurant where they frequently ate, and wished her well. Drew felt much more happy than sad about leaving.

Wiley was on her mind much of the time. They spoke daily, mostly by phone, mostly about the trip and the plans for the study, but they also talked some about Wiley's past romances and about women loving women and what that meant. Drew was doing very well with it, she thought. Those conversations were important to her, and to Wiley, as well.

They made plans to spend Saturday afternoon doing the preliminary hypothesis testing, Phase I, using Judith as the subject. "She's not having second thoughts about it, is she?" Wiley asked.

"No, she's not," Drew said, "but *I'm* having some trouble with it. Actually, I've been thinking of erasing her awareness of my power, wiping it from her memory. She's still real uncomfortable with it, with me, I guess. I don't like that."

"Hm-m," Wiley said, "I wonder how it would affect her if you did erase it."

"What do you mean?"

"Well, there is a lot of connected memories. The rape attempt itself, your talk with her that night explaining your power, and everying you've told her about it since; her awareness of how you used it on people, things like that. I wonder what would happen to all that."

"I suppose she'd forget it all."

"Possibly. How would she explain the rapist suddenly stopping his attack?"

"I don't know." Drew paused. "*He* must have come up with some explanation."

"True. It would be interesting. But it would certainly be preferable to have her as a subject. You could erase it all from her memory when we're done."

"This is weird."

"What?"

"Do you realize what we're talking about? Erasing people's memories. God, I feel like God. Sometimes I hate it."

There was silence on the phone. Wiley waited to see where Drew would go with it.

"I think I'll let *her* decide."

"That's an interesting option."

"*Interesting option*," Drew mimicked. "Wiley, sometimes you're a creep."

"Thank you."

"You're welcome. I'm going to talk with Judith about it. I'll see you tomorrow then. Maybe Judith will be there with me for the studies, maybe not."

The next day at 2:00, Drew and Judith arrived at Wiley's office. Judith had been angrier than Drew had ever seen her when she suggested the memory-erasing possibility.

"No fucking way, Drew," she had said. "How could you even think of such a thing. Erase my...God, control my awareness that way. You know, every time I think of what you're capable of, I get a creepy feeling." She didn't look pretty when she twisted her face that way. "I hate the idea that you have the ability to control my thoughts. I hate it, absolutely hate it!" Her generally warm eyes were cold and hard.

Drew felt a sinking dread, like the time she'd received a call from Becka's school that Becka had fallen on her face off the monkey bars and was in the hospital. Her eyes filled. "Judith, please, no, it's not like that. I'll never use it on you unless you want me to, I swear." She was sobbing then. "Trust me."

Judith took Drew in her arms.

"It's like a knife, Judith," Drew said, letting herself be held. "Even though it could be dangerous, it depends on how I use it. I can use it for positive things. I won't ever hurt you with it."

The two women held each other for a long time, each needing the other's consolation. She's so important to me, each thought silently.

"All right," Wiley said, when they'd settled into seats with their coffee, and finished discussing the removal of Drew's cast. "Here's the protocol." She handed Drew a manila file full of papers. "You understand that Drew will be implanting beliefs in you, Judith. We'll stop whenever you want us to, all right?"

"Fine. Hit it."

64

"Any apprehensions?"

"Sure," Judith said, "I feel like Twilight Zone." She removed her blazer and draped it over the couch. "I'm glad you're doing it this way though, you know, approaching it scientifically. I'm not crazy about being a guinea pig, but at least I'm not the first, right Wiley? The wizard here has zapped you and you seem OK." With a glint in her eye, she pretended to scrutinize Wiley. "You are, aren't you?"

Wiley smiled. "Same as always."

"That'll do. Fire away."

Drew read over the first segment of the protocol which spelled out, step by step, what she was to do. Wiley and Judith watched her read, both of them clearly very fond of Drew. The first few zaps, simple ones dealing with temperature and other sensations, went like clockwork, Judith responding exactly as expected. Then the instructions called for Drew to explain one of the zaps to Judith to test whether being aware that it was a zap would enable her to overcome it.

"Since you know I zapped you to believe your coffee tastes bitter, Judith," Drew said, reading from the page, "you realize that, objectively, it tastes the same as the cup you had earlier. Think about that and then taste it again."

"OK," Judith said, nodding slowly as she spoke. "You just suggested to me that the coffee would taste bad. God, this is amazing," she added, smiling. A beautiful smile, Drew thought. "You told me it would taste bad and it does, to me; it tastes awful. But, actually the coffee hasn't changed. OK, I can buy that. It should taste all right now." She brought the cup to her lips. Drew thought them very lovely lips. "Uk! No way. It really is terrible coffee. Or maybe my taste is off today. I might be getting sick of coffee, I drink so much of the stuff."

Wiley smiled and wrote in her notebook. "OK, Drew," she said, "let's go on to the next step."

Drew glanced at the protocol. "Judith, listen to me, I have something important to say to you." She waited until Judith's stare was intent. "In a minute you will notice that it's beginning to get dark outside. Within another minute after that, it will be completely black, like nighttime. Then, quite rapidly, illumination will return to normal." Drew waited. Judith's glazed eyes cleared.

"Are you aware  of anything having just happened?" Wiley asked Judith.

"No. You told Drew to go on to the next step, that's all. Hey, look, there's a storm coming." She gestured toward the window, then looked back at Wiley. "Why, did I miss something, did something happen?"

No one answered.

Judith kept looking out the window. "Is that weird! Can't even see clouds. It's just suddenly getting dark." She rose from her chair and went to the window, nearly tripping on the rug. "Can you believe this? It's like midnight. Pitch black." She thought of the tornado and felt fear. "Do you think...? No, no it's OK, it's passing. It's almost back to what it was. No rain or anything." She returned to her seat. "You two don't seem interested in the aberrant weather conditions. That was fascinating. Maybe it was an eclipse, not a storm at all. Yes, it must have been an eclipse, a total solar eclipse, but I didn't know we were going to have one, did you? And it happened so fast."

Neither Drew nor Wiley responded. Drew wondered if she'd ever get used to it, being able to...

"So, OK, I'm distracting you from mind science; to hell with the solar system. Let's go, I'm ready." She folded her arms. "Zap away."

Drew did. Judith smelled a pine forest and decided the janitor was deodorizing; she heard music and concluded there was some street entertainment going on outside. The protocol then instructed Drew to vary the form of the induction.

"You know, I'd like you to listen to me a moment, Judith," Drew said in a casual tone, smiling. "I have something kind of important to say." She continued smiling and so did Judith. They held eye contact, but Judith's eyes did not change. She blinked normally, still smiling and no glaze came.

Drew then again told Judith she would hear music. Judith nodded and said all right, she'd listen for it, and she did, but heard none. "Was that supposed to be a zap?" she asked.

The same thing happened with the next two attempts. The casual induction did not lead to the trance-like state and the implantations did not take.

Wiley continued writing as Drew went down the list, following the instructions step by step. They moved from perceptions to values, and soon Judith was arguing strongly for the banning of cars in the downtown area of the city, something she previously felt neutral about. Drew erased the zap, then proceeded with more tests.

"You feel happy," Drew said, and Judith became jovial; cracking jokes, smiling, behaving very warmly towards Drew and Wiley. That was the best part of the experiment, Drew thought later. "You feel angry," and Judith cursed and paced and talked of things that annoyed and frustrated her.

But when Drew told Judith she would go to Wiley's desk and type a letter, Judith did not. Questioning revealed that Judith had neither any memory of the suggestion nor any inclination to type a letter. Wiley and Drew talked briefly off to the side.

"You believe that it's important for you to type a letter now," Drew said.

When her eyes cleared, Judith gave a quick fabricated explanation and went to Wiley's desk to type. Drew waited until she'd finished, then went on to the next item.

"Today is Sunday," she said. "You fell asleep on the couch here yesterday when we were doing the experiment and you slept all night and into the next day. It's now Sunday afternoon and you just woke up."

Moments later, Judith's face twisted into a surprised, then worried, look. "Shit, I can't believe it." She looked at her watch. "Oh, no. I've never done this before. Where were you two all that time? I've got to pack. I'm sorry, I must have been exhausted." She stood and put on her blazer. "You should have awakened me. I have to go." She was moving around the office, looking for her purse. "I was supposed to call my aunt last night. She'll be worried. And I missed a brunch date with Vic this morning." Judith looked at the others. "I wonder why it happened. You must be pissed. I spoiled the experiment. How did this happen? I've never slept twenty-four hours straight in my life."

"What makes you think you slept twenty-four hours?" Wiley asked.

"Makes me think? What are you talking about? I did. I wonder if I'm coming down with something."

"How do you know you slept?" Wiley asked.

Judith continued searching for her purse. She finally found it behind the couch. "I have to leave. Why didn't you wake me?" She had the purse over her shoulder now. She looked like a businesswoman in a hurry.

"How do you know you slept?"

"Wiley, you're getting on my nerves with your goddamn questions. Drew, are you packed?" Judith looked at her watch again. "We're leaving in nineteen hours. I have to go."

"Judith, sit a moment. Just relax. Take five minutes to talk with us, OK, before you leave."

Judith hesitated. "OK, five minutes," she said anxiously. "No more. I've got a million things to do."

"How do you know you slept for twenty-four hours?"

Judith took a deep breath. She gestured with her hands as she spoke. "It's 3:30 now, right? We came here at two o'clock yesterday. I dozed off right in the middle of the experiment. I slept here, on the couch. That makes about twenty-four hours I slept."

"It's Saturday. You didn't sleep at all. Drew implanted the belief in you that you slept for twenty-four hours," Wiley said. She was sitting on the edge of her desk, facing Judith, arms folded in front of her.

Judith looked from one to the other, her face strained. "No way," she said. "What you're saying is feasible, theoretically, but that's not what happened. Possibly you two slept, too, and didn't realize it. It's simple to check." She rose, grabbed Wiley's phone and dialed.

"Aunt Grace, hi. Sorry I didn't call sooner. Were you worried?...No, I said I'd call you last night. I fell asleep, slept all night until just now...That's ridiculous...Oh, OK...No, I'm fine...No, I was just confused...No, I'm OK...I'll call you later tonight, then. 'Bye."

"You bastards," Judith said angrily. "Drew, you zapped my aunt. You must have left here while I was asleep and gone to her house and zapped her into believing today is Saturday. You better get to her quick and straighten her out. She'll be confused as hell. Go now, all right!"

"Drew didn't talk to your aunt, Judith. Today *is* Saturday."

Judith rubbed her temples. Then she grabbed the phone again. "Operator, I'm sorry to bother you, but could you tell me today's date...Oh? And the day of the week?...I see. Thank you."

Judith went to the window and looked down. The Loop was full of traffic, the stores open, the sidewalks jammed with shoppers. "I wonder why the stores are open on Sunday," she said slowly.

Wiley waited, observing with fascination.

"Somehow, everything stood still for the last twenty-four hours," Judith said. "That's what happened." She rubbed her head again. "Suspended animation. I wonder if your power caused it somehow, Drew."

"Wouldn't it be more reasonable to conclude that Drew zapped you into believing you slept for twenty-four hours, though you actually didn't?" Wiley asked.

"All right." Judith was nodding. "That's what happened then. All right." She moved her fingers absently along the leather strap of her purse, then shook her head from side to side. "But, I know I slept." She stopped. "No, it was a zap. It's a delusion. OK." She paused, tapping her fingernail on her lower tooth, an act Drew had often seen Judith do when she was in turmoil. "Maybe it's Sunday but I'm the only one who knows it," she said. "Could the clocks have stopped? This is absurd. It's impossible, and yet, it happened. Everyone apparently thinks it's Saturday. Even you two. Twenty-four hours lost."

Drew looked worried and tried to get Wiley's eye.

"Maybe everyone slept, and I'm the only one who realizes it." Judith shook her head. "No, that's impossible. If everyone fell asleep, the city would be a mess. Car accidents, fires. No. But how could it be? You two tell me. You're responsible somehow. You did it, didn't you, Drew?"

"Yes, Judith." Drew did not like seeing her distressed. She looked so vulnerable and Drew felt a powerful urge to go to her and hold her. "I told you you'd believe you slept for twenty-four hours and now you believe it."

"No, that's not it. I know I slept. You zapped the world somehow. Your power is more immense that we imagined." She laughed. "It's OK, though, about the trip I mean. Since it seems everyone believes it's Saturday, then there's no risk. Our flight will leave Tuesday instead of Monday, but everyone will think it's Monday."

"Amazing," Wiley said. "It's like a core belief. Seems to be virtually unshakable."

"But erasable," Drew said vehemently, and zapped Judith's delusion away.

The work continued following the protocol; more and more hypotheses were tested. Wiley was pleased with the results; Drew was intrigued; Judith was growing restless. At the end, they talked about the experience and filled Judith in on just what they had done.

"Scarey," Judith said. "That's too much power, Drew. It shouldn't be."

"I know. It keeps blowing my mind." Drew was stretched out on the couch, her legs, in light brown jeans, draped over the edge. "But it's there. I have it." She pointed to her head, her eyes closed. "And I'm going to have to live with it." She sat upright, her blouse pulled halfway out of her pants. "I'm glad we're doing this. It helps. I like knowing that I can reverse any of the zaps, get the person back to where they were." She turned to Judith. "I tested that one before, but this helps confirm it. That's important to me. It's like a safety valve to know I can reverse them."

"It's also important to realize that you can't directly induce behavior," Wiley said. "You have to go through beliefs or feelings. Your power is over other's ideas, not their actions."

"One leads to the other, though."

"Yes, but you have to take the indirect route. It's a matter of wording."

"If I had simply told the rapist to stop, he wouldn't have," Drew said.

"Not according to what we learned today."

"I was lucky."

"You were following what had worked with the other people, probably without realizing it."

Judith pointed to Drew's blouse. Drew tucked it in. "I'm glad I need to say it strongly, that I can't influence people in casual conversation, zap them unintentionally. That's another safeguard." Drew's eyes narrowed. "If that weren't so, it would really be dangerous. Like I might say to someone, 'you're a jerk' and they'd start jerking around, or I might say, 'you idiot'. I've been known to say that." She smiled sardonically. "I could end up making retards out of anyone who got on my nerves. Or I might say..."

"Hey, Drew," Wiley said.

"Yeah?"

"Stifle yourself."

"Hey, Wiley."

"What."

"Eat shit and die."

"Hey, you two, back to business. What else did you learn, Wiley?"

Wiley looked at her notes. "That the person being zapped has to understand what you're saying. You, for example, Judith, are immune to zaps in French."

"I might learn French some day."

"Then you wouldn't be immune."

"All right, then I won't learn French."

"And people seem to be immune to zaps using vocabulary they're not familiar with," Drew said. "I told you you were feeling a *boranding* sensation in your *globus pallidus* and nothing happened, Judith."

"My what?"

Wiley laughed. "It's some part of the body, I forget which. I looked it up in an anatomy book."

Judith chuckled. "I feel it boranding now." She wiggled on her seat. "You know," she said, "the part that really bothers me is that even when I tried to resist, I couldn't."

"That's another way that it's different from hypnosis," Wiley replied.

70

"Wiley, I've been thinking about you," Judith said, stretching out her legs. "You certainly are working hard on this project." She watched Wiley closely.

Wiley acted as if she did not notice. "Yes," she said, lightly, "and I'm having a hell of a lot more fun than I had doing my dissertation." She laughed hoarsely, then grew serious again.

She looks more like herself when she's serious, Drew thought, though she loved it when Wiley laughed and got silly and often tried to provoke it.

"This is a bit more important, too," Wiley said.

"So, how far along are we?" Drew asked.

"This was a good start. The pilot study is complete, Phase I is over. I'm glad you did this, Judith. It made it so much easier than if I had to be the subject. Thanks."

Judith nodded. "Say, Wiley." She angled her body away from Drew.

"Yeah."

"Does it make you nervous at all, about Drew, I mean? She's not a regular person anymore."

"Damn right it makes me nervous."

"I mean...like, for yourself?"

"What Drew could do?"

"Mm-hm."

"To me?"

Judith nodded, avoiding looking at Drew.

"Drew and I have discussed that," Wiley said.

"So did we," Judith replied, glancing at Drew. "I feel better about it, but it's still freaky."

Drew shifted uneasily. "I'm the same person I always was, you two. Trust me, will you?"

"Sure you are," Wiley said, "but power does strange things to people, even wonderful people like us. We have to move cautiously, look at our reactions."

"You mean *my* reactions," Drew snapped.

"All of ours, but, yes, mostly yours. You're more burdened, of course. You have the ultimate control."

Drew didn't reply. She looked out the window. The day was ending, the sun getting lower in the sky. "That was quite an eclipse," she said teasingly.

"Wasn't it!" Judith responded. "I'm surprised there was no warning. Those things don't come unpredictably, do they? And it came and went so fast. I'm sure the news will be full of it."

"Judith, that was one of the zaps, remember? There wasn't an

71

eclipse."

"Oh, right, yeah, maybe not."

"Will she always believe it happened?" Drew asked Wiley.

"Unless you erase it, I suspect she will, on some level, even though she also knows it was imaginary. Is that how it seems, Judith?"

"Yes, I think so." Judith took a stick of gum and bent it into her mouth. "I know it didn't really get dark out there, because I believe it was a zap. How could I not? I read the protocol." She was chewing juicily. "I know everything you did, yet it's real hard to shake it. I keep thinking, well, maybe it was a coincidence and maybe there really was an eclipse, at that moment, just when you said it would happen. Now, obviously, that's ridiculous, but..."

"Core belief," Wiley said. "Almost impossible to dislodge."

"Does it work this way in hypnosis?" Judith asked.

"No, at least there's not that intensity. No, hypnotic suggestions are much more fragile, more easily overtaken by contradictory beliefs the person already holds."

"So, it's not a form of hypnosis?"

"I don't know what the hell it is," Wiley said. "Of course, no one really knows much about hypnosis either. How it works, at least. This is way beyond hypnosis; it's beyond anything I've heard of, and believe me, I've been searching. This seems to be a first."

"You're sure into it, Wiley," Judith said, snapping her gum. Wiley ignored her.

For some reason, Judith thought of Jesus. "I wonder if you can get people to do things that are physically impossible," she said to Drew, "like turning water to wine or something."

"Let's try," the child in Drew responded immediately.

"That comes later," Wiley cautioned.

"There's no harm. I'm curious. Are you up for it, Jude?"

"Go."

Drew placed her thumb on her forehead, winking at Wiley as she did. "OK, I'm ready," she said. "Judith, listen to me, I have something important to say to you. Listen carefully." She paused. "You have an extraordinary power. You know this. You are able to suspend objects in the air just by willing it. You can really do this, amazing woman that you are."

When Judith's eyes cleared, Drew asked her if she could lift the pen off Wiley's desk without touching it.

Judith looked at Drew with curiosity, surprised Drew knew she could. "Yes," she said, "yes, I can do that." She stared at the ball-point Bic as if penetrating it with her eyes. Several seconds passed, then a minute. Judith smiled and looked at the others. "Isn't that something?"

"What?"

"You're not impressed? What do they call it? Levitation. No, telekinesis, yeah, that's it. I've got that power. You're not the only one with powers, Drew baby." She leaned back, self-satisfied.

"The pen didn't move, Judith."

Judith laughed. "Can't handle it, huh? That was my mental energy holding that pen in the air. I'm an amazing woman." Judith puffed herself up, quite pleased.

"Judith, Drew zapped you into believing you could lift objects by willing it," Wiley said. "You believe you can. You believe you did, but you didn't"

"I did too." Her jaw set stubbornly.

"See what I mean. Drew, I think you should erase that one. In fact, I'd include the eclipse and, let's see, are there any others we didn't remove?" She looked over the protocol.

"You guys think it was a zap, huh?" Judith said.

"Listen to me, Judith," Drew intoned, "I have some important things to say to you..."

## 14.

They spent the first night at a sea resort on the outskirts of Athens. Drew lay still listening to the surf and to Judith's soft, rhythmic breathing. She couldn't sleep. Jet lag, she thought, or the excitement of the trip. But it was not the memories of their walk among the ruins of the Acropolis that filled her mind, nor the blueness of the sea, or the ringing sounds of the Greek language. Drew's thoughts, instead, were on the nearness of Judith's body to her own as they lay side by side in the bed they shared. Only inches away. She felt a tingling warmth as her eyes drifted over the soft contours of Judith's shoulder. For a few moments, she let herself fully acknowledge her desire. Allowing her imagination to take her where she longed to go, Drew saw herself slowly reach her hand toward that smooth shoulder until she made contact with the flesh; and she pictured Judith awakening and dreamily reaching back.

In the past, Drew would brush such thoughts from her mind with rationalizations or with disparaging labels, guaranteed to inhibit the thoughts and bury the feelings. Tonight, lying beneath the white sheets miles from home, the breeze rustling the curtains, the smell of the Aegean filling the room and filling Drew with romantic stirrings, tonight she gave her feelings and imagination more rein. Maybe it was because of Wiley. Maybe learning of Wiley's love for women freed Drew to allow herself to think it less unthinkable. She knew Judith's lips would feel soft and warm and giving against her own. Drew felt tingling between her legs, and wetness. She made herself turn her back and close her eyes and wait until finally her yearnings mixed with dreams and she slept.

After their morning swim, they played tennis. Drew and Judith were evenly matched. Each took one set and then they sat at a table on the veranda, an umbrella shading them from the hot Greek sun. They sipped their drinks and watched the players on the court and tried not to hear the whiney voice of the graying woman at the table next to theirs.

"It's outrageous," she said, adjusting her straw hat, "the prices go up, the service deteriorates. Did you see how that waiter looked at me? Surly little man." She made a face. "And I didn't sleep a wink. Not a wink. That air conditioner rattled all night. It didn't bother you, though, did it, Albert? Your snoring was about as loud."

Her husband nodded, half listening, watching the tennis players on the courts below.

"They say American cuisine. What a joke! Eggs floating in oil. Stringy limp bacon, probably from sheep. God, it's hot." The woman fanned her face, then caught Drew's eye, and smiled. "Are you girls from the States?"

Drew nodded. "Yes, Chicago."

"We're from Cincinnati. This is the third time we've been to Greece. How about you?"

"First time here."

"Do you like it?"

"So far," Drew replied cordially. "We just arrived yesterday."

"Well, it *is* a beautiful country, but the people...," she said, lowering her voice, "...very pushy. They'll try to cheat you so watch out; count your money carefully. Have you been shopping yet? What a nuisance! One line to pay, then another line to pick up your purchase. So inefficient."

Judith got up looking at Drew apologetically. "Sorry to leave

74

you at a time like this," she said quietly, "but I have to go to the john. Hope she doesn't convince you to take the next flight home."

Moments after Judith left, soft pink Albert said something to his wife and wandered off.

"Isn't the sun piercing," the woman said to Drew. "I don't see how Albert can stand to go for a walk in it. At least there's a breeze. I'd go swimming, but I never did like to get salty water all over me. We've been here a week so far and it's been dreadful. And we have another two weeks to go."

Feeling generous as well as irritated, Drew leaned toward the woman. "Listen to me," she said, "I have something important to say to you."

The older woman's bright red lips no longer moved. Her jaw dropped slightly as she stared at Drew.

"You can allow yourself to enjoy your trip. There are interesting and pleasant things here and you can focus on them, focus on the positive. You feel relaxed. You know you don't need to complain. You can let yourself enjoy."

When her eyes were clear again, the woman looked upward. "Oh, the sky. So blue, not a cloud in it. My husband wants to drive to the Peloponnesos, stay at some of the smaller hotels, visit a monastery. I thought it would be too hot and nasty, but, you know, it might be fun. And I do love the islands. Maybe Albert would like to go to Mykonos. We've never been there. They say it's full of *homosexuals.*" She whispered the word. "But I suppose that would make it even more colorful."

"Lively and gay," Drew said.

"The Greek people are so friendly if you give them half a chance. I bought a phrase book, but I haven't looked at it. I think I'll learn some phrases, maybe this afternoon. Right now, I'm going for a swim in the sea. Nice talking with you, dear," she concluded, smiling happily, and she was gone.

Drew watched Judith approach. So entranced was she by Judith's movements and the bright glow of the sun on her bare legs, that she barely noticed the man accompanying her.

"This is Tom," Judith said. "Sometimes known as 'Mr. Tennis'. Tom, this is Drew. He talked me into playing a set or two with him."

"You can be next, if you dare," Tom said. His grin was cocky. His clothes were tennis whites and his blond, wavey hair looked almost silver against the deep tan. "It gets boring here," he said. "I'm always on the lookout for worthy partners." He smiled suggestively. "So far I've never been defeated by a woman. I don't suppose that will change today. If you two are as good as Judith says, though, I may have to play right-handed."

"Sit a minute," Drew said, rolling her eyes at Judith. "I like to psych out my opponents before I demolish them."

Tom laughed. "I love it." He rested his Adidas-clad foot on the chair. "The more they boast, the sweeter the victory."

"Ah, then our victory should be most sweet," Drew said to Judith.

"It would be most surprising," Tom stated. He slung his well-cared for body onto the chair. "So you two are from Chicago, huh? Traveling alone?"

"No, together," Judith responded.

"Tom," Drew said. "Listen, I have something important to say to you."

Though uncharacteristic for him, Tom did listen, he listened very intently to what Drew had to say and when he stopped staring, he went with Judith to the court.

His style was excellent and assured, but inexplicably, he'd falter on easy shots, and Judith took the first game, then the set. Tom began to sweat profusely as he lost again and again. He talked about how late he'd been out the night before, dancing with some Australian girls, and how Judith's lucky streak was just a fluke. It was Drew's turn. She too defeated him consistently, game after game, until, his face flushed, his shirt hanging out from his shorts, his hair matted to his forehead, "Mr. Tennis" threw his racket down and stomped away without a word.

"That was fun," Drew said.

Judith laughed. "He deserved it." She had ordered both of them an iced coffee. She sipped pensively on hers. "I was wondering...what do you think would have happened if, instead of zapping him to play poorly, you'd zapped me to play especially well?"

"I think you would have played even better than usual," Drew said. "I like to watch you play, the way you move; it's very...nice." She felt herself begin to blush and so she looked away.

Judith was not unaware. "How would you feel about zapping me sometime, if I asked you to?"

"I wondered when you'd ask about that. I'd feel fine, I think, I mean depending on..."

"I was thinking about my sister, Paula."

"Yeah?"

"You know how I am with her."

"Mm-hm, intimidated, sort of."

"It's always been that way with her, you know, ever since we

76

were kids. She always bullied me." Judith's hand closed tightly around the tennis ball she held. "I don't know why I let her. I mean, I don't let anyone else push me around, do I?"

Drew shook her head. "I don't think so." She wiped the table absentmindedly with a paper napkin. "I always used to wish I could be as assertive as you."

"*Used* to? Oh, yes, that's right, that hasn't been much of a problem for you lately."

"No it hasn't. For some reason, I feel a lot more self-confident lately."

They both laughed. "I wonder why," Judith said.

"What about your sister?"

"Yeah, well, I was wondering. What if you zapped me to believe I didn't have to view her the way I do, you know, see her as somehow having authority over me? She still has my favorite jacket. I can't get up the nerve to ask for it back."

"You know, now that I think of it, it's not just your sister. Remember how your aunt Grace talked you into going to that Tupperware party a few weeks ago?"

Judith rolled her eyes. "Oh, that was awful. She's always getting me to do things I don't want to. She guilt-trips me into it. You know, it's that way with all my family, I think. Not Trish, she's more like me, but the rest of them. My mother especially. I've got a shopping list twelve feet long of things I'm supposed to bring her from Greece."

"Would you want me to zap you to be more assertive with them?"

Judith smiled conspiratorially and moved her head up and down. Drew liked the way the glistening strands of her hair moved.

"Just my sister, though, for starters."

"OK, what should I say?"

Judith closed her eyes a moment. Very delicate soft eyelids, Drew thought. "How about telling me I believe that I don't have to be afraid of Paula, that I can speak up to her and not be frightened by her sarcasm and criticism."

"I'll use just those words," Drew said. "Now?"

"I'm ready."

"Listen to me..."

After the zap, Judith sat quietly for a while, smiling to herself. "Just thinking about Paula now gives me a different feeling," she said. "I don't get that sinking sensation." She laughed. "I can hardly wait. She'll probably come over as soon as I get home. That's another thing. She's always coming over and she stays way longer than I want her to. I've always been afraid to say anything about it."

"Not any more," Drew said. "Anything else I could do for you?"

Judith looked off into the distance. "God, what an offer." She laughed. "It's like those fantasies I used to have; you probably did too, you know, *if you could have three wishes*... Let me think. Money's not a problem to me, although I could always use more, but no, not money. My job is fine; I don't need any changes there." She was squinting now, still looking into space. "I don't think I'd want you to zap people to love me more or treat me in a certain way or feel different ways about me. I wouldn't like that. It wouldn't feel real, so it wouldn't mean anything."

"Like with David?"

Judith looked at Drew but didn't answer. "Could I ask you to zap someone else for me?"

"Sure, you could ask."

"Zap my next door neighbor to play his music softer."

Drew laughed. "You're like the man and his wife with the three wishes, you know, wishing for pudding."

"Trivial, huh?" Judith shrugged. "What I'd really like is to feel happy and fulfilled all the time."

"You would? I mean, would you really want me to zap you into that?"

Drew's response made Judith take pause. "I suppose not," she said. "It would be kind of like being high on drugs rather than *on life*." She said the last mockingly. "There's a woman I know at work," she said more seriously now. "Kay Dane, I may have mentioned her to you."

"Yeah, I think so, the one with the pig husband who beats her?"

"Yeah, it tears me apart to hear about it. I'd like you to zap him to stop. Maybe other wife beaters, too."

Drew took the last sip of her coffee and lit another cigarette. This was beginning to remind her of Wiley and she didn't like it.

"I don't know, Drew. I think I'd really have to give it more thought. I keep thinking of things like wanting not to have headaches and wanting people to like the poems I write and to be able to write even better ones and to be able to take a trip around the world and things like that. I'd have to think about it more. I mean, I'm not sure *what* I want. I think anybody would have to think about it first." She rolled the tennis ball around in her palms. "Like that guy over there, for example. I wonder what he would ask for." She pointed to a busboy wiping off a table. "Or those women coming out of the bathhouse. What zaps would they want? People aren't used to thinking about something like that."

78

Drew laughed and felt overwhelmingly warm towards Judith and wanted to hold her. She changed the subject, talking of their plans for the trip to Corinth.

They left after lunch. It was Judith's idea to go there, to see the isthmus. When they arrived late that afternoon, she remained on the bridge for nearly an hour photographing the isthmus from every angle, shooting down the stark, steep walls to the strip of blue below, the narrow channel of water linking the Ionian and Aegean Seas. She took at least ten pictures for every one Drew took and, though they were very amateurish, enjoyed herself immensely.

While waiting for Judith to run out of film, Drew bought a lemonade at the souvenir stand and an ornament woven from strands of twisted wheat. It was because of that ornament that she and Judith came to dance with the people of Pelosai and spend the night in their little village. Drew held the wheat in the air admiring it. "This is really neat," she commented to another tourist. "I wonder how it's done."

A young Greek couple overheard. The woman, Niki, small and plump like a ripe fig, said that her mother weaves them in the village nearby and invited Drew and Judith to come and see exactly how it is done.

With Judith behind the wheel of their rented Fiat, they followed Niki and Taki Petrakis the twenty kilometers to Pelosai where they met Niki's parents and other relatives and many of the three hundred villagers whose world this was. They visited on a wooden balcony eating creamy white candy served on a spoon that was placed in a glass of cold water, and later, ate rabbit slaughtered for the occasion. From a distance, children stood in groups to stare at the strangers. Drew learned the secret of twisting and weaving wheat into pleasing ornaments, and made one for little Antonia, a next door neighbor, who accepted it shyly. Niki's parents were happy to have these guests, and insisted that they spend the night and come to the baptism celebration that would take place that evening.

The party was held in a large, tin-roofed storage building, lined with tables, and gaily decorated for the festivities. Bouzoukia music blared and dancers snaked in a line around the tables singing and yelling *opa* as they jumped and turned.

Taki told Drew and Judith the story of the Petrulios brothers. Every guest who came to the village of Pelosai heard this story and all would shake their heads sadly and say, "What a shame".

"Over there, you see that one, the tall man with the blue shirt.

He is Yorgios. And there, across from him, the man with the little boy on his leg. That is Nikos. They are *adelphi*, brothers. Such brothers they are. All their lives, like this." Taki held up two fingers pressed tightly together. "Everywhere you see one, you see the other. But then, they had this very big argument, who knows what it was about. I think even they have forgotten, but no matter. Ever since that day, there's no talk. Not one word. They both are stubborn guys. They love each other so much, but not one will take that step. So, they go on, now two-three years like this. No talk. When they see each other it is like they see air. And they both live here in Pelosai. This is a small place. Their families are always together, they are in each other's house, their children play together, their fields are next to each other. Everything together day after day, but they never say one word, ever since that big disagreement. So many people try; their wives, the priest. I have tried myself. No one can help them to mend the bridge, and so it goes, day after day. Like now. They sit at the same table with their families, but it's like Nikos is not there for Yorgios and Yorgios is not there for Nikos. Inside I know they both are in pain for each other, but they are so stubborn and neither one will move."

Judith and Drew agreed it was a shame and Judith shook her head, but Drew smiled to herself and later asked Niki how to say certain phrases in Greek: *Listen to me. I have something important to say. What a nice party. It is time to go. It is time to talk with your friend. Will you travel with your brother?* She wrote them down phonetically and practiced with Niki until her pronunciation was good. Niki was pleased to help though she thought Drew's choice of phrases somewhat strange.

They ate chicken and roast lamb and potatoes and okra and the music played and everyone seemed happy. Drew practiced some of her phrases on the villagers who were delighted and spoke back to her rapidly and incomprehensibly. She sought out Yorgios whose eyes became glazed as she spoke to him; then she found Nikos, and he stared and listened raptly to her as she spoke some of the Greek words she had learned. When his eyes cleared, she told him this was a nice party and returned to the table where Judith sat with Niki and her family. Drew told Judith to watch, across the room, to watch Yorgios and Nikos.

"They're looking at each other," Judith said. "I thought they never did. Hey look! They're walking toward each other."

Now others were looking as well. In fact, the whole room stopped and watched with amazement as the brothers embraced and spoke their first words to each other, spoke them simultaneously. Everyone watched them hug again and kiss each other's cheeks and hug some more and talk together with big tears flowing from their eyes. Then the two brothers walked around the room, arms about each other's shoulders, talking, crying, laughing.

"How nice," Drew said.

Judith looked at her powerful friend and shook her head, smiling.

When they returned to the home of their hosts, Drew and Judith were shown to a room, off the kitchen, where they were to sleep. It contained a large bed and a narrow canvas cot. They ignored the cot. The evening was cool and the two women slid beneath the sheets and pulled the rough, scratchy wool blanket up to their chests. Through the open window they could see the stars, many, many more stars than they'd ever seen at home.

"I'm having a good time," Judith said.

"Me too." Drew hesitated a moment. "I like traveling with you."

Judith did not reply.

"I like *being* with you." Drew could feel her heart beat.

Judith's hand rested on the blanket and Drew looked at it, so graceful and soft, illuminated by the starlight. Without knowing she would, she slowly moved her own hand toward Judith's until their fingers touched. She felt daring and afraid.

Judith did not pull away but gently moved her thumb back and forth over the skin of Drew's hand. "I feel very close to you," she said.

"I feel it, too." Their hands remained connected, softly stroking.

Judith turned toward Drew, lying on her side now, facing her, and touched Drew tenderly on the cheek. Drew's whole body responded with a hot, tingling rush. She smiled. "That feels very good."

Their faces were only inches apart. Slowly, Drew lifted her chin shortening even more the distance between their lips, and Judith turned her neck a fraction so that each could now feel the heat of the other's breath and skin. Their lips touched. Barely at first, just the softest contact which slowly deepened until it became a kiss, a tender kiss, a filling, warm and loving kiss between two very loving friends. Then they moved apart and were quiet for awhile.

"Did you know that would happen?"

"No, not really." A few seconds passed. "But I wanted it to."

"Me, too. It's...I feel kind of scared."

"So do I."

"I never kissed a woman before." There was a pause. "I've been thinking about it, though, about you, I mean."

"About making love with me?"

81

"Yes."

"What a coincidence."

Again their lips came together, this time less tentatively, deeper. They could hear music. It began faintly then grew louder until it filled the room where they lay. With the music came a cacophony of whoops and shouts, singing voices, and the clatter of footsteps.

"*Koritsia, elate.*"

Drew and Judith sat up in bed.

"*Pame no horevome.*"

They looked at each other, uncertain. Then came a soft rap on the door.

"Are you awake?" It was Niki's voice.

"Yes," Judith said. "What is it?"

"A celebration. They want you to join them. Come. We are going, too." Niki opened the door and poked her head in. "It's Yorgios and Nikos. They're gathering the villagers in the square for more dancing. Will you come?"

Judith and Drew looked at each other and shrugged their shoulders. "I guess we will," Drew said.

They found their clothes and the moment they emerged from their room, were taken by the hands, a villager on each side and led outside where they joined the growing crowd gathered around Yorgios and Nikos, who, clearly drunk, danced side by side, connected by a white handkerchief, jumping and turning and bouncing gracefully to the clarinet and bouzoukia sounds. Drew and Judith were pulled into the line of dancers encircling the joyous brothers and the celebration went on into the night.

When at last the villagers headed toward their homes, Niki walked between Judith and Drew. "My cousin, Toula, there she is, with Taki. She's fourteen," Niki said. "She has fights with her mother sometimes and sometimes she comes to my parents' to sleep the night there. You know how those things are. They had a fight tonight. Would you mind to have another guest in your room? She will sleep in the cot."

## 15

The sun was getting high when Drew awoke to the sound of bells. Judith sat at the window leaning out over the sill. Toula had risen an hour earlier, neatly made her bed, and was gone. A donkey was passing outside, its back piled with branches and twigs, a bell around its neck.

With her eyes, Drew traced the graceful curve of Judith's spine.

"What's happening?" she asked, sitting up in bed.

"This place is full of animals," Judith replied. "A bunch of sheep went by a few minutes ago and now there's a donkey. It's going down the main street."

Drew laughed. "It's the only street there is. What happened to the kid?"

"I kicked her out."

"Good for you. But you know what?"

"What?"

"It's lonely in the bed."

Judith's eyes were sparkling as she moved toward Drew.

A knock sounded. "Good morning," Niki said brightly. "I have some towels for you. Shall I bring them in?"

The two tourists showered in cold water and drank thick Turkish coffee from tiny cups and, after thanking their hosts and sharing warm goodbyes, climbed into their dust-covered car and drove the twisty yellow dirt roads to the highway and then on towards Sparta. They were well inland now. Grove after grove of silver-leafed olive trees and occasional jutting cypresses decorated the mountains and valleys.

Both women were very high, very happy. They sang every song they knew and many they barely knew and stopped frequently along the road to take photos. They laughed a great deal, got silly, even giddy. They talked of the people of Pelosai. Drew wondered how Becka would like staying in a little village like that. She loved farm animals. There were periods of silence, too. Each thought her own thoughts, separate thoughts, but very similar, thoughts of the other, loving thoughts. Several times their arms would brush and the exciting chills each felt were similar as well. Only once during the drive did they speak of it.

"Do you feel OK about what happened?" Drew asked, her eyes glued to the road.

"Yes. I'm nervous, though."

Drew didn't respond.

"I want to touch you everywhere."

Drew swallowed, her hands tightening on the wheel. She took a quick glimpse at Judith. "Oh, I can't believe this. I was so afraid you'd feel...that you..."

"I just feel that I want to be as close to you as I can possibly get."

"Yes."

Sparta was a beautiful little city, nestled in the green mountains, landscapes far plusher than those they'd seen near the sea. The hotel was small, containing perhaps twenty rooms. Theirs had a balcony looking out over miles of rolling hills.

It was ten o'clock. They'd had their dinner in a vine-covered, outdoor restaurant and, without discussing it, had silently walked back to the hotel and begun to undress. Drew put on a t-shirt, her usual sleep attire; Judith, a sleeveless pajama top of soft, loose cotton. Both eager, both afraid, they stalled and dawdled in their preparations, alternating periods of nervous chatter with moments of weighty quiet. When they finally found their way to the bed, they lay for several minutes, neither of them moving or speaking, a foot of space between their bodies. Each knew that the day was not yet done. At last, Drew spoke. "I'm loving you," she said.

Judith reached for her. Both women knew just what they felt and what they wanted, and each had made love to the other in her mind. They held each other tightly, savoring the feel of it, and then their lips touched. It was a long, soft, tender kiss.

Judith ran her fingers slowly, sensually, along Drew's back then over the contours of her hips. "I'm tingling all over."

Rising to one elbow, Drew brought her head down slowly until she covered Judith's mouth with her own. Her tongue explored Judith's lips and the hot inner lining of her cheeks, and then she slid her tongue along Judith's neck and downward until she reached cloth. She undid the first button of the skimpy top, smiling into Judith's eyes as she did, then let her tongue go further down. She undid the second button and then the rest, spreading the fabric wide.

The light from the stars and moon coming through the balcony doors glistened on Judith's breasts. Drew moved her hand slowly toward the soft peaks, cupping one breast lightly, tenderly caressing with her fingertips. She felt the heat rising as she took Judith's nipple into her mouth, softly sucking the erect flesh, rolling her tongue around and around, doing finally in actuality what she had so many times imagined. Judith's whole body rose in response, and Drew's hand moved downward over the swell of her hips, along the firm smooth thighs. She loved the softness and the smoothness of Judith's female flesh and lingered over her buttocks and thighs until finally her hand went to the moist inviting place between Judith's legs. It was velvet smooth and slippery, even warmer and softer than Drew had expected.

The love they made was sweet and tender and lingering; it was new, and long in coming. Drew had not doubted that if it ever was, it would be very good, wonderfully good, but could not have known just how strongly she would feel and how much pleasure she would get. This is different, she thought. This is more, and she told Judith so, and Judith said she felt the same. They fell asleep in each other's arms and woke that way, warm and content, and then excited by the feel of the other so close. They skipped breakfast that day.

In the days and nights that followed, back in Athens and then at Hydra and Rhodes, the mutual excitement and joy of their bold discoveries grew stronger, the lovemaking more passionate and free and wild. They spoke openly of their feelings, their love and what it might mean, and each soothed the other's anxieties. The bond between them grew deeper than either had thought it could ever be with anyone.

One evening, at a beach cafe in Rhodes, they joined three other women, young lively women from the states. Two were students at the University of Pennsylvania, the other a cab driver. A few minutes into the conversation, both Drew and Judith suspected the women were lesbians; ten minutes into it, they knew for sure. Judith felt self-conscious at first, but relaxed as she saw Drew being so pleased and comfortable.

The women talked about a music festival that took place in Michigan every year, a place where only women went, to camp and make music and be together. They had been there a couple weeks ago, they said, before coming to Europe.

"It sounds great," Drew said. "Four or five days of no men. What a joy."

Judith, too, thought it sounded appealing. "Maybe we'll go next year," she said, looking at Drew.

"I wish it lasted longer," the woman called Angie said. She called the waiter over. "*Nero, parakalo.* I wish it lasted all year long."

"Yeah, we could build cabins and permanent buildings and work the land and have our own town."

"Lezzie town."

"We could secede from the union."

"Lesbian Nation."

Everyone laughed and the fantasizing went on. "We could expand," Tanya said. She was the cab driver, a tall thin woman with
very short hair and rosey cheeks. "Bring in more and more women,
take over more and more land. We could start with the festival
and towns around there and then maybe all of Michigan."

"Michigan gets so cold; maybe we should have it out west
somewhere."

"How about taking over California and Oregon," Drew said.

"All right." Everyone laughed.

They talked for several hours at their beachside table, and then
the trio had to leave. They were going to Pireaus the next morning for their boat trip to Brindisi, Italy.

Drew and Judith were up late that night and the night after, in
their room, in their bed. Drew so loved the softness of Judith's skin,
she never tired of touching her, nor of kissing her. And she was
getting more comfortable and more pleasure now from going down
on her. It wasn't until the third time they made love that Drew
had done that. It was Judith's own boldness that gave her the
courage. They were still in Sparta. Judith was kissing Drew's belly and then her mouth skipped down to Drew's thighs, then back
up but not as far, then down, stopping at the hairs. Drew's back
arched and Judith stayed there going closer and closer until Drew
could barely breath, wanting it so much. There was a tenderness
and a knowingness in Judith's mouth and tongue as she vibrated
and licked and sucked and Drew felt the ecstatic rising that left
her body coated with sweat.

"Yes, we enjoyed our trip to Greece very much," they told the
hotel clerk in Athens on their last night. They smiled as they spoke
to him and let their fingers touch below his view.

_16._

When Wiley saw Drew coming towards her at the airport, her
blue bag hanging from her shoulder, walking with that familiar
bouncy step, she breathed easy for the first time in two weeks.
Becka spotted her mother and ran ahead, jumping into her arms.

"...and Susie's bird got out of the cage and flew into the bathroom but it didn't find any windows and Jeffie Jackson had to get four stitches 'cause the robot's arm cut his mouth when he fell and...Oh, you're crying." Becka smiled wisely. "I know. It's tears of happiness, right, mom? From missing me."

Drew held her girl at arms length, absorbing the sight. She nodded. "Yep, tears of happiness."

"We sure love each other," Becka said, "more than anything. Look what I made you."

Wiley stood patiently as Drew read the dozen pages of one-line poems and admired the drawings and hugged Becka again. "Nice tan," she said, finally having her chance to greet her friend, and take her back under her wing. She knew without a word from Drew that something very special had taken place in the land of Aristotle, more special than the snorkeling and boat rides between islands and visits to ancient ruins that Drew described on the drive home. Wiley did not need to ask and Drew knew she knew and knew that soon they would talk about it and Wiley would be happy for her. Drew's own happiness had added a perpetual glow to her cheeks. She was vibrant and looked more attractive than ever. Almost beautiful, Wiley thought.

Not surprisingly, Wiley had been quite productive during Drew's absence, proceeding with plans for the next stage of the study which required using naive subjects. She was also compiling her "consultant/resource" list, a roster of feminists which included political theoreticians, economists, sociologists, psychologists, historians, philosophers, and various activists.

Three days after her homecoming, the transporting feelings that had peaked during their travels still did not dissipate at all for Drew, but seemed, instead, to be growing in Judith's absence. Judith had stopped in New York to stay a few days with her parents. Drew longed for her, feeling a void, but fought the recurrent urge to call. She could wait. Only one more day. She knew there was need for caution, for discretion, that she must avoid arousing suspicion, especially in Judith's parents.

The photography studio was ready. Wiley had the carpenters and painters in while Drew was gone and Drew handled the final decorating herself, pleased at finally finding a use for the impressionist prints she'd been storing in the closet at home. These went in the reception area along with some samples of her photos, primarily portraits, but she couldn't resist including several of her abstract shots. The studio section of the shop was in back and here they put a stool, table, a couple of chairs as well as the lighting equipment and tripod. The washroom doubled as the darkroom.

Drew was looking forward to starting her "business" even though she wasn't as convinced as Wiley that it was necessary to go through all of this. She also was having some doubts about the ethics of the zappings. Like before, however, she ended up deciding that as long as she was doing them for good reasons and since no one was getting hurt, it was OK to proceed.

Drew sat now at the counter in the front of the shop waiting for her first "customer", Caron Sharp, who was due any minute. She felt a little nervous. This time it was she who worried about the risk, but Wiley insisted their precautions were adequate. "Once the door to the studio is closed, it will be virtually sound proof," she'd assured Drew, and they had already determined that amnesia for the zaps occurred.

A young woman walked through the door, scanned the scene with her heavily made up eyes, and presented her coupon to Drew. Drew tried not to stare at Caron Sharp's hair which fell to her shoulder on one side and was cut blunt short on the other. In the studio, the door tightly closed, Drew took the photographs, varying the backgrounds (Caron preferred the fuschia drape) and having her subject take a variety of poses. When they were done, she told Caron she had something important to say to her and proceeded with the implantations, following the protocol step by step. Drew engaged her in conversation, inquiring about her ideas on abortion, her taste in literature, her political views. It sounded strange to hear this flamboyant-looking woman spout such conservative ideas.

"It all rests on the old-time values," Caron said, "the nuclear family, return to the churches. That's our only hope."

Wondering what Caron's friends would think if they could hear such talk from her, Drew zapped her again, restoring her original views. They set up an appointment for Caron to come and look at the prints, and after she left, Drew made some entries in the notebook Wiley had provided, then closed the shop and left for the airport.

She drove fast even though she was early and she paced impatiently and smoked several cigarettes until the plane finally arrived and Judith was there. Drew's heart pounded and her smile made her whole face glow like sparklers as she hugged Judith tightly, welcoming her. Judith's body felt stiff.

"Are you OK?" Drew asked.

"I'm fine," Judith said, looking away.

Drew felt an immediate tension, and fear.

Judith began walking and Drew had to rush to keep up. "So, how was the visit? It was hard for me not to call."

"It was fine. I had a good time." Judith did not look at Drew, but continued her rapid pace toward the baggage area.

Drew wanted to scream: *Hey woman, it's me, Drew, the woman you love. Remember?* But she remained silent. Perhaps Judith is self-conscious in the publicness of the airport, she thought. Yes, that must be it.

But it was no different when they were alone. The drive to the city was excruciatingly uncomfortable. Judith spoke little, making only casual comments about her stay in New York, mostly staring out the window.

When they arrived at Judith's apartment, she said there was no need for Drew to come up, that she could handle the luggage herself, and that she was tired and needed to rest.

"Bullshit," Drew said. "This is ridiculous. You're damn right I'm coming up, and we're going to talk."

"There's nothing to talk about," Judith said simply.

"Shit," Drew moaned. "You freaked, didn't you?"

Judith tugged at a suitcase, not responding, and Drew grabbed it from her hand and proceeded with it to the lobby. They waited together, silently, for the elevator. Inside the apartment, Drew stood watching as Judith busied herself checking plants and putting things away. "Judith," she said at last.

Judith looked at her, her face a mix of anger and anguish.

Drew felt terrible, for Judith, clearly in pain; for herself, frightened, mystified. "Come on, you. Let's have a cup of coffee and talk about it. Obviously you've been through a lot since I last saw you. Let me in, will you, Judith? Please!"

Judith's face began to tremble. She fought the tears. "I just don't feel the same," she said. "I don't feel that way about you, Drew. What happened in Greece was a...an aberration. It's not for me. *You're* not for me."

The tears came then. Drew went to her, to hold and comfort her, but Judith tightened and pulled away, turning her head.

"It never occurred to me," Drew began slowly, "that it would affect you like this. I just assumed you'd be feeling like me. Happy about us. Eager for more."

"Stop!" Judith yelled. "I can't stand listening to that." She got up and walked to the window, leaning on it, her shoulders shaking. "I can't stand being with you," she sobbed. "I hate it, the whole ugly thing. It's not me. It's not normal. It was a mistake." Tears ran from her cheeks onto the window pane. "I...can't...stand...it." Her shoulders heaved with her heavy breathing.

Drew felt a sinking nausea. She was lightheaded, dizzy. She had to leave, but didn't know if she could make it to the door. She drove straight to Wiley's, nearly side-swiping a brand new Cadillac on the way.

"It's just temporary, isn't it?" she asked, her face blotched and tear-streaked. "That's my only hope. I keep thinking: she'll get over it, she'll get past it. The love is real. She's just scared. What do you think, Wiley?"

"I don't know." They sat side by side in Wiley's big old living room on the comfortably worn leather sofa. "I agree she's scared and maybe needs to blame you, but what will come of it, I can't say. She must have pretty heavy homophobic attitudes. Most likely being with her parents didn't help. That was real unfortunate timing." Wiley rubbed Drew's back softly. "We'll just have to wait and see."

"I could zap her," Drew said angrily.

Wiley's hands stopped in the middle of Drew's back. She did not move.

"Zap the homophobic bullshit out of her head."

Wiley said nothing for a while, then softly: "I suppose you could."

Drew cried quietly, her head in her hands. "I love her so much." She moved her head forlornly from side to side. Wiley's eyes were also full of tears.

It was getting late and Becka was waiting for her mom and so Drew left. It was hard to cover up her pain, but Drew did, and she and Becka went over Becka's supplies—pencils, notebook paper, erasers, for the summer was ending and school would soon resume.

Several days passed, wrenchingly painful ones. Judith did not call and Drew made herself wait. She photographed three more subjects, two men and a woman, though her heart was not in it. Each had been carefully screened by Wiley prior to receiving their coupon for the free portraits. Each walked out thinking all that had occurred in the studio was a routine picture-taking session.

One week after Judith's return, Drew called her.

"How are you doing?"

"I'm OK, Drew."

"Well, ah...so how've you been?"

"Did you call for something in particular?"

Drew felt the pain dart downward through her ear, ending at her stomach. "I'd hoped maybe you were feeling better...different. That we could talk."

"I'm feeling the same."

"Oh." Drew hesitated. "Judith, can we talk about what hap-

90

pened, what changed you, how you're thinking about all of it?"

"I'd rather not. I want to just forget it."

"And our friendship?" Drew was afraid to hear the answer. Judith did not respond for a long time. "I have a lot of mixed feelings," she said at last. "A lot of thinking to do and I need to do it on my own, Drew."

"I see."

"I'd rather you didn't call me."

"I see." Drew struggled to keep her voice from breaking. Tears came down each cheek. She took a deep breath. "Call me when you...call me sometime, OK?"

"I don't know, Drew. We'll have to see."

"Yeah, well...well...so long, Judith." She hung up before Judith could reply. The tears wouldn't stop and she didn't try to stop them.

_17._

Over the next few weeks, it was Wiley who helped Drew avoid sinking deeply into the depression. She would commisserate with her, hearing and accepting Drew's pain and grief, and comfort her, but she would also spur her to keep moving, to keep open, and to take what she could that was positive from what had happened.

Eventually, Drew did. She was able to acknowledge that, despite the outcome with Judith, the experience had been freeing to her for it had allowed her to open herself to her love of a woman, to feel it and acknowledge it. That was a lot, and somewhere alongside the pain came something almost like joy.

Wiley, very openly, talked with Drew of her own experiences, of her feelings for women, what her relationships meant to her, of being woman-identified and why, of her thoughts about what lesbianism means. Drew learned a great deal, very quickly. She was ripe to learn, overripe maybe, wishing she'd been able to let it come sooner; at times, resenting the years of effort to find with men what now seemed so much more possible with women—equal, role-free, non-competitive bonding with those who did not need her to be less than she could be.

Wiley brought books for Drew to read and journals and a variety of feminist newletters. She took her to a women's music concert where Drew was moved to tears by the feeling of unity and sisterhood she sensed, and to a discussion of lesbian literature at a women's bookstore, which opened Drew's eyes even more. She introduced Drew to some of her friends whom Drew had never met and who made her feel welcome. Bit by bit, between the crushing walls of Drew's pain came that sweet, refreshing air of her rising awareness of another way, a very positive alternative that felt right to her. It's been there all the time, she thought, and I never knew.

Through it all, Wiley was as caring and supportive as a friend could be, and Drew appreciated and valued her more than ever. Finally, she believed, she had come to know her good friend very well. She did not suspect that there were aspects of Wiley Cavenar she did not know at all.

As gratifying as Drew found her discoveries, they were painfully tarnished by the recurrent thoughts of Judith, and some days she mostly stayed alone and felt her sadness.

It was Monday morning. Becka was safely ensconced in the third grade classroom at Brenan Elementary School, the new school year having begun two weeks before. Drew was home alone, sitting at the window watching the wind picking up the red and brown leaves and tossing them over sidewalks and lawns. She hadn't had a real crying session for over a week and now even the numbness was beginning to leave her. The worst was over, Wiley had said, yet Drew felt sad today. I could turn on the music again, she thought, and let myself mourn some more. It was tempting. Damn, I miss her. There was nothing Drew had to do that day; the one appointment she'd had for a portrait/zapping session had been cancelled. She was free to do as she pleased until 3:30 when Becka would get home. A couple walked by on the sidewalk below, not touching, but clearly very close. That's how it was with us, Drew thought. On the island of Hydra, they had walked along the coastal highway, feeling very happy, totally satisfied. Drew remembered scratching her nose as they watched a ship pass by and smelling Judith on her fingers. It gave her a quick rush and she told Judith who laughed and suggested they stroll on over to the hotel. The tears began, but Drew pushed them back. No, she thought, no, enough, I don't feel like sitting home and feeling sad. She took a deep breath. More and more her thoughts had been turning to her plan to learn filmmaking. Maybe that's what I'll do, she thought. Maybe today I will begin my new career.

She'd already done the preliminary work; she knew Art Trevor's schedule, had spoken with several people who worked with him and had learned some things about him, that he was generally calm and patient but prone to occasional artistic outbursts, that he was predictably sexist, but respected talent and creativity in whomever he found it. He was thirty-seven years old, divorced, and reputed to be the best there was in his field.

Yes, it's time, Drew thought, and so she dressed and pulled back her shoulders and went to the Cinequan Film Studio in Evanston. She saw Art Trevor in the corridor, in fact, almost bumped into him. She had not expected to encounter him so easily and immediately took advantage of her good luck.

"My name is Drew McAllister," she said as he began to move past her. "Listen!" She had to say it strongly for he clearly did not care to be detained. "I have something very important to say to you." She paused until the confirming glaze of the eyes appeared. "You see in me great potential for being a filmmaker, Mr. Trevor," Drew said confidently. "You wish to bring out my talent, to foster it. You want to take me on as your apprentice and teach me, patiently, step by step. You are eager to do this and you want to be flexible and supportive with me as you teach me. Your goal is for me to learn filmmaking and for me to enjoy the process of learning it."

He guided her to his office where he asked her question after question, exclaiming delightedly at her interest in film and insisting that she begin as his apprentice as soon as possible. Drew had to threaten refusal in order to convince him to accept payment. They agreed to begin today, right then. In the showing room he introduced her to the others, then began the teaching, describing his reactions to the film segments they watched, speaking his thoughts aloud, explaining everything, patiently, making sure she understood.

Art Trevor took Drew to lunch after that and told her what books to get, what films to see and what to look for, and then they went to the set to work on the scene being shot that day. When she had to leave in the middle of it to get home for Becka, he did not protest, but shook her hand warmly and they arranged to meet again tomorrow.

"It's like a job," Drew said, "and also like going to school. A little of each. So, we'll go back to how we did it last year. You go to Karen's house after school and I'll stop by for you on my way home."

"OK. Anyway, Karen's mom likes it when I go there. She said so lotsa times. If Karen doesn't want to play with me, then I'll go in that little room they have with the soft chair and read a book.

Karen's mom said I could do that if I felt like it sometime. I could close the door and be alone if I wanted."

Drew looked closely at her daughter. "Haven't you and Karen been getting along?"

Becka fiddled with her plastic brontosaurus. "Me and Lisa hid on her today. She couldn't find us anywhere."

"Oh? Why did you do that?"

"I don't know." She put the bright green dinosaur in her pocket.

"Did Karen get upset?"

Becka thought about this. "I think so. She looked kind of funny. Maybe like a sad look."

"Mm-m."

"Well, she called Lisa a 'fuck face', that's why we did it."

"A fuck face?"

"Uh-huh. So, Lisa said let's ditch her, so we did."

"I see. Why did she call Lisa that?"

"I think because Lisa said *she* was walking home with me today and Karen couldn't. But then I wanted to go back and get her, but Lisa didn't."

"What happened then?"

"Me and Lisa walked home a different way and Karen never found us. Can I call her up, mom?"

"Call Karen?"

"Yeah, I bet she feels sad and so I wanna call her, OK?"

"OK."

"I'll tell her the good news. Anyway, we're best friends."

## 18.

Wiley suggested she go. Drew had vacillated until the last minute, not sure she was ready to get that involved in the women's community, but when Wednesday evening came, she found herself joining a dozen others at a meeting of the Lesbian Legal Defense Committee. It was held at the Loop YWCA on Wabash Avenue. As soon as she walked into the room, Drew spotted a woman she knew, a receptionist in the Political Science Department at the University of Illinois where she used to work. She was surprised to see her there, and pleased, wondering how many other people she knew were more than they appeared. They spoke briefly and exchanged phone numbers, and then the meeting began.

Drew was asked to introduce herself, was thanked for sharing an interest in the committee's work and given some background information on cases the committe was working on. The group consisted of several law students and a spectrum of other women concerned about the legal rights of lesbians. They acted as resource people, Drew learned, advocates, fundraisers and advisors to lesbians involved in legal struggles.

"She says she's tired of lesbian custody cases," Joanne Lipski was saying. "Money wasn't the problem, nor were the particulars of the case. She thought there was a chance for success if it were argued well and wished us luck."

"Sounds just like Rit Avery," someone responded.

"She wouldn't budge. She agreed with everything I said about it being a worthy cause, about the need to win for this woman, herself, as well as for the precedent it could set. On and on. But, she said no, she didn't feel like getting involved in it."

"Damn her."

"I guess she can afford to be particular."

"This case is so important and she's the best lawyer for it."

"She said they're all important," Joanne replied. "All the cases she takes. But this topic just doesn't appeal to her right now."

"I wish there were someone else half as good."

"Well, we'll have to look elsewhere. There's no way to convince her. Rit Avery is out."

Drew knew *she* could convince her. She felt an immediate affinity with the women in this room and wanted to contribute. "Maybe I could help," she said.

Everyone looked at her.

"Oh?" a tall, black woman responded. "What do you have in mind?"

Drew hesitated. "I think I could persuade her."

The chair of the meeting, a very short, very butch woman, looked at Drew skeptically.

"Well, it sure would be worth a try," someone said.

"Do you know her?" another woman asked Drew.

Before Drew could reply, the chairperson spoke, her strong low voice standing out from the others. "Since the case has been continued," she said, "there's no big rush. If there's a chance of getting Avery, let's go for it. Joanne, why don't you get together with Drew and fill her in on the case."

After the meeting, Drew and Joanne Lipski went to a hamburger place down the street from the Y. Joanne ordered a double cheeseburger with fries, a chocolate sundae and a diet 7-up. She was seventy to eighty pounds overweight.

"I pretend I believe that Fat is Beautiful and I raise my fist for Fat Power and I think Fat *is* a Feminist Issue," she said, spooning in some whipped cream, "but the truth is I hate being fat. I can't seem to stop though. Maybe it does represent power to me. That's what Marian thinks. She's my skinny lover. She thinks I need to be big to feel powerful. Who knows? It's a compulsion, I guess. It's so boring. I'm sorry, Drew. Here I go again. I'm always talking about it. Let's get back to the case."

They did, and then Drew looked into Joanne Lipski's eyes and told her that her power comes from her own inner strength and that she doesn't need to eat excessively, that she can lose weight in a reasonable, healthy way, and feel good about herself as she does. Joanne did not remember that Drew said all this to her, but that night, at home, she filled her garbage can with sweets and potato chips and pastas and Marian looked on at what she mistakenly assumed would be just another frustrating, futile attempt.

---

## 19.

Art Trevor had begun putting the make on Drew. She had to admit, on some level, she felt flattered. He was a very attractive man, charming, most would say, and amazingly talented. Nonetheless, Drew was not the least interested. She remembered how one of the women at the Lesbian Legal Defense meeting had talked about men, calling them "pricks" and saying she resented any time she was forced to deal with them. "I don't want to put my woman-energy in pricks," she'd said. They had been discussing the brother of a rape victim. "He's part of the problem," she had added. "Every male has a rape mentality." The woman's name was Wildflower, which made Drew smile. Joanne Lipski told her that Wildflower was a separatist, which in itself, she quickly added, did not bother her, but she did happen to find this particular separatist to be offensive, narrow-minded, and inconsiderately negligent of her personal hygiene. "She's one of the sponge-using, goddess fawning, alfalfa sprout types," Joanne had said contemptuously. "She's also a witch." Drew thought Joanne rather harsh in her judgment, and perhaps somewhat narrow-minded herself.

No, Drew was not interested in Art Trevor, not because he was a "prick", she thought, but maybe partly it was because he had one. Having a prick does weird things to people, she mused, and wondered if she should change her name to Chrysanthymum or Flora or maybe Fauna. Daisy? Oregano? Not Petunia.

"How shall we frame this shot?" Art Trevor asked.

"Close-up of the running water," Drew offered, "then a cut to the sand, a medium shot."

He praised her for being on the right track and then explained how they would do it and why.

"Your neck is elegant," he mumbled.

"What?"

"Your neck," he whispered in her ear. "The best. I want to eat it."

"It must be time to break for lunch," she said.

"All right, a wonderful idea. We'll go to my place."

"Let's to the Main Street Deli."

"Let's make love."

"Let's change the subject."

"Why are you so cruel, you irresistible filly? Don't you see what you're doing to me? Look, I'm a wreck." He smiled at her calmly, his blue eyes sparkling mischievously.

Art Trevor seldom failed to accomplish what he set out to do, especially if it related to women. Drew considered zapping him. He took her hand, pulled it to his face, and softly licked her palm. Drew strongly considered zapping him. She was loving working with the man, being exposed to his brilliance, his flawless sense of timing, editing technique, story development. He was the best, a genius, Drew was sure, but he was acting like a prick.

"Listen to me," she said, "I have something important to say to you..."

After that, he was content to teach Drew, and be friendly and playful, but no longer did he seem to feel a need to seduce her. It seemed he liked her even more then, though this hadn't been part of the zap.

Today, Art Trevor was instructing her on lighting. Drew showed some knowledge and he asked her about her experience with photography, which she told him, though she did not mention her latest venture. She thought of Wiley, of the project and the secrecy. Wiley also was thinking of the project. At that moment, she was at her desk facing varying-sized stacks of papers, all related to the research, and was deep in fantasy. She was picturing herself in a large meeting room, furnished with rich mahogany tables and chairs and gilt-edged paintings. Maps of various parts of the world lined the walls. She sat at the table's head, with Drew at her side, listening to reports from representatives of the different sectors.

"Argentina has moved to stage two," the woman was saying. "So far it's bloodless. The coalitions have solidified and are communicating according to plan. No power ploys, Wiley, although there is a minor oppositional movement developing. The leaders have been identified. We may need to invite them in to meet Paz, although it's still too early to tell. We're watching them closely."

Wiley nodded as she listened. The room was filled with people, primarily women. The meeting was taking place in New York, in the U.N. building. It had been Wiley's decision to make this their headquarters.

The phone interrrupted her thoughts.

"Luann...Yes, I did call you, to invite you over for a get-together. Are you free on Sunday evening? I'm having a few eggheads. Snacks and 'lively conversation'. Can you come?...Well, good...Just a few people, five or six. Alexandra Prell, you know her. Eleanor Clark, and a few others...I know, it's been too long. I'm looking forward to seeing you. Around seven o'clock...Great, see you then."

Wiley went back to reading the paper in front of her. Hypothesis 8 was getting strong support. So far, every subject was susceptible to every zap regardless of I.Q., socioeconomic status, or personality variables. The other hypotheses, too, were being supported. Next we'll try the first post-implantation suggestion, she thought. She read over the protocol Drew would use: *When you go for your follow-up appointment with Dr. Cavenar, you will talk with her for a while, then suddenly realize that you want to talk about Michaelangelo. You will feel a strong desire to discuss this topic with Dr. Cavenar and not be satisfied until you do.*

Wiley smiled, pleased with herself, pleased with how the research was progressing, pleased with the prospects for the future. Nothing will ever be the same, she thought, and again drifted into fantasy.

## 20

That night, right after dinner, Becka ran to the piano. She'd had two lessons now and was eager to show off what she'd learned. *Robin in the Cherry Tree* never sounded so good to Drew. Watching her daughter's little fingers carefully pick out the silly tune brought sentimental tears to her eyes. Still, more than eight years later, she had not gotten over the miracle of having created a child, and she continued to marvel at Becka's growth and accomplishments and her exuberance for life. For a while, this is what had kept Drew going. Recently, though, since the tornado, she rarely slipped into the melancholic crevices that used to trap her. The pain about Judith was different. It was still there but it was different.

The phone rang.

"Hi, Drew, this is Judith."

Drew's face fell. Her heart thundered in her chest and she had to sit. Through her mind flashed the scenario she'd longed for repeatedly over the past three weeks: that Judith had been able to get over her fear, or whatever was blocking her, realized their love for each other transcended everything else, and was calling to ask Drew to be with her again. "Judith, how are you? It's good..."

"I'm worried, Drew. I've gone over this a thousand times and I decided I have to talk with you."

The words were ambiguous. They could be interpreted hopefully, but the tone was wrong. "All right, good, let's get together, Jude. When would...?"

"I mean now. On the phone."

That wasn't good. Anxiety edged out Drew's hope. "OK," she said, "then let's talk now." She rubbed her hand tensely against her jeans.

"It's about your power, Drew," Judith said. Her voice was strained. "It's eerie. It scares the shit out of me. It shouldn't be. I think it's...it's evil."

Drew was painfully frustrated. This was not what she wanted to talk about with Judith. She was also puzzled. "Evil? What do you mean?"

"It's not natural, not normal. I'm frightened in a lot of ways, Drew, afraid of what's going to happen to you. No human being is meant to be able to interfere with the world that way. It's wrong, and could be...I don't think anything good can come of it."

"What are you suggesting, Judith?" Drew hated this, hated the conversation. She longed to declare her love for Judith, to get her to come back and let their love unfold, to plead to give them a chance. She longed to hold Judith close to her and touch her soft warm skin and kiss her eyes and lips and...

"That you stop. That you vow never to use it again."

"I miss you," Drew said.

"Drew, please don't. Please listen to me. I'm doing this for you because...because I care about you and..."

"You do? God, Judith, you don't know how much I've needed to hear that. I've been..."

"No, Drew, not that way. Our friendship, our past. All of that. I don't want to see you destroyed."

"What are you talking about?"

"Drew, all I want to say is that you must...I'm asking you, for your sake, and for everyone else's, to stop. Don't use the power. Pretend you don't have it. Go back to what you were. Will you promise?"

"Promise? I can't do that, Judith. I don't get it. Can't we get together and talk. Maybe then it would be clearer to me."

"I can't. Things have changed, Drew. I..." She hesitated. "Vic and I are engaged," she blurted. "We're going to get married soon, probably before the end of the year."

The plunge Drew took was bottomless, an immediate hurling crash into a black, deep hole that sucked her down and had no end. There was no way she could respond.

"Drew, are you there?"

Nothing.

"Drew, say something."

Silence.

"I know it's a surprise. It's probably what I should have done long ago. Vic wanted it for over a year now as you know. It's what I want, too."

"I see," Drew said, numbness taking over.

"Please think about what I said. This call was very hard for me to make. Will you stop using the power?"

"I don't know what I'll do," Drew said tonelessly.

"I wish you'd..."

"Well, take care," Drew said, her voice emotionless.

"Yeah. You too, Drew. Are you...?"

"Goodbye, Judith."

Drew did not hear the little tune coming from the piano. Several minutes later, when Becka spoke to her, Drew replied mechanically and Becka wisely moved away and went to play. Drew remained in the chair near the phone. An hour passed. She continued sitting, motionless.

"Mom, can I invite Wiley over? She's your best friend for sadness, isn't she?"

Drew nodded, not really registering what her perceptive daughter said.

"Hi, Wiley...Nothing much, playing the piano and doing a puzzle...and drawing...One picture of a horse with a cat riding it. And, let's see, one of a long, long house with twenty-five rooms all in a line, like a train, but it's a house...Wiley, will you come over to our house now...Yeah, she's here...She's not happy right now...Mostly she's just sitting on a chair and looking out the window...I don't know...just talked on the phone and then sat...I don't know who. Maybe somebody said something mean to her...Yes, I asked her if I could invite you and she said yes...Oh good! Bye."

Drew was still sitting when Wiley arrived.

"So, can you talk about it?"

As always with Wiley, Drew did. She told her their conversation verbatim.

Wiley held Drew and let her talk.

"Vic's a jag off," Drew said.

Wiley listened.

"Judith is nuts. She's acting like an asshole."

Drew continued to ventilate and Wiley listened, comforting her. At last, Drew grew quiet and resigned. Wiley stayed until Drew thought she'd be able to sleep and they sadly said goodnight.

## 21.

In her office several days later, Wiley looked over the face sheet of the subject due at 10:30 that morning: Dorothy Briggs, sixty-nine years old, white, female. Good, Wiley thought, we need another older woman.

So far, the subject recruitment was going well. Through the newspaper ads they'd placed and the notices they'd sent to various groups and organizations, they had already been contacted by twenty-six people. Drew had now zapped fifteen of them and all the hypotheses were continuing to be supported.

Mrs. Briggs turned out to be a pleasant, talkative widow who easily passed the screening for cooperativeness, reliability, and absence of severe psychopathology, and so was accepted as a subject. Wiley assessed her attitudes toward various social issues, determined her preferences for foods and magazines, and ascertained her susceptibility to hypnosis by having her enter trance. When Mrs. Briggs went to another room to take the I.Q. test and fill out the attitude questionnaire, Wiley readied herself for the next subject, Andrew Zayre, who was due to arrive in fifteen minutes.

"Yes, insurance," he said, "you can never have too much." He chuckled, but his eyes remained cold. He wore a navy blue sports coat and a plaid shirt and carried a tattered leather briefcase. Andrew Zayre was a large man who made the chair across from Wiley's desk creak when he moved.

"And what else do you do besides insure people?" Wiley asked.

"That's it," he said perfunctorily.

"I mean, in your spare time," Wiley added, imagining him pushing policies every day from morning 'til night.

"Oh, you mean hobbies?"

"Or whatever."

"I collect guns," he said.

Wiley nodded, concealing her disgust. "How did you get interested in that?"

"I don't know," he said, looking around the room. "I just like them, always have."

"What else do you like to do?" Wiley asked.

The questions continued. Andre Zayre informed Wiley he had a wife, but no children, and that his parents were dead. His responses were brief and minimally self-disclosing.

"You understand the purpose of my questions, Mr. Zayre," Wiley said at one point. "It may seem like idle curiosity but, as I said, we're trying to correlate hypnotizability and various characteristics of people and so..."

"Oh, that's all right. Fire away. Ask anything you want."

Andrew Zayre clearly did not like being asked questions. In fact, Wiley got the impression that it was a strain on him to be cordial. Strange for someone who sells insurance, she thought. She was tempted to reject him as a subject, but since he did meet the criteria of inclusion, she went on. It amused her that, like Mrs. Briggs, Andrew Zayre, too, had an aversion to brussels sprouts. However, he also had an aversion to abortion rights, Communists and homosexuality. His susceptibility to hypnosis was average.

When Andrew Zayre left Wiley's office, he caught a cab to his near north apartment. It was small and cluttered. There was no sign that anyone lived there except Andrew Zayre. He removed a tape recorder from his brief case, rewound the tape and listened to himself being interviewed by Dr. Wiley Cavenar.

## 22.

Drew figured the appointment with Rit Avery shouldn't take long, fifteen or twenty minutes at most. They'd talk briefly, she'd zap the attorney who would then agree to take the case, and then she'd leave. On the way downtown, Drew found herself again questioning the morality of what she was doing, of zapping people to get them to do what she wanted. She didn't want to think about it. Besides, my zaps are for good ends, she argued to herself. She was walking up the stairs of the subway station. I'd never harm anyone with a zap. The Loop was crowded as usual this time of day. Who's to say what's harmful, though, she thought, feeling uncomfortable. Is it any worse than other forms of persuasion? She knew this was not simply a form of persuasion, but did not want to think about it. Not yet. I'll think it through later. You're being selfish, she chastised. Yes.

Instead of the customary bland furnishings, Rit Avery's waiting room was full of beautiful objects. There were two magnificent oak end tables, a grouping of antique chairs, a slim elegant silver lamp, a rich tapestry wall hanging, and several gilt-framed oil paintings. Drew was absorbed in examining the intricate design of the tapestry when she heard a voice that caught her immediately, drawing her full attention. It was a woman's voice. The sound was rich and deep. Through the sliding glass panel of the receptionist's office, Drew could see the profile of a tall, dark- haired woman. Her heart sped up at the sight. She felt flushed. She stared at the striking figure, gaped actually, her mouth slightly open, her heart pounding. Then the woman moved away and was gone.

What an extraordinary person, Drew thought, still staring at the place where she had been. She assumed the woman was Rit Avery.

I can't believe my reaction, she thought. Nothing like that had ever happened before. She shook her head as if trying to clear it and took several deep breaths. The image of the face remained etched in her mind, the wavy black hair, strong angular bone structure, the full lower lip and flash of white teeth. And the sound of the voice—resonant, full, sure, captivating.

"Ms. Avery will see you now."

Drew felt nervous as she rose. How ridiculous, she told herself, but the tense excitement persisted. The receptionist led her down a short corridor and opened a door for her.

Rit Avery rose from behind her large oak desk and approached Drew. Drew felt faint. Rit held out her hand and Drew's lifted of its own accord. Though it lasted only a second or two, Drew still could feel the touch of Rit's hand on hers after the attorney had re-seated herself and directed Drew to an easy chair at her left. Drew's palm burned. She wanted to look at her hand to see if it had changed, but she could not take her eyes off of Rit Avery's face.

Rit observed this and smiled slightly. The smile softened what otherwise might be judged a stern face, and Drew regained enough composure to avert her eyes momentarily and break the stare.

"I understand you're with the Lesbian Legal Defense group," Rit said. "What can I do for you?"

The voice grabbed Drew again, almost stunning her. She fought for enough control to say something, for she was sure she'd been asked a question. Her heart pounded against her sternum. "You're Rit Avery," was all she could manage.

Rit frowned. "That's right," she said slowly, scrutinizing Drew. She waited. Drew did not speak. "You wanted to talk with me about something," Rit prodded, not kindly, but not impatiently either.

"Yes."

Rit waited.

"There's a case," Drew said at last. She bit down on her teeth, forcing herself toward control, trying to calm enough to function. "Linda Morely."

"Yes, I'm familiar with it. Is there a new development? I already spoke to one of your people about it."

The voice again reverberated in Drew's ear. She lit a cigarette. Her hand trembled slightly. Talk about the case, she ordered herself. "Yes," Drew said. "There are several new developments." Her voice was lightening and she began to speak with more confidence. "This may surprise you for I doubt that you often change your mind, but when you finish hearing what I have to say, I think you'll be interested in taking the case."

Rit raised her heavy eyebrows. "Oh? Try me."

Drew talked rapidly for nearly five minutes, adrenolin rushing through her. She outlined the merits of the case, the issues it involved and their importance. She tapped an eloquence she didn't know she had. She was uncertain why she was doing this, for she knew she merely had to zap this woman and save her attempts at persuasion.

"An interesting perspective," Rit said. "I'm almost tempted to yield to your charming rhetoric." She smiled flirtatiously at Drew. "Almost, but not quite. No, Drew McAllister, I'm not interested enough, not in the case. What about you? Why such a moving appeal? Is Linda Morely someone special to you?"

"I've never met her."

"Hm-m. You're with the Committee. You're a lesbian then?"

Rit could have been asking if Drew were a Democrat or an art lover or bookkeeper.

"A lesbian?"

"Yes, lesbian."

"I suppose."

Rit laughed. "Yes, of course you are," she said, "but you're just finding it out, aren't you?"

Though it registered dimly in Drew's mind that this woman was getting much too personal much too fast, she seemed unable to prevent herself from answering candidly. "Yes," she said.

Rit leaned back in her chair, smiling. "Would you like a drink?"

Drew realized she was feeling lightheaded, as if high from some strange illicit drug. She nodded.

"Over there, do you mind?" Rit gestured toward the credenza. "I'll have a scotch."

Drew rose immediately and poured them drinks as if it were quite natural for her to be performing this service. She handed Rit hers and, in the process, their fingers brushed. An electric jolt entered Drew's fingertips and shot down her spine. A film of perspiration coated her forehead.

"You interest me," Rit said.

Drew took a gulp of her drink, hoping for a calming effect. What's happening, she thought.

"Tell me about yourself."

"I'm beginning a new life," Drew said, surprising herself by her response.

"Yes, I see that. A domesticated wildcat breaking free, discovering her true nature."

"I can have anything I want."

"Good. And what is it you want?"

"That's part of the beginning, to find out."

"To transcend limitations."

"To go as far and deep as I wish. There are no barriers."

Rit rose. Slowly, she moved toward Drew and stood very near to her, towering over her, seeming very strong and powerful. She took Drew's chin in her hand and lifted it. She looked into Drew's eyes. Drew felt as if her bones were melting.

"There's something quite unusual about you, Drew McAllister. Something special...almost strange."

The grasp on Drew's chin altered gradually into a brief fingertip caress along her cheek. Drew's whole body tingled with heat and cold darting shivers. Then Rit moved away and walked to the window. She continued speaking, her back to Drew as she looked down onto LaSalle Street. "Forget the Morely case. With me, that is. Try Shar Benz. She may be interested, I'm not." She turned to face Drew, her eyes softening. "But I am interested in the new life you're beginning."

The allusion to the case brought Drew back to her mission and she knew she must proceed with the zap, get it over with so they could talk some more.

"Rit Avery, listen to me."

Rit watched her visitor curiously.

"I have something important to say and I want you to pay close attention."

Rit was looking deeply into Drew's eyes.

"You want to take the case."

Rit continued staring at her, her eyes clear.

"You know that you can do a fine job advocating Linda Morley's right to custody of her children and you want to involve yourself in the case. You are deeply interested in it."

As Drew spoke, Rit Avery moved her head back slightly, frowning, still maintaining eye contact with Drew. Her eyes remained clear. "What are you doing?" she demanded.

Drew was flustered. "What do you mean?"

"What did you do...or try to do just now?" Rit's eyes were fierce.

"I don't understand."

"Don't mess with me, McAllister. You told me I'm interested in the Morely case, that I want to work on it. You said it as if by so saying it would be. I want you to explain."

Drew felt liquidy and weak. It was fear, undoubtedly, that had taken hold of her, but excitement too. This woman is extraordinary.

The zap didn't work on her. She's too powerful, Drew thought, growing even more excited. She felt unable to resist Rit's command, either to lie or refuse to discuss it or make a joke of it. For some strange reason, she felt unable to do anything but what Rit Avery demanded she do, and, stranger yet, she liked the feeling. "I can make people believe things...most people. It didn't work on you."

"Tell me more."

Drew did. She told Rit Avery everything. As the story unfolded, Rit asked pointed questions, probing until Drew had spoken for nearly an hour giving every relevant detail, fully, truthfully.

When Rit allowed her to stop, the powerful attorney leaned back in her big oak chair looking at the ceiling. She did not express her thoughts to Drew. She gave no verbal reaction to what she had heard, but remained sitting that way for several minutes. "I'm going to bring Alice in here," Rit said at last, turning her steady gaze on Drew. "I want you to zap her. Tell her that she believes we need to relocate our offices to another building; that it's crucial and we must do it within a week."

It didn't even occur to Drew to refuse or question Rit, and clearly Rit expected no resistence for she immediately spoke into the intercom.

When the receptionist entered the office, Rit spoke pleasantly. "Alice, our friend here has something she'd like to say to you."

"Oh?" Alice looked expectantly at Drew.

"Yes," Drew said. "Something important. I want you to listen very carefully."

Rit observed, looking from one to the other, watching as Alice's eyes became glazed, listening as Drew told Alice she believed it was crucial that their offices be moved. Rit waited until Alice became animated again.

"Yes, what is it?" Alice asked Drew. She seemed impatient.

"I just wanted to say that you remind me of a an old friend of mine who I haven't seen in years. From college. Are you Alice Weber? University of Wisconsin?"

Alice looked annoyed. "No, sorry," she said. "I must have a common face." She looked eagerly at Rit. "I don't want to rush you," she said, "but there's something I need to discuss with you right away."

Rit looked quickly at Drew then back at Alice. "What is it?"

"I'd rather..." She glanced at Drew.

"It's all right, go ahead," Rit said.

"You know I'm not superstitious," Alice began, her intense

motivation overriding her embarrassment, but this building is unsafe, Rit. Don't ask me how I know. You've said many times what an uncanny ability I have to sense things. Well, I feel this very strongly. We have to get out of here, move our offices. Soon. Within a week. Trust me on this. The building should be evacuated. I'll begin checking for available space. We should do it quickly, within the next few days, if possible."

Rit leaned back and looked at Drew approvingly. "Have a seat, Alice."

She continued looking at Drew. "All right," she ordered. "That's enough. Cure her."

"Alice...," Drew said.

Alice was sitting now, on the edge of her chair. She looked at Drew and listened and soon, after Drew stopped speaking, was again composed and calm. "Is there anything else?" she ased Rit.

"What do you think of this building?" Rit said.

"This building?" Alice looked puzzled. "It's a building. I don't know. It's adequate, I guess. Why do you ask?"

"OK, Alice. That's all for now. Thanks."

After Alice closed the door behind her, Rit remained seated at her desk, leaning her chin on her hands, staring at Drew. "Interesting," she said at last.

Drew nodded.

"Quite a power you have."

Drew smiled.

"What are your plans?"

"I'm not sure. Like I told you, I've just been playing it by ear so far, zapping people here and there when I feel like it or want something."

"And your friend, Wiley?"

"What about Wiley?"

"What are her plans?"

"She likes to investigate things."

Rit frowned. "For knowledge's sake?"

Drew shrugged her shoulders. "She's an idealist. I think she wants me to save the world or something."

Rit was still frowning. "Maybe." She smiled then and stood. "As to the Morely case, it appears you haven't been able to change my mind, though I've enjoyed your attempts." It was clear that she was finished with the meeting and was dismissing Drew.

Drew stood and walked to the door with Rit at her side. "I'll tell the Committee you suggested Shar..."

"Benz. B-e-n-z. Yes. I imagine you will be the one to discuss it with Shar," Rit said, smiling, "in case she needs some persuading. Of course, you could always take a short cut and just have a talk with the judge."

Not wanting to leave, Drew saw the chance to prolong the contact. "You don't approve? Of my using the power?"

"It must be hard to resist," Rit answered, leaning against the doorway.

"Would you resist if you had it?"

The attorney smiled broadly, showing her straight white teeth. "Ultimately."

"Why?"

Rit paused as if considering whether to answer. "Because I like the game," she said. She held out her hand. "Goodbye, Drew McAllister."

## 23.

It was "Ladies Night" at the baths. The regulars were there, wrapped in white sheets or sitting naked, playing pinochle in the card room. Some of them were napping on the rows of cots in the sleeping area. Most of the women were older, European immigrants who lived in the neighborhood, women who came here each Wednesday to sit in the whirlpool, sweat in the sauna, take a swim and be among friends.

Drew and Wiley were stretched out in lounge chairs at the side of the pool. Becka wore a diving mask and bobbed up and down in the water. The first time they came, Becka had insisted on wearing her swimsuit. Now she obviously felt fine in the freedom of her nakedness, swimming and jumping around in the pool. She was the only child there tonight.

"Look, mom!"

Drew watched her daughter's somersault "Good one," she called.

"I've been thinking," Wiley said. She stretched her arms then crossed her hands behind her neck. The muscles of her slim tan body were nicely toned and defined.

"Again?" Drew smiled at her friend. "Tell me, Wiley Cortex,

tell me exactly what you've been thinking."

"About my work as a therapist."

"Ah ha," Drew said, settling in to listen. "Go on."

Wiley ran her fingers through her hair. The few gray strands were barely visible when her hair was wet as it was now, though the gray did not bother her at all. "Much of what I do essentially involves helping people become aware of the central constructs they hold," she said, "the beliefs that rule their lives, that form the bases of their personalities."

"Good," Drew said, "someone needs to do it."

"Drew, I'm trying to have a serious conversation with you."

"Yes, Wiley."

"People's cognitions, what they tell themselves, what they think, believe—these generate many of their feelings and actions."

"Ain't it the truth!"

"Drew."

"Yes, Wiley."

"I'm working up to asking you something important. Is there any chance of you being serious for a moment."

"Mm...it's possible."

Wiley shrugged. "Never mind, we can talk about it later."

"About what?"

"My idea."

"Oh."

"Don't you want to hear?"

Drew laughed, the deep hearty kind that transformed her face into glowing cheerfulness. "Wiley, I love it," she said. "You're too funny. There is no way I could *avoid* hearing. I love to watch you when you're like this." Then she made her face more serious. "Go on, I'm ready. Tell me about your idea."

Wiley swung her feet over the footrest of her chair and leaned toward Drew. "As I work in therapy with people," she began, "one of the things that happens is that their beliefs become more and more clarified; the core ones, the central ones, as well as the more peripheral ones. The beliefs we focus on, of course, are those that interfere with their functioning, that impede their growth, stifle their potential for fulfillment."

"Mm-hm."

"For example, if you believe you're a bad person, unloveable, worthless, et cetera, then that belief affects your feelings and your behavior and your interpretations of your experience. Your interpretations of your experience, in turn, affect your feelings and behaviors and so on."

"That makes sense," Drew said. "They're all tied together."

"Many beliefs people hold," Wiley continued, "especially core ones, formed early, accepted without rational critique, become very rigid, very solidified. Other beliefs get built on top of them. They're hard to alter, even though the person, as an adult, can see that some of them are not reasonable or realistic, and, in addition, are debilitating or self-destructive."

Drew watched the rippling movement of Wiley's arm muscles. Her skin looks so smooth, she thought. Very nice breasts.

"For example," Wiley went on, "I'm working with a woman now who is convinced that her worth is a function of her appearance. She's an attractive woman, but she's obsessed with her looks. She spends hours on grooming and always finds some minor flaw to worry about. She's constantly dieting, even though she's thin. We've traced it back. It has to do with the societal expectations for women, in part, but it also connects with the messages and the contingent strokes she got from her parents, especially her mother, and it has some symbolic meaning, too. It's deeply rooted, more complex than I need to go into. She's critiqued it. She knows it's ridiculous, but it's very difficult for her to let go of the notion that for her to be cared about, she must be physically perfect. She's engaged now, seems to really love the guy and he her. They basically have a good relationship, but she's tormented with insecurity. She fears he'll reject her if she gets a pimple or a hair is out of place or if he discovers the little birthmark on her thigh that she goes to great lengths to conceal. They've talked together about all of this. He assures her that he loves her for many things about her—her character, personality, endearing quirks. She'll let it in part way, but can't seem to go further. Deep down, she's still convinced that her loveableness resides in how she appears. Clearly, this interferes with her life."

Drew nodded. "I can see how. It's like my belief that I can't rely on my own judgments sometimes, that I have to look to others." She smiled. "That's changed recently, but I know it used to really stifle me, and depress me."

"Yes, you got a lot of messages that making mistakes was awful, didn't you? So, you got too cautious, wouldn't trust yourself. You gave other people a great deal of power over you because of that."

"Like Steve."

"Yes, especially him."

"I have an aunt, Aunt Betty, who's terribly afraid of moths. She's so extreme about it that she really restricts her life. It's funny, in a way, but it's really sad. She hardly ever goes outside in the summertime."

Drew shook her head. "I ought to zap her."

Wiley smiled. "That's my idea," she said. "Using your zapping power to..."

"Wait a minute..." Drew looked displeased.

"Let me finish. What I want to suggest is that we try something with one of my clients, that you be my 'consultant' on a case—not the one I mentioned. Someone else. We've got it down to three main beliefs that are blocking her. It's been a bitch for her, trying to let go of them. We've tried all the usual methods; she's made some progress, but it's so slow and in the meantime..."

"So, you want me to zap her."

"Yes," Wiley said, "if she's willing. I'll explain that you're a hypnotist and tell her exactly what suggestions you'll give her. It could turn her life around. She can tell you herself what the blocks are, the irrational beliefs, and then you can...what's the matter?"

Drew did not answer. She was feeling itchily uncomfortable. The concerns about her life being taken over surfaced again, about becoming nothing more than a useful resource, a zapping machine. The gnawing uneasiness churned in her. It was worse than the discomfort she felt about whether it was right to zap people. Those doubts she was fairly successful at rationalizing away. But the fear of being taken over by the power ate at her. She closed her eyes as the images came. There she was, perched high on a golden, cushioned, throne, wearing a silken robe. Her fingers were weighted with rings, her body adorned with jewels. Lackeys hovered around her and before her came the petitioners, a line of people, an endless line stretching beyond the ornate room, beyond the castle, beyond the city, a never-ending line. One by one they came to her with their requests. They spoke humbly, standing at her feet, beseeching her to grant their zap, wooing her with gifts and sad, moving stories.

"I've got to be careful not to lose myself," Drew said.

Wiley frowned. "How do you mean?"

Again, Drew did not answer for some time. She watched a woman swim across the pool, cutting slickly through the water with smooth, well-coordinated strokes. "And if it goes well with that one, I suppose there will be other clients you'll want me to consult with and then..."

"Mom, let's go in the sauna, OK?" Becka yelled from the pool.

"In a minute," Drew called back. "And then there will be the temptation to let some of your therapist friends in on it, to be their 'consultant', too." She looked sharply at Wiley. "We can cure the

112

world, wipe out all neurotic ideas..."

"Drew."

Drew's lips formed a tight line.

"You're getting carried away," Wiley said.

"I know."

"One step at a time, huh?"

"Yeah." Drew grabbed her towel. "Me and my girl, we're gonna go saunatize," she said. "I gotta clear out my pores."

Wiley watched her walk away, watched the graceful movements of Drew's naked legs and hips and gently swaying breasts. Her own body stirred and she went to the edge of the pool and dived.

# 24.

All the people at Joanne Lipski's party were women. Most of the members of the Lesbian Legal Defense Committee were there and about a dozen others. Drew felt comfortable; she liked the relaxed atmosphere. The lack of males did not seem like a lack at all. She leaned in a doorway talking with Joanne and another woman from the Committee.

"You're losing weight," Drew said, smiling. Though they had talked on the phone several times, this was the first time she'd seen Joanne since she zapped her in the restaurant nearly a month ago.

"Yes, I've tried a thousand times before, but this time it feels like it's just happening naturally. I actually only eat when I'm hungry. I'm two sizes smaller already."

Wildflower walked past and nodded to them. A few minutes later she came back with a glass of apple cider and spoke to Drew. "I'm not surprised you couldn't get Rit Avery to help us. She's male-identified."

Drew cocked her head. "Male-identified? What do you mean?"

"It's obvious," Wildflower said. "That woman's more involved with pricks than she is with sisters. She's been co-opted and doesn't even know it. Of course, she's probably just a genital lesbian anyway...if she's even a dyke at all."

Drew wanted to laugh at her, but felt a furious anger. "My, you're a bitter one," she said.

"Bitter? Shit, I'm enraged. Look around, woman, look at the world they made."

Drew took a long drag on her cigarette. "Right," she said, blowing a huge cloud upward. Wildflower despised smoking. "So we have a lot of work to do, a lot of changes to make in the world, in men's attitudes." She was working hard to hold herself in check.

"Oh bullshit, that's not our job. Besides, you'll die trying. Me, I'm not wasting my energy on pricks. They're hopeless aliens. Let the Rit Avery's of the world suck up to them."

Joanne Lipski had silently slipped away and joined another conversation. Drew and Wildflower stood near the doorway, out of earshot of the others at the party. "Listen to me," Drew said, bringing her face close to Wildflower's, "I have something important to say to you."

Wildflower's eyes focused sharply on Drew's, then glazed.

"You are becoming aware of a strong attraction to males," Drew said. "You feel drawn to them. It's a powerful urge, a need, to get close to men, very close, to be emotionally intimate. You may choose not to get physical or sexual with them, but you feel an intense drive to become caringly involved. The attraction is growing. You're aware of this and you cannot resist it. These feeling will be there in you for the next week, and then, if you want them to, they'll fade away. While they're there, they'll be very intense."

Drew waited.

Wildflower stared at her awhile, then blinked her eyes rapidly. Her close-cropped hair glistened as she shook her head back and forth, the thin locks at the nape of her neck brushing over the collar of her flannel shirt. "I feel weird," she said.

"What is it?" Drew asked.

"I don't know." She shook her head again and looked around the room. "All these women," she mumbled, "it doesn't feel right. I...I've got to get out of here."

Drew felt a little guilty as she watched Wildflower bolt to the door. She wandered toward the dining room table and its stacks of raw vegetables. As she was drawing a small piece of broccoli coated with creamy dip toward her mouth, someone took hold of her wrist from behind and pulled her hand slowly back.

Rit Avery took the vegetable into her mouth and continued holding onto Drew's wrist. She chewed, smiling, then, very slowly licked off the drop of dip from Drew's finger. "Thank you," she said pleasantly, releasing Drew's hand.

Drew was speechless, her face flushed.

"You have a delicious finger." Rit stood very close to her. "In addition to your other gifts."

Drew could feel Rit's body heat, and unconsciously moved toward her a fraction of an inch until their hips touched. "We'd better dance," Rit said. She rested her hand on Drew's neck and drew her finger softly across Drew's cheek, then led her to the living room where they joined several other dancing couples. Each time Drew's hands touched Rit's or they brushed against each other, she felt electric surges through her body. After a while, Rit guided her to the edge of the room, to a sofa where she bid her sit, her eyes never leaving Drew.

Drew squirmed beneath the scrutiny. "I'm surprised to see you here," she said, groping for conversation to ease her tension.

Rit seated herself next to Drew, sinking into the soft maroon cushions. "I knew *you'd* be here," she said.

Shifting nervously, Drew looked away.

"Am I being too direct?"

Drew turned back. Rit's dark hair waved past her ear and fell lightly to jaw level, but it was on her mouth that Drew focused, on the full, succulent lips. She took a deep breath. "Maybe so. You...uh, I find you a little overwhelming for some reason."

Rit nodded. "I find you delightful...enticing. I've decided I want to get to know you."

Drew's pleasure was overridden by a suddenly defensiveness. "Why?" she asked.

"Ah, yes," Rit said. "You *should* be cautious. Have you zapped anyone lately?"

Drew looked down, biting her lip.

"I see. Tell me."

"Do you know a woman named Wildflower?"

Rit nodded. "Oh, yes. Dear little Wildflower. She's going through the worst phase now: righteously angry, conceptually blinded by her indignation, rampantly overgeneralizing."

"Well put," Drew said. "She had some rather unpleasant things to say...about you, so I zapped her for it."

Rit chuckled. "Defending my honor. I'm flattered. What happened?"

Drew told her and Rit laughed so hard heads turned. "That's marvelous," she guffawed. "And I'd been thinking you might be a little too serious-minded."

"It was nasty."

"Yes," Rit said with mock seriousness.

Drew laughed. "I wonder where she is now. Probably rummaging through her drawers, looking for her discarded makeup."

"To go on the hunt."

"For pricks."

They laughed together. "Very nasty, Drew." Rit stared at her, a light smile softening her sternly attractive face. "I'm going to enjoy making love to you."

Drew had just taken a drag from her cigarette and began to cough; her face got red.

Rit patted and rubbed her back. "You're quite excitable, aren't you?"

Drew coughed some more. "I don't know what to make of you," she said finally, catching her breath.

"Yes you do."

An hour later, they left together.

"Where are you parked?"

"That way."

"Good night, then," Rit said, turning in the opposite direction. "Call me at the office Monday. Early afternoon."

She disappeared around the corner as Drew watched, feeling disappointed that nothing more would happen tonight, but also relieved.

## 25.

On Monday morning, Andrew Zayre entered the studio. He placed his briefcase on the floor near the wall and took his place on the stool while Drew adjusted the camera and lights. "Put your chin slightly up and to the right," she said.

After snapping a half dozen shots of his expressionless face, Drew asked him to listen for she had something important to say. One after another, Drew implanted into the mind of Andrew Zayre beliefs which were to become more truly part of him than what his eyes saw or his ears heard, beliefs that would supercede those he had acquired in a lifetime of sensing, experiencing, and interpreting. She told him her book was a footstool, her age was 65 and height six feet three. She told him two plus two are five, that he limps, and loves to eat brussels sprouts. She told him he enjoys romantic love stories, but cannot read; that he feels favorably towards abortion rights, communism, and homosexuality. She told him that he believes animals should wear clothing and that Allah is the true diety. And finally Drew told Andrew Zayre that when she begins to engage him in conversation, he will feel motivated to be cooperative, to talk with her and answer her questions.

She was silent then. Gradually, after nearly a minute had passed, Zayre rose from the stool and paced the room, limping as he walked.

"Any more pictures?" he asked.

"That's it," Drew replied. "I think we got some good shots."

Zayre looked at the photos on the walls. "These your grandchildren?" he asked, pointing to a shot of two teenagers.

"No," Drew said. "How old do you think I am, Mr. Zayre?"

"Oh, I don't know."

"No, go on, tell me."

"Sixtyish," Zayre replied.

Drew smiled. "You know, I was quite an athlete in my younger days?"

"Basketball, right?"

Drew smiled again. Zayre was about three inches taller than she, which would make him five feet ten. She walked over and stood by his side. "How tall would you say I am, Mr. Zayre?"

"Oh, about six three," he answered.

"Really, but look, you're taller than I."

Zayre frowned. "I don't understand," he said. "Why do you say that? It's obvious that you're nearly half a foot taller. Unusually tall for a woman."

"Look," Drew persisted. "The top of my head comes to your nose."

He looked at her as if she were crazy. "All right, all right," he said. "So you don't like being tall. I can understand that. It's probably hard for a woman."

Drew sat down. "Now, what happened to that footstool?" she asked, looking around the room.

Zayre limped over to the table and brought a book to Drew, placing it on the floor near her feet.

"Thank you," she said, resting her heels on it. "I notice you're limping, Mr. Zayre. What happened?"

"Injury."

"What a shame."

"Hunting accident."

Drew had a pile of magazines on the table—a gun magazine, a detective pulp, a True Story, and several others. She gestured toward them. "Do me a favor, would you," she said. "I've had a headache all morning." She put her hand to her temple. "Sometimes they go away when I'm read to. Would you mind reading aloud from one of these? It doesn't matter what. Choose something you like. Just read for a few minutes, I'd appreciate it."

Zayre hesitated.

"Please," Drew said, playing up her elderly image. "It would help."

Zayre reached toward the magazines, then drew back. "No," he said. "I'd rather not. How about an aspirin?"

"Just a few lines," Drew coaxed.

"I can't," Zayre said. "I...I can't read."

Drew looked at him in mock surprise, then tilted her head. "Why, you're serious, aren't you? But how could that be?"

"I...it's...it's from the leg injury...neurological damage...I just can't...it spread to my brain...somehow..."

"Oh, you're kidding me," Drew said. "Just relax. Help an old lady's headache."

Zayre grabbed a magazine at random and flipped it open. He stared at the page of print. "I can't," he said. "It's just...they're just marks. They mean nothing to me. I can't read." He was perspiring.

Drew erased that zap.

When his eyes cleared, Zayre sighed with relief and then selected another magazine and began reading to Drew about the torrid romance of Brett and Julia.

"I feel much better now," Drew said. "I get a headache whenever I worry about money. I never could balance my checkbook. Here, let me show you the problem." She wrote out a column of numbers. "Now you add this up for me, will you?"

Zayre's addition was clearly distorted by the new math he'd been zapped into accepting. The testing continued for the next ten minutes and Zayre, like those before him, revealed his total acceptance of each belief Drew had implanted.

It was time now for the erasures. As the protocol directed, Drew left some of the implanted beliefs intact in order to test the longer-term effects of the implantations.

"Three weeks, yes, that's fine," Zayre said. "I'll see you then." He took his briefcase and left.

Drew made the required notations in his file, wondering how something so astounding could begin to seem routine. They all react the same, she thought. Except for Rit. Rit was different.

118

## 26

To Rit Avery existence was a series of stimulating games and she an avid player. Drew McAllister stimulated her and so she was making room for a new game in her life.

She smiled thinking about the powerful effect she had on Drew. This wasn't unusual. Many people had strong responses to her, she knew; she accepted it and sometimes used it. Ordinarily she would have made little of Drew's reaction, except that the intrigue in this case was mutual. Drew McAllister was a rarity and Rit anticipated pleasurably the adventures to come.

She poured herself a scotch. There's a hungry look about her, Rit thought, especially in those sad green eyes. Beautiful eyes. She liked Drew's frowns, too, and the little twitches at the sides of her mouth when she was about to speak. Rit took a large swallow of her drink. A sensually appealing woman, extremely so in Rit's estimation, and she was glad of that. It would make it much more fun. Rit had attended Joanne Lipski's party last Friday because Drew would be there. She expected some resistance, just enough to intensify the game and the pleasure of the ultimate resolution.

The intercom buzzed.

"Cora Jorganson on two."

"Thanks." Rit picked up the phone. "Yes, Cora....Mm-hm, it's taken care of. Relax, huh? Go to the beach...You're welcome...Yes, that's right, I've entered the writ. I'll call you when something new develops...Yes, goodbye, Cora."

In the pursuit of law, Rit found a game that had kept her stimulated for the past decade. She had lived forty years, the period between her twenty-fifth and thirtieth being the most unusual. At age 25, after one semester as a University of Chicago graduate student in Philosophy, she suddenly left the university and the city, giving little explanation to her professors, who were disappointed with her decision, or to her friends, who were confused. For the next five years, Rit Avery's life was a mad cacophony of endless adventures. She played in a rock band, lived on a commune, worked in a factory, farmed, taught, spent time in jail, traveled much of the world, went on a treasure hunting expedition, associated with politicians, actors, writers, socialites, Socialists, Birchites, Arabs, Japanese, French, athletes, criminals, and more.

She had become very wealthy; no one knew how. It is true that she burglarized a jewelry store once, to see how it felt, she'd said, but that hadn't yielded much. Her experiences during that half decade of her life seemed far beyond what any one person could possibly have.

At age thirty, when a lover was convicted of computerized embezzlement, Rit began reading law. The criminal justice system was an unruly, complex, lumbering giant, she discovered. It fascinated her. And so, Rit Avery found an abiding interest that remained and deepened. Her life quieted then, seemed more ordinary, although she never took a case nor pursued a legal question that didn't excite her, and that was not ordinary. Even now, as she was preparing to take a break from it, she knew that, like her interest in women, her interest in law would never wane.

Drew McAllister certainly was not the first woman to capture Rit's imagination, although Drew did present a new twist. There had been many others. Men too. While some men still intrigued her, especially their power games, they held little appeal to her deeper passions or her softer emotions and never really had.

A new beginning, Rit thought, recalling her first conversation with Drew McAllister here in her office. I'll be part of that, a major part. She glanced at her watch, 5:30. So, she decided not to call. Interesting, Rit thought, smiling. She spoke into the intercom. "Alice, one last thing before you go. Will you get Drew McAllister's number for me."

Drew was doing dishes when the phone rang three hours later. She wiped her hands on her jeans. "Hello."

"You didn't call." The voice was deep and rich, even on the phone. The words were spoken matter-of-factly.

Drew caught her breath. "I thought about it," she said softly. "But...?"

"I don't know."

"Scared?"

"What would I be scared of?" The response was reflexive. "Yes, I think so," she amended.

"Mm-hm. That's OK," Rit replied. "A little fear can make it more intense. I want you to meet me tonight, for a drink."

"Yes," Drew said, without even considering whether Sarah was available to stay with Becka.

"Good. In an hour, at The Found."

"All right."

When Drew replaced the receiver, she remained motionless. What will I wear, was all she could think. She didn't think about the fact that she did not know where The Found was, although she had heard of it and knew it was a women's bar. She didn't think of Becka and who would stay with her. She thought only of being with Rit and felt tension and excitement and wondered if she was attractive enough for Rit or smart enough. She felt scared.

An hour later, Drew squeezed her compact Chevy between two beat up vans in front of The Found. If someone had asked her how she had found the place or how she'd arranged for her friend, Marie, to stay with Becka, or why she was so entranced with Rit, she could not have explained.

Rit watched her enter, enjoying her hesitancy and the look of strain and anticipation on her face as Drew scanned the crowd. Walking over to Drew, she took her wrist. "This way," she said. "I have a table." She led her through the main room into a smaller, quieter section in the rear of the bar.

"I like your eyes," Rit said. They sat across from each other at a small round table, Rit looking fixedly at Drew without smiling. "What would you like to drink?"

"To drink? Oh, a beer, I guess."

"Are you sure?"

Drew looked at her.

"You don't seem sure," Rit said.

"No, I'm not at all sure." Drew smiled then, her eyes dancing, "but, I *would* like a beer."

After Rit left to get their drinks, Drew looked around at the women, small groups, and pairs, talking, laughing, couples dancing. It seemed comfortable to Drew for women to be with each other this way. Lesbians, she thought, smiling to herself. Yes.

Rit guided the conversation. They talked about the people they knew in common; there were only a few, all members of the Lesbian Legal Defense Committee. They talked about music. Rit played bass guitar, she said, and drums. Drew acknowledged that this was the first time she'd been to a lesbian bar.

"It won't be the last," Rit replied. Her smile was warm.

They sipped their drinks, and Drew felt a tingling relaxation begin to enfold her.

"I want to know about you," Rit said. "Your version. Who is Drew McAllister and how did she grow?"

Drew smiled remotely. "I'm still trying to figure that out."

"And what have you found so far? Start early, I like to hear about childhoods."

Drew was still smiling. "I think you really would like to hear."

"Yes," Rit said. "Were you raised in Chicago?"

"Mm-hm. Northwest side. Middle class family. My father was an actuary, an expert on the odds." Drew chuckled. "And odd

121

himself. He's a quiet man, unlike my mom. He's very inward. I have some of that."

There was the little twitch near the corner of her mouth which Rit observed.

"He just retired. My mother, too. She was a teacher, a real spunky woman. They moved to Florida, where else? They have a condo and a section of a big garden. They don't seem to miss the city. How about you? Are you a native of Chicago, too?"

"No, I'm from the East, New York. I may tell you my story, someday, but not now. Tell me more. What was it like growing up middle class on the northwest side of Chicago with a quiet, odd father and a spunky mom?"

Drew laughed. "It was ordinary, I'm afraid."

"Something made you special."

Drew blushed and was thankful for the darkness in the room "I'm special?"

"Yes."

"Oh, you mean..."

"No, not that. Not *just* that." Rit raised her chin and narrowed her eyes. "What stands out about your life back then?"

Drew thought a moment. "Being a tomboy," she replied.

Rit laughed. "Of course."

"And loving it. Until puberty. I hated puberty."

"Why was that?"

"It all changed. The guys weren't supposed to be my buddies any more."

"No, you were supposed to become a 'lady', or at least a 'chick'."

"It didn't work."

"You sound glad."

"Yes, God, yes. But not then. Then I wanted to want it. I wanted to be like the *popular* girls, to be cute and flirtatious and coy...I mean I really wanted it, but at the same time it made me sick."

"Nauseating."

"You said it. God, I hated it. I'd sit around the hangout, you know, one of those corner hamburger places. I'd sit there with my girlfriends hoping some loudmouth male would talk to me, maybe ask me out. Oh, how I wanted a *boyfriend* . If you had a *boyfriend*, you had it made. Did you go through a boyfriend phase?"

"More or less."

Drew laughed and looked deeply at Rit, still smiling broadly "You fascinate me."

"I know."

"You do? It shows?"

"Yes."

"I can't be coy."

"Good. So, did you get a *boyfriend?*"

"Yes, unfortunately. Several. I would much rather have been playing ball than being..."

"Balled?"

"Gross."

They laughed together, and ordered another drink.

"I was shy all through high school."

"And still are a little, I suspect."

"You can tell?"

Rit just smiled.

"I felt different."

"You were."

"You mean...what do you mean?"

"You were different, that's all."

Drew let it pass. "I heard the phrase 'marginal man'. That's me, I decided. The 'man' part didn't offend me back then. I was a marginal man. No solid reference groups, no ethnicity, a melting pot product. No religion. My attempts to embrace one of them was short, though I did get confirmed into some church. I think it was Lutheran. My best friend at the time was Lutheran. I was thirteen."

Drew's eyes looked especially sad just then. "What is it?" Rit asked.

Drew reached for a cigarette. Rit lit it for her. "You know, high school's a place of cliques, right? Or categories, at least. I wasn't a jock or a doper, a cheerleader or a brain. I was on the edges of lots of groups but not in the center of any of them. It was a painful time in some ways."

"Paying your dues."

Drew didn't hear this. She had entered the past too deeply and was temporarily lost there.

"What then?"

Drew blinked.

"After high school."

"I had an abortion. I was pregnant at my graduation. That always amused me in an odd way. I was seventeen. My cousin took me to Washington for it. She was a good friend. The guy was a creep."

"So, what's new?"

"All men aren't creeps," Drew said defensively.

"That's true," Rit replied.

123

Drew had been ready for an argument, had suddenly wanted an excuse to lash out angrily, but Rit's simple response disarmed her and Drew let go of it. "College was much better. I felt less alienated there. The sixties. I needed them, and Madison, Wisconsin, was a great place to be during those years. So much was going on and I got swept up into it."

"And became a radical hippie freak."

Drew laughed. "We sure didn't drop out. We were in the middle of things—my group was. Of course, I never felt quite in the middle. More like pulled along the edges. Half really in and half watching, observing it. I guess I fell in love. Anyway, I ended up marrying Steve Tremaine. He's a dentist now, in Winnetka. We've been divorced for four years." Drew paused, staring at the dying embers as she put out her cigarette. "I liked college," she continued.

"What was the best part?"

"My film."

"Oh?"

"I took some courses in filmmaking and made a documentary about the stuff going on on campus, the protests and strikes, marching on the R.O.T.C. building. It was a real hit locally. They showed it over and over at different events. I felt like a celebrity...sort of, actually Steve, somehow, got much of the credit. He helped me with it some."

"I'd like to see the film."

"Sure, I'd like you to. Nostalgia for a dead era."

"You miss it, those times?"

"No, not really. I wish there was more going on now. Of course, we do have the anti-nuke stuff and the Women's Movement."

"Yes, more or less. So you like making films."

"I love it. I'm really learning how now. I'm working with Art Trevor."

"I heard of him."

"He's brilliant, and he's teaching me so much. He's great!"

"You're lucky. How did you get connected with him?"

Drew didn't answer.

Rit frowned. "You're involved with him? Romantically?"

Drew shook her head. "No, even less upfront than that."

"Oh, I see. You used your outstanding powers of persuasion."

Drew didn't reply.

"Why not?" Rit said. "So filmmaking is a real high for you. What else pleases you?"

"Becka," Drew replied instantly. "My daughter. When she came into my life, I changed inside. It was a real shift. My life took on a kind of meaningfulness like I'd only glimpsed before. I really got into motherhood. Still am, but it wasn't enough, of course."

"And what happened to your interest in film back then. Did you pursue it?"

"Not much. I've got reels of Becka, and vacations, things like that."

"So, how come you let it go into the background for so long?"

"I don't know. I had a kid to raise and a husband to help through dental school, and not a lot of confidence."

Rit nodded. "There's a deeply sad part about you, Drew," she said.

Drew looked away. "That's changing too."

"Because of the power?"

"I guess. It's a rather major aspect of my life now."

"Yes, I imagine it is."

"What are your thoughts about that, Rit? You seem disapproving somehow."

"Disapproving? No, not at all. It's quite a gift, but also an encumbrance."

Drew's shoulders dropped. "I suppose I ought to use it for the good of the world somehow. But, then I just go about my business zapping people when it seems like a good way to make something happen that I want." She watched the smoke from her cigarette in the ashtray curl past Rit's shoulder. "At first it scared me. I felt more alienated than ever. I wonder why it didn't work on you."

Rit shrugged her shoulders. "Apparently, there are some limits."

"Yeah." Drew suddenly felt drained. "Would you like to take a walk?" she asked.

"Let's go."

They didn't walk far, only to Rit's car and then they drove down to the lake, near the aquarium, and looked at the stars and lights and saw a rat run by.

"Give me a cigarette, will you," Rit said.

Drew did and lit it for her. It pleased her to do this and she felt a strange yearning to do more for Rit, to do whatever she wanted. Drew leaned back against a tree, thinking about it. Rit had wanted to hear about her life and so Drew had told her, told her quite a bit. She certainly hadn't gone into much detail, but realized that the highlights she gave were not those she would have told to anyone else she was just getting to know. Why, she wondered? Even with Wiley, it had taken months before she divulged some of those things, the alienation, the sadness. With Rit, there seemed to be no question that Drew would respond as Rit wanted her to. Almost as if she had no choice. Suddenly Drew felt anxious. "What do you want from me?" she asked abruptly.

Rit looked at her pensively, not at all taken aback by the question. "I haven't fully decided yet," she said. "We'll see. You're doing OK."

Drew wanted to feel angry, indignant at this, but she did not. "Do you have a lover?"

"There are women I make love with," Rit replied, "and people I love."

There was silence for a while. They watched the ship lights far out on the lake, two sets of them, moving towards each other. Gradually they met and seemed to coalesce, the larger lights taking over the smaller.

"You have a strange effect on me," Drew said.

"Do you like it?"

"Yes."

Rit looked at her. They were sitting side by side on the grass beneath a cluster of trees. Drew felt scrutinized, penetrated, and unconsciously pulled the zipper of her jacket up to her neck. Rit continued watching her.

"You're not cold," she said. "Just feeling a little chill, perhaps, or thrill."

Drew felt transparent.

Later, she wasn't sure if Rit had moved toward Drew or had pulled Drew to her, for the touch wiped out awareness of anything but the hot, rushing, pulsing excitement in her body. Rit's hand was touching the back of Drew's neck, their faces inches apart. Drew only knew sensation at that moment. She felt weakened, liquidy.

"Very nice eyes," Rit said, placing a soft kiss on each of them.

Drew's memory of exactly what happened next was blurred. She knew that as they walked back to the car, Rit's hand rested on her shoulder, but she did not remember if they spoke or how it was decided they would leave then or much about the drive. Rit had dropped her at her car at The Found, and said goodnight.

## 27

Becka was at school; Sarah was out somewhere (she hadn't been spending much time at home lately); and Drew was sitting in the round cushioned chair she used when she wanted to think. One could sleep in the round chair; it was big and comfortable enough for that, but Drew never slept in it. One could lounge in it and talk and lie around, but Drew didn't use the round chair for that either. She used it when she wanted to think through something or let her mind savor some experience. Now she sat in it, or sort of laid in it, her body curled slightly to fit its contours, and was thinking of Rit.

Her thoughts had been of Rit all morning and even through the night, images in her dreams. She tried to focus on their conversation by the lake, the words, but shifted again to the feel of the soft pressure of Rit's lips on her eyes, and of Rit's warm strong hand on the back of her neck. The heated feeling came again, and the chill. It was different from what she felt for Judith; more concentrated, it seemed, and more mysterious. Judith was a friend, or used to be, Drew thought sadly. Their closeness had grown slowly, woven by numerous contacts and shared experiences and confidences and intimacies. Rit was a sudden, overpowering, jolting force in her life, rattling her, tingling the edges of her nerves, arousing her imagination.

Making love with Judith had been soft, rising, sensual, tender, enveloping. Drew stroked the cushion with her fingertips. Making love with Rit will be vibrant, breathtaking, transcendent. Drew opened her eyes. "I'm planning to make love with her," she said aloud. She shifted on the chair, smiling, then closed her eyes again. Her hips stirred with the fantasy and her hand found the zipper. Drew's fingers and her imagination took her and Rit Avery on a very pleasurable journey, Rit's lips never leaving Drew's eyes though going to every other part of her body at the same time. Drew went on for fifteen or twenty minutes and several peaks that left her wanting more.

What's the attraction, she wondered, readjusting her jeans. She did not mean her own, for she felt no need right now to analyze that; it was so overwhelmingly there. But Rit's? Why would she be interested in me? It was always hard, deep down, for Drew to accept another's love for her, or even their interest in her. Somewhere, welded among the strands of her self-concept, was the sense that she was not worthy of other's attention and affection.

It must be my zap power, she thought, that interests her. It's not me at all. The familiar heavy gloomy feeling came.

But she said it was more than that. Drew felt some relief.

Of course, she could be lying, but, no, I doubt that Rit would use lies that way.

She likes my eyes.

Drew twisted in the round chair. I don't know, she thought. I have to be careful. It's hard to resist her. A tingle rose along the tiny blond hairs at the base of Drew's neck. She took a deep breath. Why haven't I told Wiley about her? Another person knows about the power and I haven't told Wiley. She pictured the psychologist's serious pensive face. Wiley thinks I should erase Judith's memory of it. I suppose I should someday, if I ever see her again. She fought the sad feeling. I suppose it would be safer. Oh, God, Judith. Why? Drew sighed, switching the memories to the last phone call. You were so upset about the power, Judith. It's evil, you said. Drew's face twisted with pain. What happened to her? Tears came then, tears of loss and missing Judith and tears of pain and confusion. I'm in love with her. A woman. I've loved a woman, Drew thought. I've loved a woman and it felt so right. I love women. The next thought came harder, but it came. I am a woman who loves women, a lesbian. Drew let it settle. She let the thought feel its way into the deep places of her being.

She lay on the round chair without moving for some time. It's almost too much, she realized, reaching for a cigarette. Too much to deal with all of this at once. I don't need the power; it's like an appendage, almost intrusive. An encumbrance, Rit had said. I don't need it. She ran her fingers through the strands of her reddish brown hair. Last night's conversation with Rit came back again, and Drew thought about the shy part of herself, the sense of alienation that she'd always had, of being apart. What is it, she wondered. Rit said it's because I'm different, "paying my dues". I don't know. I think it has something to do with the sense that others don't really want to know me, and with my not really allowing them to. Drew paused on that awhile and then her face brightened. I can help them now, can't I, she thought. Help them free themselves to let me in.

She put her cigarette out in the ceramic ashtray, a gift from Wiley. She was smiling. Yes, but who, she wondered? She let her head fall back on the soft cushion. Whoever I wish, she concluded, and then she thought of the words she'd use in the zap: *You feel warmly and benevolently towards me and you wish to let me know you, the real you, and you want to get to know me.* It felt like an inspiration. Lifting up her head, she looked through the window, and thought of all the people out there and the excitement of connecting with them, of *really* connecting with some of them. Whoever I choose, she thought—the neighbor woman next door who talks with me about the weather and about the kids throwing their candy wrappers. Who is she really? I can find out now if I choose. The achievers. The talented people. The thinkers. The creators. The sad and lonely people. They're all mine if I want them. Drew was feeling exhilarated. *You feel warmly and benevolently...* She was eager to test it. I'll go for a walk, she thought, and stop people on the street. No, let's see, I'll go...I know, to the Art Institute. I'll test it there, where people aren't always in a hurry.

Drew finished dressing in about two minutes, eagerness rushing her, and when she walked onto the porch of her three-flat graystone and felt the Indian summer air, she decided to go by moped. A flash of memory, of her and Judith riding together down Ravenswood Avenue on their matching red Hondas brought the heaviness back, but Drew determinedly shoved it away and went to the garage.

She didn't make it to the Art Institute. She couldn't get past the zoo. It called her in and it was there, on the bench by the buffalos, that she did it.

"They're almost extinct," she said to the aging woman seated next to her.

"Yes, it's a shame."

The woman seemed typically leery, Drew thought, leery of a stranger talking with her, but cordial. "Listen to me," Drew said.

The woman looked at her.

"I have something important to say to you."

She continued looking, her eyes drawn to Drew's magnetically.

"You feel warmly and benevolently toward me..."

They talked for two hours and exchanged phone numbers and Melinda Stevenson remarked over and over how fortunate it was that they both sat on that bench at that time for she couldn't remember ever feeling such rapid rapport and openness with someone. It was the pleasantest time she'd spent in ages, she said, and Drew said, "I've enjoyed it more than I can tell you," and meant it, for that afternoon she and Melinda Stevenson, widow, retired nurse, grandmother of four, bridge player supreme, loving, warm, frightened, lonely woman, had connected deeply. They each felt they'd found a new friend.

Every person is a gold mine, Drew thought, skirting her moped boldly between rows of traffic. Every one of them. Deep and complex, full of needs and hopes, and fear and humor. They're all interesting, but mostly we never get beneath the surface, never find out. Melinda Stevenson. How nice to have touched, to have been allowed inside, and to have let her in. She stopped for a light. No one has to be alone, she thought, the barriers aren't necessary. She took off, pulling ahead of the cars which soon overtook her again. Maybe next time I'll do it with someone famous, she thought, someone the world has decided is more extraordinary than Melinda Stevenson. Are they different inside? A star. Who? Drew braked for another red light. A politician? Actor? Intellectual? Who's in Chicago? She accelerated and made a right turn, preferring side streets. Somebody from Channel 2 News? The Chair of the Board of something? The mayor? Drew laughed aloud. Anyone I want, she thought. A car pulled in front of her. "Asshole." She yelled the word mechanically, too excited to feel anger right now. Who are the famous people here? Who would I like to connect with, maybe over lunch. It was nearly 2:30 when Drew locked the moped in the little slice of garage she rented. She had a 3:30 appointment at the photo studio. As she climbed the apartment stairs, Drew searched her memory for Chicago celebrities she could meet. She had a quick snack, changed her clothes and left again.

A man in a turtleneck sweater and trench coat was waiting outside the photo studio. What's he doing here, Drew wondered. He's not due back for three more weeks. "Hi. Mr. Zayre, right?" She unlocked the door.

"Hello, yes, I hope you don't mind my coming by. It's not about the photographs. There's something else I'd like to talk with you about."

Drew felt uneasy. "Sure, come on in." She looked at her watch. Fifteen minutes until her subject was due. "I only have a few minutes, though." She went behind the counter and removed her coat. "What can I do for you?"

"Can we talk in the back room?"

"What about?"

"About what else goes on in there besides picture-taking. About two and two equalling five and books being footstools."

Drew's chest was crowded by the pounding of her heart against her ribs. A half-dozen thoughts ran simultaneously through her mind. Call Wiley. Neutralize him immediately, erase it all. How does he know? Is he like Rit, immune? Who is he? Is he dangerous? How did this happen? "Yes, come on in." I'll hear him out first, she thought. I just hope he's not immune. Anything but that.

"So, what's this about," Drew said, trying to sound calm. They sat across from each other on the white enamel folding chairs Drew had picked up at Woolworth's.

"That's quite a thing you have," Zayre said, "being able to force thoughts into people's heads like that. I'd like to hear more about it."

"What do you want to know?" Drew's mind was still racing.

"How do you do it?"

"What is your interest in it, Mr. Zayre. Just curiosity?"

"No, more than that. I want to make a proposal to you."

"Tell me this, first, what vegetables have you been eating lately?"

Zayre laughed. "Brussels sprouts, of course. You didn't remove that one. Actually they *are* quite good. I have had a problem, though, with my interest in clothing animals. People think I'm nuts. They are wrong, however, and I have some very good arguments. For one thing, it's unsanitary for animals..."

Drew knew he could be faking. She dreaded the possibility that he was immune. "Mr. Zayre, listen to me," she interrupted, "I have something important to say..."

"Oh, no you..." But his words trailed off as his eyes locked on hers.

"You want to be totally honest with me. You wish to tell me what you know about me and how, and who you are and what you want. You want to keep nothing from me, but to tell me all this and to answer all my questions fully and honestly."

She waited until his eyes moved. "Tell me exactly who you are and why you've come today, Mr. Zayre."

"I'm a private investigator. I was assigned by one of my employers, Mr. Abram Granser, to investigate your operation. I tape recorded my session with you and discovered that you told me many unbelievable things and that I believed them. Some of them I still believe even though I know where they came from. I can't shake them."

"Who is Abram Granser?" Drew asked. She was shaking inside, but her voice was calm.

"I'm not sure. He's with a company called Stillwell Import-Export. I work for him occasionally. That's all I know."

"Why did he want you to investigate me?"

"I don't know. That's part of our understanding. I ask no questions. It's fine with me, I don't care what he's about. I'm not interested in the information I obtain for him. At least I wasn't until...until this time. All I know is I was told to become a subject

131

in this hypnosis study and tape record my conversations. I did that. It seemed routine. I was listening to segments of the tape of our session on Friday—to make sure that it was audible—and I became...I was astounded at what I heard. Much of it I had no memory of, but clearly, it had happened. Your ability is quite impressive. Is it hypnosis?"

"Who else knows about what you've discovered?"

"No one."

"Granser?"

"I didn't give him the tape. Not the one with you. I gave him the one with the psychologist. I told him the tape of my meeting with you was defective. I told him it was a routine photo session and he accepted that."

"Where is the tape of our meeting?"

"In my apartment. In the bathroom cabinet."

"No one else has heard it, besides you?"

"No one."

"And you've told no one."

"Correct."

"Are you taping this meeting?"

"Yes."

Drew glanced at his briefcase, feeling anger along with her fear. "Why did you come to me now? What's your proposal?"

"I came to blackmail you into using your power for me."

Drew shuddered. "How?" she asked. "What did you have in mind?"

"That I would agree to tell no one what I know if you would use your power for me from time to time."

"Use it how?"

"Mostly to get money for me. And some revenge. I have a few enemies. I figured I could keep using you occasionally as I thought of things I wanted. The first thing I was going to do was to have you and me meet with some banker guy, probably at First City, privately, you know, and he'd hand over a bundle for me and then forget it ever happened. Then, I thought..."

"That's enough," Drew said. She felt nauseated. "Have you told me everything relevant, everything you know about this?"

"Yes, I believe so."

"All right, listen carefully, I have something important to say to you." Drew paused briefly, watching his eyes. "You cannot remember the conversation we just had. You believe you came here because you were anxious to see your photographs. You're now aware that they're not ready yet. You remember when

132

you listened to the tape of our previous session that the tape was defective; it did not record. You remember clearly that in our meeting Friday, I took pictures of you, and we made some small talk. Nothing more. You have no memory of anything more than that in regard to me or our sessions. All the implantations, all the suggestions I gave you last time, you no longer believe. They're erased. You're convinced that this investigation was a waste of time; that a psychologist is studying hypnosis and giving coupons for portraits as incentives to get subjects. You're convinced of this and have no interest in it. You're angry, however, that the tape was defective and when you leave here, you want to go home and you want to destroy that defective tape, totally destroy it. In a moment, you will want to give me the tape that's in your briefcase and forget that you were taping this."

Drew stood up and waited.

"Well, I'm sorry to have bothered you, then." Zayre said after a moment. "So, I'll just have to be patient about the photos." As he spoke, he reached into his briefcase, turned off the tape machine and removed the cassette. He did all this as if unaware of it, handing the cassette to Drew, and then pleasantly saying goodbye.

Drew felt relieved. She reviewed everything that had happened. It seemed she'd left nothing out. She needed to shift gears, quickly, and proceed with the subject who had been waiting in the outer office, a young man with a trim mustache and cheerful, outgoing manner. She went through the protocol according to established routine, but she added one thing.

"Soon I will ask you about your motivation for coming here today, for being in this study, and you wish to answer this question honestly. You believe it's important to be truthful with me about this."

Zayre went directly home after his visit with Drew. The moment he opened his apartment door, he sensed that someone had been there. The cues were subtle. Drawers were not pulled out nor the mattress cut open nor was anything in obvious disarray, but Zayre knew. He went immediately to the bathroom cabinet. The terra cotta box, which he had bought from a street vendor in Mexico, was on the top shelf as always. Zayre removed the cover. Inside were his toenail clippers, the little packet of amphetamines, and his ear plugs. That was all the box contained; the tape cassette was no longer there.

## 28

Wiley was visibly shaken. She paced as she fired more questions at Drew, and then she paced some more as she listened to the tape again.

"Nothing else. Damn! No hint of who Granser is. No clue as to why they're investigating us." She banged her fist on the phone directory. "And no listing for Stillwell Import-Export. You know, Drew, neutralizing Zayre isn't enough. We have to get to Granser."

Drew did not respond immediately. She felt irritated with herself. Despite how adequately she thought she'd handled it, she obviously hadn't done enough. "I wish I'd thought to set it up through Zayre while I had the chance," she said angrily.

"Yeah, well you did real well, Drew. Great, in fact. You stopped Granser from getting the tape. You got rid of Zayre. You couldn't have thought of everything." Wiley sat on the edge of her desk, tapping her hand rapidly on her knee. "We've got to find out what Granser knows." She stood. "How does this sound? You call Zayre tomorrow and tell him that since he was so eager for his portraits, and you had some free time, you decided to do a rush job, and that they're ready now."

Drew thought about it. "He does believe that he really wants those photos. It would probably work. He'd come."

"I can't imagine how it happened," Wiley said again. "Let's think...is there any reason anyone would be suspicious of us? Maybe it has nothing to do with your power. Maybe Granser's investigating psychological researchers for some reason, maybe totally unconnected with what we're really doing." Wiley was pacing again.

"Maybe," Drew said, unconvinced.

"I don't think so, either. No, they're onto us somehow. Drew, have you been careful? Shit, you've been zapping people left and right." Have I been careful enough, Wiley wondered. The meeting...no, surely none of those women would...She shook her head and looked at Drew.

Drew shrugged.

"Someone got suspicious. Maybe the zaps don't work on everyone."

Drew thought of Rit.

"Maybe some people don't get amnesia for them. Maybe it was one of the subjects we ran." Wiley was leaning on the desk, now, tapping its surface with the palm of her hand. "Maybe it's Judith. Maybe she told someone, David maybe, and he's feeling vengeful enough to..." She walked a few paces away, then turned back to Drew. "Maybe Sarah overheard us or found something at your apartment and put it together and... Andrew Zayre, I should have trusted my instincts about that bastard. Shit."

"So, we'll find out." Drew said. Wiley's anxiety was exacerbating her own. "I'll have a talk with Granser and then we'll know, and then we can decide what to do. In the meantime," Drew added, standing up, "I'm going to go home and see my girl. We have a hot dog and spaghetti date tonight. Give me Zayre's number."

Wiley had one more therapy appointment that day and then she, too, left for home. She had not yet reached the streets below when the door to her office opened again. The person who released the lock did not use a key. After succeeding in getting into her locked file cabinet, the intruder removed a file labeled "Paz" and, page by page, laid the contents on Wiley's desk and photographed them. Outside, the rush hour traffic was beginning to thin.

---
## 29.

Becka had the table set when Drew arrived. She couldn't find the napkins, so she'd taken two dish towels and folded them carefully into triangles and placed them beside the plates.

"I knew you wouldn't be late. I knew you'd come in the middle of *Wild World of Animals* and you did."

"Yep, just like I said. Sarah picked you up all right? From Karen's?" Drew stretched out on the living room carpet and Becka immediately lay down beside her.

"Mm-hm. She's not going to eat with us again even when I told her we were having spaghetti."

"Hm-m."

"Doesn't Sarah like us anymore, mom?"

"I think she does. She's just busy, I guess. New boyfriend, maybe."

"You know what happened at school today? The bell got stuck and everyone had to do this." Becka placed her hands over her

135

ears. "And then we all went 'oohh', like that, real loud and the teacher was yelling something but no one could hear."

Becka lay down atop her mother, hugging her. "Teacher said I should put my crayons in order in my box, like blues in one part, reds all in another."

"Why's that?" Drew asked. She kissed her daughter's neck and blew at it noisily.

Becka giggled. "I don't know. I can always find the one I want without any trouble anyway."

"So, what did you do?" Drew asked.

"Put 'em like she said."

"Oh."

They were sitting up now, leaning against the sofa. Becka, ever sensitive to her mother's reactions, frowned. "What, mom? What's wrong?"

"Well, it doesn't seem to make much sense."

"I know, but that's what she said."

"Yeah, well, maybe you could talk to her about it. You don't have to do things like that if they don't make sense."

"I don't?" Becka said, obviously giving this idea serious consideration.

Drew tickled her and rolled over on the floor again, then jumped up. "I better get the spaghetti cookin'."

Becka stayed on the floor. "Not if they don't make sense...," she mumbled to herself.

While they were eating, Sarah came from her room. "Got a date," she said, smiling. "See you later."

After dinner, Drew and Becka were engrossed in the photo album, adding a new batch of pictures, when the doorbell rang.

"Drew McAllister?"

"Yes." There were two men.

"I'm very pleased to be speaking with you, Miss McAllister," the younger one said. He was a tall man, balding, thirty-five or forty, dressed in a blue knit suit. "My name is Abram Granser. This is my colleague, Will Stokely." He held out an identification card. "We're with the President's Special Peace Mission. May we come in?"

Drew had not moved a muscle. All her strength was directed at keeping a calm facade. The men had entered the hallway and the older one, Stokely, closed the door behind them.

"I don't understand," Drew said at last, standing in the hall with them, feeling as if the air were too thin to breath.

"Let us explain. May we sit down?"

136

They led Drew to the dining room table. Becka remained in the living room, watching.

"Is anyone else at home?" Stokely asked, glancing at Becka.

"No, just us. Why? What is it you...?"

"The President's Special Peace Mission, as you may or may not already know," Granser said, "seeks alternative avenues to world peace." He stroked his pale chin as he spoke. "We work quietly, looking for hitherto unexplored means to achieve our goal. Recently, we've become aware of *you*, Miss McAllister, and are here to discuss the possibility of your helping us."

"You're with the government?" Drew was trying to clear her head.

"Well, yes, but in a non-typical way." Granser cleared his throat. "We have lines of communication with the president and with various governmental agencies, but we're not subject to the political pressures of the more known departments." His mouth formed what might have been a smile. "So you see, we're freer, thereby, to seek...peace, to avert potential crises..."

Drew was feeling extremely anxious. "I never heard of..."

"I'm not surprised. Most people aren't aware of us, but that's OK. It's better actually."

Becka fidgeted across the room, staring at the men.

"Do you think your daughter might want to go watch TV or something?" the gray haired one, Stokely, asked pleasantly. "I'm sure this must be quite boring to her."

"Becka, hon," Drew said, "we're going to be talking for a while. Why don't you go into your room and play, OK?"

Becka rose silently and made a sluggish exit, looking over her shoulder at them all the while.

"Cute child," Granser said, sort of smiling. "Now, let me proceed."

He leaned forward in his chair. "In order to carry out our mission, we make it our business to become informed of anything that may relate to our goals. Recently, we've learned about you, Miss McAllister, about your most amazing ability to...uh, to control minds, to impart ideas into the minds of others. Quite impressive."

He smiled approvingly, as if just congratulating her for writing a brilliant essay or playing a flawless sonata.

"We think it's possible that you could make a significant contribution to peace in the world. We'd like you to consider working with us."

Drew's mind was racing. She had no trust in government, especially "secret missions". She wanted these men out of here,

137

wanted no part of this, any of it. She wanted to be back on the shore of the river, with Judith, watching the leaves being carried by the current, feeling the budding love. She wanted to be there and for no storm to come, but instead a peaceful growing of her and Judith's attachment with no magic evil power to come and fuck it up. "Listen to me, Mr. Granser, I have something important to say to you..."

Minutes later, slowly, gradually, the heavy blackness began to give way to returning consciousness. Drew's head was on the dining room table, her cheek resting on its cool, smooth surface. She could see that someone sat across from her, someone with a blue suit. She blinked her eyes several times and lifted her fuzzy head.

"Are you OK?" Granser asked.

Drew was breathing heavily. She was confused. She wanted to cry.

"Sorry about that," Granser said. "I should have let you know. You see, I want you to hear me out, consider what I have to say. I don't want you to use your power on me, Miss McAllister. We've taken precautions against that."

"What happened?" Drew asked, numbly.

"Chloroform. Sorry, but as I said, I don't want you to use your power on us."

"How do you know...how did you find out about...?"

Granser half-smiled. Drew was uncomfortably aware of Stokely's presence behind her.

"That's all part of what we do, as I mentioned," Granser said smoothly. "We know all about your powers and how they work. That's why we're here. Would you like a glass of water or something?"

Drew shook her head.

"We want you to come work for us. It's quite a job offer I'm prepared to make you. It would involve attending some conferences. Have you ever been to the Capitol? A chance to travel, possibly to other countries. Opportunities like this are rare. You're a lucky woman. Of course, the most gratifying part for you, I'm sure, would be the contributions you could make to the world. The money, the luxuries, no doubt would only be little side benefits."

Drew was trying to figure some way to zap them without alerting them. Could she risk another attempt? "I'm not sure that all this appeals to me," she said, as if thinking it over. "I enjoy my life now, the way it is."

"We can work out the details," Granser said obligingly. "If you want, we can arrange it so your work with us interferes minimal-

138

ly with your present life." He paused, pursing his lips. "However," he went on, "you may come to find that the attractions we can offer compare favorably to what you now have. Wealth. Respect. Contribution to mankind. Travel."

"I feel overwhelmed."

"Of course. I'm sorry. I don't want to go too fast. Let it settle in a minute. Think it over. Ask all the questions you want." Granser lit a small cigar. "Do you mind?" He leaned back smoking. Stokely remained standing behind Drew.

"What exactly do you want me to do?" Drew asked.

"That depends," Granser said. "It's up to you, partly, what feels comfortable to you. We'll brief you and decide together. The first step is to meet with the commission so that we can all discuss it."

"All right," Drew said. "I'd be willing to go to a meeting. When? Where?"

Granser looked pleased. "At our offices in Vermont. Tomorrow afternoon. We'll arrange the flight."

"Vermont?" Drew drew back. "It's too sudden," she said. "I can't just...I have things to do. I can't just leave town. There's my daughter and..."

"No problem," Granser said. "I'm sure the little girl would enjoy the adventure—an airplane ride, a chance to be in the country. Beautiful scenery in Vermont."

"No," Drew said, shaking her head. "It's too fast. Let me think about it."

Granser scrutinized her, the light from the overhead tiffany-type lamp reflecting on his bald spot. "Certainly," he said. "Could you come to our Chicago office tomorrow? Discuss it with us again at that time."

Drew nodded. "All right, I'll come. But tomorrow's impossible. I have plans; I'm working on a film. I could come Thursday."

Granser hesitated. "OK, Thursday it is," he said, giving her the almost smile again. "We're at 75 East Washington, Suite 1602. The sign says Stillwell Import-Export, but don't let that bother you. Say ten a.m.?"

"All right. Seventy-five East Washington, yes, 1602."

As soon as the two men politely took their leave, Drew locked the front door and collapsed on the sofa.

Stokely drove the green sedan two blocks to a gas station on Fullerton Avenue where Granser got out and went to the phone booth.

The phone's ring roused Drew from her thoughts. She walked to it briskly, trying to regain her sense of control. "Hello."

"Hi, sexy," Rit said seductively. She laughed in her deep throaty way. "I've been thinking about you."

Despite her state, Drew felt the familiar excitement. "Oh?" she said, "Tell me more."

"Greedy woman. Why aren't you here, with me, where you belong?"

Drew laughed. "I've had quite a day," she said. She reached for a cigarette. "Actually, I was thinking about calling you. Somehow it seems the government got wind of things. Some Peace Mission group. They were just here and..."

"Drew, don't say anything more." Rit's voice had lost all its playfulness. "Meet me as soon as you can at...at the place where you told me about your *boyfriend* period. Meet me there right away. Leave now. Bring Becka with you." She hung up.

Drew felt an ominous sinking chill, a feeling of terrible dread. Only for a second did she consider not complying. Rit's alarm augmented her own. She felt the urgency. "Hey, fruitloop," she called, "we're going for a ride. Get your jacket."

## 30.

Only a handful of people were at The Found when they arrived. Rit was not there. Drew felt uncomfortable bringing Becka to this place.

"You're Drew?" the bartender said.

"Yes."

"Come back here."

She led Drew and Becka past the john to a storage room. "Rit Avery called," the woman said. "She said you're to wait here." The woman looked around the little room. "Sorry it's not very comfortable. Can I bring you a drink?"

Drew shook her head. She sat down on a box. Becka looked around at the cases of beer and bottles of liquor and the boxes of little napkins.

"Lookit this, mom." She'd found a box of drink stirrers. "Can I play with them?"

Absentmindedly, Drew took a handful from the box and spread

them on a shelf where Becka could reach them. "Just these," she said, preoccupied.

Becka began arranging the red plastic sticks.

What the fuck is going on? Drew stared at the door, hoping it would open and Rit would come in and they'd talk and then there'd be laughing and everything would feel safe again.

The door opened. A woman with short, graying hair and a ski jacket entered the room. "Drew, I'm Randy, a friend of Rit's. She asked me to take you to her. We'll use the back door."

"What? Hey, wait, what is this? Why are...?"

"Let's go, OK? We'll talk later."

Becka was watching silently.

"Becka, we're going to leave now."

They got into the white Oldsmobile parked in the rear of the bar and drove off quickly, turning frequently at intersections, cutting through alleys.

"What are you doing?" Drew demanded.

"Rit's afraid you may have been followed," Randy replied. "We're just being cautious."

"Followed?" Drew turned around and scrutinized the traffic behind them.

"Mom."

"Yeah, hon."

"Does it make sense to steal?"

"To steal." Drew was still looking out the back window. "No, not usually. Sometimes it might. Why do you ask?"

Slowly Becka withdrew her little hand from her jacket pocket and spread it open. Across her palm lay five red plastic drink stirrers.

"Oh, you took them."

Becka nodded, her lower lip protruding.

They took a sharp right, then another into an alley.

"It would have made more sense to ask. I don't think anyone would mind if you took those, but it's better to ask, just in case."

"Can we call up that lady and ask?"

Drew smiled and hugged her girl. She looked back over her shoulder again at the pairs of headlights behind them, all now seeming ominous. "I love you," she said, squeezing Becka tightly. "Yes, later. You can call the bartender later and talk with her about it."

Randy pulled into a parking place at the south end of Rogers Park. "This way," she said, leaving the car and leading them up the street. She got them a cab and they rode north on Clark Street

141

through the city until they were in Evanston.

"Where are we going?" Drew asked again.

"To Rit's," Randy said softly, gesturing toward the cab driver and putting a finger over her lips.

"She doesn't live in Evanston," Drew whispered.

"She has a house there. Turn right on Dempster," Randy said to the driver.

When they left the cab, they walked three blocks down a side street then turned, walked another block, turned again, then went another two blocks east. They were on the other side of Sheridan Road, near the lake, when they turned into a driveway and went up to the entrance of a large, old mansion.

Rit answered the door. "Any problems?" she asked Randy.

"No, everything seems OK."

Rit closed the door behind them. "So, this is Becka! What would you like first—icecream or a game of Pac-Man?"

"You got Pac-Man?" Becka's eyes were wide. "Far out!"

Rit nodded. "Upstairs. Randy, will you show our guest the game room."

Drew was torn between annoyance at the cloak and dagger games and bristling excitement about being with Rit.

Rit looked at her. Her eyes were soft, maybe a little sad. She reached toward Drew and Drew felt a rush shoot down her spine. Rit unzipped Drew's jacket, then led her to a room down the hall. A fire was just getting started in the fireplace and Rit poked at it a few times.

"So the 'government' is aware of your power. How do you know? Tell me what happened."

"That's what the guy said. Presidential Peace Mission or something."

Drew was standing next to the fireplace. "It started with one of our subjects...he taped the session and found out what I can do, then he tried to get me to use my power for him, but I zapped him out of it. Then tonight, this other guy, Granser, the one the first guy was working for...he came and asked me to work for them, somehow, for world peace, he said." The words flew out of Drew one atop the other.

Rit moved to the sofa and gestured for Drew to join her. "OK, tell me everything step by step," she said calmly and, of course, Drew did. Rit frowned deeply the whole time she listened.

"Not good, not good at all," she said. "Too bad it happened so soon."

"So soon? What do you mean?" Drew's voice had a sharp, almost irritable edge. "You sound like it was inevitable."

"Yes. If not the government, then some other group or person. Who knows, maybe this Granser isn't with the government at all. At any rate, it's all over for you now, cutie. The fun part's done, at least for awhile. Now begins the run."

Drew leaned back, her face very near Rit's shoulder. "I'm getting a headache," she said.

Rit smiled indulgently. Slowly she reached her hand toward Drew's face and began caressing her temples. Drew closed her eyes and let herself slip into the comforting pocket of Rit's strength and sureness.

"You'll have to stay here awhile," Rit said gently, "until we can arrange for you to leave town, you and Becka."

Drew sat up. "Leave town?" She shook her head vigorously. "Damn," she groaned, "here we go again. I run my own life, can't you people understand that?" Her voice had raised appreciably. She felt uneasy about it, for some reason worrying about Rit's reaction to her sharp response.

Rit frowned at her. "You could use a drink," she said.

Just then Becka ran into the room. "Mom, I got 3200 points. Mom, it's Atari. Come on, you wanna play?" She was jumping up and down, her face bright and animated.

"Not now, Beck. Rit and I have to talk for awhile. You OK without me? You having fun?"

"Yeah, 'bye." And she was gone.

"She's a sweetie," Rit said. She handed Drew a glass and sat next to her again on the sofa, looking at her face. She stroked Drew's brow from the center of her forehead, over her eyebrow to her temple, then did the same on the other side. "This is one worried-looking woman," she said.

"I *am* worried." Drew didn't want the stroking to stop.

"For good reason," Rit replied, withdrawing her hand. "You won't be able to go back home, you know."

Drew stared at the fire for a long time until the small red stick resting across two logs crumbled and fell into ash. "All lawyers are paranoid," she said.

"All generalizations are inaccurate."

Drew smiled. "Including that one?"

"They know what you can do. They have to have you; at best, to work for them; at least, to make sure you don't work for anyone else."

"What about what *I* want?"

Rit took Drew's hand. "I hope you want to leave the country," she said strongly, but with compassion.

Drew pulled her hand away and sat up straight. "I want to meet with Granser again. Get some more details and explain my position, then..."

"No," Rit said. "That's out of the question."

Drew was tempted to concede, but fought it. "Hey, Rit, it's *my* life, remember? *I'll* decide."

Neither woman spoke for a while. Drew settled back on the sofa, painfully aware that, despite her anxiety about Granser, she was experiencing a feeling of delight from the closeness of Rit's body to her own. "If I have to, I can zap them. I'll insist that I speak to Granser alone."

Rit shook her head. "They won't let you insist on anything, my dear. It's not safe to meet with them. I'm surprised they let you go tonight."

"I think you're exaggerating all this," Drew said.

Rit did not respond.

"Tomorrow morning," Drew said flatly, "I'm meeting Art Trevor at the set at 8:30. Becka has school tomorrow. It's 9:30 now, and she should be in bed." Drew's face was set. She did not look at Rit. "We have to leave. Don't worry, I can handle this." She began to rise. "I'm going to call a cab."

Rit reached out and held Drew's arm, restraining her. "No, Drew, I can't let you do that."

Drew felt a strange rush of pleasure. She took a couple breaths, deep ones, letting her body savor it, then faced Rit, who still held onto her. "I will assume," she said calmly, "that you're genuinely concerned, that you think you're doing what's in my best interest." She was fully aware of the feel of Rit's strong hand on her arm. "However," she continued, "we obviously have a difference of opinion. I don't know you very well, Rit, but I'm convinced that you would not attempt to coerce me, that you'll accept my need to do what my own judgment demands, to handle it my own way."

"Wrong." Rit did not loosen her grip.

"Dammit, Rit," Drew hissed, fighting her excitement. She twisted her arm, attempting to break Rit's hold. "Stop this. You have no right. I'm going home now." She looked Rit in the eye. "I'm very powerful, remember. I'm not as vulnerable as you seem to think."

"You're just barely beginning to learn about power," Rit said.

"Listen to me, Rit, I have something important to say to you."

Rit looked into Drew's eyes, smiling.

"You want to let me leave. You want to help me, but on my

terms. You..."

"It won't work, Drew." Rit continued looking into her eyes. "Listen to me!"

"If you want Becka to sleep now," Rit said calmly, "I'll show you to the bedroom you'll be using."

"We're not staying."

"You're staying."

Drew wrenched her arm free and got up. She hadn't gone two steps when Rit's powerful hands again constrained her. "Stubborn and difficult," Rit said, shaking her head. "Now, *you* listen. I'd rather not have to restrain you physically, all right? It would be upsetting to Becka for one thing, but I will if you don't cooperate. You are *not* leaving. Now, sit down and listen."

Drew let herself be led back to the sofa. Her blood was rushing. She felt a strange, delightful excitement.

"You and your daughter are in serious danger. At this stage, they may not have bugged your phone or be following you, since you told them you will meet with them on Thursday. It seems they're trying to get you to cooperate voluntarily. They probably don't want to arouse your suspicions yet."

"I need more information. I...I'm not convinced it's as bad as you say."

"Right, except that getting that information might be the last thing you ever get as a free woman."

Drew shuddered, then shook her head vigorously. "I disagree with you, Rit. Whoever they are, their approach seems reasonable. I don't see the risk of hearing what they want from me."

"They'll want everything."

Drew chewed on her lip.

"To own you, so they can control your power."

"No one would want to do that."

Rit laughed.

"You think I'm naive."

Rit said nothing.

145

## 31

Drew's sleep was not calm that night. The bedroom she and
Becka were given was large and furnished in richly grained woods
and tapestry and brass. She pulled the pillow under her, then tossed
it aside twisting with her thoughts and feelings, trying not to disturb
her daughter who slept peacefully beside her. Being in Rit Avery's
home was thrilling; being here under these circumstances was vile.

At breakfast, Becka chattered happily, delighted with her day
off school, eager to play some more video games and explore the
garden with its luring swing, and to visit the workshop in the shed
with the wood pieces. Rit told her she could build a boat with the
wood if she wanted, to float in the pond with the goldfish.

"You got a pretty home, Rit. It's like a castle. Don't you love
it here, mom?" She emptied her milk glass. "Mom, can I use Rit's
phone because you remember what we said... you know, about calling that lady. Will you stand next to me when I call her?"

Drew sipped her coffee from the big earthen mug, smiling at
Becka, feeling especially loving toward her right now. *You and
your daughter are in danger*, Rit had said. "Sure, but not 'til later,
hon. It's pretty early now. We'll call later."

"I'm gonna go outside, OK? I'm done eating." She held up her
empty plate.

Drew nodded. "Stay in the yard, though."

Rit walked with Becka to the back door and outside; she was
gone for ten minutes. "What's the phone call she's talking about?"
she asked sharply when she returned.

Drew felt irritated despite the other feelings Rit's presence
brought. "The bartender at The Found. Becka's concerned because
she ripped off some swizzle sticks last night."

Rit laughed. "Such ethics," she said. "We do have to be careful
about phone calls. That one would be OK, but check with me about
any others."

Drew's face reddened. She pounded her fist on the table, upsetting her coffee cup and rattling the dishes and silverware. "Goddam, that does it! Who the hell do you think you are telling me
who I can call and who I can't? I've had it!"

Again the fear came. She looked at Rit for a reaction. Rit returned her look, coolly, and did not reply.

Drew wiped at the little pool of spilled coffee. "I've been giving
a lot of thought to the situation," she said, more calmly now.

"Good," Rit responded.

"I understand your perspective." She wadded the wet napkin into a ball. "It's possible that there is some danger; possible, but far from certain. I'm willing to take some risks at this point." She tossed the ball of paper across the table at an empty bowl, missing. "I want to zap Granser and find out the real story. I'm not willing to run away and hide. I refuse to accept that as my only option."

"It's not your only option, Drew," Rit said. She retrieved the napkin which had rolled onto the floor and tossed it deftly into the wastebasket across the room. "You could join Granser's so-called Peace Mission and become a dupe for the CIA or whoever he really represents, until someone decides you're too dangerous to have around and..."

"CIA! God, Rit, you've been seeing too many movies."

"Whatever."

"I could tell him I'm not interested."

"You're being drafted, my dear. You don't tell Uncle Sam you're not interested."

"That's not the impression I got from Granser."

"That's not the impression he chose to give."

"Everyone wants to use me," Drew said in exasperation. She picked up a fork and began tapping it angrily on the table. "And you, Rit? What do you suggest I do? Anybody you want me to zap for you?"

"I suggest you come with me to Arizona. I have a place there. Hang out until we can arrange for you to leave the country."

Drew's fantasies soared at the thought of being with Rit in some remote mountain cabin.

"When you get to France, forget you have the power, or if you can't do that, don't tell anyone, anyone at all. Use it discreetly."

"France?"

"Yes, for starters at least. I have a little house there."

"You have a little house there," Drew mocked. "You have a little house everywhere, it seems. This is insane?" She almost screamed it. "Goodbye, I'm leaving." She piled up her dishes in front of her and those Becka had used. "I'm going to meet Art and shoot film. Thanks but no thanks for your...for your *help*." She pushed the chair back abruptly, carried the pile of dishes to the sink, and stomped out of the room and upstairs to get her purse.

Rit rose, too, and walked that way. She knocked on a door as she passed it, then she followed Drew upstairs, slowly, taking each step easily. Soon, Randy was there, beside her, and then another woman. Drew came out of her bedroom and stopped. Three women blocked her way. She stared in disbelief.

"I can't let you go, Drew," Rit said softly.

"Where's Becka?"

"Becka's fine."

"Rit," Drew said with determination, "I'd like to take Becka now and leave." She adjusted the purse on her shoulder. "Please don't do this."

"I know," Rit said, standing firmly with the other two, still blocking Drew's way, "but you can't. It wouldn't be wise to push it, Drew."

"Let me pass."

"Don't push it, Drew. Randy has a brown belt in karate, Bo a black. Accept the situation."

Drew looked from one woman to another. Rit was tall and powerful-looking. She stood in the center. Randy, shorter by a half-foot, to her left, and the other one, Bo, slim and sleek, boyish-looking, to Rit's right. Drew's eyes stayed on Randy. "Listen to me," she said. "You feel weak! You can barely move."

As Randy began sliding limply to the floor, Bo grabbed Drew in one lightning movement, twisting her around, pinning her arms, holding her from behind. She dragged Drew down to the end of the hall, nudged her into the room there and closed the door. Drew heard the lock click. There was shuffling down the hall and then Drew could hear Rit speaking soothingly to Randy. They'll have to let me go now, she thought. How dare they try to stop me. She went to the window. It was fastened shut with a brass safety lock; below the two story drop was a cement patio.

"Drew." It was Rit's voice outside the door. "Drew, are you listening?" She rapped on the door.

"Yes," Drew said.

"I want you to take care of Randy. Unzap her."

Drew was at the door now, her head separated from Rit's by only an inch of oak. "If you let me go home, I will."

"I can't do that, Drew. Randy's scared. It isn't doing you any good to leave her this way. Will you take care of it if we let you out?"

There was no answer.

Drew was back at the window. Off to the right, she could see Becka happily hammering near the shed. She pictured Randy collapsing beneath her words and felt frighteningly powerful, but not enough. She wished she could zap more than one person at a time. How easy it would be then, she thought, picturing herself on a high platform, a balcony like the Pope's, overlooking throngs of people who stared up at her and simultaneously succumbed to the mass zap.

"Drew." Again the tapping on the door. Drew ignored it. She looked around the room. The walls were pale lavender. The wood, as in the rest of the house, was richly grained. The room contained a large bed, an oak four-poster, with a maroon quilt. There was a desk, a dresser, two easy chairs, a footstool, and two doors in addition to the one Rit stood behind. Drew opened one. It was a closet, large, empty except for a robe, several cotton nightshirts, and some thin strands of some kind of leather. The other door led to a john. Drew examined it. The window, in the shower, was high up, and very small.

"...especially Becka. She doesn't need to be aware of this. You might as well negotiate now...Drew..." Her voice remained low and calm.

Drew looked at herself in the mirror. "They all want to use you," she said aloud.

It was silent then. Drew went to one of the chairs and sat. Negotiate, she thought. Yes. They won't let me go, that seems clear. They need me to fix Randy. How can I use it? What can I trade for it? I don't want to go to Arizona. She smiled. Yes I do. Rit's image filled her mind. This is absurd. I can't...no, I don't want to go, not this way. She placed her feet on the footstool. Why is she doing this? Protecting me? Maybe. She wished she had a cigarette. No! I *am* naive. She wants to use me, like everyone else. Even Wiley. Wiley wants to make me her super-therapist-cure-zapper.

The lock clicked. Drew stood, alert. The door opened. Drew watched as Rit entered, calmly, and walked toward her.

"Becka's asking for you."

"So, you're going to coerce me using Becka, you bitch." Both fists were clenched.

Rit's angry expression sent a shiver of fear and remorse from the nape of Drew's neck downward to the small of her back.

"Here's the situation," Rit said harshly. "The power you have to control others' thoughts is now known by people who will dispassionately attempt to force you to use it for them. You're not convinced of this, but I am. I'm choosing to intervene despite our difference of opinion. You don't like that and I don't blame you, but that's how it is. In my garage is a van. You and I and Bo are going to drive to Arizona. I have no doubt that Granser and his crowd will try to pursue you. It's safer for us and for Becka if she doesn't travel with us. They'll be looking for a woman with a child, for

one thing. She will stay with a friend of mine in another state."
Drew pulled back, almost tripping on the footstool. She began
to speak her protest. but Rit intervened.
"Temporarily, until it's safe for her to join us. She'll be all right.
You'll be in touch by phone. She'll be with good people." Rit moved
in closer. "We're going to change your appearance some." Her
face softened for a moment. "You'll look good in curls," she said,
almost smiling. "I like curly hair."
"How dare you!" Drew uttered hatefully, fighting the other, contradictory feelings. She folded her arms across her chest.
"We'll get papers for you," Rit continued. "That will take a
while. Then, if all goes well, you and Becka will leave the country. Someone will go with you. Probably me. As it seems apparent
that you'll not accede to this plan willingly, you will have to be our
prisoner, Drew." She said this almost apologetically. "Protective
custody," she added, chuckling then. "Unfortunately, your apparent proclivity for zapping my friends does present a problem."
Drew was shaking her head. "No way," she said. "Not a chance.
I won't let you do it. Randy will stay crippled until you get the hell
out of my way and let me live my own life. My way. I don't want
your protectiveness bullshit. I don't need it. I don't believe it." She
was yelling now. She rose from the edge of the chair where she'd
been leaning and approached Rit threateningly.
"I see," Rit said calmly.
Drew strode to the door and grabbed the handle. It was locked.
"Tell them to open this," she demanded.
Rit didn't move. She seemed deep in thought. "I didn't want to
have to do this," she said.
Drew still stood by the door. She glared at Rit.
"There is Becka's welfare to be considered."
"You slime!"
"Don't force me to elaborate," Rit said firmly. "I'm going to
take you to Randy now. Will you remove the zap?"
Tears wet Drew's face, slipping down her cheeks to her angry
set jaw. "Yes," she said through clenched teeth, her head lowered
in unjust defeat, her eyes filled with hate and pain.
"Come on."
Rit had Bo unlock the door and led Drew down the hall to the
study. Randy lay motionlessly on the couch. Her eyes darted with
fear and hope when she saw Drew.
Drew felt a painful tug of compassion, mixing with the anger.
"Go ahead," Rit said.
Drew bent on one knee. "Randy, listen to me," she began, speak-

ing firmly. "I have something important to say. You feel fine. Your normal strength is back. You're OK."

Randy flexed her arms. A slow wide smile took over her face. She jumped from the couch, ran in place, did some jumping jacks, boxed the air. "All right," she yelled. "Hey, hey, anybody wanna Indian wrestle?" She glanced at Drew. "Not you," she said, averting her eyes. "Don't you look at me."

Rit accompanied Drew back to the room and again the door was locked. "We need to do some more negotiating," she said, settling into the arm chair. "I need you to agree not to zap my people."

Drew stood away from her and did not speak.

"I could keep you gagged or blindfolded, maybe that's what I'll have to end up doing. Can you think of any alternative?"

Drew turned and faced her. "Yes," she said. "I won't zap them if Becka can stay with me."

"That's impossible. Any other suggestions?"

"Those are my terms."

"Impossible."

Drew took several deep breaths. "Then let her stay with her father."

"Not safe."

Drew paced the room, her face twisted in anguish. "I need a guarantee that you'll never harm Becka."

"Harm her?" Rit might have looked hurt; Drew couldn't tell for sure. "Jesus, what are you thinking, woman? Of course I won't harm her. That's an absolute."

Drew sneered. "I'm supposed to believe that? You just threatened her."

"I wouldn't have done anything to Becka."

Drew looked pointedly at Rit, trying to look inside. Despite the many reasons she could think of not to, she believed her. She was beginning to relax a little when Rit spoke again, her voice firm now.

"However, if, through the use of your power, *you* cause harm to me or to my friends, then Becka..."

"Don't say it!"

"I have to."

"Don't! I'll hate you."

"Then Becka will be taken away..."

"I hate you."

"...until the damage you did is mended. And if that's impossible, then we'll keep her from you permanently. She'll be cared for by..."

"Stop!"

151

Rit nodded her head slowly. "Be careful how you use your power, Drew."

"You disgust me."

"Keeping Becka from you is my ultimate back up. You leave me no alternative than to present it to you. I do mean it, I will follow through if you force me to but I'm confident I'll never have to. You're basically too reasonable." She paused, folding her hands behind her head, and leaned back against the chair. "That's the ugly bottom line part. I think it will never have to be discussed again."

"Why don't you leave me alone," Drew said. It was not a question, nor was it a plea.

"There's more to negotiate," Rit continued, "concerning the milder zapping you might consider. I propose that you give me your word not to zap my people in exchange for my agreement not to keep you blindfolded. Do you accept?"

Drew felt nauseated. "I feel like I'll never see Becka again."

"Nonsense." Rit reached over and took Drew's hand. "I have no wish to hurt you," she said, "in any way. I wish you could believe me. I think mostly you do."

Rit was right. Most of Drew did believe it, but part of her could not.

"The plan we have is good," Rit said, still softly touching Drew. "It's best this way." She gently pulled Drew to sit on the footstool facing her. "I have a friend, Naomi Brown. She's a good friend and a good person, a teacher in a little school, alternative education, parent's school, or whatever they call it. It's in a small rural community in northern Kentucky, Cutler Springs. She has three kids of her own and lives on a farm with them and her lover. Becka will stay with her until we're sure it's safe for her to join you. I don't want to alarm you, Drew, but you're not the only one in danger. They could use Becka..."

"Stop...please. I don't want to hear. Go on, about Kentucky and..."

"Randy will take Becka there. You'll be in contact with her by phone, frequently. It'll be OK, Drew. Becka will be safe. She'll love it on the farm."

Drew nodded. She felt there was no escape. "You're going to an awful lot of trouble."

"Yes."

"Why? To convince me?"

"To protect you."

"That's patronizing."

"I suppose it is."

Drew wished she could be sure. "My friends will be worried if we just disappear, you know. Wiley especially, and Becka's father. They'll think we were kidnapped or something. They'll call the police..." She was standing again, her voice rising. "The plan is no good. It won't work."

"Relax, my sweet, your *patron* will tend to those things."

Drew had to stifle a giggle. This woman was unbelievable.

"Do I have your word about the zapping?" Rit asked. "No blindfold in exchange for a moratorium on zapping. Deal?"

"I guess." Drew dropped into the empty chair. "I want to see Becka now."

"All right."

"When are we leaving?"

"Tomorrow morning."

"I have no clothes. Becka needs things from home. We'll have to stop there first."

Rit shook her head. "Don't worry about those details, it'll all be taken care of. Go see your daughter."

"I wish I could trust you," Drew said sadly.

"That will come."

Drew helped Becka finish nailing the wood together and they used a piece of rag for the sail.

"Will it work?" Becka asked excitedly, carrying the clumsy craft to the pond.

"We'll soon find out," Drew said.

It wasn't very stable, it bobbed and tilted, coming very close to falling over, but the little sailboat managed to stay upright. Becka gave it a shove and they watched its shakey journey across the pond.

"Rit was right," Becka declared. "She told me how to make it so it wouldn't tip." She went around the pond, retrieved the boat and sent it across again.

Drew kept her eye on it expecting it to capsize any moment. "How do you like Randy?" she asked.

"Oh, she's funny. She knows more jokes than Bobby Sanders at school. What did the parents name their daughter who was born with one leg shorter than the other?"

"What?"

"Ilene." Becka laughed. "Randy told me that. Isn't she funny?"

Drew grunted.

"I like Rit, too, and everything here. This is like a vacation, huh, ma?"

"Yeah, sort of," Drew said, her enthusiasm significantly less than Becka's. "How would you like to go on a real vacation? Stay on a farm?"

"A farm! Oh, boy! Can I take my boat? Is there a pond like this on the farm?"

"I'm not sure. We'll find out about that."

"Can we ride horses?"

"The farm is in Kentucky, Becka. Do you remember where that is, from your map puzzle?"

"Mm, no." Becka reached for the boat with a stick.

Drew took a stone and began drawing in the dirt. "Here's Illinois," she said. "That's where we live, right here." She pointed. "This is Chicago."

"Where's our apartment?"

"About here," Drew said. "Now right down here is Kentucky. Not too far, is it? That's where the farm is."

"When are we going?"

"Tomorrow."

"Oh, goodie. You think my teacher will be mad?"

"She'll understand." Drew hesitated. "Becka..."

"What, mom?"

"There are some things I have to do, some business things, so I can't be with you right away."

Becka tilted her head, her greenish eyes looking worried, like her mother's. "What do you mean?"

"That I can't go with you to the farm."

Becka's face took on that sad, scared, pouty look that never failed to melt Drew. "But I don't want to go without you." She plopped down and sat cross-legged on the dirt.

Drew touched her corduroy-covered knee. "I know. What a pain, huh? It won't be long though, we'll be together soon."

"I don't think I want to go on vacation, mom." She picked up the boat and dropped it in the center of Drew's dirt map. "We're having a spelling test Friday so I can't go. Let's just go home, mom. Anyway, I miss my bedroom."

Drew laughed and sad tears clouded her eyes. "The business I have to do means I have to go away for awhile."

"Oh, fuck a duck!"

"Becka!"

"Can't I go with you?"

Drew shook her head.

Becka was silent.

"It won't be too long. I'll talk with you on the phone, probably every day."

"I'll stay with daddy while you're gone."

"No, hon, you're going to go to the farm. There are children there."

"I'll stay with dad."

"No, that won't work. Randy will go with you. She'll probably tell you a bunch of jokes on the way."

Becka laughed. "What is Irish and is always outdoors?"

"I don't know," Drew said.

"Patty O'Furniture," Becka replied, laughing. "I don't get it, but it's funny, don't you think, mom?"

"Mildly."

"Mom, let's think about something else. Let's go home now." She tugged on her mother's arm.

Drew hugged her, wishing she could stop her tears.

"What, mom?" Becka cried with her, her fear growing.

Suddenly Drew jumped up. "It's an adventure," she shouted, running around the pond, then hiding behind a tree.

Becka began the chase. They darted through the yard for several minutes until Becka caught her mother. "You're it," she said, and Drew chased her until she was exhausted.

They went and sat on the swing.

"In a way, we're real lucky to get to have this adventure. You get to go and stay on a farm and play and go to a little country school, and I get to call you every day and talk on the phone and hear about your adventure."

"They have a farm on the school?"

"You mean a school on the farm?"

"That's what I said." She giggled. "Isn't it?"

"There's a little school nearby."

"What else do they have?"

"Let's go find Randy. She's been there. She can tell you all about it."

Drew fretted and sulked on the porch while Becka listened to Randy's stories in the kitchen. She could hear their laughter, Becka's sharp little giggles and Randy's robust guffaws. She'll be OK with her, Drew had to think. The rest of the day and evening, Drew and Becka played and talked and rested and drew pictures together. Becka was far the better of the two at Pac-Man. They called Chris, the bartender, who was quite understanding about the theft and barely lectured Becka at all. They made a dock for the boat and ate lunch and dinner which they prepared together. When it was dark out, Drew read poetry to Becka by the fire until

155

Becka's sleepy yawns came.

Drew had not spoken to Rit since their encounter in the morning. She avoided her and Rit accepted this, spending much of the day on the phone and pouring over papers. Alice, her secretary, brought over some files at noontime. Drew also ignored Randy and Bo, whom she encountered from time to time in the house.

She stayed by the side of the bed long after Becka had fallen asleep, looking at her daughter lovingly, occasionally stroking her cheek or forehead. There came a soft tapping on the door. Rit told Drew she'd like to talk with her before she went to bed and so the two went to the study.

"We've got to cover our tracks," Rit began. "Put off the people who might inadvertently get in our way. You can't contact your friends by phone because the paranoid lawyer thinks the bad guys might be tapping the lines of anyone close to you. You'll have to inform Wiley right away, so she doesn't panic. Who else do you need to inform that you'll be gone?"

Drew wished she only felt anger, but the pleasant excitement of Rit's presence insisted on permeating and overpowering the negative feelings. "Art Trevor. Steve Tremaine, Becka's father. I made plans with Dana, a friend of mine, for Saturday night. To go to a play. I've got the tickets. My parents. They call fairly frequently. They'd worry if I were never home. Becka's school. My friends, Janice and Marie; they'd wonder if they couldn't reach me. And there's..."

"OK, stop. You'll have to get the word out to your other friends through Wiley. Can she do that?"

"I suppose."

"Good. Write a letter to Wiley telling her about Granser's visit and that you thought it best to go into hiding. Don't mention me. Tell her to inform your friends that you're vacationing...let's see, what would make a sudden vacation believable?"

"You figure it out, this is your game."

Rit smiled at the word. "Yes," she said, "but yours, too." She grinned sweetly at Drew. "I like the way you play."

"Get fucked."

Rit shrugged. "Have Wiley tell people you won a free trip to Disney World; that you had to leave right away, et cetera."

"Yes, boss."

Rit smiled a sad, sardonic grin. "I know," she said, "but, this has to be done. You probably should also send a note to your hero, Art Trevor, and to Becka's father, using the Disney World story. To Becka's school, too. Those can be sent by mail. The one to Wiley

156

has to be hand-delivered. That will be faster, but also because they're almost certainly watching her. We'll figure out a way to get it to her. Any questions?"

Drew pretended to be bored and shook her head. "It's perfectly clear."

"Of course, I'll have to read the letters."

"Of course."

"Tell Wiley you'll be in touch with her within a few days. Tell her not to take any action, that you're safe, et cetera, et cetera. There's paper in the right hand drawer. Pen over here. I'll be by the fire."

Drew sat at the desk, staring at nothing. She was thinking, then considering, then planning—planning to sneak upstairs, quickly get Becka dressed and sneak back down and out the back door. I'll do it my own way, she thought. Maybe I *will* go into hiding, I'm not sure. Maybe we are in danger. Her fingers tapped rapidly against the desk. I really will go to Disney World, Drew decided. Yes, and visit my folks, and I'll have time then to figure out a way to get to Granser and zap him.

She went to the door of the study. Bo and Randy were probably around somewhere, but there seemed little to lose by trying. She looked up and down the hall. No one was in sight. Walking soundlessly, she moved toward the stairs. Silence. One by one, she ascended. To her relief, none of the stairs creaked. So far, so good. She moved toward the bedroom where her daughter was, and slowly, silently, turned the doorknob. She pushed gently. The door did not move. She pushed again. It wouldn't budge.

Drew smiled through her disappointment and anger. I should have known, she thought, shaking her head. With a little bounce in her step, she returned to the study and began writing the letters.

## 32.

When Bo, the keeper of the key, awakened Drew and Becka, the sun was just beginning to rise. The whole group breakfasted together, but it was Randy and Becka who did most of the talking, chattering, really, and giggling. Randy talked about the shopping spree they'd have in Kentucky and all the new clothes and books and toys they'd get for Becka. Drew felt leadenly miserable. Becka laughed and talked about how she'd feed the chickens and maybe have a tractor ride.

After breakfast, Rit had Drew remove Randy's memory of her zapping power. The Oldsmobile was in the driveway. Randy put a small suitcase into the trunk and handed Becka a bag of nuts and a thermos. "For the road," she said. "I think we're all ready to go."

Becka took the bag numbly, then set it on the ground. Her expression, cheerful and bright a moment ago, altered dramatically. She turned toward her mother who stood off to the side looking at that moment all of her thirty years of age. Becka's soft rosey cheeks twisted and a strangled cry emerged from her throat. She ran to her mother's arms. "I don't wanna go, momma. Don't make me go."

Drew broke. Her cries blended painfully with Becka's as they clung to each other.

The others discreetly backed away.

Drew had vowed that she would never, ever zap Becka. It was a promise she'd made very soon after her discovery. There had been times when she'd been tempted, when Becka was being particularly stubborn or upset, but she had resisted. No, not to her, she'd reaffirmed, never to Becka.

"I'm scared. I'm scared."

Never to Becka.

"Something's wrong! You never go away and make me go to a farm."

Never to Becka.

"Mommie, don't leave me-e-e!"

A very tortured heart can overlook vows.

"Please!" Becka clung desperately.

"Listen to me, Becka." Drew held her daughter at arm's length. "Listen, honey, I have something very important to say."

Becka's fearful eyes fixed on Drew's, staring intently, and calmed.

"You don't need to be afraid now. You don't need to feel so worried about my going away. You have the feeling that things will be OK, that you'll be fine and I'll be fine and we'll be together soon."

Drew continued to hold onto Becka's shoulders after she finished speaking, held her that way until Becka smiled.

"Do you have some nuts for the road?" Becka asked.

"Oh, I'm sure we'll have something," Drew said, trying to smile herself. She handed Becka a sealed envelope. "I wrote you a letter," she said. "Save it in case you feel lonely for me, and then read it, OK? Don't open it right away. Can you save it?"

Becka took the envelope and brought it gently to her chest, holding it as if it were a fragile flower. Randy was in the car waiting. Drew walked Becka around and helped her settle in and fasten the seat belt.

"I love you, mommy."

"Drew watched them drive off, fighting the tears. When the car was out of sight, she turned abruptly and went inside, not looking at Rit or Bo.

They left Drew alone for a half hour, then Bo came to her and said it was time for them to leave. Rit's van was a fully customized, decked out compact home on wheels. Drew was surprised. From the outside, it looked quite ordinary. Within was a refrigerator, stove, sink, john and shower, chairs that became beds, tables that concealed storage areas and doubled as extra sleeping space. There was a stereo system and a TV. It was done in shades of gold and soft yellows and browns. When Drew climbed in, she wanted to exclaim and praise and comment on how beautiful and clever it was, but she did not. She silently settled into a chair in the back and looked out the window. She was a prisoner, she reminded herself. She could not feel pleasant excitement or delight. Her actions were being controlled forcibly, her basic rights being violated. She could not feel anticipation about a cross-country trip under these circumstances. Against her will, her daughter was separated from her. She could not feel drawn to someone who would do such a thing. And so, Drew sat sullenly, staring out the tinted window at the passing buildings and traffic, not letting herself look around at the van's interior, not letting herself look at Rit.

Rit was driving, her left arm resting partially outside the window. Bo sat in the seat at Rit's side, humming with the music. Drew was thinking about her future, the future Rit had outlined for her. Were she and Becka to live under false names and identities in a foreign country away from everything that they knew? Was she to live in fear, always to be looking over her shoulder for the predators? Was Rit right? Was she in danger? She recalled the times she and Wiley had discussed such possibilities, the risks involved if other people, the "wrong people", learned about her power. She had always cut such conversations short. Was Rit a wrong person? What did she really have in mind? Will she try to blackmail me like Zayre did? Was that her plan? Drew watched a huge truck tear past them. Or is Rit really trying to protect me? She let herself take a surreptitious glimpse of Rit. I hope she's telling the truth about that. Yes, I think she is. She's just trying to protect me like she says. Why didn't she do it some other way though? I'm reasonable, Drew thought. She could have tried harder to convince me instead of grabbing me and locking me in rooms. She's a pig. She's like Granser or Zayre, wants my power. She's no different from thém.

Drew glanced at Rit again, at her profile; the wavy black hair, the smooth, tanned skin of her angular face. She was talking with Bo, sharing something and laughing with her. They seemed close, intimate. Were they lovers, Drew wondered. She felt a sharp pang of jealousy and looked away. There were fewer and fewer houses now. They'd left the city behind, heading away from the recently risen sun, away from Becka and Wiley and Judith and Abram Granser.

"You comfortable back there?" Rit called to her.

"I'm OK," Drew responded crisply, not looking at her. How can this be? How can just a word and a glance from her do this to me? Drew focused on her heart, beating out its response, contradicting her conscious thoughts.

I'm not going to Arizona, Drew affirmed. She'd thought earlier that she'd escape tonight, as they slept. Now, seeing the van, she feared they'd be sleeping here which would make escape impossible. First chance I get, she decided. When we stop somewhere for food or gas. I've got to believe her when she says she wouldn't harm Becka. I do believe her. Whatever she's about, it can't be that. She's not...evil. No, she's wonderful, she's...Drew slipped into reverie then, remembering their brief and special times together, before Granser and this sudden shift. She remembered each touch and interchange and felt the kisses on her eyelids over and over again.

Rit and Bo were passing a joint and offered her some. Drew declined. She watched the boring flatness of Illinois. The next state would be Missouri. That would be somewhat better, she thought. The sooner I get out of here, the easier it will be to get to Cutler Springs, Kentucky. I don't want them to be suspicious. Maybe I should be more friendly. No, they might see through that. I'll be dejected, resigned. Drew smiled to herself, beginning to enjoy the plotting. As long as I don't harm them, I'm OK. No problem. She began to whistle, then immediately caught herself. I'm dejected. They went another ten miles. Drew listened to the conversation of the two women.

"It won't happen," Rit was saying. "The prosecutor's too smart to even try it." She chuckled. "I'd enjoy it if he did, though. Defeating some of those jagoffs at their own game is almost as much fun as those rare occasions when I actually get the system to work."

"Who are you up against?"

"Murphy."

"Ugh," Bo groaned. "Superprick. So, you'll fly in then for the deposition?"

"Yes, if the timing's right. Ella will take over from there."

"With this sudden departure, I bet you've left a lot of loose ends."

"No, not really. Ella can handle things. In fact, she's glad for the opportunity. She's been looking forward to it; it's just coming a bit sooner than we expected."

"Right. I have to piss."

Five minutes later they pulled off at a gas station. Drew pretended to be dozing.

"Hey, gorgeous, pit stop. You gotta go?"

Drew groggily turned her head. "No, I'm OK," she mumbled.

She watched Bo go for the washroom key, then disappear around the corner of the white tile building. She clutched her purse, ready, waiting for the opportunity. Rit was standing off to the side near the gas pumps stretching her back and arms. Drew waited until she walked toward the station, then tried to open the rear door. Not surprisingly, the lock wouldn't release. She slipped into the driver's seat, keeping low, then slowly opened the door and slid out. Beyond the gas station was the highway, then fields. The sign had said there was a town two miles north. If I can make it to that field without being seen, I'll be OK, Drew thought. She took a couple steps in that direction.

"You're awake!"

Drew jumped. "Yes," she said guiltily. "Uh, where's the john?"

"Over there," Bo answered in her friendly way, "around the corner. Rit's there now. Do you want anything to drink? There's some beer and pop in the fridge, but I'm going to have a Kayo. I always drink Kayo when I travel. Other times, I can't stand it."

"No thanks," Drew said, trying to make her voice sound dejected.

As soon as Bo walked into the station, Drew looked behind her, gauging how long it would take to get to the field. She was edging around the van, about to sprint, when she heard whistling. Rit was walking toward the van looking right at her. Drew sauntered toward her trying to look innocent and bored as she silently ac-

161

cepted the washroom key and went around the corner. She could feel Rit watching her. Inside the john, Drew quickly used the toilet then opened the door a crack. They were leaning against the van, each drinking a bottle of chocolate soda pop. Drew slipped out and behind the building. Her captors could not see her there.

There was a dirt road, some bushes and then an orchard. Drew ran. She didn't look back, but ran straight ahead, crossed the road, and pushed her way through the brush to the edge of the orchard. She lay down flat and waited. A twig poked at her ribs. As she shifted positions, a grasshopper flew over her back. She waited a few minutes then, slowly, she raised her head. The gas station looked like an ugly white sore rising from the vacant landscape. Drew could not see the van, nor Rit or Bo. She moved further into the orchard, keeping low. Surrounded by the apple trees, she began to feel bolder. It seemed so easy. Of course, they'll realize it soon, she thought, picking up her speed. She ran among the straight rows of trees until she caught a glimpse of some wooden buildings ahead, probably a farm, she decided. That didn't seem safe so she headed the other way, toward what appeared to be a forest.

The only sounds she heard were her own footsteps and breathing. She continued until she reached the woods then into the woods to a path and onward heading what she hoped was north. She walked for another ten minutes, planning how she'd get to Kentucky, considering calling Wiley, feeling relieved that her captivity was over. The path was coming to a road, a gravel one, which, Drew was sure, would lead her to a highway. When I reach it, I'll be on my way, she thought. When she reached the gravel road, Bo was there.

Drew jerked back, unbelieving, suddenly covered with sweat. She stumbled backwards a few paces, then turned and started running back into the woods. Her perspiration stung and cooled her as she ran. She crashed over logs and brush, scraping her leg, running wildly for she knew that Bo had seen her. Drew was fast but Bo's lean wirey legs were faster still. Drew came to the stream she'd crossed minutes earlier, jumped it, but slipped as she landed on the other side. There was no time to sooth her screaming ankle, twisted in the fall. She pushed on, limping, leaving the dirt path for the thicker woods and felt Bo close and heard her and soon felt the steel hand on her shoulder. She couldn't jerk free. There seemed to be so many hands, turning her, then holding her arm behind her back so she could not move. She stood bent over to the side, panting, sweating, knowing she was caught, but, nonetheless, she gave a final futile twist within the vice of Bo's strong hands.

"OK," Bo said, "relax. It was a good try but you didn't make it." She was panting herself. "So stop struggling and I can let go of you, all right?"

Drew let her muscles unflex and Bo loosened her grip. Drew turned and the two women stood facing each other, both breathing heavily. For some reason, they began to laugh. One fed the other and they nearly keeled over with it. They sat then on a log, side by side, recovering from the chase and from the giggling which neither could explain.

"You know, Bo," Drew said, another snicker escaping, "I've got to hand it to you..." Her voice shifted suddenly. "You will listen to me carefully now." Her smile was gone. Bo stared into her eyes. "You want to help me escape. You know what you're doing isn't right. You want to be clever about it, not confront Rit, but without her knowing, you want to help me get away, and make sure I get to Becka. You're determined to help me with this."

Bo remained transfixed for nearly half a minute, then broke the stare. "OK, now, be cool," she said. "You're gonna make it, but not just yet. I'm with you, Drew. Now, play it cool. Rit's just up the road with the van. Take your cues from me. I'm going to help you get away. We have to time it right."

Drew smiled, rubbing her ankle, then stood and walked a few steps.

"You hurt your foot?"

"I think it's OK."

Bo took Drew's forearm, holding it gingerly, and they walked back to the gravel road and to the van.

"So you wanted a little exercise," Rit said. She laughed. "You look worn out, girl. Sit up here."

Bo went in the back and Drew took the seat next to Rit. They re-entered the highway and drove for several miles.

"I assume you zapped her."

The words made the tiny hairs along Drew's neck and back stand on edge. "No," she replied. She couldn't let her victory slip away. "I wish I'd thought of it, though."

Rit drove on silently for awhile. "Tell me exactly what you told her." She kept her eyes on the road, not glancing at Drew. "Don't bullshit me. That would displease me which would be highly inadvisable. Tell me what the zap is."

Drew rubbed her hand nervously across her knees. She did not speak.

Rit pulled the van to the side of the road, turned the engine off and faced Drew. "Tell me. Now. Exactly what did you say?"

Drew knew she could stay with her lie, deny it, but knew, too, that for some reason, she could not. "I told her she'd help me escape."

"Mm-hm. What else?"

"That's all. That she wouldn't let you know, that it was wrong to be forcing me."

Rit laughed. "OK, that's it?"

"Yes."

Bo was listening from the rear. "Rit, it is wrong," she said. "No matter what our rationale, we can't justify..."

"Erase it," Rit commanded.

Drew knew she could refuse, knew that's what she should do, but she did not. Instead, she turned to Bo and told her to listen, for she had something important to say to her. Afterwards, they sat silently for a minute, Rit looking out the window at a flock of crows, Bo waiting patiently, Drew nervously.

"You know what this means," Rit said at last. She looked pointedly at Drew.

Drew felt limp. She wanted to move closer to Rit, bury herself in her strong arms. She wanted to despise her.

"You've forced us to go the blindfold route." She looked over her shoulder. "Bo, there's a scarf in the closet drawer. Would you get it, please."

"Rit, don't," Drew protested.

"Would you prefer a gag?"

"I can't zap her from here, with you right next to me."

Rit leaned back against the bucket seat. "It would be more difficult, that's true," she said. "However, it's also important that you realize things like that trick will have consequences, unpleasant ones. I can't have you pulling stunts like that."

"I understand," Drew said. "I had to try. I won't do it again." *She has all the power. She's so powerful. She's magnificant. It's disgusting.* "Will you give me another chance?"

Rit looked at her, her eyes softening. Slowly, her full lips turned upward. "All right," she said. "You stay up here. If you want to talk with Bo, don't turn around to do it. Don't look at her."

Drew nodded. For the next hour of the drive, they spoke very little. Drew was glad Rit did not try to engage her in conversation. She didn't think she'd be able to speak, so occupied was she with sensations, strange exciting feelings, all having to do with Rit and how close she sat to her and every movement that she made and how it would feel to be held by those powerful arms.

When they stopped for lunch, Drew was watched very closely.

Still she spoke little, listening to Bo and Rit, watching Rit all the while through the corners of her eyes. At 2:45 they pulled into a medium-sized town. "Time for your new look," Rit said.

They found a hair stylist and, over Drew's protestation, she was subjected to a haircut, a dye job, several shades darker than the original, and a permanent wave.

"You look great," Rit proclaimed.

"Oh, you do," the hair stylist said. "You're a new person. Gorgeous. Now, aren't you glad your friend talked you into this?"

Drew continued looking in the mirror. It was certainly different, she thought. No more reddish highlights. And she hadn't had curls since her freshman year at Wisconsin. After that she let it grow long and wore it flowing and wild, until after college when she changed to her more tame shoulder length style.

From the beauty shop, they stopped at a department store. Drew got a couple pairs of heavy cotton slacks, some jeans, several shirts, underwear and a few other things she'd need. She also bought a large leather shoulder bag to keep them in. Rit tried to pay but did not argue against Drew's adamant refusal.

"Now, one more stop," Rit said.

At the photography studio, a half-dozen shots were taken, developed, and printed on the spot, passport size. Then they took to the road again.

When it had been dark for about an hour, Rit pulled into a roadside motel. Drew was pleasantly surprised that they wouldn't be sleeping in the van, thinking she might get another chance. Too bad Bo's not on my side now, she thought. Again Drew was surprised, and doubly pleased, when she realized she would have her own room. They're making it easy, she thought, and wondered why. She was already planning to set her watch alarm for two a.m. figuring they'd be deep asleep at that hour.

"We're going to call Naomi's now," Rit said in the motel lobby. "You can talk with Becka."

Drew felt relieved after the conversation. Becka was bubbling. She described each child that lived on the farm and listed the animals. She told her mother how different the food they ate was and how quiet it was outside and then she told Drew another joke she'd heard from Randy and they said goodnight.

Rit had gotten them adjoining rooms and accompanied Drew to hers. They'd dined several hours before and everyone seemed tired "We're going to have a nightcap," Rit said. "Do you want to join us or stay here?"

"I'll stay," Drew replied.

"OK, take your clothes off."

Drew felt the adrenalin. Is she going to...? No, of course not. The bitch is going to take my clothes away. "You're going to take my clothes away," she said.

"No."

Drew was puzzled. "I'd rather not undress just yet."

"Take them off."

Strange thoughts passed through Drew's mind again, but she discarded them along with her shoes and long sleeve cotton shirt. She left her corduroy pants and t-shirt on. Rit leaned on the edge of the dresser, watching.

"Go on."

Drew resented the excitement building in her. "I don't understand," she said.

"Take off the pants."

Drew hesitated.

Rit glared.

Drew unzipped the corduroys and slipped out of them feeling painfully vulnerable in her semi-naked state, not unaware of Rit's steady gaze.

"OK, sexy, that's enough," Rit said. She didn't move right away, but continued looking at Drew for what seemed like days. Then she reached into her bag.

Drew watched as Rit withdrew a long, heavy, silver chain. She sucked in her breath, unconsciously drawing back. Attached to the chain was a smooth narrow shackle.

"You understand now?" Rit asked, padlocking one end of the chain to the bed base and holding the shackle end in her hands.

"Obscene."

"That's a rather strong word. Sit here." Rit slipped the shackle around Drew's ankle and clicked it closed. She stood back, again absorbing Drew with her eyes. "It looks good on you," she said, in her suggestive way, and left the room.

Drew sat on the edge of the bed for a long time, staring at the chain, recalling long-buried fantasies. Disbelief and outrage competed with the same strange pleasure she'd been feeling for the past two days. She could hear Rit and Bo's muffled voices next door.

The chain was long enough to allow Drew access to all areas of the room. She showered, then lay in bed, in the darkness, sleepless, thinking, very aware of the metal on her ankle. She did not feel unhappy. The more she didn't want to leave, the more she thought about escape.

## 33

They breakfasted early, in the van, on rolls and steaming coffee they got at a truck stop. Drew had been awake long before Rit came to free her from the chain.

"Did you dream of me?" Rit asked.

Not answering, Drew closed the bathroom door. The bitch, how does she know everything? It had been a strange dream. Drew was in a large bed, like the one with the maroon quilt in Rit's house, lying on her back, naked, her arms above her head. She was unable to move, and was frightened. When Rit came to her, dressed darkly, the fear went away. Rit kissed her eyes and kissed her everywhere and Drew could not stop her from doing whatever she chose because there were chains and because she did not want to. She awoke with her hand between her legs and, awake, continued the dream.

They drove for nearly three hours before pulling into a town. Bo went to make some phone calls. Drew said she'd like to buy something to read, some "escapist" fiction, she quipped, and a few other items.

"A hacksaw?" Rit asked.

Rit accompanied her along Broadway Avenue to Banner Rose Department Store and watched her closely as Drew walked the aisles examining things, then stopped to leaf through the paperbacks. A magazine cover caught Rit's eyes. Drew was hoping for this. She waited until Rit picked up the magazine and opened it. It took only a second for Drew to slip around the book rack and bolt. She knew exactly where she would go. The men's room was empty when she entered it. She closed herself into a stall, waiting, hoping her plan would work, that Rit would not think to search here.

A boy came in, used the urinal and left. Drew chuckled to herself and was glad she wasn't wearing heels. Five minutes passed, then ten. As she was about to leave, a man in a plaid shirt pushed open the door. His jaw dropped, but his shock soon changed to indifference after he heard the words, "You see that I'm a male. You wish to ignore me." He did what he'd come for and as he was exiting, another man entered. It was the clerk Drew had noticed at the counter near the books. He listened intently as Drew spoke and then his sour face broke into a wide grin and he vigorously shook her hand. With a light step, he walked her to the manager's office upstairs, convinced that his boss would be as delighted as he to meet such a celebrity. The clerk proudly introduced Mary Tyler Moore to the balding man behind the desk, and then left them, forgetting immediately that he had been there at all and why.

Drew zapped the manager. She decided this was where she would remain awhile, allowing Rit and Bo time to give up their search and leave the town. From her amiable office companion, she learned that the only public transportation out of Evansville was a train which came through at 7:15 p.m. every day of the week including Sunday. It would take her to Cranston where she could probably get another one to Cutler Springs.

Settling in for the wait, Drew used one of her favorite zaps, and soon her conversation with the manager of Banner Rose Department Store grew lively and intimate. She was learning who Joseph Carothers was and growing fond of him. He clearly felt warmly and benevolently toward her. They talked about friendship, embarrassing moments, hopes for their futures, people they've loved, fears and letdowns, alienation and connectedness. They talked about his job at Banner Rose and about each of their work histories.

They laughed until tears came as Drew described her brief experience as a tour guide in a potato chip factory. "He was fat, I mean like over 300 pounds. He took me aside at the end of the tour and told me about how his kids never got enough to eat." Drew was doubled over. "He said...he said there were eight of them, eight kids." She had to stop for breath. "So, I gave him eight bags, you know, sample bags, and then I asked him if he'd like one for himself." Joseph Carothers laughed along with her. "It was really ly sad," she said then, giggling uncontrollably. "Poor guy." She wiped her eyes. "And then there was the health fiend. He wore a button saying *Stamp Out Junk Foods*. Every ingredient I'd mention would bring on a lecture about how we're poisoning ourselves." Drew was sitting in a chair on wheels, scooting it around as she talked. "The trouble was, I agreed with him and the whole tour group ended up deciding potato chips were awful and no one took their free sample. I almost lost my job over that one."

She took a potato chip Joseph Carothers offered her. "And then there was the German couple..."

They swapped lots of stories and shared the lunch Joe ordered for them, and Drew did some filing for him. She had no trouble getting Naomi Brown's phone number in Cutler Springs, Kentucky, and had another pleasant chat with Becka, this time learning how Becka liked to go down by the shallow stream behind the school where the bridge was, and play. I'll see you there soon, Drew thought.

She had dinner with Joe Carothers' family. No zaps were needed to bring out their warmth and conviviality. After coffee, Joe drove her to the train station, not questioning her wish to use the station several towns away rather than the one in Evansville. The train arrived there at 7:55. It was a sad parting when Joseph Carothers hugged Drew goodbye and waved as the train pulled out. They had enjoyed each other very much.

The car was about half-full. Drew settled back, confident that when she reached Cutler Springs, Naomi Brown's farm would not be difficult to find. Most likely Naomi had been warned that she might come so Drew figured she'd try to sneak Becka out and if that didn't work, zap anybody who got in the way. Rit and Bo are probably on their way there right now, she thought. She would travel all night and hopefully arrive in Cutler Springs before them.

It was hard to think further into the future than that. She could picture the reunion with Becka, their return home, but then she stopped. Partly, she knew it was because she feared Rit; partly because she missed her. She closed her eyes and, lulled by the rhythm of the train's movement, allowed the fantasies to come. They always started with kisses on the eyelids.

The train made several stops in little towns whose names Drew had never heard. A few passengers would get off, a few on. She might have dozed. In Pratford, one of the new arrivals took the seat next to her. Drew's body tightened; a rush of emotion ran through it, more from happiness than fear. "Hi," she said.

"Hide and seek," Rit replied.

Drew smiled and shrugged her shoulders. She was feeling strangely warm now and safe.

"Some game," Rit said. She was wearing a thin leather jacket that Drew thought the sexiest-looking garment she'd ever seen. "Next stop is Waynesville. It's about thirty-five miles from here. That's where we get off."

That controllingness again. Drew bristled. "Suppose I refuse."

"Don't."

"I might."

"Then there'll be a scene."

"So."

"You'll end up coming with me in handcuffs." Rit pulled out some papers—a warrant for Drew's arrest, a wanted poster with her picture, dark, short, curly hair.

"You've been busy."

"I'd like you to quit running away now. You're becoming a pain in the ass."

"That's easy to resolve, you know. You could just leave me alone."

"I considered it."

Drew's face fell. "You did?" She recovered quickly. "What stopped you?"

Rit smiled. "Your eyes." Chuckling. "And probably your spunk. Other things as well."

"What 'other things'?"

Rit didn't answer. They rode a while in silence, each with her own thoughts. "Bo talked with our contact in Chicago," Rit said.

Drew looked at her scornfully. "Contact. What do you mean 'contact'. That's B movie talk."

"You're grouchy."

"You're controlling."

"Mandy Coors. She's a friend. She's the one who got your letter through to Wiley. Your phone is being bugged. So are Wiley's, home and office. They've begun questioning people. Someone's masquerading as a long-lost cousin of yours to get the information. They know you've left town, so no doubt they're actively searching for you."

"Really," Drew said skeptically. "Granser, I presume."

"Yes, that's what I think."

Drew shook her head. "For some reason, I'm having trouble believing all this. No offense, but you wouldn't put me on, would you, Avery? Use scare tactics to bolster your position. Naw, you'd never do that. You're ethical. Let me see those papers again. What am I wanted for?" Drew looked at the poster. "Embezzlement. Good choice. Nice, clean white collar crime for a nice clean white collar girl." She ripped it up.

Rit shook her head. "I have others."

"Such trouble you go to. What are you after, Rit? Money? Fame? Who do you want me to zap for you? Tell me about your power fantasies."

"You should have hitchhiked if you really wanted to get away. Covering all the roads would have been impossible. The buses and trains were easy."

"You're better at this game."

"Yes."

"So far."

They disembarked at Waynesville, Missouri. Rit called Bo who was waiting at a motel about twenty-five miles from there. That night, again, Drew slept in shackles and, the next day, they chained her in the van as well.

"Shopping privileges revoked," Rit said, "and you'll be eating in from now on." She touched Drew's knee sending a shiver all the way up to Drew's chest. "I'm tired of chasing you, sweetheart. Besides, eventually you may pull it off if we keep giving you opportunities to practice."

"You're so arrogant."

"And you do have a significant advantage, though you still don't use it very well. Maybe you need some lessons."

"I'm sure you'd be an excellent teacher; you have just the mind for it."

"True."

Drew enjoyed each of the sparring dialogues and she and Rit managed to have a fair number of them as they continued cross-country.

_34.

They were near the border of Oklahoma. Bo was driving; Rit and Drew were in the back.

"Wiley's expecting a call from you at ten this morning," Bo said.

Drew had stretched out on a chair and was reading. "She is? Great! I thought the phones were tapped."

"She'll be at a phone booth."

"So, you're going to let me talk with her," Drew said to Rit. "You trust me? I may tell her I've been kidnapped, that she should call the cops."

"I don't think you're self-destructive," Rit said. "The police are the last people you want alerted."

"The FBI frowns on kidnapping."

"The FBI and Granser may be buddies."

"Or Granser could be a Russian."

"Could be."

"Or a Mafiosi."

"That's possible."

Drew laughed. "Rit, do you believe what you're saying?"

"Yes."

"Maybe Granser's a seeker of world peace, part of a special mission."

"Highly unlikely."

"There *are* good people in the world, you know."

This time Rit laughed.

"You don't think so?" Drew asked.

"I think so."

"You also think I'm naive, right?"

"*You* said it."

"You think I'm naive enough to believe your motivation is to protect me from evil governments and gangsters?"

"Too naive to believe it."

"You're impossible." She wished she could have suppressed the smile. "So what am I supposed to tell Wiley?"

"Whatever will put her mind at ease. We don't want her complicating things."

"No censorship?"

"Use your own judgment."

"Then I can tell her where we're going and who it is who puts chains on me?"

"Poor judgment."

Drew turned the corner of the page down and closed her book. "Why can't I tell Wiley everything?" she asked.

"Because, my dear, the less anyone knows, the better off you are. Sometimes you're exceedingly dense."

That hurt, but Drew let it pass. "Wiley's an exception," she said. "I trust her with my life."

"Trust has to be conditional," Rit replied. "Wiley obviously sees the potential of your 'gift'. She's one of those people who thinks she has the answers for everyone and would feel justified in using whatever means to impose her 'truth'."

"She is not! How do you claim to know so much about her?"

"You told me."

"I never told you that."

"I draw my own conclusions. I'm sure Wiley would not sit back idly if she knew our plan." Drew started to say something, but Rit cut her off. "Besides, Granser might decide to coerce Wiley into telling him whatever she knows. Better that she know nothing he could use to find you."

"Coerce her?" Drew felt sick to her stomach, and tried to push away the images. "It's your paranoia again."

Rit said nothing.

172

"If Wiley really might be in danger, then she should hide too."

"Possibly," Rit said. "That's up to her."

"You didn't leave it up to me."

Again Rit did not respond.

"She could come to France with us," Drew said.

Rit shook her head. "Given the opportunity, I'm sure your friend, Wiley, would be full of ideas about what to do."

"Yes," Drew said eagerly.

"She's not getting the opportunity. Apparently, I'm not able to convince you to see it my way, Drew. You'll just have to accept it."

Drew turned away, angry, but full of other feelings, too. She sat silently, her book ignored on her lap. Of course I can trust Wiley, she thought. Rit's trying to manipulate me. She wants me to distrust everyone...everyone except her. I wish she wasn't so sure of herself.

At ten to ten, they pulled off at a rest stop. At ten o'clock, Drew called the number Bo gave her. "Be careful now," Rit warned.

"Drew, thank God! It's really you! Where are you? Are you OK?"

"I'm fine, Wiley. Fine. It's good to hear your voice. I hope you haven't been too worried."

"Are you really OK?"

"Yes, I really am. This Granser character may be a real baddie, though. I'm not a hundred percent sure, but, like I said in the letter, I'm avoiding him for now."

"Drew, if you're really OK, tell me this..." Wiley's voice had a pressured urgency to it. "Who won big at our last poker game. If you're not, if Granser has you, or you're in trouble, lie."

"Sharon won," Drew said immediately. "The bitch. She got twenty bucks of mine. Yes, Wiley, I'm really OK."

"You really are?"

"Really."

"That was my first thought when I got your letter, that Granser kidnapped you. Then I found out that they're still looking for you so...You're free, then, Drew, you're not being held against your will?"

Drew hesitated.

"What is it?"

"I'm fine."

"You can't talk freely, can you?"

"Yes, Wiley, I can talk freely." She looked at Rit who was leaning on the phone booth. "I know it seems mysterious."

"You can say that again. Why didn't you call me after Granser came? When I couldn't reach you Wednesday, I was going crazy with worry. I didn't get your letter 'til Thursday. I don't understand what's happening. Where are you? Are you at your folks? I don't think that's safe if you are. Why didn't you come to me when the trouble started?"

Drew felt very uncomfortable. "Wiley, I won't be able to explain everything. I'm sorry it's been bad for you, but...well, the less you know, the safer it is—for me *and* for you. If Granser really is...Wiley, it's possible that *you're* in danger, that they might try to get to me through you and..."

"I thought of that. Is that why you didn't come to me?"

Drew took the opportunity. "Yes," she said.

"We could have run away together." Wiley's throat constricted as she spoke.

"The...the people I'm with..."

Rit looked at her sternly and moved toward her.

"...convinced me to do it their way."

"Who are they? What people?"

"Wiley, I can't...I'm with two women. That's all I can say. They're trying to protect me."

"Are you sure?"

Drew hesitated, looking at Rit. "Yes," she said, trying to sound as if she meant it.

"Well, who are they, Drew? How do you know them? How did they get involved?"

"I can't tell you that, Wiley. Listen, in case you *are* in danger, is there any place you could go, disappear for awhile?"

"I haven't decided what I'm going to do," Wiley said. "The police are out. They'd really mess things up. It was going so well..."

"Yeah, you must be disappointed that the research had to stop," Drew said, disliking herself for her skepticism, but feeling the need to test her friend.

"To say the least, but that's a minor concern at this point."

"What did you mean when you said you found out they're still looking for me?" Drew asked.

"Marie called. Yesterday. She's been trying to reach you. It was what she told me that..."

"She didn't get my letter yet?"

"Apparently not, but I told her the Disney World story. Anyway, she called because of the visit she had from Brian McAllister."

"Brian McAllister?"

"Do you know him?"

"No."

"I thought not. He's going around saying he's a cousin of yours from Ireland, that you have an uncle...or *had* an uncle named Michael McAllister who died a couple weeks ago and left his fortune to you; a mansion of some sort, some other property and a ton of money."

"I never heard of Michael McAllister."

"This Brian McAllister said he traced you. He says he's sure you're the right Drew McAllister, daughter of Kevin McAllister, granddaughter of Sean McAllister."

"That part's right."

"He says that, according to the will, if he finds you within thirty days of the death of your uncle, he gets $80,000 for his trouble. If he fails, the whole fortune goes to some charity."

"I don't believe any of it," Drew said, feeling proud for not being naive.

"I didn't either."

Drew looked at Rit who still stood at the edge of the phone booth. "It may be," she said to Wiley, "that Brian McAllister is really one of Granser's men." And that Rit *isn't* paranoid, she thought, and isn't deceiving me.

"Yes, that was my conclusion. I figured he was using the inheritance story to get people to open up to him. He asked Marie a lot of questions about you. She told him quite a bit, unfortunately. She gave him my name and the names of a bunch of other people you know, including Steve. David, too. She gave him your parents' address. You're not there, are you?"

"No."

"Good. Who knows what else she told him. He's already contacted some of the people. He hasn't contacted me yet."

"Hm-m," Drew said. She ran her finger over the mouthpiece of the phone. "Well, I guess that proves they *are* after me."

"There's more," Wiley said. "My phones definitely *are* tapped. I had it checked out myself when Mandy told me why we'd be using a phone booth for this call. She's the woman who brought me here."

"So, that's true, too," Drew said. She was looking at Rit, somewhat sheepishly. "I guess it was good that I left." She paused. "Of course, I did stand Granser up Thursday. So, he's trying to find me, using the methods he has available." She scratched her head nervously. "Maybe I should contact him, try to see if something reasonable can be worked out. If there's any chance of that, I'd certainly prefer it to hiding. What do you think, Wiley?"

"No, Drew, I don't think you can trust him at all. You shouldn't

175

take any chances."

"Remember that movie you told me about? About the government chasing that guy who had the power to...the 'people-pushing' power."

"Yes, I remember. I've thought of it a number of..."

"It's sort of freaky, isn't it?"

"Very. Drew, I think we have to re-locate. Continue elsewhere, but be more discreet. Change your appearance, operate totally clandestinely."

"An interesting proposal," Drew said sarcastically, suddenly feeling the ugly distrust again. "What do you mean about continuing? Continue what?"

"Exploring your power. Actually, we know enough about it now to begin."

"Begin what?"

There was a brief pause. "This is no time to discuss it, Drew. Who knows what Granser might do. It's your safety that we have to consider now. Are you sure you can trust the people you're with?"

Drew looked painfully uncomfortable. "At times, Wiley, I feel like I can't trust anyone."

"Small wonder. I should join you, Drew. I want to see this through with you."

Drew did not respond.

"I want to be with you. If you tell me where you are, I'm sure I could get there without being followed. At least, I think I could...no, maybe I couldn't. I don't know..." There was silence. "How are you handling it, Drew, emotionally, I mean. It must be rough on you." Wiley's tone was very empathic. "Is it getting you down?"

"I'm not depressed, if that's what you mean. Just scared, uncertain. I can't go home. I miss Becka."

"Becka's not with you?" Wiley was clearly alarmed.

"She's OK. Wiley, this is very difficult. I know it's hard on you, but I'm feeling real confused right now. I've got to think, OK? I'll call you again. Soon."

"Wait," Wiley said apprehensively. "When? How?" Her mouth felt dry.

Drew looked at Rit. She covered the mouthpiece with her hand. "When can I call her again? She wants to know."

"Mandy will arrange it," Rit said. "Tell her that."

"Mandy will arrange another call, Wiley."

"I see," Wiley said.

Drew felt awful. She knew how Wiley must be feeling. "This is all pretty unreal, isn't it?" she said. "I mean, it's not dull." She tried to laugh.

Wiley picked up on it. "You should have seen the undull route we took getting to this phone booth," she said, "zigzagging through the city. I'm not even sure exactly where I am. Somewhere on the South Side. And this Mandy is quite a character." Wiley chuckled, obviously needing this change of pace. "Do you know her?"

"No."

"She showed up last Thursday, in the john in my office building, of all places. She gave me the letter from you and told me to meet her today. She's playing it real cloak and dagger. I had to follow an elaborate set of instructions, running here and there, to end up meeting her in the Marshall Field's ladies'room this morning. I'm beginning to wonder about her penchant for johns. She's not real communicative. The most I know is that she's connnected with whoever you're with."

"Yes, this whole thing is mind boggling. Just a few months ago life was so routine and now..."

"I know. I'm worried, Drew, very worried. I wish I could feel assured that whoever you're with is trustworthy."

"I had some trouble with that, myself," Drew said, catching Rit's eyes without smiling. "I wasn't completely convinced that there was any danger, any reason to leave town, but now, with the phone taps and that Brian McAllister business, I'm...now I trust her." She placed her hand on Rit's arm. "I have to," she added.

"Drew, I don't want to push you about this, but I want to be there too, wherever you are. We could do it together. Doesn't that make sense? You need support and..." Wiley stopped herself. "They might follow me, though, that's true. There is a risk, but..."

Drew felt the painful churning again. "It has to be this way, Wiley, at least for now."

"You will call, won't you, Drew?"

"I'll call."

"Whatever happens, I'm with you. Let me know what I can do. If you have to stay in hiding long, I want...I want to be there too." She paused. "You know what I'm saying, don't you?"

"Yes."

"Mandy gave me a way to signal her if I have to get in touch. Call soon, will you?"

"I'll call soon," Drew said. "Mandy will let you know."

"All right. You take care. I miss you."

"You too, Wiley. We'll get through this. 'Bye for now."

## 35

Mandy dropped her at the edge of the Loop and Wiley took a cab from there back to her office, all the while trying to convince herself that they *would* get through this. She had an 11:30 follow-up appointment with one of the subjects, Larry Silesky. He was a plumber, in his mid-forties, a pleasant man, Wiley thought, remembering her initial interview with him.

"Welcome back," she said after he was seated. "How have things been with you, Mr. Silesky?"

"Not dull, doctor." He looked worried.

Wiley was struck by the phrase he used.

"I don't know what to make of it. I hope you can shed some light 'cause I'm groping around in the dark here."

"What is it?" Wiley said with concern.

"Well, getting arrested turned out to be the least of it, though I never thought I'd say a thing like that." He folded his arms across his husky chest. "I've never been arrested before."

"You got arrested? What happened?"

"It was at the zoo, after closing hours. I got this idea..." He leaned forward in his chair, his arms now on his knees. "I'm sure of it...well, anyway, I climbed the fence. Snuck in. Nothin' to it, the zoo's a cracker box. I was with the giraffes, trying to have a conversation with them, when the keeper spots me. He thought I was nuts."

Silesky touched his temple with his thick index finger. "Called the cops. *They* thought I was nuts. They was gonna send me to Read Zone Center, you know, the mental place. Hey, I says, not me, man. So I said I didn't mean it. I told 'em I know giraffes ain't intelligent beings." He paused. "They are though," he said, looking sincerely at Wiley. "But I told 'em I went there on a dare, that my buddy dared me and that's why I did it. It's embarrassing. I ain't told my wife. She'd laugh, Lord, how she'd laugh."

It wasn't funny. Wiley had to work to prevent herself from laughing. How could this be, she thought. That zap should have been erased.

"Anyway, that's nothin' to what happened next."

"There's more?"

"You bet. And this is the part I hope you can clear up for me. That hypnosis stuff you did. Did that have anything to do with putting clothes on animals?"

Wiley's face muscles hardened angrily. That implantation was supposed to be removed, too. How could he be aware of it? Did Drew get sloppy? "What do you mean?" she asked.

"Well, I never made the connection until Fred mentioned it. You see, about a month ago, I was thinking. I was lookin' at the dog next door, you know, watching it squat in the yard. That ain't right, I thought. It should be wearing some kinda trousers or something. The more I thought about it, the more sure I got. Animals just shouldn't be going around naked like that."

Drew obviously didn't erase it, Wiley thought. Poor guy. What a ridiculous spot this puts him in. Despite her annoyance over the slip up, a smile was tickling at the edges of her mouth.

"For a while, I thought I was the only one who knows it, the only one who cares. I mean, everybody I talked to thought I was wacko. So, I put an ad in the paper. I got two answers. Two people called me. They agreed with me, felt just like I do. So we got together for a meeting. We had a great discussion. We're making plans to form a league. Animal Anti-Nudity League, A.A.N.L. We were gonna call it Anti-Nudity for Animals League, but that didn't work out so well with the initials. Anyway, Doc, we had this meeting and got to just talking and conversing about lotsa things. And, here's the weird part. All three of us—me, Jane, and Fred, we are all in your experiment. We've all been here to see you and we all went and got our pictures took. Hey, that's weird! I mean, some coincidence, no?"

Wiley's concern skyrocketed now. Maybe I made a mistake on the protocol, she thought. Her mind clicked rapidly as Silesky continued.

"Fred, he's pissed. He's sure you did it, did it with hypnosis. He thinks that's rotten, you know, to hypnotize someone and not tell 'em. I say, hey, Fred, man, you're in an experiment. A psychologist, for God's sake. You gotta expect stuff like that. Fred didn't see it my way. He said he was gonna get to the bottom of this. He said he was gonna do some investigating himself, that he was gonna notify the authorities. I ain't sure what he had in mind, but he didn't want me to talk about none of this."

*Fred*, Wiley thought frantically. Yes, there was a Fred. . . Fred Greeley, an accountant, obsessive-compulsive, very rigid, full of repressed anger.

"I told him I wouldn't say nothin', just to shut him up, you know, but I just figured I'd ask you about it, get right to the heart of it."

"I'm glad you did," Wiley said calmly. "When did you have your meeting?"

179

"With Fred and Jane? Let's see..." Silesky tapped his chin. "It was a while ago now...Oh, yes, I remember. It was the last day of September, September 30th."

A little over three weeks ago, Wiley thought, and Zayre called a few days after that. It fits. Fred Greeley must be the leak. He must have contacted Granser. "You and Fred and who's the other one?" Wiley asked.

"Jane Wunderlust or Wonderhead...something like that. Anyway, Jane something."

Jane Wondra. Wiley remembered her well. A waitress, good sense of humor, possibly alcoholic. I doubt that she'll cause any trouble. I wish Drew were here to remove these damn zaps, she thought. I've got to smooth this over somehow until Drew...I've got to reassure them. "Well," she said, "this is wonderful. You and the others have confirmed an important psychological hypothesis. It's very exciting."

"Oh yeah?"

"Yes. You see, certain very sensitive, very perceptive people are able, occasionally, through hypnosis, to tap an inner awareness that is blocked to most of us, to get in touch with other spheres of human consciousness." She nodded as she spoke and Silesky nodded with her, looking mystified. "From what you tell me, it sounds like you and Fred and Jane have retrieved some long-lost primitive superstitions, ancient memories buried deeply in the modern brain. It's quite astounding." Wiley was sitting behind her desk. She leaned her arms on it now. "Over the ages," she continued, "humankind has held many intriguing ideas about animals. It seems that you and the others have been able to experience some of these ideas, about giraffes and about clothing animals, with the same sense of reality as our ancestors probably did."

Silesky was listening with his eyes wide, his mouth slightly open.

"How fortunate that three of you, three such sensitive and perceptive people, turned up as subjects in my study. This is wonderful," Wiley said.

Silesky nodded modestly. "My wife always says I'm pretty perceptive. Uh, Dr. Cavenar, let me see if I understand this. you say it's like a superstition, like from caveman days or something...?"

Wiley nodded. "Yes, actually believing something as *they* believed it."

"But it's not true? Giraffes really aren't...?"

"It's a *true* superstition."

"Hm-m." Silesky frowned. "A superstition."

"It's probably not a good idea to tell people about it," Wiley said. "They wouldn't understand."

"Yeah, like the cops. If they hadn't stopped me, I think I could have gotten through to the giraffes. There's a language problem. Once we get past that, it will be fascinating, talking with them, learning about what they think, how they feel about being giraffes, living in the zoo and all. I'd like to talk to some wild ones, too. My wife don't believe it. Like you said, she doesn't understand. She thinks giraffes are just giraffes, you know, dumb and all. Well, she's a wonderful lady, Gert, but just, you know, not all that perceptive. She doesn't know much about caveman ideas hidden down there in the brain."

Wiley sighed. Although it was probably futile, she continued trying to dissuade him from acting on these ideas. She suggested he and his group do some reading about primitive superstitions related to animals before they proceed with their campaign, go to the library, research it. She also asked Silesky questions to assess the effects of the other implantations, those that had intentionally been left intact. He commented on Drew's unusual height and on his recent craving for turnips which he used to dislike. Apparently, there were no other errors in the protocol. Wiley was particularly interested in the effect of the zap which changed Silesky's views on abortion.

"I been reading about it," he said. "They're right on this, the libber women. Women *do* have to have the right to control their own bodies. So they can be more in the driver's seat of their own lives, you know. That makes damn good sense. Now, Gert, she's my wife, she disagrees with me. I mean, she understands my point, all right, but she says you can't go around killing babies for convenience." Silesky shook his head. "I used to think that way, too. In fact, I used to think if a girl went and got herself knocked up, then, shit, let her deal with the results. But the other day I sent ten bucks to a pro-choice group. You know, I been thinking about other stuff, too, I mean, libber stuff, and reading about it. They got this magazine called *Ms,* maybe you heard of it. I'm a plumber, doc, I make an OK living. My wife doesn't have to work. Fact is, I never wanted her to, but lately I been thinking. The kids are growing up, you know. Gert's gonna need something for herself. She used to always be looking in the help wanted ads and I'd get mad, but now I've been kinda suggesting it for her, you know, to get out of the house, experience a little more of the world. For her, for Gert. I used to think women had it made, but I've been doing some thinking and..."

As she listened, Wiley felt a chilling gratification. It is possible, she thought. We can change things. She felt angry anew at how her plans were being interfered with. Misdirected people getting in the way. How dare they. They have to be stopped. Wiley realized she wasn't listening to Larry Silesky and brought herself back. He was talking about animals again. How many others are walking around the city convinced that animals need clothes and giraffes need a higher education, she wondered. She couldn't help smiling as she thought about it. No, it's not funny, she told herself. Poor Silesky. She felt angry that they could have made a mistake like that.

After Silesky left, Wiley looked over the protocols. She found the error immediately; she had, indeed, neglected to include "intelligent giraffes" and "naked animals" on her removal list. Six subjects altogether were affected. And damn if one of them didn't have to be a Fred Greeley type. One little mistake that was ruining everything. She felt angry at herself for being careless and at Drew for not catching it.

At least I know now how Granser got onto us, Wiley thought. She had little doubt that her inference was correct, that Fred Greeley had contacted Granser, but she wanted to confirm it. She was feeling somewhat better, less powerless. Now that I'm beginning to understand what went wrong, maybe I can do something about it, Wiley thought. She'd talk with Greeley, she decided, and then find Granser and arrange for Drew to zap him. She checked her appointment book. Greeley was due in for his follow-up appointment next week. Wiley knew she had to talk with him sooner than that.

## 36.

After the phone call with Wiley, Drew and Rit took their seats again in the back of the van and Bo drove. Rit put away the shackle. "No need for this now," she said. "Sorry we had to use it."

Drew nodded. "I put you through quite a bit, didn't I?"

Rit didn't answer.

"Sorry," Drew said, feeling almost ashamed, thinking that perhaps she *was* naive.

"You did what made sense to you."

Drew thought of her own advice to Becka. "I thought you wanted to use my power."

"I know."

"It's hard to know who to trust," Drew said defensively.

Rit nodded.

"I didn't want to believe Granser was really dangerous." She was close to tears. "I just want to live my life," she said. Rit was silent. Drew sighed. Neither woman spoke for awhile. "That Brian McAllister ploy is pretty clever," Drew said breaking the silence. "I suppose people will tell my 'cousin' everything he wants to know."

"Yes, it's clever."

"And the phone tappings...damn." Drew shook her head. "They're not about to give me much choice, I guess."

Rit nodded.

"I suppose I should thank you."

"No need."

"You're putting yourself to an awful lot of trouble, Rit. I don't feel right about it."

"I take care of myself."

Drew smiled. "I'm sure you do," she said, "but...listen, whatever help you give me, I appreciate. I mean it, but it doesn't feel right to me. You have your law practice and...I'm sure you've got other things to do. Now that I know I have to hide, I can do it myself. You don't have to..."

Rit laughed. "Stifle yourself, McAllister."

"But I feel bad for you..."

"Don't." Rit opened a can of beer, took a slug and passed it to Drew. "Don't worry, you can't take advantage of me, Drew."

Drew accepted the beer. "I believe that," she said, placing her lips where Rit's had been.

"So, cut the guilt, huh? Think of it as an adventure that I'm choosing to share with you. I know what I'm doing."

An adventure. Again Drew thought of Becka. Does Rit think of me as a child? That bitch. She's so damn arrogant and...

"Enjoy our vacation! This is beautiful country, don't you think?" Drew looked out the window but Rit continued looking at Drew. "Very beautiful," she added.

They were near Oklahoma City and planning to camp in New Mexico when they reached the mountains. The time passed quickly as they moved westward. The atmosphere in the van was significantly different now. Drew let herself fully feel the excitement of being with Rit. The three women took shifts driving. They talked a lot and laughed. Drew discovered that Rit had a very appealing, though droll, sense of humor, and this brought out her own light-hearted side. They sang songs. Bo had a very smooth, lilting singing voice. She was a member of Chicago's lesbian chorus, and entertained Drew and Rit with song after song of womanstrength and union and love and fighting back and the dawning of Lesbian Nation.

Interspersed with the singing, Rit told stories. She had had countless adventures in her life and related them in ways that engaged Drew fully and left her wanting more. Most of them took place ten or fifteen years ago, but some were more recent. Every once in a while, Rit told her, since beginning her practice of law, she would take off for a while, leave her cases to colleagues and follow a whim or an interest somewhere. The last time, a little over a year ago, she met an African woman and went home with her, spending two months in Nairobi. The time before started with a legal case, a woman accused of murdering her husband. The woman was convicted, but Rit was convinced of her innocence and pursued it privately, playing detective rather than lawyer for a while. She went to California in pursuit of the man she believed was the real killer and, within a month, came back with him, complete with confession.

The more Drew learned of Rit, the more interested she became, and flattered. Drew watched her as she napped, feeling a powerful longing to stroke her smooth face, to stretch her own body out beside this strong and intriguing woman. She did not dare make the first move.

They stopped briefly on the outskirts of Albuquerque to make some phone calls. Becka was fine. She was learning how to make bread from flour with little dots in it and how the sun can heat a house. She missed her mom some, but only once was it bad enough to read the letter and then she felt a happy sadness. Rit's calls were less comforting. Her office informed her of a new development in her civil disobedience case and she decided she needed to handle it herself, in person. Bo and Drew dropped her at the Albuquerque airport where she caught a flight to Chicago, and they continued the trip west without her.

"There they are," Drew said. She'd been driving for the past hour.

Bo had been dozing in the rear of the van. "What?" she asked sleepily.

"The big rocks."

Bo sat up and peered out the windshield. "Indeed." She got out the map. "We should be in the national forest soon."

The campground at the Cibola National Forest was vast and quiet and beautiful. Tall trees surrounded the campsites and the mountains were visible from everywhere. They picked out a spot to hook up the van then went for a hike along the stream. After three-quarters of a mile, they came to a waterfall and sat on some rocks near its base staring at the water, listening to it, not talking much.

"Hey, Drew."

"Yeah?"

"I've been thinking."

"Mm-hm."

"About that zapping you do."

"What about it, Bo?"

"Well...have you ever just fooled around with it?"

"Fooled around?"

"Yeah, like, you know, zapped someone...zapped them to feel certain things...just for their own pleasure?"

Drew smiled. "That's an interesting thought," she said. "What do you have in mind, Bo?"

"Oh, nothing in particular. I was just wondering."

The two of them were quiet again.

"Now, take that waterfall, for instance," Bo said. "Look how the water bounces around and how it sparkles, and the little balls of foam and the swirling patterns. It's really beautiful, don't you think?"

"Yeah, it is."

"You can almost get high just looking at it."

"Yeah, it's really nice."

There was another long period of silence.

"I wonder what would happen if you zapped someone to feel high."

Drew smiled at her. "I wonder," she said.

"Or zapped them to feel a euphoric oneness with the universe."

Drew laughed. "It would probably be pretty pleasurable," she said.

"Yeah, I bet it would." Bo sat balanced on a smooth rock, arms around her knees. The tawny skin of her gaunt face was baby smooth, her eyes, large and round.

They watched the water some more.

"I've always wondered what that means," Bo said, "to be 'one with the universe'."

Drew leaned toward her companion. "Would you like to find out?" she asked, smiling.

Bo looked surprised. "Who me?"

They both laughed. Bo's laugh was larger than one might expect from looking at her, and it had a little edge of nervousness in it this time.

"Are you ready?" Drew asked.

Bo sat up very straight and stared into Drew's eyes. "Ready," she said. She looked as if she were about to parachute out of a plane.

"Listen carefully, then," Drew said, "I have some important things to say to you."

Bo's large eyes grew even larger.

"You are beginning to feel very relaxed, very mellow, but also very high. It's quite pleasurable. You are beginning to experience an ecstatic, transporting feeling, a sense of unity with the universe. It's very, very pleasurable, very enjoyable. You are sensing this, feeling it, and you will continue to feel it until you are ready to stop and then you'll feel as you normally do. After that, whenever you want to recapture the high, ecstatic feeling, you will be able to do so for as long or short a time as you desire."

Drew got very involved in this implantation, identifying with Bo, wishing she could zap herself this way.

Bo looked off into the distance. Slowly, she pulled herself up from the rock, standing, stretching out to her full five and a half feet. She spread her arms, lifting them gracefully toward the sky. Her eyelids were partially closed, a hint of a smile was on her lips. O-o-oh," she murmured. "Wow!" She swayed her head sensually back and forth. "Yes, oh yes." Slowly she lowered her hands to her flushed cheeks, gently cradling her face as she continued swaying her head, her eyes opening and closing slowly and rhythmically.

"Can you describe it?' Drew asked.

"I don't know," Bo crooned. "I don't know if...if words...It's warm," she said. "There's warmth, filling me. I am the sun, the tree, the air."

Her eyes were closed now. "The water is flowing through me. It *is* me. The water, me, caressing, caressing us, no limits, no boundaries. I am the light air, solid, heavy rock. Oh, wow." She was breathing quickly through her mouth. "Oh, yes." She sat again and began moving her body, her shoulders, arms, hips, feet, moved them snake-like, rhythmically. "Oh, God, it's . . .oh, it's wonderful." Her hands drifted across her breasts. "It's everything at once." She rolled her eyes. "Oh, it's so beautiful. The colors, the way things are...everything, everything. Look, that flower...it's pure beauty." Tears were coming from her eyes. "It's so perfect." She leaned over, resting her elbows on the rock and gently cupped the flower between her palms, barely touching it, lightly caressing the bright yellow petals. "Amazing," she said. "I love the flower, I feel its love, love flowing, everything together, it's all one, all, I know it, feel it. I've got it. It's here, Drew. Yes, oh, yes."

Drew felt slightly embarrassed, as if she had stumbled into the culmination of a bedroom scene. She tried to imagine what it was like, what Bo felt, how she was experiencing it. She felt envious. "You look very happy," she said.

"Oh, Drew, I can't tell you. It's more that that, oh yes, happy." She continued to sway, to touch things around her, a stone, a blade of grass, her own knee. "Oh, yes."

Bo kept exclaiming and exhalting over everything. She continued for another half hour and seemed to have no intention of stopping. Drew suggested they walk back to camp and Bo was quite agreeable, exclaiming at the trees they passed, the feel of the ground and leaves beneath her feet, the beauty of the chipmunks, the beetle she saw, the commonality she felt with them, her love of them and theirs of her.

They gathered wood for a fire and Bo kept on and on, revelling in every movement she made, every twig she touched, the specks of earth clinging to the branches, the beautiful patterns of the brown and crumpled leaves, the glory of dying and rebirth, replenishing the earth.

For a full five minutes she extolled the miracle of her hand, of each finger and how it moved, the skin that wrapped it and the little wrinkles and tiny pores and hairs.

It seemed she would never tire of this. Then she turned her attention to Drew and began lauding her for her beauty and all the wonderful qualities she had, the joy she felt in being alive and able to be with Drew and experience the miracle of another human being. It was at about this point that Drew decided another zap was in order, and so she brought Bo back, for clearly Bo was in no hurry to do so herself and Drew was beginning to feel lonely.

They spent the next hour discussing it. Bo said it was, by far, the most pleasurable, valuable, significant experience she'd ever had. Drew told her she'd erased her initial suggestion that Bo could bring on the experience again for herself whenever she wanted.

"It's better that way," Bo said. "I'd probably never stop otherwise. I don't think I could. Yes, it's better that you changed it, but

I'll want to go there again, Drew. Sometime, probably soon. I feel exhausted. God, it was intense." Her face was glowing. "Hey, thank you, magic lady," she said, hugging Drew and kissing her warmly on her cheek.

"What's amazing," Drew said, "is that you really did it yourself. I just told you you could and then you made it happen."

Bo sighed. She spread a blanket on the grass several yards from the van, laid down using her arms for a pillow, and was immediately asleep. Drew read for a while then napped herself. When they awoke, Bo was her usual self again, the experience of her oneness with the universe a very pleasant memory. They listened to the crickets and the birds and watched the sun setting beyond the mountains and built a fire. The fire made Drew think of Judith, but she would not let the thoughts stay.

"Too bad Rit has to miss this," Bo said, draping her hotdog over the flames.

After they ate, Bo brought out her guitar. Their singing attracted a group of women camped nearby who joined them, and soon the strains of the collective voices drifted over the campground masking the country and western music from nearby radios. The women were from Charlotte, North Carolina. They were moving to San Francisco.

"Great town," Bo said.

They smoked some dope and talked about the city where they'd all left their hearts. Everyone had stories to tell, except Jamie.

"Your friend, Jamie, is so quiet," Drew said to one of the women, Irene, a tall Chicana. They had gone to get some more wood. "Is she OK?"

"Oh, yes, she's OK," Irene replied. "She's always like that with new people. Shy." She shrugged her shoulders. "It's too bad, really, because when she loosens up, she's a riot."

Drew sat next to Jamie when they got back to the fire. Somebody started a song, and when it was loud enough to conceal her words from the others, Drew spoke to Jamie. She looked into Jamie's eyes and told her she had something important to say to her.

After that, Jamie kept them laughing, and, sometime near midnight when the group decided it was time to go back to their own camp, Jamie told Bo and Drew that this was the best time she'd had in ages and that she found them such comfortable people to be with.

## 37

Wiley phoned soon after Larry Silesky left her office, but Fred Greeley said he did not want to meet with her.

"No," he said, "I have nothing to say to you, Dr. Cavenar. I've withdrawn from the study. I will not pick up my portrait. I've done my duty and I'm finished with it."

"Did your duty?" Supercilious prig, Wiley thought.

"That's right."

"What is it you did?" She felt the pull of constricted muscles across her shoulders.

"You'll find out soon enough."

"You sound upset, Mr. Greeley. I wish you'd tell me what's bothering you."

"I'm on to you, doctor. You'll be hearing from the committee."

"The committee?"

"The Ethics Committee. I've reported you to the Illinois Psychological Association. You have no right to use hypnosis in that way. No one likes to be controlled by others. Now don't get me wrong, I appreciate the fact that I am now one of the few people aware of the immoral vulgarity of nudity among God's creatures. I'm glad I now see the light on that, but that does not mean that I condone the method by which I acquired this truth."

Wiley barely listened to his speech. The I.P.A. Ethics Committee, she thought, laughing to herself. They seemed so benign relative to the phone tapping and spying that had been going on. The Ethics Committee would hardly be involved in anything like that.

"I see. So you reported me to the I.P.A. Ethics Committee, reported that I hypnotized you to believe animals should be clothed."

"That's right, after I investigated you." Greeley was clearly enjoying this.

"Oh? What did your investigation involve?" Wiley asked. She rubbed the back of her neck.

"I contacted the Department of Registration and Certification. I determined that you are, indeed, licensed to practice as a psychologist. At least your credentials are in order, but I do not believe you behaved ethically with us, doctor. And I did what I had to do."

"Did you do anything else? Discuss it with anyone else besides Larry Silesky and Jane Wondra?"

"Anyone else? No, no need. What I did was sufficient."

"Yes, I suppose that's true. You seem like a man of action."

"That's correct, when action is called for."

"I still would like to talk this over with you in more detail, and to conduct the follow-up interview," Wiley said. "No hypnosis will be involved. If you change your mind, will you let me know?"

"I won't change my mind."

"It's unfortunate that you feel that way."

"That's the way I feel."

So Fred Greeley's not the leak, after all, Wiley thought when they hung up. Who then, she wondered. Who's the link to Granser?

Wiley had no appointments scheduled for the rest of the day except a lunch date with Andrea Smith. She and Andrea had never been particularly friendly although they'd known each other for years. Wiley was somewhat puzzled by the lunch invitation and not particularly looking forward to it. She certainly could not have anticipated that Andrea Smith would have any information related to what was going on with Drew.

They met at the Hungarian Club, a restaurant midway between their two offices. They ordered light lunches and engaged in light conversation until Andrea shifted gears.

"I wanted to talk with you about Drew McAllister," she said. Wiley's boredom left immediately. "Oh?"

"I know you and she have been tight for a long time. Until recently, I always thought Drew was het. Of course, I did have my suspicions about you two. Then when I saw her at the LLD Committee I figured she was finally coming out. Anyway, I'm concerned about her and that's why I wanted to talk with you."

Wiley felt apprehensive. "You're concerned about her? What do you mean?"

"Drew seems so innocent," Andrea said, tapping a cigarette on the table, "and I'm worried about what she might be getting herself into."

There was an air of high drama in the way she spoke. She twirled one of her blond curls around with her polished-nail fingers. "Since I know you two are very close, I thought I'd talk to you about it."

"About what, Andrea?"

"Do you know Rit Avery?"

Wiley shook her head. "No."

"Drew does. She told us at the meeting, the Lesbian Legal Defense meeting, told us that she could persuade Rit Avery to take a case, an important one, lesbian custody. Rit's an attorney. Drew seemed confident she could get Rit to change her mind about the case. Well, she didn't. Instead, I think Rit got her. Got her captivated. They were at Joann Lipski's party a couple weeks ago. They left together, then I heard they were together at The Found one night. I'm worried about Drew being involved with her. That Rit is a strange one. She can affect people in really weird ways. I'd hate to see her get Drew in her spell. I don't trust the woman." Andrea jiggled her head, dancing the curls. "When I met her, I had a lover. It was a real solid relationship but, even so, Rit just took over my feelings. I mean, I threw myself at her. I couldn't resist her."

"She must be something."

"She is. She's poison. We had a fling and then she dropped me. It ruined my relationship with my lover. I don't know what you and Drew have going, Wiley, but I just wanted to warn you that if Drew's getting mixed up with Rit Avery, it won't end well. Supposedly, Rit's a dynamite lawyer, but I'd bet anything she's unscrupulous. And she's egocentric as hell. Very dynamic, I must admit. Fascinating, but poison. I thought it might help, help Drew, if I talked to you about it."

Wiley felt disgusted with the gossipy, interfering nature of Andrea's communication. She changed the topic saying something about Drew being an adult, and got through the rest of their lunch on small talk. But she couldn't get it out of her mind.

In her office, she went round and round with it. Maybe a romantic involvement *had* developed betweeen Drew and this Rit Avery, she thought, feeling the stab of jealousy. Maybe Drew didn't tell me because she thought I'd be hurt, Wiley thought, feeling hurt. No, Drew's always told me about all her involvements.

Against her better judgment, almost without willing it, Wiley found herself looking through the phone book under the A's, finding the listing, and dialing.

"Rit Avery's office."

"May I speak to Ms. Avery, please?"

"She's not in. May I take a message?"

"When do you expect her?"

"She's out of town. I'm not precisely sure when she'll return. Would you like to leave a message and she'll get back to you when she does?"

"I didn't realize she was going out of town. When did she leave?"

"Who's calling, please?"

"This is Dr. Cavenar, Dr. Wiley Cavenar."

"She left last Thursday, doctor. At what number can she reach you?"

Last Thursday, Wiley thought. Coincidence? She gave her number. "Where has she gone? Maybe I can reach her there."

"I'm afraid that would be impossible. If you need an attorney, I can refer you..."

"No."

"Then I'll let her know you called."

Again Wiley used the phone book and again she dialed.

"First Federal Savings, may I help you?"

"Andrea Smith, please, Mortgage Department."

"One moment, please."

"Andrea Smith speaking."

"Andrea, this is Wiley. I've got a question for you."

"You want to know if I can get you a loan at five percent."

"No, I want to know if Rit Avery has a friend named Mandy."

"I hope our conversation didn't upset you, Wiley."

"Does she know a Mandy?"

"Yes, I believe she does. Mandy Coors. She works for Rit, a law clerk or legal assistant or whatever. Why?"

"I just wondered. Thanks, Andrea," Wiley said flatly, ending the conversation. Suddenly she felt tired.

Again she dialed.

"Hello."

"Marie, this is Wiley. Tell me something...this guy who talked to you, Brian McAllister, did he give you his phone number?"

"Yeah, why, what's happening?"

"He hasn't contacted me yet and I want to talk with him. What's the number, Marie?"

An hour later, Brian McAllister sat across from Wiley on the easy chair that her clients used. He was a large man with a bulging paunch, fat lips and an ill-fitting toupe. He certainly didn't look Irish to Wiley, although he spoke with a brogue. "I'm going to level with you right away, Mr. McAllister, or whatever your name is," Wiley began. "I don't believe you're Drew McAllister's cousin or that there's any inheritance for her." She watched for an effect on his face, but it remained unchanged. "I think someone hired you to ask around about her in order to make her think that she's being sought." Again Wiley paused and, again, the man across from her showed no reaction. "I'd like to know who hired you to seek Drew McAllister, and why."

Finally he reacted, a frown and then a smile. "What makes you doubt that I am who I say I am?" he asked.

"Many things," Wiley said.

192

"So many mysteries," he replied, leaning back and crossing his big legs. "Truth is so difficult to unearth." He grinned soupily.

"Yes, isn't it."

"And expensive."

"I'm willing to pay you for the information."

"My, my, you're obviously quite distraught about something, doctor. Exactly what is it you suspect?"

Wiley weighed this carefully before she replied. "I suspect you're working for an attorney here in Chicago and the reason has nothing to do with an inheritance."

The man's face registered no emotion. "Why?" he asked.

"It's not important that you know that."

"But I prefer to know."

Again Wiley paused, considering. "I think this attorney is taking advantage of Drew McAllister and using you to frighten Drew into allowing this."

"That's interesting. Taking advantage in what way?"

"*That* I can't divulge. Will you tell me who hired you?"

The man hesitated briefly, then replied. "That's the $2500 question."

"That's steep."

He shrugged.

"All right," Wiley said. "$2500, but you must convince me that what you say is the truth, the attorney's name for starters, and some information about the circumstances under which you got hired."

"I'm an investigator," the man began in a monotone. "I do some work for attorneys occasionally. Rit Avery is one of them. Last week she hired me to pose as Drew McAllister's cousin, gave me some data about McAllister's background and told me to ask around using the inheritance story."

Wiley's heart thumped. "Where is Avery now?"

"Not in Chicago. That's all I know. Word is she's closing up her practice here, not taking any more cases."

"When did you hear that?"

"When? A week or so ago. I guess she's got something better going for herself."

That bitch, Wiley thought. "Why did she want you to pose as Drew McAllister's cousin?"

"She didn't say, I'm afraid. I assume that whatever this is about, Miss McAllister is all right. I've grown rather fond of her through my investigation. She's not really visiting Disney World, you know. I am a bit worried about her. Is she all right?"

"I don't know," Wiley said.

"You do know where she is, I assume."

"Do *you* know?"

He shook his head.

"Who else is working on this with you?" Wiley asked.

The man smiled. "Who do you suspect?"

"You tell me."

"My partner's helping, and another private dick we hired."

"What are their names?"

"I can't reveal that..."

Wiley's eyes narrowed.

"...but I suppose I could tell you their cover names."

"Yes?"

"Abram Granser and Andrew Zayre."

Wiley felt pulsing rage toward Rit Avery. "What else can you tell me?"

"Your phones are being tapped."

"Why?"

He shook his head.

"What else do you know about this?"

"That's it." He wet the corners of his mouth. "I gave you the information we contracted for. I trust you'll keep your mouth shut about your source."

"I have no interest in you," Wiley said. She opened a drawer and removed a checkbook. "To whom should I make this out?"

"I'd prefer to remain anonymous," the man replied, smiling condescendingly, and I'd definitely prefer cash."

They went together to Wiley's bank. When she returned to her office, she took a rolled up poster from her drawer, taped it onto her window, drew the draperies and waited for Mandy Coors to respond to the signal.

## 38.

Rit sank the last of the stripeds in the middle pocket. She didn't particularly like pool but people frequently challenged her to play because she was good and because she didn't flaunt it. She squinted, lining up white against black, fired, and the game was over.

"Hey, Rit!" The woman approaching smiled with pleasure. "I didn't expect to see you here. Let me buy you a drink and have a deep and meaningful conversation with you." The woman was short, slightly overweight, and clearly very energetic. "I thought you were away on another vacation."

"I am," Rit said. "The lawyer part of me flew back for a meeting tomorrow, then I disappear." They found seats at the end of a long table. "So how are things in academe, Ellie?"

"Not bad, not bad at all. The research is going well and I'm teaching a new graduate seminar this semester, *Social Impact of Bureaucracy*. I've got some very bright students. I expect to learn a lot."

After an hour of drinking and talking with Eleanor Clark and several other friends, the discussion began evolving into an argument. Eleanor was slightly drunk and growing increasingly frustrated that she could not convince Rit of the validity of her position.

"The systems we've created now run *us*," she said vehemently. "They're out of our control. It's become so complex that none of us—no individual, no group, can even comprehend the whole picture, much less significantly affect it. We cannot control it and it's accelerating geometrically."

It wasn't that Rit disagreed with Eleanor's thesis; she simply was not particularly upset about it, but she challenged Eleanor on several points because the game was interesting to her.

Eleanor shook her head. "We're at an impasse, Rit Avery, my friend. You're too stubborn to see the truth." She smiled and stared intently at Rit. "Listen to me," she said, "listen carefully." Her voice became low and slow and almost hypnotic. "Zap! You believe I am right; you know what I'm saying is the truth. You're totally convinced." She laughed and took a long drink.

Rit did not laugh. In fact, Rit looked as if she'd been struck. "Eleanor, let's get out of here. There's something I have to talk with you about."

"Oh, oh, watch out," Clair said laughingly to Eleanor as she and Rit left the bar.

They went to a coffee shop up the street.

"What was that 'Zap, you believe me' business?" Rit asked pointedly as soon as they were seated. "Where'd you get that idea?"

Eleanor's eyes gleamed. "Now, wouldn't it be something, Rit, if I could actually do it, if I could implant into your meager little mind my more enlightened, profound ideas."

"It would be something all right. Where'd you get the idea?" Eleanor looked at her quizzically. "What are you getting at?" "You tell me."

"Why, have you heard something about it?"

"Something. How about you?"

"You've been talking with Wiley Cavenar."

"She told you about it?" Rit asked, raising her thick eyebrows.

"I was part of the 'pilot study'."

Rit frowned "Oh, yeah? Tell me more."

Eleanor's round faced crinkled with her laughter. "Well, how much do you know?" she asked. She placed her hand on her chest. "I'm sworn to secrecy. That's part of the study, that we don't discuss it yet. I suppose I shouldn't ask you what you know about it, but I am curious."

"What I know about what?"

"About Paz. About zapping the world into a utopian state. It's an intriguing fantasy. I've been giving a lot of thought to it since Wiley's party. You know what struck me?"

"What?"

"The way Wiley talked about it. Supposedly she's working on some kind of a study, possibly on group consensus or group leadership dynamics or maybe creative thinking processes. Those were my guesses, but from the way she acted, it was almost like she really believed it."

"Believed there was someone who could zap people?"

"Yes." They ordered their coffee. Eleanor ordered a slice of lemon cream pie as well. "I don't know Wiley very well. I was on a committee with her a few years ago. That's where I met her. And I've seen her around socially, but it seemed like she was obsessed with the idea of really figuring out the best way to use Paz's power, as if it were really true and that she, somehow, would be in charge of it." Eleanor raised up her hands. "The Grand Emperor of the new world," she said, laughing. She poured more cream into her coffee. "'Paz is the key', Wiley told us, 'and our job is to find the right locks to insert it in'. What do you think? Is Wiley losing it?"

"So you had a meeting. She told you to figure out how to use Paz's power, that it was a psychological study."

"Yes, an exercise, she called it." Eleanor looked very serious now. "I've seen it happen to other people like her, social activists, idealists. They get so frustrated with not being able to make the changes they want that they start to flip out, become delusional even, look for magical ways to achieve their goals. Now, I'm not saying that's what happened to Wiley. It's just that there was something odd about her...I don't know..."

"And you weren't supposed to discuss it with anyone?"

"Well, *you* don't count since obviously you already know about it. Are you involved in the study, too, or what?"

"Not exactly. Tell me more about the meeting?"

"It wasn't really a meeting. It was a little party. At least that's what Wiley told us when she invited us. It started out with five guests and ended with four. Alexandra Prell left."

"What happened? Exactly. I'd like to hear the whole story."

"All right, sure." Eleanor winked. "Actually, I've been dying to tell someone. Let's see, it was a week or so ago. We were all at Wiley's house and we'd been talking and drinking and eating for a while and then Wiley asked us if we'd be willing to take part in what she called 'an interesting exercise'. There was some quipping, Sandra said something about a six-way." Eleanor laughed. "Wiley took us into the dining room..."

"I'm going to ask that you suspend disbelief for a while and let yourselves really get into this," Wiley began. "I think you'll enjoy it."

She was sitting at the head of the antique dining room table, on an old captain's chair; two women sat on either side of her and one across. Wiley knew all five of the women personally, though only two, Luann and Sandra, did she consider friends. She had chosen the list carefully; they were all bright, articulate, educated women. *For snacks and conversation,* she had said when she invited them.

"I'm going to present you with a situation," Wiley continued, "and I want you to accept what I present as factual and then have a discussion about how you'd handle it." She smiled. "Are you willing?"

"Oh, sure, why not?" Greta Weitz said. Greta was the "hard" scientist of the group, a physicist. She liked a good time, and for her the best good times were those that were intellectually stimulating.

"Is this a parlor game or what?" Eleanor asked.

"An *or what,*" Wiley said. "It's kind of an experiment, but a game, too."

"All right, so, what's the situation?"

Wiley looked around the table. Her dark eyes were very bright. "I've recently made a phenomenal discovery," she said in a low serious voice, "something incredible, but which is, nonetheless,

197

quite true. This discovery has the potential of deeply affecting our lives, everyone's lives, of helping us achieve our goals as feminists, of radically altering the social structure of the world."

"M-m, this sounds like fun," someone interjected.

"Sounds heavy to me."

"Sounds like a pipe dream," Eleanor said, laughing.

"You five are my consultants. No one else is aware of my discovery."

Wiley crossed her hands on the table in front of her. "Before I go on, though," she said, "I'd like you to agree not to discuss the exercise outside this group."

There was some shuffling and frowns. "I'm a little confused. Are we supposed to believe that you actually made this 'phenomenal discovery' or is that part of the exercise?" The speaker was Alexandra Prell. She was fifty-five years old, sat ballet dancer upright, and was the only one drinking tea. She was an historian, and the coordinator of the National Women's History Project.

"For the exercise," Wiley said, "I'd like you to accept the discovery as actual."

"But it isn't," Luann Brown stated. "Right?"

"It's an exercise," Wiley said.

"You're being very mysterious, Wiley." Luann laughed. "I have no problem keeping my mouth shut, though. Sure, I'll agree not to talk about your mystery exercise to anyone. Let's get on with it." Luann was an old friend of Wiley's, a tall, robust woman with a voice that filled the whole room. She was a long-term political activist and a financial wizard. Recently, she had helped found the Lesbian Political Action Committee, and she was also engaged in the development of women's banking networks.

The others around the table nodded their agreement.

Wiley took a deep breath. This moment was a very exciting one for her, though she was trying not to show it. She leaned forward on the table.

"I'm sure all of you," she began, looking at each woman in turn, "has dreamed of a world far different from this one; a world without patriarchy, life free of sexism and racism and all the other forms of oppression. I've had many dreams like that, but I always thought they would essentially remain dreams in my lifetime. Now, I've discovered a way to actually make them happen, and much more."

She paused for a breath. Her mouth felt slightly dry.

"The key is a woman whom I shall call Paz, a woman with a

very special gift. Paz is the key. In this exercise, I want you to find the right locks in which to insert this key."

Wiley's excitement increased as she spoke.

"Several months ago," she continued, "this woman, Paz, experienced a brain trauma. She has not been the same since nor have I..."

Wiley spoke for twenty minutes, uninterrupted. She built the story layer by layer, describing the actual feats Drew had performed, her own investigation of the power and her speculations about how the implanted ideas affect the recipient's belief system. "We are a committee with the task of deciding how to utilize Paz's power," Wiley concluded.

"All right!" Eleanor Clark said. "It's an interesting premise. I'm willing to discuss it. This is a research project, isn't it?" Eleanor Clark was a sociologist, a teacher, a researcher and an outspoken social critic.

"I want to hear your ideas," Wiley answered. "Imagine that everything I said is true."

"I generally find science fiction and fantasy boring," Alexandra Prell said, "but I suppose we might have some fun with this. I won't be a wet blanket. I'd like to hear more about the purpose of your study, though, and I wish you'd told us this is what you wanted to do tonight. I'm feeling a little used."

"It's not a formal study at this point," Wiley responded trying not to be defensive. "I'm just toying with the idea of it. You might consider yourselves my pilot group." She laughed nervously. "I didn't think it was important to tell you the entertainment I had planned. If you don't feel like doing it, that's OK. I just thought we'd all enjoy it."

"Sure. It's a hell of a lot better than charades," Sandra Raye said. She looked at Alexandra teasingly. "Quit giving Wiley a hard time."

Wiley appreciated Sandra's intervention. "So why don't you just start," she said. "Discuss how you would recommend proceeding, how to tap Paz's power."

"The potential for social change is mind-boggling," Greta Weitz said. She was the chair of the Chicago Committee of Scientists for Nuclear Freeze.

"The end of patriarchy," Luann added.

"Of poverty."

"Even injustice eventually."

"Utopia," Luann said. "I've always held that the potential to create a utopia exists. If enough people want it, if their ideas, and values, and goals support it, then they could make it happen. We can imagine it and we could create it. It all depends on what's in people's minds."

"And our friend, Paz, can control people's minds."

"Oh, one more thing," Wiley interjected, "when Paz discovered that she had this power, she found it pretty overwhelming. She's still in the process of adjusting to it and doesn't feel like jumping right in and using it to make major changes in the world. That's another variable I want you to consider."

"So, we must sway her to our side somehow. Maybe that's the first problem we should tackle then, how to get Paz to be the 'key' to utopia."

"I imagine that if someone really had such a power, she might not choose to use it to change the world. She might be satisfied just using it for herself."

"Yes," Wiley said, "but we can't allow that. She has a moral *obligation* to use her gift for social change, don't you think? We must convince her of this."

"Are *you* going to participate in the discussion?" Eleanor Clark asked.

Wiley looked offended. "Yes, from time to time," she said.

Eleanor shrugged.

"I don't think anyone has the *obligation* to use their talents for the benefit of other people," Sandra Raye said, "though, hopefully most people would want to." Sandra was a professor at Northwestern University and an authority on international politics.

"So our first task would be to convince Paz to allow us to use her as our instrument."

"That's an unfair way to put it," Wiley snapped angrily, then she quickly calmed herself. "Paz would participate fully, as I see it, not be a robot for us or a martyr. Her needs would have to be considered."

"They'd have to take priority," Sandra said.

"They'd have to be *considered*," Wiley said, "but I don't think you can deny that such a gift creates a moral obligation for her to use it for the general good." Wiley appeared to be uncomfortable. "She would have to come to realize that..."

"It would be wrong for Paz to use her power at all," Alexandra Prell said definitively, "regardless of her willingness."

All eyes turned toward her.

"I agree that there definitely *is* an ethical issue involved here," Eleanor Clark said, "but that's not the point. Wiley's asked us to speculate on how such a power might be used rather than whether it's ethical or not to use it."

"The ethical issue must come first," Alexandra said, sitting up even straighter. "If we're to accept as true that there is a Paz who has these powers and is willing to use them, then we must address the ethics of the matter. Mind control is not something to play with. Our focus first should be on whether or not the power should be used, rather than on what ways it could be used."

"Would it be unethical to zap a habitual criminal to change his ways?" Greta Weitz asked.

"Yes," Alexandra said.

"You're not serious. Are you implying he has a right to be a criminal and zapping him to stop would be an infringement of his rights?"

"In a sense, yes. Remember *Clockwork Orange*. We have the right to choose, and the obligation to bear the consequences of our choices. Controlling another person's thoughts in the way Wiley has described removes from that person the freedom of choice."

"Following that argument," Eleanor said, "the only ethical use would be with the consent of the recipient."

"That's right, fully informed consent," Alexandra said.

"That certainly would limit its application."

Wiley felt irritated and uncomfortable. She didn't want to hear this. "What about what you said earlier," she asked, "eliminating injustice, poverty, all of that, creating a utopia?"

"A community of robots," Alexandra hissed, "is no utopia."

"You're distorting it, Alexandra," Sandra Raye said. "As I see it, the task we have in this exercise is to figure out productive, *ethical*, humanistic ways of using the power."

"If it's to be ethical, then we're back to the limitations—the necessity of informed consent."

"Do you think we could ever get the world's leaders to *consent* to giving up war and other forms of force to get what they want, or convince them to voluntarily change what they want? Will they voluntarily agree to be zapped to renounce greed and power? Is anyone who has power over others going to voluntarily give it up?"

"Unlikely."

"So then Paz's power would be reduced to...it would no longer be power at all if consent were required."

"Not power *over* others," Alexandra said.

"For that principal you'd sacrifice all the good that could come of it?"

"Yes, without such a principle, you'd just be creating another form of oppression."

Sandra shook her head. "Would you be willing to suspend, Alexandra, for the sake of discussion, the rightness or wrongness of using the power?"

"No I would not, but I won't interfere with the rest of you."

Alexandra stood.

"You're leaving?"

"No offense. I simply wouldn't enjoy further discussion and I would have nothing to add. May I have my coat, please, Wiley."

There was a pall over the group for several minutes after Alexandra Prell left.

"I think she's wrong," Luann said. "To consider freedom of choice as an absolute is to live in the proverbial ivory tower. How much choice does a kid born in the ghetto have, or someone coming out of a crazy family, or any victim of another's perverted thinking or cruelty or violence? We're talking of speculating about an opportunity to stop all that. Should we be stymied by some high blown moral absolute?"

"I'm willing to go on with the discussion," Eleanor Clark said. "Maybe beginning with setting the criteria for what sorts of zaps can be given to whom."

It was moving again. Wiley sat back, relieved, and listened intently. She made few comments herself, preferring to hear what the others had to say, now that they were going strong. They talked of the need for goals around which to build steps, the zapping order, when to implant what in whom. The women began to give full rein to their thoughts. Sandra threw forth idea after idea, building one atop the next, as if she had worked for years conceiving such a plan. The others contributed their perspectives. Disagreements arose on specifics, but not regarding the general goals, creating a world free of hunger, war, violence, abuse and every other social evil that has plagued humankind since its beginnings. The discussion went for three hours, until Wiley finally brought it to a close.

"This was wonderful," she said. "I, for one, had a very good time. I hope you all did, too. What a powerhouse of ideas in this room." She smiled broadly.

Her guests began to stretch. Greta started to excuse herself.

"Let me ask you one more thing," Wiley said quickly. "Still assuming that there is a Paz, would you want to be involved in implementing what you talked about? Be a part of the planning? How about you, Greta?"

Greta had pushed her chair back from the table. She stood. "If there were a Paz," she said, "you're damn right I'd want to be involved." She picked up her purse. "In fact, I'd feel I had no choice

202

but to dedicate myself to the task. And furthermore, I would propose that this group, as well as other members we might include, be the Board of Directors of...what the hell, The Board of Directors of the *New World*."

There was self-conscious laughter.

"How could anyone refuse such an opportunity," Luann said. "I'd want to be part of it." She laughed. "Too bad it's just an exercise."

"Yes, too bad it's just an exercise," Eleanor repeated, looking closely at Wiley.

Wiley was tremendously gratified with how the discussion had gone. It was even more valuable than she had hoped and, with the exception of Alexandra Prell, she was very pleased with her choice of participants. We'll need to get ahold of Alexandra, she thought. Soon. Perhaps Drew and I will drop in on her tomorrow.

"She told us she'd contact us soon," Eleanor concluded, "to debrief us about the experiment. I'm curious about it. Like I said, there was something odd about Wiley that night. Something's going on with her."

"Yes," Rit said, "I believe you're right." She was looking out the coffee shop window. "Wiley definitely does seem to have a problem."

---

## 39.

They were en route to the Flagstaff Airport to pick up Rit when they got lost. Bo was studying the map, trying to get them found while Drew drove randomly on unheard of streets. Suddenly, a big red Buick tore out of an alley across their path. Drew slammed on the brakes. Bo's hands shot forward to cushion the impact, but she only succeeded in mashing her fingers against the windshield as well as her head. Drew's seatbelt held her. Just as they skidded to a stop, a police car flew from the alley catching the right front fender of the van and spinning them.

"Are you OK, Bo?"

The police did not stop.

"Pigs," Bo said, feeling her head gingerly with sore fingers.

"It's beginning to swell."

Down the next alley, the police had cornered the Buick and had the occupants spread eagle, leaning over the trunk.

"We should get you to a hospital," Drew said.

"No, that's not...God, look at that. The cops are punching up those kids."

Drew started the van and drove slowly up the alley. One of the officers, a dark, stocky man, maybe thirty years old, was looking through the aging Buick when Drew and Bo approached; the other was searching the handcuffed prisoners.

"Cocksucker," one of the youths mumbled. "Uhh." He caught it in the groin.

"Slimey spic," the cop hissed, shoving the kid against the squadrol and whacking him again. "I told you to keep your fuckin' mouth shut."

"Excuse me, officer," Drew said.

The cop pushed the three youths into the back of the police car then turned to face Drew. "Whadda you want, lady?" He looked at her as if she were a gnat.

"Listen to me, this is very important."

Bo stood to the side.

"You realize that you don't have to brutalize the people you deal with. You want to be courteous and considerate and fair to them."

The officer didn't move for several seconds, then he spoke. "Was it your van we hit?"

"Yes."

"I'm sorry that happened. We do all we can to avoid incidents like that. Of course, you'll be reimbursed for the damage. We'll need to fill out some forms."

The stocky officer joined them, carrying a cellophane bag. "Our taco friends are naughty boys," he said, grinning, swinging the bag of grass.

Drew hesitated, looking from the scared kids squashed in the back seat to the smug-looking cops. "Can I talk with you a moment, officer," she said to the stocky one.

"Hey lady, can't you see we're busy. Move back, I'll be with you in a minute."

She smiled sweetly. "It will just take a second," and beckoned him to the side.

He went to her.

"Listen carefully," Drew said.

His expression changed from the leer to intense concentration.

"You know there's no need to make anything out of finding the marijuana. You can just forget that you found it. You want to put it back in their car and forget about it."

Drew went to the other officer then and, after listening to her, he, too, forgot about the grass. He spoke to the young men telling them he would have to take them to the station for trying to evade police officers. "When we tell you to pull over," he said, "you'd be a lot better off doing just that and not making it worse for yourselves." There was no hostility in his voice. "Do you know what I mean?" he added, almost kindly.

One of the young men nodded. "I was afraid to get a ticket," he said. "It's my father's car and he would be crazy with anger."

"Yeah, well, I can understand that, but you know, you did make an illegal turn, so that's the risk you take. Have you had any other moving violations?"

"No, sir, never."

The kid was probably barely sixteen. He was clearly frightened, no longer playing tough.

"OK, come out of there, all of you," the officer said. He removed their cuffs. "Let me see your license, son."

"What's going on?" the other cop asked.

"I'm going to give him a citation for the turn and let 'em go."

"Hey, gettin' soft, Burns?"

Drew was checking with Bo again about her injuries. "I'm fine," Bo insisted, "but the fender's definitely looked better. Let's get out of here. Rit's probably already arrived."

Before they left, Officer Burns very courteously explained how they should file the report and gave them directions to the airport. He apologized again for the collision and pleasantly said goodbye. The stocky cop kept staring at him in disbelief.

They had no trouble finding the airport and Rit was waiting outside with her bag when they arrived. She drove the two and a half hours from Flagstaff to her A-frame in the hills, the last forty minutes on a two lane county road, then a narrower, dirt one.

The house was airy and rustic and much larger than Drew had expected. Drew insisted on making their dinner saying she had a way with steaks. She liked the idea of doing something that would bring Rit pleasure.

After eating the huge meal, the trio relaxed with drinks on the balcony and watched the sun set, slowly, redly, behind the trees and mountain tops. The balcony was, in fact, a large, furnished, outdoor room. The air was mostly still, just a bare ripple over the plants every so often. On the large lounge chair, nearly as big as a double bed, Rit and Bo stretched out together. Rit caressed Bo's injured fingers soothingly.

"I don't like to think of your body being vulnerable," she said. "How's your head now?" She felt the bump tenderly for maybe the tenth time and kissed it softly.

"It's fine, Rit. I've got a thick skull."

"Even thick skulls aren't invulnerable," Rit said, looking at Drew. "Do you know what happened to our little girlfriend, there?"

"What?"

"A skinny little piece of mirror blew right into her skinny little brain. That's why she's so weird."

Bo hadn't heard the story and Drew was not unwilling to tell it. The hardest part was the memories of Judith. Someday maybe I'll be able to think of Judith without the pain, Drew thought. "The doctors kept looking for changes in me, from the brain damage. They have some strange ways of testing for it. I had to say 'puh-tah-kuh, puh-tah-kuh' over and over as fast as I could and 'methodist episcopal' and go like this." Drew held her hand up and rapidly brought her thumb and middle finger together, over and over. "You try it, Bo."

Bo sat up and alternated "puh-tah-kuh, puh-tah-kuh" and "methodist episcopal" and "roman catholic" and "orthodox jew" and "zen buddhist" as she slapped her finger against her thumb. "Oh," she said, "I must have brain damage, this is killing my fingers."

"You know, you two aren't as elite as you may think," Rit said. She stretched her long muscular body out on the lounge chair and yawned. "I had a head injury myself."

"Really?" Drew was ready for another story.

"Fifteen years ago this month."

"So, what happened?"

"I took nearly 100 volts through the brain." ·

"That's shocking," Bo said.

"Yeah, it was. Unplannned shock therapy. It cured me."

"Of what?"

"Playing with electricity. It was a very bizarre accident in a physics lab at the University of Chicago. A friend of mine worked there; she was one of those weird scientist types. I used to hang around while she'd play with her electrodes and other toys."

Rit told the story in vivid detail, though her awareness of how it actually happened was fuzzy. "There was sort of a buzz-hiss sound, then the smell of something burning. It scared the shit out of Susie. I was unconscious for a while and, of course, she thought I was dead."

"And?" Drew said. She'd been on the edge of her seat through the whole story.

"I wasn't dead." Rit was quiet for a moment. "That was it. In the meantime, my friend, Susan Baines Forsythe, has become so esoteric she can only communicate with a tiny group of other specialized eggheads. I still see her once in a while. She's still at the U. of C. I hear it can be hard to leave that place. Hey, I need some popcorn. Any volunteers?"

Drew wanted to make popcorn for Rit. She had a strong, sometimes disconcerting, wish to do anything that would please Rit, that would bring that little smile to her full, soft lips. But before she could respond, Rit had already jumped up.

"All right, then I'll do it myself," said Rit. "Drink refills anyone?"

Both women watched Rit leave. "You kind of like her, don't you?" Bo said.

Drew was not sure what to make of the comment. "Have you known her long, Bo?"

"All my life."

"What do you mean? Not literally."

"Literally. We're cousins."

"You are?" Drew was beaming. "I didn't know that." She was still smiling. "I thought you two might be..."

"We're that too, sometimes."

"What?"

"What you thought we might be."

Drew giggled. "And what did I think you might be?"

"Lovers."

Drew looked almost shocked. "A game the whole family can play, huh?"

"Don't be crude, Drew. We don't worry about inbreeding."

Drew laughed. "You must have quite a family."

"We do. Rit's the brightest and we're all brilliant. Some of them are odd."

"But not you?"

"No, but I'm the only one who's experienced unity with the universe."

"It's been quite a trip," Drew said.

"Yeah, it sure has. I'm glad you're feeling better about being with us, Drew." Bo was sitting cross-legged on the lounge chair. "It was pretty bad for you at first, wasn't it? Believing we were kidnapping you and all. What did you think of us?"

Drew laughed. "I thought Rit was an arrogant, presumptuous,

power - hungry egoist, and you her similarly-inclined right-hand woman."

Bo smiled. "And now?"

"The same."

Bo laughed. "Really?"

"Yeah, basically," Drew said nonchalantly. "Well, I've modified the power-hungry part some. I don't think Rit's so impressed by my power that she wants to use it, or make me use it for her. That's changed. But I still believe she likes power, mostly her own."

Bo laughed again. "I know what you mean."

"I don't know if I'll ever be able to forgive her for..." Drew's eyes narrowed. "...for one thing she did."

"The shackles? Chaining you?"

"No." Drew chuckled. "Actually, that amuses me for some reason. What nerve!"

"What then?"

"She threatened to harm Becka before we left Chicago. She implied that something would happen to Becka if I didn't de-zap Randy."

"She wouldn't have followed through."

"I know, but it was an awful thing to do."

"It was."

"I guess she felt she had to," Drew said.

Bo nodded. "Well, it won't be long now before you and Becka are together again."

"I really miss the little twerp. It feels strange without her. The same thing happens every time we're separated."

"What did she have to say on the phone tonight? Is she excited about coming?"

Drew reached for her cigarettes. The pack was empty. "She is, but I think there was a little note of disappointment, too. Just a little. I may have to get her a farm."

Bo laughed. "She'll be arriving day after tomorrow, right?"

"Right. She'll love it here."

"Too bad we can't stay for long," Bo said. "Mandy tells me the I.D.'s and passports are almost ready. When they are, someone will bring them here."

Drew nodded. "I'm getting used to the idea of going. You don't want to go with us, huh? to France?"

"I can't. I'd love to, though. I've been there. Rit's place is beautiful, her 'chateau'. No, my partners think I already spend too much time away from the job. We're in the middle of renovating a three flat now. Like I told you, I'm the dry wall pro and they're getting impatient. They also need me for the wiring.''

"Back in a sec'." Drew went inside and returned with a pack of cigarettes. "How did you learn all that stuff, carpentry and all that?"

"Not from my father," Bo said. "That's for sure, though he could do it all. He taught my brothers. One's a school teacher now. The other writes poems, smokes dope and collects unemployment. They both hate working with their hands. I smell popcorn."

Rit brought the heaping bowl and drinks and they crunched and watched the stars, almost as many as in Greece, Drew thought, and enjoyed the warm night.

The phone interrupted them. When Rit returned she told them Mandy was envious of their sojourn in the mountains. "She informed me there are no mountains in Chicago."

"Observant girl."

"She also said that Wiley wants to talk with you, Drew. She'll be calling tomorrow morning." Rit looked away.

"Good," Drew said. "I'm missing her. I bet this is worse on her than it is on me. She's always kind of watched over me." Drew sighed. "However all this turns out, I can't ever lose touch with her. She'd probably like France. She speaks French, you know. I love the sounds."

Rit said nothing.

"Well, I'm wiped," Bo said after a while. "I'm going to crawl into bed with my woman, *Woman on the Edge of Time*. I'm reading it again. I'll see you two mañana."

Drew did not pretend she wasn't glad Bo had left. Bo was one of the pleasantest people she'd ever met, and still she was very delighted when Bo said goodnight and disappeared within the house. She didn't look at Rit but felt Rit's eyes on her and felt the goosebumps tingling across her shoulders and down her arms.

"Come on over here, woman."

Somehow Drew managed not to knock anything over in her rush to get from her chair to the roomy lounge on which Rit lay.

"Do you like it here?" Rit asked.

"It's a wonderful place."

Rit smiled. "Very wonderful." She stroked Drew's arm, then lay back looking upward, out into the sky. They were silent for a long time.

"What are you thinking?" Drew asked.

"About how fortunate I am."

Another few seconds passed. Drew was waiting for Rit to elaborate; Rit was toying with the possibility of doing so.

"I'm fortunate to find people who give me so much pleasure."
Rit turned and looked at Drew. "Take you, for instance. It gives
me a great deal of pleasure to look into those big, green, fabulous
eyes of yours. I don't know why. Who cares? It pleases me the way
you are." She chuckled. "Your struggle was wonderful. I loved
your escapes."

Drew tightened and was about to speak.

"Now, don't get me wrong," Rit said rapidly. "I'm not making
fun of you, and I'm not *patronizing* you. I'm very sincere about
this. When I find someone interesting, I observe them very closely. Sometimes I miss something, sometimes there are surprises.
I love that. I love the way you're falling in love with me and how
you've been fighting it."

Again Drew began to respond, but Rit went on, continuing to
touch Drew up and down along her arm as she spoke.

"I enjoy the person you are and what's happening to you.
Sometimes it's almost as if I can see the wheels in your head spin,
and then you do something...and, oh...I don't know, I'm just lucky."
She chuckled again. "That shy boldness. The doubting and then
the assertive bursts. The solid core of decency. Your relationship
with Becka. People can be wonderful. Look at you *now*, for example. You're torn. You love what I'm saying, but you're embarrassed and trying to figure me out at the same time. You're excited to be alone with me like this, but a little frightened, I believe.
Could that be?"

Drew squirmed. "Sometimes I think you know too much."

"There's always more. Always surprises." She pressed her lips
over Drew's, enfolding them deeply into her own. The heat from
their mouths worked its way down into Drew's body, filling every
part, tingling nerves and making her woozy.

Rit slid her hand down Drew's face to her neck, unbuttoning her,
then to her breast. Over the inviting topography of Drew's body,
Rit explored, generating wave after wave of radiating pleasure
in both of them.

It wasn't like with David, hard muscles contracting tightly all
around her, taking his with her, through her. It wasn't like with
any man. It wasn't like with Judith, slow, tentative, tenderly
enveloping. Rit took Drew where she'd never been. Rit's mouth
and hands set off long silent synapses, now charged and pulsating.
She knew Drew's body as her own and responded knowingly to
every twitch she created in her. Drew's senses took over, her
cerebrum becoming dormant except to register and magnify feelings generated by each caress, feverish, then soft, tender,

demanding.

When Rit's mouth took Drew's nipple in and sucked it powerfully, the sensation reached downward through the dark passages of her insides, going everywhere. Rit brought her to the edge of pain, close enough to make Drew moan in ecstasy and cling and pull and push herself against Rit's sure and powerful body. Slowly, Rit brought a hand downward. It paused to slip Drew's pants away, then went on, over the curve of her hip and glided toward the center, stroking gently, skimming the hairs there.

Drew's body arched, seeking. Rit withdrew herself, just a bit, a fraction of an inch, making Drew come for her. She slipped a finger over the creamy slit and held it there as Drew held her breath, then vibrated it, slightly at first, just enough to bring from Drew a gasp and another grasping of her. Granting Drew's hungry wish, Rit slid fingers inside and part way out and in again, her own body moving with Drew's until Drew ascended fully, coming noisily to a pause.

Rit let her rest, holding her, speaking in her rich, throaty way about Drew's eyes and other parts. She shifted then, removed her pants, and taking hold of Drew's curly hair, pulled her slowly down. The message was clear and Drew felt she had no choice, and wanted none. She tasted Rit and knew the taste and feel and felt it herself, knowing just how it was and just where Rit was and brought her further to rising gasps of moaning, arching pleasure.

They paused entwined gazing upwards to let the stars fill their eyes, to feel the universe. Rit moved, sat up. She looked at Drew, into her. "Spread you legs," she commanded.

Drew's legs moved themselves and Rit slid her head between them, her tongue, her mouth, her lips finding all the places, drinking, sucking, elevating Drew, and herself.

Drew lay quietly afterwards, her head on Rit's chest, enclosed in her strong embrace and soon they dozed. An hour passed, perhaps more, until the chill of the night aroused them again and they aroused each other again. At last, they said goodnight and tiptoed to their rooms.

## 40

Drew awoke to the smell of coffee and then smelled Rit on her fingers and sighed. She lay in bed remembering, living it again, then hurried to dress; for Rit was real and she was right there in the next room.

But it was Bo Drew had heard and who gave her coffee and cheerful conversation. Rit had gone for a walk, she told her. It was a long dragging hour before Rit returned. Drew felt the rushing excitation when she heard her coming. Rit joined her in the living room, frowning heavily.

"What is it?" Drew asked.

"I have to talk to you. About Wiley. I have to tell you what I learned. It's not pleasant."

Drew's face lost color. She sat upright on the wicker chair. "Did something happen to her?" Every muscle tightened in preparation for the blow.

"No, nothing happened to her. I learned some things about her the other night, that's all, when I was in Chicago." Rit took the rocking chair across from Drew, looking very much like she was not enjoying herself. "I ran into a friend of mine, Eleanor Clark. She said some things that confirmed my suspicions about your friend, things it won't be easy for you to hear."

Drew was still recovering from the fear-evoking image of Wiley hurt or in trouble. "What things? What do you mean?"

"Let me start by putting it together the way I see it."

Drew's teeth were clenched. She did not want to hear this, and yet she did.

"You said yourself Wiley's an idealist..."

"There's nothing wrong with that."

"...and frustrated by the way things are in the world."

"Who isn't?"

Rit gave her a stern look. "Then you turn up with your magical powers..."

"I didn't 'turn up'. I've known Wiley for years."

"Do you want to hear?"

Drew shook her head no. "Yes," she said.

"So, suddenly Wiley has the means to actualize her idealistic dreams. Only, unfortunately, another person's involved. You. Your power is the means. The rest of you is an obstacle."

"Oh, come on. You don't know her, Rit. She's..."

"I have no evidence that she set up the Granser/Zayre business to scare you. It's possible that she had nothing to do with it."

"What! Wiley...you *are* paranoid!" Drew said the last words through clenched teeth. "You're making me very angry, Avery."

"I'm not sure how far she'd go to get you to cooperate, to put yourself in her hands. At any rate, her plan backfired because, instead of your running to her, you came to me."

"I didn't *come to you,* I..."

"Your welfare is not her prime concern. You're a means to an end for her. Her motives are, at best, questionable. Her methods are despicable. She's become a megalomaniacal..."

"Megalo...oh, come on, Rit. This is making me sick. What are you talking about? What do you know about Wiley or her motives?"

"I know she told five women about your power and asked them to help her plan ways to get you to allow them to use it as she wants."

"She told no one!" Drew shouted. "She worries about Judith knowing. She'd never tell a soul."

"She told five women, one of whom is my friend, Eleanor Clark. It was just by chance that I found out. They were sworn to secrecy."

"I don't believe a word of it."

"Will you try to listen without interrupting me?"

Drew sat back in the chair and crossed her arms. "Go ahead."

"Eleanor Clark is an old friend of mine," Rit began. "She teaches at DePaul. Night before last, in Chicago, I ran into her at..." Rit gave the details of her encounter with Eleanor Clark, repeating exactly what Eleanor had told her about Wiley's meeting.

Drew listened sullenly. "Well, then she didn't actually tell them," Drew said when Rit finished. "She told them it was a psychological study. I'm sure none of them believed it was actually true. Who the hell would? She never mentioned my name. She probably had a good reason for..."

"Drew, goddam it, don't be so..."

"Naive?"

"She's planning how to use you, step by step. She's in the process of gathering information. She believes you have a mission, Drew, to use your power the way she believes it should be used. Regardless of what you want."

"Wiley's my friend," Drew said stubbornly. "That comes first. She'd never try to force me..."

"I didn't say anything about force, not direct force, at least. Her goal, as I see it, is to use your vulnerability, and I'm afraid, your

213

'naivete' to get you to do exactly what she wants. She got you to do that stupid nonsense at the photo studio."

"That wasn't nonsense. We had to learn about the extent of the power - who it works on, what kind of beliefs can be implanted, the effects on people's thinking, things like that."

"You sound just like I imagine Wiley sounds. She's got you brainwashed, Drew. You're like her puppet."

Drew's eyes were suddenly stinging with tears. Her throat felt constricted and painful. Is it true? Has Wiley been manipulating me? Drew chewed on her lip. She *has* changed, Drew thought. She's been different since the first night I told her. Maybe Rit's right about her. Oh, Wiley, how could you? Drew swallowed hard, keeping her eyes closed, shaking her head. "When all of this first started," she said slowly, "way back before we began the research thing, I went through a period where I didn't trust her."

Drew spoke without looking at Rit, as if speaking to herself.

"I had the sense that somehow she might use me. I felt awful about it, being suspicious of Wiley who's so decent and good. That was the day she came out to me."

Drew lit a cigarette. Her eyes were dry now and had an angry cast.

"I guess she thought that would help me get over my distrust."

She threw the match at the ashtray and watched it bounce out and onto the table.

"It worked, too. At the time, it was like she had given me a gift, to trust me with that information, to share that part of herself with me. Maybe she *was* manipulating me. Maybe all along, ever since I told her about the power, her main concern *was* how she could use it, use me, to get what *she* wanted, to be in charge of changing the world according to *her* image." Drew laughed hollowly. "Remake the world in her image with me the sacrificial daughter." Grabbing an empty candy wrapper from the table, Drew crumpled it and threw it angrily across the room.

"She was always telling me how cautious I have to be and, behind my back, she's having meetings, telling people about it, conspiring with them. Idealism is dangerous," Drew said with disgust. "She does want to take over the world, doesn't she? Megalomaniac." Drew felt the sinking pain of disillusionment.

"We all have dreams," Rit said softly. "Apparently, Wiley thought your power was a way to make hers come true."

Drew's eyes were full of tears again.

"I'm sorry, Drew," Rit said, "but I thought you should know before she calls." She paused. "People," she added, "are just that,

214

Drew, human. They all have bottom lines."

"Wiley's a rock," Drew said feebly. "I always thought she was so...noble, I guess, fair, and humanistic." Drew lifted her chin, then. "She is. It's not power for herself she's after. That's not it; it's the chance to improve life for everyone. That's her motive. She's not seeking power for herself." She took a deep breath. "Wiley likes to be in charge of things." Her eyes looked very sad. "Maybe she didn't tell me about the meeting because...because..." Drew's face contorted. Her shoulders drooped. "I guess her plan is spoiled now."

"Maybe," Rit said. "There was a message from her at my office."

"She called you? Well, how...?"

"I don't know. I chose not to return the call."

Drew thought a while. "I wonder how she knows about you. Mandy wouldn't have slipped and..."

"No way."

"She's still trying, then. I guess she's not about to give up easily."

Rit was silent.

"The bitch!"

Rit waited.

"Some friend!" Drew spat. She wiped at her eyes. "I wonder what she'll try next."

Drew's tears were angry ones now and she went to Rit and felt consoled in Rit's warm, strong, solid arms.

_____ *41.*

Judith Brodie was wondering if they actually had to get *married*, whether living together wouldn't be sufficient. She laughed out loud. Mom would love that, she thought. *You can't wait much longer, Judy. Being a mother is the most fulfilling part of a woman's life. Believe me, I know. How I hate that foolish women's liberation garbage you've been filling your head with. You've postponed marriage long enough.*

Judith was on the twenty-fifth floor of Sear's Tower. She didn't have an office with a view yet, but some day she would, she thought. *I can't tell you what a relief it is to know that you're finally going to settle down. Vic is such a nice man. You did get yourself a real gentleman, so I suppose I shouldn't complain that you waited until you're almost thirty to do it. But, you can't wait for children. Vic's salary is good, thank God, so that's no problem. Judy, are you listening?*

A "gentleman", Judith thought, sneering, rolling a paperclip back and forth through her fingers. The thoughts of Drew sneaked up on her, catching her off guard and filling her with a warm glow before she tightened her hand into an angry fist and threw the paperclip across the room. She looked at it sitting, shining dumbly on the flat functional carpet. Judith loved her office. She loved it because it was hers, because she had earned it. Her business degree was paying off. She had earned that, and her promotions, and the responsibility she handled so well, as Mr. Blackman had recently told her. She was succeeding in the so- called man's world, making it her world.

Those *lesbians* are wrong, she thought, recalling once again the conversation she and Drew had had in Rhodes with the three women from Pennsylvania. Men are *not* hopeless. She shook her head angrily. *They* are. They just can't make it, can't succeed playing by the rules so they want to tear it all down—build *Lesbian Nation.*

Judith felt the familiar wave of nausea, her body's reaction to the puzzling mix of anxiety and longing. They're harmless as long as they don't get Drew, she thought. The pictures returned, the images of the two of them in Greece and how wonderful it felt. Her fear and rage grew.

She dialed the phone.

"Vic, honey, I was just thinking about you." Her lip was quivering. "I just called to say I miss you. I love you."

## 42.

When the phone rang, Drew did not move, although inside she stiffened.

"It's Wiley," Rit said. She looked at Drew sadly and left the room.

216

Drew forced herself to the phone. "Hello."

"Drew, can you talk freely?"

"Yes."

"No one can hear our conversation?"

"No, Wiley, no one can hear. It's all right. What's up?"

"Unbelievable things have happened. I've been trying to call you for two days. I know you're with Rit Avery. That's true, isn't it?"

Drew hesitated. "Yes," she said. "It's true."

"She's trouble, Drew. You may not want to believe this. I'm sure she's been working hard to convince you otherwise, but listen to me, all right?"

"All right," Drew said sadly.

"Somehow Rit Avery found out about your power. If you told her, Drew, I'm sure it made sense to you at the time. But, Drew, Rit Avery is out to use you. The government isn't involved in this. The only danger you're in right now is from Rit Avery herself. No one's pursuing you. They're all Rit Avery's people—Zayre, Granser, the guy posing as your cousin. Rit Avery hired them all to convince you you must put in with her. It's she who's tapping our phones. She's a sharp one, but very bad news. Drew, are you listening?"

"Yes," Drew said flatly.

"I talked with Brian McAllister, which obviously isn't his real name. He admitted that Rit Avery hired him to pose as your cousin."

"She hired them all, huh?" Drew's voice remained emotionless.

"Drew, you've got to believe me." Despite the chilly weather, Wiley was perspiring as she stood in the phone booth. She'd barely slept the last two nights. Her head ached almost constantly. Her need to free Drew from Rit's web had become the overriding goal of her life, possessing her unrelentingly. "Rit Avery is not who she appears to be. She's been deceiving you. You've got to get out of there. Drew, are you reading me?"

"Yes," Drew said sadly. "I get the picture. It...it bothers me, Wiley." Her eyes were red and wet, her stomach close to rejecting the breakfast Bo had prepared for them.

"Yes, of course, I understand. It really stinks. Can you get Becka?"

"She's coming this afternoon."

"Terrific. You've got to take her and leave. I know this must be hard to believe."

"It's very hard to believe but I believe it now."

"Good. I was worried that your feelings about her...that you might have grown attached and... Anyway, I've got a plan. Do they

217

trust you? Are they guarding you?"

"They trust me."

"Can you get away without their knowing, get yourself and Becka to an airport?"

"I could."

"Great. Where are you?"

"Texas," Drew said.

"OK, then we'll take the western route. I want you and Becka to fly to Los Angeles, all right? Call me through Marie when you arrive there. Marie will give me the message. We'll leave the country, Drew, the three of us. Rit Avery is dangerous and I think she'll try anything to get what she wants. I'll bring your passport. Do you understand the situation, Drew?"

"I understand."

"You sound...what...what is it?"

"I understand the situation."

"Your affect doesn't fit, Drew. You don't sound right. What's going on?"

"I'm upset."

"Of course, but...you sound sad...disillusioned. Yes, that's it, isn't it? You're disillusioned by what I'm telling you. You've grown to trust her, haven't you and...?"

"It feels like betrayal," Drew said. She was crying now.

"Yes, damn. It must hurt like hell. It *is* betrayal. You understand then. You're willing to leave the country."

"Under the circumstances, I think it's the best thing to do."

"Call when you arrive in L.A."

"Goodbye, Wiley."

"Drew, wait! You sound awful. Can you handle it?"

"I'll have to. I'll handle it."

"OK, I'll be waiting for your call."

"Yes, goodbye, Wiley."

Wiley remained in the phone booth staring at nothing long after they'd hung up. Mandy approached her.

"You done?"

"Oh, yeah. Yeah, I'm ready. Let's go."

Again Mandy had traveled around the city before stopping at a phone booth, this one at a gas station on the far north side. She'd dialed the number then waited at the car for Wiley to finish her conversation. Wiley was annoyed at the farce of evading fictitious pursuers.

After the call, Mandy drove her to an el stop. Wiley was silent on the car ride, reviewing the conversation with Drew, full of

218

unanswered questions. Mandy left her alone.

Her train came and she found a window seat and looked at the passing back porches of the apartment buildings without seeing them. I should have gotten the phone number from her, she thought. Damn! Something is very wrong. She didn't respond like Drew. Has that woman brainwashed her? The train stopped at the Bryn Mawr station. Closed faces left; other closed faces got on. She hardly said anything, Wiley realized. I don't know what she's thinking. She didn't react as I expected. No anger at Avery, or fear. No relief that the government doesn't know about her, that no one's following her. The train moved on, Wiley's closed face one of many peering from closed windows. I should have talked to her more. Damn!

### 43.

The mother and child reunion was full of laughter, a few tears and many farm stories and comments about Drew's curls. Naomi had put her on the plane and Becka made the flight to Flagstaff alone. She was very proud of herself for that. "I wasn't even scared," she said, "because I knew you'd be right there when I got off the plane, mom, and that's why I wasn't scared."

She described the airborne meal in great detail, how she put the icky peas in the little white cup, but ate all the potatoes and the chicken except for the skin. She said the "airplane waitress" was very nice to her and that she didn't want a pillow because she liked looking out the window even if all she could see most of the time was clouds. The stack of drawings for Drew was thick and, sitting on the balcony floor, they went over each of them together. Most were pictures of cows and chickens.

From the moment they arrived at Rit's until they slept that night, Becka and Drew were together. Yet, not for a moment, did Drew forget Rit's presence, whether she was with them, talking, listening, eating dinner, or somewhere else in the house. While Drew baked cookies with Becka and talked about the school with big kids and little kids in the same room, her mind was also on the feel of Rit, the smell, the way she smiled, the overwhelming happiness she gave Drew. From time to time, against Drew's will, came thoughts of Wiley and of her ugly lying betrayal, which made Drew grow silent until Becka noticed.

"What, mom?"

"Nothing, hon, I was just thinking. Look at all those stars."

Becka resisted bedtime until nearly midnight when Drew went too, sleeping beside her girl, cuddling her, loving her and longing to be holding Rit, wondering when they'd be together alone again. The next day they all hiked, then Drew and Becka rented horses to ride through the sandy hills. They counted the different kinds of cacti and how many branches they had, and took photographs with Rit's camera. In the early evening, mother and daughter sat on the hill outside the house waiting for the sunset.

"In a way, it's prettier here than on the farm," Becka said.

"It sure is beautiful."

"But there's no animals."

"There are snakes."

"Yeah, that's neat. But I mean real animals, like cows."

Rit came out the side door and walked toward them. Drew felt her body stir as her focus shifted from her daughter to the woman she found more exciting than any human being she'd ever encountered.

"Just got a message from Mandy," Rit said, tossing Becka a banana and sitting down with them. "The good news: passports, et al are on the way. Starting tomorrow, you'll be Sandra O'Leary. Are you getting used to the name?"

"No."

"And this is Kathy O'Leary," she said to Becka. "Can you remember that, Kathy? This pretend game is really important."

"I know, but I'll still be me, right?"

Rit laughed. "In every way," she said. "A name is like a shirt. You can take it off whenever you want and still be you."

She turned to Drew. "The bad news: Wiley contacted Mandy again. She wants to talk with you. Mandy put her off until tomorrow night. We'll be gone by then."

Drew nodded sadly.

Rit turned to Becka. "So are you two having a good time?"

"You have pretty houses, Rit. Mommie says you have another one, far away, where people talk a different English."

"French, *mon cheri*. I bet you'll learn it in no time."

"I can say 'I love you' in German. My girlfriend, Margie, is German and she taught me. Listen. *Ick liebe dick.*"

"*Gut, und Ich liebe dich, mein Kind.*"

"What?"

Rit laughed. "Tomorrow you go for another airplane ride. Are you excited?"

"Well, I sorta miss my friends."

"I know. Won't you have a lot of stories to tell them some day."

"Yeah, and about the cow's milk. I know just how to do it. Naomi said I'm a natural."

"She did?"

"Yep." Becka tilted her head. "What's a natural?"

Rit took the banana from Becka's hand and peeled it. "A pure and simple sweetheart and that's just what you are." She took a bite and offered some to Becka. "I think we should all go down to the river and watch the sunset from there. What do you say?"

"Yeah, come on, mom. Let's go to the river, OK?"

It was OK with Drew, and the rest of the evening was OK except for the sadness weighing on her, the fear about the life they'd have and the worries and the disillusionment about Wiley, and the longing to touch Rit. It was OK.

Terri Silverman arrived in Flagstaff on a morning flight. She would take the next plane back to Chicago. "Silverman Courier Service," she said in the airport lounge, removing the sealed manila envelope from her briefcase and handing it to Rit. "This is all quite mysterious. Mandy wouldn't tell me a thing. Just fly to Flagstaff and give this to Rit. As long as I'm here, I really ought to stay awhile, but I can't."

Terri chatted on as Rit looked through the papers. Their plane for L.A. would leave in three hours. From there, they would take a flight to Paris.

"Naomi never drinks coke," Becka said, sipping her coke. "She says sugar's bad for you and something else in here." She stared at the dark liquid. "What else is in here, mom?"

"Caffeine."

"Yeah, that's it. I sort of missed cokes on the farm. I told Naomi when I get old enough to understand that sugar and that other thing is bad for me, then I'll stop having cokes."

Bo laughed. "I'm going to miss her," she said to Drew, ruffling Becka's hair.

Becka pulled her head away and smoothed her hair.

A half hour later, Terri left to catch her plane and the others—Drew, Rit, Bo and Becka—went to the observation deck to watch planes take off. Their own would leave in two and a half more hours. Three other people were on the deck, a woman in polyester, a man in cowboy boots and a stetson, and their noisy child. Becka asked for a coin to look through the telescope.

A few minutes later, a man in a business suit came through the glass door of the observation deck. He walked to the side wall and leaned against it, nonchalantly watching the women. Another man came a few seconds after that, and then another. Rit was talking to Bo, reviewing the instructions for Ella who would be taking over her active cases.

"So you won't get your chance at Murphy," Bo said.

"No," Rit replied. "Everything has a cost."

Rit noticed the men, four of them now, two near the wall at opposite corners of the deck, one on either side of the door. She began to feel uneasy. She looked from one to the other and each one caught her eye, then looked away.

The couple and their child moved toward the door, the woman dragging the kid by his arm. They left and it was very quiet on the deck, except for the sounds of airplanes coming and going. Now only Rit, Bo, Drew, Becka and the four men were there. Rit's uneasiness increased and Drew, too, was noticing the men. Rit looked around to see if there was any other way off the deck besides the glass door. There wasn't.

At that moment, one of the men, the one who'd been standing in the far corner, threw down his cigarette and began walking slowly toward them. He went up to Drew. "Miss McAllister."

Drew felt the adrenalin.

"My name is Jed Humphreys. I'm with the Central Intelligence Agency." He showed her a card. "We'd like to talk with you."

Oh Christ, Drew thought, feeling an hysterical panic. It's just like the movie Wiley talked about. She was afraid she might burst into moronic laughter. "Talk about what?" she asked instead, struggling to keep her voice from shaking.

"We have a car downstairs," the man replied. "I'd like you and your party to come with us."

Rit stepped between Drew and Humphreys. "Tell us what this is about!" she demanded. Her voice was steady and firm. "We have the right to know why you want to talk with us. Are we under arrest?"

Jed Humphreys looked at Rit coldly, his upper lip curling subtly into a sneer. "You have the right to remain silent..." he began, his steel eyes glaring into Rit's.

Drew looked around as he finished reciting their rights. The two men at the door were watching her. The other man, his face pasty and lined, had moved closer and was watching, too.

"We're going on a trip," Drew said trying to deny what was happening. "We haven't time to talk now." She took Becka's hand and clutched it tightly in her own.

Bo placed her hand on Drew's arm. "I think we're going to have to go with them, Drew."

The procession descended the stairs. They walked through the terminal to a side door which took them outside to the fringes of the airstrip. Two cars were parked there, a blue sedan and a cream-colored chevy. As they were walking towards them, like lightning, Bo suddenly went into action. With one swift karate blow, she downed the first man, then kicked another. Rit pushed Drew back toward the terminal door.

"Run!" she yelled, pushing Becka too.

Bo started for the next man, Humphreys, and Rit turned to join her, but they now faced three crouching men, each holding a revolver with its black hole pointing toward the two women, and a fourth, recovering from Bo's blow, getting up and reaching for his weapon. Humphreys and the pasty-faced one tore after Drew and Becka. Rit was grabbed and handcuffed and so was Bo, and they were taken to the cream-colored car.

Drew and Becka were only about a hundred yards ahead of the pursuers running as fast as they could, Drew holding Becka by the wrist. There were people ahead. Just a few more yards, Drew thought, and we'll hide in the crowd. She turned a corner, sharply, pulling Becka after her. Becka stumbled. Drew was bending to pick her up when she felt a heavy grip on her upper arm. One man got on each side of her, each holding an arm. Becka screamed, "Let go of my mommie," and kicked one of them in the leg. People turned to look.

"Cool your brat," the pasty-faced one said.

"Listen to me," Drew said sharply, facing him. "You can't walk."

She turned to zap the other man, Humphreys, but his hand went over her mouth,,tightly, painfully. She could smell tobacco on his fingers. The zapped man stood frozen in the hall, his leaden legs unmovable. Drew was led away, with Becka following, holding onto her shirt, crying. They handcuffed Drew and gagged her and shoved her and Becka into the back seat of the blue car. Humphreys got in the front and turned to face Drew.

"I know you can reverse what you did," he said.

Drew did not look at him. Her eyes were on her frightened daughter. The gag cut tightly across her mouth.

"I want you to restore Anderson's ability to walk." Humphreys spoke calmly, but clearly was furious. "It's serving no useful pur-

pose now. Things will go better for you if you do as I ask." Jed
Humphreys was a handsome man but Drew saw only the coldness
of his black eyes, cruel inhuman eyes, she thought, looking away
again.

Two airport security guards came toward the car, supporting
Anderson whose useless legs hung stiffly, dragging on the ground.
They pulled him into the seat next to Drew.

"You're to tell him he can walk," Humphreys said. His cold eyes
held Drew's until she nodded.

"Take her gag off," he said to Anderson.

Anderson fumbled with shakey fingers until the cloth was removed from Drew's mouth. From the corner of her eye, she could
see Humphreys watching her. In a flash she turned her head, met
his icy eyes and spoke sharply. "Listen, you're blind."

"Wha...?" His hands were up, spread wide. "What happened?"
His voice was frantic. "I can't see!" He kept blinking. "Fucking
bitch. Anderson, are you there?"

"Yes, I'm here. She said you're blind." He would not look at
Drew.

"Get Helms over here. Helms," Humphreys yelled out the window. "Get over here!"

"He's on his way, Jed."

"Don't look at her. Is he here? Tell him not to look at her. Helms,
is that you?"

"Yes, Jed. What's the matter?" He was leaning over the car at
the driver's seat. "What happened?"

"Don't look at McAllister. Something happened to my eyes. She
blinded me. Mother-fucker, goddam." He was reaching wildly,
touching things around him. "Get her to reverse this, Helms.
Where is she? Is she there?"

"She's here."

"Cover her eyes. She's a demon."

Anderson tied the gag over Drew's eyes. Helms got in the front
seat, next to Humphreys, and began speaking to Drew. Drew felt
calmer now. She was in their custody, but not powerless. She felt
the control she had and it calmed her. She felt Becka next to her
and rubbed legs with her.

"You're making it worse for yourself and your friends by what
you're doing," Helms began. "We're going to take you to our compound in Vermont. We want you to work with us, for the government, for the country. We don't want to harm you in any way, do
you understand?"

"Too well," Drew said calmly.

"Our assignment is to bring you in. We want to be fair with you. We don't want anybody hurt. You've hurt two of our operatives and I want you to fix them. Will you do that?" Helms was the youngest of the four. He reminded Drew of a science teacher she'd had in high school, Mr. Ruggles. Everyone called him a "sex maniac", and the girls stayed out of his way. "If you don't," Helms continued, "we're still taking you in, but we'll naturally feel less kindly toward you and your daughter and the others. Will you do it?"

"If you let my friends and daughter go."

"We can't do that. Our orders are to bring you all in."

"There's no need for my daughter to go. This is frightening for her. I want her to go back to Chicago."

"Impossible."

"That's my offer."

"Make another."

Drew brushed Becka's leg again with her own. She wanted to touch her with her hands but they were locked behind her back. "Let my daughter stay with me all the time," she said. "Don't separate us."

"All right, you got it. Now you..."

"For that," Drew interrupted, "I'll take care of this one." She gestured with her head toward Anderson who still sat next to her. "For the other guy, we'll have to negotiate some more."

"Fix Anderson then."

"Hey, wait," Humphreys said.

"It's OK, Jed. We'll get to you. Hang in a while longer."

Drew turned her head toward Anderson. She could hear his heavy breathing. "I have to be able to see him," she said.

Helms reached over and removed the blindfold, averting his eyes from Drew's.

"Listen carefully," Drew began, "I have something important to say to you." Anderson's frightened eyes glued to Drew's. "Your legs are fine. You can walk normally now and you're determined to help me and my friends escape from here and..."

Her head was grabbed from behind by such force that her neck cracked and a hot pain shot across her shoulders.

Anderson held his gun on Helms. "It's over, man. Let her go. Reach over and unlock the bracelets." The revolver was pointed at Helms' forehead.

"She's making you do this, Dave. Fight it."

"Shut up. Do what I say. Now."

Helms got his key and was starting to lean over the seat toward

225

Drew. Humphreys, groping around next to him, tried to prevent it. Helms pushed him away.

"Groberski!" Humphreys yelled.

"Shut up, Jed," Anderson said to him. "My gun is pointed at your head."

Joe Groberski had been leaning on the other car where Rit and Bo were. He left his post and moved toward the others. "What is it?"

"Nothing," Anderson said. "It's under control. Go watch your prisoners." Anderson's gun was pointed at Helms. "There'll be a bullet in your head if you say anything," Anderson whispered to Humphreys. "We're going to let these people go. I'll take full responsibility."

Helms freed Drew's wrists from the shackles. Her sore neck was forgotten in her scramble from the car. Taking Becka by the arm, she ran toward the terminal. Almost immediately she heard the crack of a gun, then a command to stop. She stopped.

Anderson lay on the ground, bleeding. Helms told Drew to come to him, but to walk backwards. She did and Becka followed, silently, stunned now, moving robot-like.

They were taken by car to the end of the airstrip. Helms drove. Drew sat next to him in the front seat, handcuffed again and blindfolded. Becka sat silently beside her, her arm through her mother's. In the back were Groberski, Rit, and Bo. No one spoke.

Becka and the three women were herded onto a small jet and handcuffed to their seats in a lounge-like room. Drew remained blindfolded, each hand shackled separately to an arm of her chair. Becka, too, was shackled.

"You OK, Drew?" Rit asked.

"Who's here?"

"Us, the four of us. That's all."

"Can you get this blindfold off me?"

"I can't reach it, Drew."

Drew twisted her head, pushed and rubbed it against the headrest of her chair until the blindfold slipped up, off her eyes, then all the way off her head.

She looked at Becka, sitting in a seat across from her. "Hi, fruitloop. This adventure's kind of a scarey one."

Becka's lower lip began to quiver. "What did we do, mom? Why are they being mean to us?"

"They want me to work for them. They want it so badly they're doing this to us."

"You don't want to, huh, mom?"

"No."

"You want to make films, right, ma?"

"Right."

Becka was very close to tears. "I saw a man get shot."

"I know," Drew said, feeling rage at the shackles preventing her from holding her girl.

"I think he was hit in the shoulder," Bo said quickly. "He'll probably be OK."

"He wanted to help us," Becka said.

"Yes, he tried."

"I'm scared, mom."

"Me, too, hon. It's hard to be brave right now."

That comment gave Becka the permission she needed. She let go, sobbing painfully. She tried to reach her mother, but the shackle on her narrow wrist would not allow it.

"Becka, listen to me."

Becka lifted her head and her teary, frightened eyes connected with Drew's.

"This is scarey, but we can handle it," Drew said. "You can keep calm enough to handle it even though you're scared. You can let yourself relax some, even though you don't like what's happening because you feel that we'll get through it." Drew tried to believe the words herself.

When her eyes cleared, Becka visibly relaxed. She even managed a slight smile. "It's like TV," she said.

"Yeah, a real life TV adventure," Drew replied, "or a movie."

Becka settled back into her seat. She played with the chain on her wrist. "What if I have to go to the bathroom?"

"Do you?"

"No. Look at the clouds. This is the fanciest airplane I've ever been on. Where are the other people?"

"It's a private plane," Drew said. She was thinking about Humphreys, about how she had blinded him just like in that movie. She felt a shudder down her spine.

A few minutes later, Helms walked into the room. "Hey." He turned his face from Drew's. "Damn you." He took the blindfold and tied it, tightly, over Drew's eyes, and gagged her mouth as well.

## 44

When the plane landed, they went by car to a complex of buildings in an isolated rural section of what Drew assumed was Vermont. She and Becka were taken to a suite of rooms in one of the larger buildings. It was actually a small apartment with a living room, bedroom, bath, a stocked kitchen, books on the shelves, even some toys. She and Becka were escorted inside by two silent men then left alone. The door was locked; the windows, which were covered with a heavy plastic grid, faced the grounds. They did not know what had happened to Rit and Bo. Becka immediately fell asleep on the couch. Drew paced.

An hour later, Drew was taken for an interview. She insisted that Becka come too, or else be allowed to stay with Rit and Bo. Blindfolded, Drew was led down some stairs and through several corridors, the escort holding her arm while Becka clung to her hand. Becka waited in the next room with crayons and paper Drew brought for her. It was not really an interview for it seemed Drew was not expected to talk, just to listen. The man who spoke to her was Sandor Smith. Though Drew could not see what he looked like, she pictured him as large and pale with small eyes, bushy eyebrows and thin bloodless lips.

Sandor Smith told her in a matter-of-fact, but cordial way that they, the government, were fully aware of the parameters of her power; he told her what they expected from her and what she could expect from them. They did, indeed, seem to know nearly everything about the zapping. They knew eye contact was necessary. They knew the recipient had to understand the message and that everyone was susceptible. Drew took some pleasure in the fact that they were unaware of Rit's immunity. They knew she could erase zaps, that people could not resist zaps, and that the beliefs implanted became strongly held, central ones.

"Where did you get all this information?" Drew asked.

"That's the business we're in," Smith answered.

"How did you become aware of me in the first place?"

Drew waited in the dark for Smith to respond. "I'm afraid I won't be able to satisfy your curiosity, Miss McAllister. Sorry."

Her head began to ache as Smith rambled on about how the U.S. Government was interested in peace and harmony in the world and how she should consider it an honor to be able to help bring this about. "Through your decision to attempt to avoid us, however," he said, "you've made it clear that your cooperation will not be totally voluntary. Therefore, we're forced to confine you for now, until we can reach an agreement."

There was a pause. Drew wished she could see him, wished she could zap the moron into total idiocy.

"The first thing we would like you to do is cooperate in some preliminary demonstrations of your powers. Included in this will be erasing the implantations that remain in two of our agents, Anderson and Humphreys. We'll also require several other simple demonstrations. If this goes well, then we'll want to negotiate with you terms under which you'll agree to implant, from time to time, certain beliefs in certain people."

Drew felt suffocated, burning up and cold at the same time. She kept thinking of that damned movie Wylie had told her about. She wished she hadn't gotten Wiley to tell her the whole plot. Things hadn't ended well for the "people-pusher".

"In exchange for this cooperation, we will try to grant some of your wishes, make your life comfortable. Miss McAllister, the fact is that you have very little choice at this point. You are too valuable and potentially dangerous a person to be on the loose. For your own protection and for the welfare of your country, from now on, you have a very special mission with the U.S.Government. Your only real choice is whether to cooperate immediately and make it easier on yourself and your friends, or be obstinate and make it difficult. I'm sure you will choose to be cooperative. You're a reasonable woman. Think about what I've said. We'll meet again soon."

Drew felt utter contempt for this faceless cockroach. Back in the suite, she did, however, give serious consideration to what he had said. Becka was watching TV. Drew sat next to her, facing the tube but neither seeing nor hearing it. Obviously they'd much rather have me alive and cooperative than dead, she thought. She knew she must bargain.

The rest of the evening passed quietly. Drew prepared a tuna cassarole for their dinner though neither she nor Becka were very hungry. They went to bed early, Becka sleeping immediately, Drew tossing much of the night. The next morning dragged. Becka began to squirm.

"Mom, can't I go outside and play. I'm bored of this place."

"Not yet, hon. I'm afraid we're stuck here for awhile. Do you want to play a game or something? How about checkers?"

"I hate checkers."

"Oh? That's new. Well, what other games are in the closet?"

"I don't want to play any games. I want to go home. I miss daddy."

"Do you want to color?"

Becka shook her head. She went to the window. There were a number of buildings, plain red-brick ones, set around the nicely landscaped grounds. "I wonder if they have a pond with fish like Rit."

Without realizing it, Drew had been trying to keep thoughts of Rit out of her mind. Now the flood of longing and concern poured back. "You hungry?" she asked. "There's some spaghetti in the cupboard. How about it? Shall we have an early lunch?"

"I hate spaghetti."

Drew laughed. "Poor babe, you're getting cabin fever, aren't you?"

Becka felt her forehead. "I've got a fever, mom. I'm too sick to stay here. I think we better go home so I can go to bed and drink orange juice."

The intercom buzzed. Drew flicked the button. "Yes?"

"Two visitors are coming to see you. Will you please put the blindfold on."

Drew flicked the switch again. "Get fucked," she said.

Five minutes later, the door opened and two men stormed in. Keeping their eyes averted from Drew's, they grabbed her arms, shackled her wrists behind her back, blindfolded her and sat her in a straight backed chair. Then a woman entered the room.

"Becka," she said gently, "would you like to come for a walk with me? I have a doggie I want you to meet. Do you like dogs?"

Becka clung to Drew. "I'm staying with my mommie."

"Your mommie is going to be busy for a little while. No one will hurt her. They had to do that to your mom because your mom got nasty, but they're not going to hurt her."

"Who are you?" Drew asked.

"I'm Madeline Drury," the woman replied. "We thought your child could use some outdoor recreation. I'll bring her back in an hour."

"You're sure? We have an agreement, you know. My daughter's to remain with me."

"I'll bring her back soon, no problem."

"Where will you take her?"

"For a walk on the grounds."

Drew was silent for a moment. "Why don't you go with her, Becka," she said gently. "I'll be OK."

"What are they going to do to you, mom?"

"Just talk, I imagine. They really don't want to hurt me, Becka. It's OK for you to go."

"Why are they afraid of your eyes?"

"I told you, hon," Drew said, trying to adjust her hands so the shackles weren't so uncomfortable. "Sometimes when I look at people and tell them things, they just have to believe me even though they don't want to. These people don't want me to do that to them."

"Do it anyway, mom."

Drew chuckled. "They don't make that easy," she said.

"I could take that cloth off your eyes."

"Thanks, hon," Drew said, smiling, "but they'll just put it right back on. You go ahead now. Go with the lady." She turned toward where the woman stood. "There really is a dog, I hope."

"There certainly is," Madeline Drury replied. "His name is Teddie. He's a cocker spaniel and he loves kids. Shall we go, Becka?"

As they left, Drew could hear people enter the room.

"Miss McAllister, we're going to take some face and head measurements."

Drew turned toward the voices. "Why?" she asked.

"To fit you for some glasses."

"I don't need glasses."

"That's not the opinion around here." He chuckled.

They measured various distances on Drew's face and head, then removed the handcuffs and left. This was the first time Drew had been alone since arriving here. She wanted to think and wished she had her round chair. Yes, she wished more than anything that she was home in her round chair safe and comfortable. She went into the bedroom and stretched out on the bed, shifting around until her body was curled up in a semi-circle. She needed to continue assessing the situation.

The first thought was of Rit. Feelings predominated for a while, feelings of desire. Next came worry. Where were Rit and Bo? Were they OK? At the airport, they had been put in a separate car and that's the last she'd seen of them. Her next thought was of how this had happened, how the CIA found out about her. There was no doubt in her mind that Wiley had nothing to do with any of these people. Wiley may share their wish to use her power, but they were competitors. She'd have nothing to gain by putting in with them. It was too painful to think of Wiley. Memories came, good memories of their long friendship, Wiley's caring and loyalty. Drew felt an overwhelming sadness and made herself go back to figuring out how the CIA found out.

Was it one of the experimental subjects who told them, she wondered. Someone who got suspicious and reported it and they sent Zayre to investigate? But how? How would a subject know anything was unusual. Maybe someone besides Rit was immune. But, no, Drew thought, they all believed what I told them to believe. Why would they fake it if they were immune? She twisted on the bed. Maybe it was one of the people at Wiley's meeting. Maybe they found out it wasn't just an exercise, and then got scared or something and reported it. She stayed with that possibility for a while but it didn't go anywhere. Maybe it was Judith. This thought sickened her. Judith said the zapping is evil. Maybe she...Drew shook her head, shuddering, and shifted her line of thought.

What to do? They're determined to coerce me to work for them. They surely have the resources to force me, unless...Drew's eyes widened. What if I made it public, she thought. What if I inform newspapers and TV stations of what's going on. That was the people-pusher's plan; it didn't work for him, as I recall, but maybe I could pull it off. Certainly the CIA wouldn't treat me like this if everyone knew. There'd be an outcry about my rights. The Civil Liberties Union would get involved. It would get international coverage. Then the government would have to leave me alone.

Drew smiled and stretched her legs. I could let them think I've agreed to go along, then as soon as I got the chance...She removed her shoes and threw them on the floor. Of course, if I did that then everyone would know, she thought. That could be awful. I'd be public property—a freak. I'd get no peace. There'd be nowhere to hide. Maybe I'd get police protection, body guards. She felt sick. What a way to live. I couldn't walk on the streets without being inundated with requests for zappings. Worse than that, Drew thought, if it were public, people would probably try to kidnap me, all kinds of people. God, am I valuable, she realized. She realized it in a way, with an impact, that had never struck her so powerfully before. She went back to thinking of her list, of what she would insist on, and the limits of her cooperation.

The door opened.

"Mommie, look what Madeline gave me." Becka ran into the bedroom holding out a box filled with toys. "I know how to make this top spin. Watch."

Drew and Becka remained undisturbed until early the next morning when the intercom buzzed. "We'll be coming for you in one hour, Miss McAllister. Please be ready." The speaker did not wait for a response.

An hour later, they buzzed again and said someone was coming to her quarters and for Drew to put on the blindfold. Drew did. The person who came stood behind her, removed the blindfold and replaced it with a strange pair of metal goggles. They covered her eyes completely, curving around the edges. A section went over her ears on each side and under them and the goggles fastened in the back. They darkened the room somewhat, like sunglasses. The outside of the lens was reflective, so that anyone looking at Drew's eyes would see only mirrors.

Madeline Drury came for Becka and Drew was taken through some hallways then down in an elevator to a tunnel, then a hundred yards or so to a small office with a desk, a table and several chairs. The last time she had come here, Drew was blindfolded, but she was sure this was the same place where she'd met with Sandor Smith. A man sat at the table. He was not large, nor pale as Drew had imagined, but he did have bushy eyebrows.

"Good morning, Miss McAllister."

Drew sat down across from him as directed. Her escort left the room, closing the door.

"I trust you've been comfortable."

Drew refused to play the game of pleasantries. She did not answer.

"I asked you to think about what I said the other day. I'd like to hear the product of those thoughts."

Drew wanted to laugh at his pomposity, but she frowned instead. "I want to trade."

"Trade?"

"Yes."

"Tell me more."

"Where are my friends?"

"They're fine."

"Where are they?"

"They're with us. They're comfortable, I assure you."

"I want to see them. Now. Before I talk with you."

Smith looked at himself in Drew's glasses. He went to the phone. "Have Avery and Clemmens brought down here."

While they waited, Smith tried to converse with Drew but she remained fixedly silent. In five minutes, the door opened. Drew moved rapidly to Rit's side and took her hand. "I really was looking forward to seeing the Eiffel Tower," she said, smiling sadly.

Rit embraced her. "*C'est la vie,*" she replied softly. "Let me look at you." She held Drew at arm's length, her strong hands on Drew's shoulders, and smiled, her eyes glistening. "You seem OK. I miss the green eyes. Your glasses are interesting but I don't think they'll

233

catch on."

Drew laughed. "I believe they're called 'functional'." She turned to Bo. "What a drag, huh? I'm sorry I got you involved in this, Bo."

Bo smiled. "I'd say Rit and I pretty much volunteered." She hugged Drew. "Where's Becka? Is she staying with you?"

"Yes," Drew said. "She and I have a light, airy, one-bedroom on the second floor. Wall-to-wall carpeting, but no fireplace. How about you? Do you have an ocean view?"

"The rooms are fine. No bare cells, no torture. Just some attempted brainwashing. Are they treating you OK?"

"They're gestapo."

One of the men who had escorted Rit and Bo made a slight movement toward Drew. Smith put up his hand to stop him. "Miss McAllister," he said, "you can see that your friends are well. Let us resume our talk now." He gestured for the men to take Bo and Rit away. Drew stared at the closed door after they had gone.

"You see we're being quite accommodating to you. Now you must reciprocate. Let's start with Humphreys."

"Not yet," Drew said. "There's something else you must do before I do any zapping."

Smith waited.

"I will do what I can to give your man his sight back if you free my friends and my daughter. When I receive proof that they're safely back in Chicago, I'll zap him to see again."

"We have no intention of harming your friends or your little girl."

"In case you're not aware of it," Drew said caustically, "in the liberty-loving, democratic, American way of life, imprisoning people is looked upon as a form of harm."

"We're not prepared to release them yet. We need proof of your willingness to cooperate first. Let me propose this..." Smith's hand went to the knot of his necktie. "You perform a demonstration thought implantation, and we'll fly your two friends home. When that's accomplished, then you tell Humphreys he can see."

"And my daughter?"

"She stays for now."

"Why?"

Smith did not answer. "That's as far as I'm willing to go."

Drew worried about Becka, about the effects this experience would have on her, and about her safety. At the same time, she did not want to be apart from her. "I'd like to meet with Rit and Bo, privately, before they leave, and I want your assurance that they will be left alone after they're home."

Smith nodded. "Agreed."

"And I choose the zap for the demonstration."

"We'll come up with a mutually agreeable one," Smith said, amicably. "When you're assured that your friends are safely in Chicago, you meet with Humphreys."

Later that afternoon, her goggles in place, Drew was accompanied from her suite to a room with a one-way viewing window. Sandor Smith was in the room with another man. This one looked more like Drew's original image of Smith only his lips were even thinner and his skin more pale.

"This is Mr. Greenspan. He'll be your subject. Behind the window there is a group of people who've come to observe. Look over this list of possible implantations. Choose one you find acceptable."

Some of the items on the list were the same zaps Drew and Wiley had used in the experiment. There was even the one about animals needing clothes. "I like this one," Drew said, pointing to number eight. "Let's use it."

Smith smiled. "That's the toughest one on the list," he said.

After Smith left the room, Greenspan unlocked Drew's goggles and the demonstration began.

"Mr. Greenspan, listen to me," Drew said, "I have something important to say to you." She paused briefly. "You know you are a very convincing speaker," she said, glancing at the paper. "You're quite persuasive and you want to use this ability to convince your colleagues of something that you believe very strongly. You want to convince them that the CIA should be disbanded." Drew decided to elaborate some on this point. "You believe that such an organization is counter to the principle of individual freedom and that it, therefore, should no longer exist in the United States."

Satisfied with her addition, she went back to reading. "You believe that your best tactic is to persuade those presently in the CIA, not others. You're convinced that you should begin immediately and make your points directly and overtly. You know you cannot allow yourself to be swayed from or frightened away from this conviction."

Behind the window, one man turned to another. "Impossible," he said. "Greenspan's one of the most loyal company men we've got. He'll never buy that 'principles' crap."

Greenspan had remained motionless during the implantation, staring into Drew's eyes. Now, he shifted positions. "Is something wrong? What's the delay?"

Drew said nothing. From the intercom came the directive for her to put her goggles back on. Then seven men joined them in

235

the room taking seats around the formica conference table.

Greenspan seemed very antsy. "Sir," he said, as soon as people were settled, "I'd like an appointment with you, as soon as possible. It's a top priority matter, Mr. Marshall."

"Then let's not wait," Marshall replied. "You can speak to me here, now."

"Good, I do want everyone to hear. But what about the girl, sir?"

"She can stay. Go ahead."

Greenspan looked around the table. "Gentlemen," he began, "please give serious consideration to what I am about to say." All eyes were on him. "As you know, this country is founded on the principles of individual freedom and respect for individual rights. We not only espouse those rights for our own citizens, but also for all people of the world. It is my strong conviction that the covert operations of our agency often conflict with these principles. While, in theory, the goals of the Company are noble and consistent with the principles on which this nation stands, in fact, we are often forced to violate the very rights we purport to uphold."

"What drivel," someone muttered.

Greenspan seemed not to hear. "I would like to propose that a committee be established, a committee composed of our own people, to develop alternative ways by which we can protect the security of our country without violating the principles on which it stands."

"Greenspan," Marshall said, "I'm shocked at what you're saying."

"Our organization needs to be re-evaluated, sir. I'm suggesting that we begin by creating a committee to do just that, re-evaluate the function of the Central Intelligence Agency."

"It's verging on treasonous, Greenspan."

"I sincerely care about our country." Greenspan looked extremely sincere. "We need to examine our consciences."

"You're leaving me no choice but to relieve you of your duties..."

Greenspan began to sweat. "Mr. Marshall, consider my record. Don't act hastily, I...allow me to formulate my arguments. Let there be a committee to..."

"...and possibly proceed with a hearing for subversion. Would you like to reconsider what you're saying?"

"I must insist that we proceed with the committee, that we explore options to this agency, that we work toward disbanding totally."

"Greenspan," Marshall said calmly, "this woman implanted these ideas in you. This is not your thinking. Now, stop yourself.

Use your head. What do you really believe?"

"I've never been more convinced of anything in my life. If these ideas came from Miss McAllister, then I'm grateful to her, for they are the truth. One way or another, I will persuade you, all of you. I will be requesting an appointment with the Director."

Throughout his recitation, the group observed silently, occasionally glancing at each other. An eyebrow raised or a head tilted from time to time.

"This is astounding," one of them said.

"Quite a gold mine we have here," said another, gesturing toward Drew. "How does she do it?"

Sandor Smith shook his head.

"How long will his irrational thinking last?"

"The data we have show there is no diminution over time," Smith said. "We know the implantations last at least several months. They may last forever. There's an orderly at a hospital in Wisconsin we've been watching. Miss McAllister implanted some beliefs in him months ago. We're going to try de-programming Greenspan," Smith continued. "If we fail, then we'll have Miss McAllister remove the implantation...unless you guys want to be harangued by Greenspan's eloquent arguments from now on."

Several men laughed. "The demonstration is impressive," Marshall said to Smith. "You may proceed with the plan."

"Yes, sir."

"Nice having you with us, Miss McAllister."

Drew stared stonily at him, but he could not see the absolute disgust in her mirror-covered eyes.

## 45

That evening, not long after darkness came and Becka stopped staring out the window, Rit and Bo were brought to Drew's suite. At the sight of Rit, a fantasy flashed through Drew's mind, a fantasy of the two of them in a bamboo hut somewhere on a plush tropical island. Rit was stretched out on a mat and Drew sat before her massaging her feet and legs.

They all embraced in turn. Bo took Becka to the side. "I think your mom and Rit want to talk, so let's you and I go in the bedroom and have our own talk; just the two of us."

"They're releasing us," Rit said to Drew. She was writing something on a pad of paper as she spoke. She pointed to the pad and gestured for Drew not to mention it.

"I know," Drew said.

"How are thing's going?" Rit asked, showing Drew the note. *This place is probably bugged. Keep up a conversation with me. Follow my lead.*

"Well, I'd rather be sailing," Drew said.

Rit wrote some more. "I'll miss you." *Say: More than anything, I wish you could stay, but I want you to be safe.*

"I wish you could stay, Rit, more than anything. But I want you to be safe."

"I don't want to leave you, hon...I'm not afraid for myself. Drew, have you been cooperating with them? I think that's the best thing to do at this point. Oh, Drew, I love you so much. I don't want anything to happen to you." *Pretend you're crying.*

Drew made some sniffling, sobbing sounds while Rit wrote.

*We need to get them to let me stay here with you, in this apartment. They know we're lesbians. You need to imply that I'm your lover and convince them you'll be more cooperative if I stay.*

"I've been thinking," Drew said, "that once you and Bo and Becka are safe, I'll stop zapping totally, never do it again."

"No, Drew, you shouldn't do that. They'll make life miserable for you. You have to go along, at least part way."

"Do you think so, Rit? I don't know what to do. Sometimes I think I should just accept it and do what they want, but other times, I get so angry at being forced that I just want to refuse to do anything."

"Poor babe," Rit said. "This is awful for you." She wrote some more.

*Perfect. Bo and I aren't scheduled to leave until tomorrow, so you have some time to get them to let me stay.*

Drew nodded.

"I want to be with you, whatever happens. Maybe you can get them to let me stay," Rit said.

"Yes, I'll ask. If they refuse, they'll get nothing out of me."

"Oh, Drew, I love you so much." Rit pulled Drew to the couch and made some sounds as if they were embracing.

While Rit wrote on the notebook, her words replayed in Drew's head and even though it was a farce, Drew felt excited by them. Rit showed her the note: *Help me search for cameras.*

Silently, interspersed with occasional soft, loving, comments to each other, the two searched the room. They found several tiny microphones, but no cameras.

"How's Becka doing?" Rit asked, continuing the search.

"I'm not sure. I worry about her. They won't let her leave. She shouldn't have to go through this. I wish they'd let her go stay with her father."

They found no more microphones. Rit sat on the couch. *Where is the video tape that Wiley made?* she wrote, *of her friends singing and talking politics?* "Yes, it's not fair to her." She handed Drew the notebook.

*She still has it as far as I know. Why?*

*Where is it? We need it.*

*Her pantry. Top shelf.*

*Do you have a key to Wiley's house?*

*No. There's an extra one under the ceramic planter on her back porch.*

"You're wonderful."

Rit went to get Bo and Becka from the bedroom and the four talked in the living room for the next half hour or so. Drew told them about the medical exam she'd had in the building next door, the EEG, X-rays and various tests. "One of the doctors talked about the possibility of surgically creating the same thing in other people," she said.

"Make zappers out of them?" Bo asked.

"Yes, I wonder if it could be done."

Through the intercom, they were informed that it was time for Rit and Bo to return to their own rooms.

"How come they can go home but we can't?" Becka asked.

Drew sat her daughter on her lap. "There are more questions than answers," she said, pulling at Becka's shoe string. "Let's get ready for bed, fruitloop. I think it must be story time. You pick the book."

Early the next morning, her goggles locked in place, Drew again was taken to Smith's office for a meeting. *She* had requested it.

"I've changed my mind about something," she said.

"Oh?"

"I'd like Rit Avery to stay here with me."

"To stay?" He looked at her as if trying to figure out her motives.

"Yes, how much longer will I be here?"

"That depends. I can't say at this point."

"I'd like Rit to share the apartment with me and my daughter."

"Maybe we could make some trades," he said, leaning back in his chair. "A conjugal visit now and then in exchange for certain..."

"No," Drew said vehemently. "I mean that she stays with me, not just visits."

"We've already arranged for her to leave."

"I want her to stay. It's important to me."

"Aren't you worried about corrupting your daughter?"

Drew glared at him. He could see the anger in her mouth, but not the contempt in her eyes.

"Sorry," he said. "I must admit I have some trouble with your way of life. I'm kind of old-fashioned, I guess. You know, convinced that men and women belong together and all that. But, of course, your sexual preference is no concern of mine. If it will make you feel better to have your...to have Miss Avery remain with you and share your living quarters, then we'll accommodate you."

"Good."

"The other one will leave for Chicago this afternoon. As per our agreement, you may call her to verify that she's safe, after which you are to take care of Mr. Humphreys' vision problem."

"You realize, of course, that I may not succeed."

"What do you mean?"

"He can't look at my eyes. The zap may not work."

Smith frowned. "Just do what you can," he said.

Rit arrived early that evening. A cot was brought in and set up in the living room. Becka insisted that she be the one to sleep on it and Drew told her that if she really wanted to, it would be OK. She smiled to herself.

Rit had begun putting her things away when Drew was told, via the intercom, that she should get ready to go make the phone call to Bo. *Try to remember every word she says,* Rit wrote. She gave Drew a phone number. *This is where she'll be.* She watched Drew put on the goggles.

"Can't get these off, huh?"

"Nope, once they're fastened, the only way to remove them without removing my ears is with a key. They do things thoroughly."

During one of Drew's absences from the suite, a peephole had been installed in the door. Someone looked through it now to make sure her goggles were in place then opened the door. After checking the lock on the goggles, the silent young man accompanied Drew down the increasingly familiar hallway to an office, and told her she could use the phone.

"I'd prefer a pay phone."

Without comment, her escort took her outside and then into the next building. Near the entranceway was a pay phone. Drew dialed direct. She had brought a handful of coins with her.

"Hello."

"Is this you? You're OK?"

"Drew, yes, no problem. They took me to the airport, presented me with a ticket to Chicago and even were kind enough to walk me onto the plane. How are you?"

They talked for a few minutes. Drew felt reassured.

"By the way," Bo said, "you can tell Rit she was right about the cat. She did shit on my bed. Her paws are still swollen too, the front ones, so I'm taking her to the vet tonight."

"I hope she's OK. I'll try to call you again soon, Bo."

"Be well, Drew. Love to Becka."

*The cat stuff means Bo really is OK and that she got the video tape from Wiley's and will mail it tonight to a lawyer friend of mine in New York, along with an explanation. It will all be made public if Bo doesn't hear from us within two days.*

*I don't understand,* Drew wrote in response.

*It's our ace-in-the-hole, green eyes. The insurance we'll use if things here look worse than the price of going public.* Rit started to hand the message to Drew, then made an addition. *It won't get us out of here, but it should be enough to insure us against death, dismemberment, or mysterious disappearance. Dig?*

Drew nodded, feeling fear and appreciation both.

*Bo is staying at a friend's now but will be leaving Chicago tomorrow. I don't trust these bastards one millimeter. I wouldn't be surprised if they've already picked up Wiley and Judith.*

Drew closed her eyes in dread. Rit poked her and handed her another note. *Say: Rit, do you think there's any way we can escape from here?*

Drew took a deep breath. "Rit, do you think there's any way we could escape from here?"

"I wish there were, hon, but they watch us every minute we're not locked up. I think we just have to accept it, try to make it as unoffensive as possible for ourselves."

There was a knock at the door and Becka returned from her swim with Madeline.

"It's a real big pool, like the one where all the naked women swim," Becka said excitedly. "And there's a sauna, too. H-O-T. Mom, can I have a peanut butter toast?"

## 46.

At 8:15 that evening Drew was taken to the room with the one-way mirror for her talk with Jed Humphreys.

At about the same moment, in Chicago, Bo left her friend's apartment carrying a thick, stamped manila envelope. She looked carefully up and down the street, then began walking swiftly towards Addison Avenue. Maybe the neighbor who was looking out her window would have called the police if she had seen it, but just as the two men jumped from their car and started scuffling with Bo, the woman's husband called her. Bo managed only one sound kick to the taller man's knee before they subdued her. The blue-black Pontiac drove off with Bo inside.

Jed Humphreys seemed to have lost much of the assurance and confidence he'd had at the Flagstaff Airport. He sat nervously in a vinyl-covered, upholstered chair. Smith put the key to Drew's goggles in Humphreys' hand and turned to leave.

"Hey, Smith," Drew said.

He turned back to her.

"This may not work, you know."

"I know. Try it." He looked with pity at Jed Humphreys.

Drew helped direct Humphreys' hands and the key to the little lock which kept the goggles fastened to her head. They succeeded, and she sat now directly across from him and turned his head so his unseeing eyes pointed toward hers.

"Listen to me, Mr. Humphreys, I have something important to say to you." She paused, but his eyes did not change. There was no indication that he was in the trance-like state she assumed was crucial to proceed. She proceeded. "You realize that your vision is back to normal. You can see as well as ever. You are no longer blind."

Drew waited. Humphreys waited, little pearls of perspiration forming on his brow.

"It's not working," he said.

"Do you know what I said to you?"

"Yes, that I can see, but I can't, goddamn it. I can't see a fucking thing."

Drew turned toward the mirror and shrugged. "Shall I try again?" she asked, looking at her own reflection.

"Do you have any ideas?" Smith asked her through the intercom.

"Not really. I've never blinded anyone before. This may be the one zap that's irreversible."

"Son of a bitch," Humphreys grunted. He reached across the table, caught Drew's shoulders, then moved his powerful fingers to her throat and, bending over the table, began squeezing.

"Humphreys!" Smith's voice blasted over the intercom.

Using a maneuver Bo had taught her, Drew bent backwards the little finger of each of Humphreys' hands and broke his grip. She moved away. He came for her. She dodged around the room as he stumbled after her.

"Humphreys!" Smith yelled again.

Humphreys stopped. He shook his head, rubbing it and rubbing his eyes. He sat. He was breathing heavily and struggling to calm himself. "Try again," he said at last.

Drew did. She told him he did not have to see her in order to believe the implantation. It didn't work. She told him he could imagine her eyes, remember from looking at her before and that would allow him to receive the zap. It didn't work. Drew was fully involved in her attempts, nearly as motivated as Humphreys for success. It didn't work. Nothing worked and Humphreys was led from the room in blackness, shoulders drooping.

"You owe us one," Smith said as he accompanied Drew back to the suite.

Rit and Becka had three-quarters of a house constructed in Lincoln Logs when Drew returned. The logs were another gift from Madeline. Rit was not as sympathetic as Drew when she learned that the attempt to cure Humphreys' blindness had failed. Nor was she surprised. Their cover conversation turned to filmmaking. The written one was about other things.

*Tomorrow morning, I'll tell them about the 'insurance', Rit wrote. We'll insist on frequent contact with Bo. Bo knows that if* two days go by without a call from us or if we say, "I wish I were a cat," she's to tell my friend in New York to duplicate the tape and her notes and send them to newspapers and TV stations. Drew was trying to read the note before Rit finished. Wait, piggy, there's more, Rit wrote, and teasingly shielded her paper as she continued. If Carole (my New York friend) doesn't hear from Bo for three days and can't reach her, she's to go public. They have a code, too, just in case.

Drew read and smiled approvingly. "Yeah, I think Spielberg's overrated, too. The content's pretty adolescent. He'll broaden with age, possibly." I'm impressed, she wrote.

We'll tell the boys here all this except, of course, about the cat code and who has the documentation.

You're too clever.

True.

I'm loving you.

Rit looked at her, smiling. "I love your eyes," she said, "or have I mentioned that before."

"Once or twice."

Rit kissed her softly. I have a secret, she wrote.

Tell.

We have to find a way to talk.

Will I like it, the secret?

Rit smiled. I'm not sure. Yes and no, maybe.

Give me a hint.

Power.

I like it.

Wait and see.

Becka came back into the room.

"So they have a nifty swimming pool, huh?" Rit said. "Boy, I could sure use some exercise. You got any pull around here, Miss Becka. Can you get us a dip in the pool."

"Sure, I'll ask Madeline. She really, really likes me. She'll say it's OK."

Becka was right. The next morning, after Drew removed Anderson's motivation to free them, they all were taken to the pool. On the walk over, several people stared at Drew and whispers could be heard as she passed. Word had gotten around the compound about the prisoner with the magic eyes. Drew's goggles made the swim somewhat annoying since they kept filling up with water, but she enjoyed the swimming anyway.

"We'll talk in the sauna," Rit said as she swam past her.

Drew's mind was filled with the memories of their quiet

lovemaking the night before, how they giggled as they stifled the sounds of their pleasure, and the silly comments they made about audio porn.

Their escorts did not object when the two of them asked to go to the sauna. It was small. Rit checked for microphones, fairly sure there'd be none, then peeked out the door. One of their guards was sitting thirty feet or more down the hallway on a stool, reading.

"You ready?"

"Very."

Rit kissed her warmly, deeply, and the melting feeling in Drew was not from the heat of the sauna coals. "Is that the secret?"

"That's no secret. Pay attention now." Rit looked Drew pointedly in the eye. "Look at me and listen." Rit paused, assuming Drew was staring at her, but unable to verify this because of the mirrors over Drew's eyes. "Look at my eyes...you can hear music, a Strauss waltz."

She waited. Drew cocked her head. "I always hear music when I look at you."

"Yes," Rit said, "but can you actually hear it now?"

"Well, not actually. Do you?"

"I didn't think you would. You're immune, too."

"What do you mean? Was that supposed to be a zap?"

Rit nodded.

"Rit, darling, do you think I'm infectious?"

"No, I didn't get it from you. It was probably from the electric shock I got fifteen years ago at the University of Chicago."

Drew laughed. "You're too amusing." She reached for Rit's naked leg and caressed it slowly, raising goosebumps on her own flesh.

"All you like me for is my body," Rit said. "You don't care that I'm a zapper, just like you."

Drew looked at her, her hand stopping its movements on Rit's leg.

"I mean it," Rit said.

"You?"

"Yes. Obviously, that's why I'm immune to your zaps, as you are to mine."

"You can zap people?"

"Yes."

"Don't kid me."

"I won't. You're the first person I've ever told, in fifteen years. Now, *that's* a secret. I decided as soon as I discovered it that it would be suicidal to let anyone know." She took Drew's hand in hers. "You're not as much a realist as I, Drew, sweetie, so you told a few people. You're more trusting."

"You have the power?"

"That makes two of us as far as I know. Though there are probably others."

"Well...what...I can't believe this...it's...do you use it?"

"Rarely now. For the first five years I used it a lot. I told you about some of my escapades. I really milked it."

"Why did you stop?" Drew was still skeptical.

"I got tired of it."

"Tired of it?"

"Yes. I like the regular game better, playing by the same rules as everyone else. I had plenty of fun with it, though. Got rich, too."

Drew shook her head, staring at Rit incredulously. "Far fucking out," was all she managed to say.

"It's quite a coincidence that we happened to meet."

"Far fucking out."

"We're going to escape from here, Drew."

"We are? How?"

"Now that we're staying together, we'll figure out a way. They don't think I need goggles, which gives me a definite advantage."

The door opened. "There you are." Becka squirmed in between the two women. "Is that your swimsuit?" she asked Rit.

"The closest thing I have," Rit said. She was wearing cut-off jeans and a black tank top. "You ready to teach me to dive?"

"No, silly, you're supposed to teach me," Becka said.

"Oh, right. Let's go then."

## 47.

Wiley had a headache again. She felt like she was living upside down. Several times she was sure someone was following her. Every day she signaled Mandy and still got no response. She looked for her in the john near her office, in the coffee shop downstairs. She called Rit's office enough to have truly perturbed the receptionist. Wiley had had her suitcases packed for days, ready to leave as soon as she heard from Drew in Los Angeles.

She took two aspirins, knowing it had been barely an hour since she'd taken the last two.

She'd told her clients she unexpectedly would have to leave town for an indefinite period. Her head throbbed thinking how difficult that had been for some of them. Those who were willing, she'd connected with other therapists. She felt guilty, that she was letting them down, deserting them. Countertransference, she told herself. She'd canceled the workshop she'd planned. She'd arranged for the experimental subjects who hadn't yet gotten their portraits taken to get photographed elsewhere, and footed the bill herself. Wiley had gathered as much information as she could about Rit Avery. While Avery certainly had managed to make some enemies, few people, she discovered, shared Andrea Smith's opinion that she was unscrupulous. Little did they know, Wiley thought. She tortured herself with fearful images of Drew attempting to escape Rit's clutches and being caught and constrained forcibly. She was unable to reach "Brian McAllister".

Wiley felt drained, awful. She needed to talk with someone, someone who knew about Drew. There was only one person.

Judith hesitated at first but finally agreed to meet with her, to have dinner at a restaurant in Old Town.

"You know Drew is still gone," Wiley said after they'd ordered drinks.

"She must really like Disney World."

"That's not where she is. She's in trouble."

Judith did not respond.

"Because of the zapping."

Wiley paused and Judith felt the press to say something. "I thought it would lead to no good."

"I'm very worried about her."

Judith nodded.

"How can you be so indifferent," Wiley said hotly. "My God, Judith, you've been friends for years. She's in trouble. Don't you hear me?"

"She's not part of my life."

"What the hell's going on with you, woman. Are you dead inside?"

Judith had known Wiley for many years. Never before had she seen her like this. Tears escaped her eyes, settling in the corners.

"You do care," Wiley said. "Tell me, Judith, what's happening with you?" Her voice, once again, contained its customary empathy and concern.

"That damned zapping power made a monster out of her."

Wiley looked puzzled. She waited for more.

"She was the best friend I ever had. I felt closer to Drew than

I ever had to anyone, ever. We...clicked. We were...so close. It was always easy to talk with her, to be with her." Judith's eyes drifted with the memories. "You know what I mean, Wiley, how it is to find someone like that, someone you fit with so...so perfectly."

"Yes, I do know what you mean."

"It changes your life. It adds so much. I always felt so lucky to have her and then...then that goddamn fucking son of a bitchin' tornado destroyed it—destroyed everything."

"How, Judith? What do you mean?"

"She didn't tell you what happened in Greece?"

"What happened in Greece?"

"Wiley, I don't know...I want to talk...I need to. Can I trust you to...to not tell anyone. It's confidential, Wiley, all right?"

"All right, Judith, of course."

"In Greece, Drew...she zapped me. She used me. She made me do things, disgusting things. She perverted our friendship, destroyed it, made it sick...sickening. She turned my feelings, my deep feelings of friendship for her into a repulsive, twisted..." Judith stopped. Tears dropped down her cheeks and onto the table.

Wiley touched her wrist. "You've been through something just awful about this, haven't you?"

"Wiley," Judith said, her face contorted with pain. "Do you understand what I'm saying?" Her voice was barely a whisper now. "Drew made us have sex together, her and me, two women." Judith's face was twisted with nausea and scorn.

This was certainly not the first time someone, unaware of Wiley's sexual orientation, had discussed with her their feelings of disgust about homosexuality. This was the first time her reaction was so intense, however, and it took all her will power to remain with Judith, to stay in her frame of reference, and continue listening. "So you and Drew made love," she said gently, "and then you realized that it was unacceptable to you, to be lovers with a woman."

"Of course it's unacceptable, worse than unacceptable. It's...it's reprehensible, obscene. That's not me. I'm not like that. I'm not sick, Wiley. I'm a normal person, a normal woman. Drew used her disgusting power in a filthy way, defiling everything we..."

Her sobbing stopped her. The waiter, who had begun to approach the table, discreetly moved away.

Wiley waited, understanding now more clearly what she had suspected. But she was still puzzled. Judith's homophobia seemed more extreme than she would have predicted. She knew that Judith was not particularly religious, that she certainly had never seemed ultra-conservative, that she was at least part way in the feminist camp. Why this extreme reaction? Clearly the attraction between her and Drew was mutual and the garbage about being zapped was Judith's defense against her own homosexual feelings. But, why with such vehemence? "It sounds like you have some real strong feelings about lesbianism being sick, Judith. How come? Do you know?"

Judith had regained control of herself. She took a sip of the drink the waiter swiftly set on the table. "Yes, I do," she said strongly. "But that's not the point. The point is that Drew used me. That's what it's about."

"Quite a violation."

"You said it."

"What about your strong feelings against lesbianism, Judith? What's that all about?"

"You act as if I'm weird to feel this way," Judith said sharply.

Wiley frowned. "Well, it's not unusual to have some negative feelings, considering the cultural attitudes, but to be honest, I'm surprised that you're so condemning. I thought you always seemed rather open-minded about various..."

"You never met my mother."

"No," Wiley said, feeling more and more like this was a therapy session. "What's she like?"

Judith wrinkled her face. "I don't know...she's hard to describe. I guess powerful in a way. To me, at least. I never could quite feel like...like a grown-up around her. She still jerks me around like I was six years old. Now she's on the baby kick—pushing me to have a child. I'm not sure I want a kid, Wiley, but she acts like I'd be a pariah if I don't become a mother, or at least a tremendous disappointment to her."

"Seems like you're still working your ass off to. get her approval," Wiley said.

Judith sighed. "That's it, gold stars from momma so I can feel acceptable. God, I know it, but I can't help it. When I'm away from her, sometimes, I feel free of it, but as soon as I hear her voice— zap—I'm right back..." She laughed. "Did I say 'zap'?"

Wiley smiled. The waiter approached their table again and they ordered their food.

"I have a cousin, Jennifer Anne Pearson. She's twenty-two years old. Last year, she made a big announcement to the family. 'I love women', she said. God, my mother flipped. She's written her off, totally, and they used to be pretty close, too. She'd always buy Jenny dresses and toys when Jenny was a kid, and have her stay overnight at our house. She invited her for dinner whenever Jenny was in town after she started college. She used to tell me what a sweet person Jenny was. Then, dear perfect Jenny 'came out', as they say, and mom closed the door, slammed it tighter than a vault. Jenny's out. She's sick, lost, not a decent person any more. Refuses to get help so write her off; flaunts it, too, nasty girl. Taboo. Dead."

It seemed Judith barely knew she was talking with Wiley, so absorbed was she in what she was saying and feeling.

"So if you were ever attracted to women, it would be quite a threat, huh?"

"I'm not attracted to women, Wiley. I'm engaged to Vic. We're getting married. I'm planning the wedding now. We're going to have a big, old-fashioned wedding. My mother..."

Again the sobs constricted Judith's throat, cutting off the words.

"What a conflict," Wiley said softly.

"You know what I found out," Judith said, again composing herself. "I found out that Drew began hanging around with lesbians when we got back to Chicago." She shook her head angrily. "We met some women in Greece. They were lesbians. They talked about destroying the so-called *patriarchy,* taking over, getting rid of men. Drew really got into it. So did I at the time...from the zap. We talked about Lesbian Nation, Wiley, and I just know...I'm sure that's what Drew wants to do. She wants to zap everyone, destroy what we have, make everybody queer, make all the women lesbians and take over the world. Dominate men, push them down, take away their power, make them serve women and pay, get revenge. She's dangerous. Her power is evil."

"Drew said this?" Wiley asked. "That she wanted to do those things?"

"She didn't have to."

Wiley was silent, not sure where to go with it. She felt concern for Judith, for her pain, but she felt very angry at her, too. Mostly her sympathy went to Drew.

"She's not Drew to me any more," Judith said. "Drew is gone, the Drew I knew. She's just a fond memory. The person she's become is...is a menace!"

Wiley looked at Judith's red angry eyes. "You really think she's dangerous?"

"She could have been."

"What do you mean?"

Judith appeared frightened. "I had to do something."

"What did you do?" Wiley couldn't imagine, yet she felt an ominous heaviness as she waited for Judith's reply.

"You have to understand my motives, Wiley. I know how close you two are. You have to realize, though, that she isn't really Drew any more."

"Your motives for what?"

"It's like Drew is dead and someone else is inhabiting her body."

"What did you do?"

Judith hesitated, clearly torn, vacillating. "I reported her," she blurted.

"Reported her?" Wiley's whole body tightened. Her mouth was suddenly cotton dry. "To whom?"

"She had to be stopped."

"Who did you report her to?"

"I didn't know who to call, who would handle such a thing, so I ended up calling the Secret Service."

"You called the Secret Service?" Wiley was dumbfounded.

"Yes, then someone came to talk to me. They said they'd investigate. Wiley, understand, will you. She had to be stopped."

"I think I do understand," Wiley said reeling with disbelief. Her mind clicked in an attempt to integrate this new information. "Who's Brian McAllister?" she asked sharply.

"I don't know. Why?"

Wiley shook her head. She was feeling both pity and contempt. The contempt was winning. "Never mind. So what's happened since? Have they kept you informed?"

"No, I told them everything I knew about it, except what happened in Greece, what she did to me. I couldn't tell them that. I couldn't tell anyone, but I have told you, Wiley. I trust you to keep it to yourself. I know you have to do that with your patients. I'm sure you'll do the same with this."

"And then what?"

"What?"

"After you told them everything."

"They said they'd look into it. I told them about the file in your office, too."

Wiley tried not to sneer. "When did all this happen? When did you first contact them?"

"It was in October sometime, late October."

"Have you heard from them since?"

"No."

Wiley was silent. She pushed her food around with her fork. Her jaw was tight. She had never felt so much like strangling anybody before.

## 48

Becka was asleep on the cot. Rit had temporarily disconnected the microphone in the bedroom. She took Drew's wrists and, without speaking, led her there, closed the door and pushed in the doorknob lock. She was wearing a pair of faded jeans and a brown jersey that clung to her breasts in a way that sent shivers through Drew. Without removing her boots, Rit stretched out on the bed, leaning on the pillows she'd propped against the headboard. She never took her eyes from Drew. Drew began to feel self- conscious as well as excited.

"Take them off," Rit said.

Drew smiled and tugged on her blouse. "This?" she asked.

Rit nodded. "All your clothes." She wasn't smiling. "Every stitch."

Drew felt that little edge of fear that so enhanced the pleasure in this game. She began unbuttoning, watching Rit watch her. When she'd removed her blouse and tossed it on the dresser, Rit beckoned for Drew to come to her. Drew stood at her side, bending slightly toward her, sinking into the liquidy rush she got when Rit cupped her breast then slowly squeezed her nipple. Drew began to crawl into the bed, onto Rit's powerful body.

"Not yet," Rit said, pulling slightly back from her, holding her off. "Finish what you started."

Drew stood again and removed her slacks and socks and underwear as Rit watched each move. Drew shivered from the scrutiny, and the anticipation. She stood before Rit now, naked, slightly hesitant, waiting for Rit to take the lead.

"Remember what you did this morning?"

Drew looked puzzled. "What did I do?"

"You dropped a spoon on the floor." Rit looked very serious. She swung her legs over the side of the bed and stood only inches away from Drew, her boots making her several inches taller, and looked down at her. "It made a noise. That displeased me."

Drew began to laugh, then stopped. She backed up a step. She knew the game, but felt a twinge of fear along the back of her neck and in her stomach, nonetheless.

"When you displease me, you must be punished. I have not forgotten."

Drew smiled.

Rit looked at her sternly.

The smile faded from Drew's mouth.

"You must be taught not to displease me."

Drew waited, her heart bumping noisily within her chest.

There were now several feet of space between them, Drew standing at a slight angle away from Rit, feeling the vulnerability of her naked body, and the excitement at Rit's manner and words.

"Come here."

Drew took a step forward. She could feel Rit's warmth against her breasts.

"Do you know what your punishment is to be?"

Drew shook her head. You do this so well, she thought, not wanting it to stop.

"I'm going to fuck your brains out, woman. Get on the bed. There's no escaping me."

Drew couldn't help giggling. "I don't want to escape," she said.

"On the bed."

Rit did not smile, but Drew could see laughter in her eyes. If it were a man playing with her this way, Drew would have been incensed and repelled. Why did it make a difference? Why should she enjoy such a game with a woman? Drew did not know and did not have time to think about it further for Rit's mouth covering hers wiped away all thought, and then Rit's fingers entered her possessively. The mix of roughness and tenderness, the power of Rit's domination and surrender tapped the deepest centers of Drew's body, the deepest parts of her being.

The appointment Rit had requested with Sandor Smith was set for nine a.m. They came for her at exactly 8:55.

"Drew McAllister's invaluable to you," Rit began.

"Not the way she is to you," Smith replied suggestively.

"Drew can be stubborn, and sometimes foolish," Rit went on. "I don't like you or what you stand for, but I do understand you. I've taken a step to protect Drew's interests. I'm cynical enough to suspect you may intend to cut Drew off from the world, except to utilize her abilities as it suits your interest. Anticipating this, I took some precautions. If you become unreasonable in your treatment of us, if you push my hand, then the whole world will know, not only of Drew's powers, but of your devious ways of trying to harness them."

Smith listened attentively but with no apparent affect.

"There is a person somewhere in the United States, an attorney, who is in possession of documentation of Drew McAllister's abilities. The documentation consists of a videotape of an implantation session. It also contains a detailed description of Drew's powers as well as Bo Clemmen's detailed memoirs of her experience at the Flagstaff Airport and at your little resort here, including, of course, the fact that I have been kidnapped along with Drew McAllister and her daughter. Unless we are allowed daily, uncensored contact with Bo Clemmens, the contents of those documents will be duplicated and sent to major news media. Unless we are allowed such contact, Bo Clemmens will present herself to an investigative reporter, a friend, who will follow through on the story. He will also protect her from you and your friends."

"We could use you," Smith said. "You seem to have a knack for this sort of thing."

"Drew's cooperation will be limited. She will not zap for you indiscriminately. We need to set up a negotiation session to work out terms. As you now understand, you can't have it all your way."

"Of course you simply haven't had the training or the experience to be competitive with us." He smiled. "I'm afraid, Miss Avery, that you underestimate us." From his desk drawer, Smith withdrew a thick, manila envelope and tossed it on the desk. "The documentation you refer to, is this it, by any chance?"

The package was addressed to Carole Berman in New York City. It had already been opened and Rit removed the contents. There was a video tape and, in Bo's handwriting, pages and pages of written material.

Rit let her anger show, but not her wrenching disappointment and fear. "Where is Bo?"

"In our custody."

"I want to see her."

"You're hardly in a position to be making demands. At this point, Miss Avery," Smith said coldly, "it still seems to our advantage to allow you to remain with our subject, with McAllister, but be careful. If that should change, we will not hesitate to remove you."

When Rit was returned to the suite, neither Drew nor Becka were there. She pulled a chair near the window, already starting to feel energized by the challenge, and began to plan.

Within a half hour, Becka returned with Madeline. Drew was still away. She was being briefed for the implantation she was to perform that day. She sat at a table with a small camera and a manual, reading a section, then playing with the camera. A technician sat with her answering questions and explaining in detail the camera's operation. An hour and a half later, Drew put on the tailored suit they had given her and was taken to an office to wait for her subject, John Luther. It felt odd to Drew, being in a skirt. They had removed the goggles. The camera sat on the desk and

Drew stared at it as she waited, wondering where this would all lead and rehearsing her lines.

John Luther was a large, athletic-looking man, tanned, energetic. "So you're the camera pro," he said, bouncing into the office. "This one's a bit tricky, they tell me." He picked it up. "I'm ready to learn."

Drew began explaining the device. During a pause, she looked at him intently, telling him to listen for she had something important to say. She began to recite the words she had memorized during the practice session.

"...and you realize now that it is much wiser to follow that protocol. From now on, you want to keep your superiors fully informed as to your operations and consult with them more frequently. You no longer wish to take the sort of risky, independent actions that have annoyed your superiors in the past."

Drew paused until his eyes cleared, and then continued discussing the camera.

"Excellent," Smith told her later. "Luther's a top rate agent. I'd hate to lose him. It looks like this will do it." Smith was obviously very pleased. "He went directly from his meeting with you to his immediate superior and proceeded to update him. I'd say this was a resounding success, Miss McAllister. You did very well."

He told her about her next assignment which was to begin that afternoon. Drew was then escorted back to her apartment where Rit and Becka were playing checkers. The guard unlocked the goggles and left. Drew sat down on the floor between her daughter and Rit. "Who's winning?"

"No one," Becka said.

*Bad news,* Rit wrote. *They intercepted the tape. They're tightening up. We're getting out today.* She double jumped and got two of Becka's pieces. "So how was your morning?"

Drew was pale. "I zapped a guy," she said flatly. *Is Bo OK?*

Rit shrugged her shoulders, looking worried. "What are your plans for the rest of the day?"

"I have a session with Smith after lunch. This time I'm supposed to zap a woman to get her to reveal some information they want." *I won't do it,* Drew wrote. *How are we going to get out?*

"They're keeping you busy," Rit said. "I just got back from another swim. Miss Becka and her friend, Madeline, invited me to join them. I met a guy at the pool *He's a big shot here.* "Brad Dorian is his name. Very pleasant man. I invited him here for lunch." *I zapped him. He's our ticket out.* "Of course, you'll have to wear your lovely sunglasses while he's here." *He's going to take us to the Reception Center. We're going to switch places with some artists working on a mural there. Dorian will drive us out of here. I'll try to get you out of the goggles.*

Drew read the note and nodded. "Let me check to see what we have in the kitchen," she said. "Since this is the first entertaining we've done here, let's make it good." She felt nervous. The plan seemed fuzzy. She feared for their safety, for Becka's welfare. She worried about Bo.

Brad Dorian didn't seem like an especially pleasant guy to Drew. He seemed detached and pedantic. They were having a drink and he was talking about Mr. Marshall's mural. "As you may know, he's the chief of this installment," Dorian said. "He's partial to murals so I hired some local artists. They're doing a fine job."

"I'd like to see it," Rit said.

"I think that could be arranged," Dorian replied immediately. "How about you and your daughter, Miss. Would you like to come too?"

"Yes," Drew said, "we would."

"If you want to see the artists in action, we should go right now before they break for lunch."

"Fine," Drew said. "Our sandwiches can wait."

Dorian went to the intercom. "I'd like to take our three guests on a visit to the mural. Clear it, will you?"

"Yes, sir."

A few minutes later, Dorian was told that the tour was OK'd and they would send an escort over.

They walked across the campus past several red-brick buildings to the Reception Center which was in the front of the compound. In the lobby, Dorian and the prisoners admired the artists' work for several minutes while their escort, a tall red-headed man, leaned against the wall in the corner watching them. Rit approached the escort. They were out of earshot of the others.

"That's quite a mural," she said, facing him.

He grunted indifferently, but when Rit told him to look at her and listen well, he became much more attentive, staring intently into her eyes. He said goodbye, then, and walked through the lobby and out of the building.

Next, Rit took Drew, Becka and Dorian into the large storage room where the artists' supplies were kept. She told Dorian it was time to fetch the saw. After their swim together, he had procured an electric jeweler's saw and stashed it in a nearby office. They waited silently in the storage room until he returned. Rit plugged the tool into the wall socket and quickly sawed through the narrowest section of Drew's goggles. In the meantime, Dorian fetched two of the female artists who Rit and Drew immediately zapped. They put on the artists' smocks and took their ID cards. They were about to leave the storage room when Drew noticed the goggles sitting accusingly on the floor. She stuffed them in a pocket.

Rit, Drew, Becka and Dorian walked together out of the Reception Center to the front parking lot. There were few people around and those present paid little attention to the group. Dorian spoke to the lot attendant, was given a car, and drove them through the grounds to the main entrance gate. Becka was crouched on the floor in the back seat next to Drew, a drop cloth concealing her.

"I'm taking these people to town," Dorian told the guard.

"Yes, sir. I'll need to see your ID's, ladies." He flashed a warm white-toothed grin at Drew, his eyes focused on the breast bulges beneath the smock.

As Drew was pulling the ID card from the hip pocket of the smock, her wristwatch caught on the goggles and, for a split second, they were visible. The guard stopped leering. His eyes narrowed.

"What's that?" he asked. "In your pocket." He stared at Drew.

"Sonofabitch! You're the Code Six!" He started to back away.

"Listen to me!" Drew said through the open window. Her firm voice captured him.

Rit saw the other guard approaching. She got out of the car hoping she would not have to zap him herself.

"Any problem?" he asked the first guard.

"...and you want to let us pass, now," Drew concluded.

The second guard saw his co-worker staring at Drew as if hypnotized. "Hey, what the fuck's going...?"

"And you..." Drew turned her powerful eyes to the second guard, but she wasn't fast enough. He understood and quickly averted his eyes, brushed past Rit, and ran to the phone.

Rit got back into the car. The zapped guard opened the gate as his companion was making the call. Dorian drove off at high speed.

The compound was in a restricted area surrounded by thick trees and brush. They left this behind and zoomed down the highway.

"Turn there," Rit said.

Dorian wheeled the car off the main road, drove for several hundred yards, then turned again as Rit directed. They entered a two-lane, black top country road.

"Can I get up now?"

Drew helped her daughter from the floor. "Keep your head down, though, just in case," she said.

257

Becka lay her head in her mother's lap and their speeding vehicle raced on.

"We need a different car," Rit said to Dorian. "Where can we find one? Where are some houses or farms?"

"The town's in the other direction," Dorian said, "but there are some farms up ahead. We may be able to get one there."

Drew's hand rested on Becka's head, stroking it. Becka was trembling.

A half mile later, there was a farm. A pickup truck stood in the driveway. "We may have to zap the owner," Rit said to Drew. "I doubt if the keys are in the truck." She turned to Dorian. "Drive around the back. We need to hide the car."

Rit went to the back door of the farm house.

"What is it?" The woman appeared nervous, a young woman, puffy and sickly looking. She stayed behind the screen door.

Rit looked into the woman's watery eyes. "You want to give us the keys to your truck, then forget that we were here."

They drove for nearly a mile, Drew's thoughts racing ahead, far ahead, to the safety of some hideout, to the eventual flight out of the country, to living somewhere far away from U.S. Government officials, perhaps Brazil, she thought. Rit had a resort there. She was trying to imagine how it would be in Brazil when the first pursuers appeared. The chase was brief. It lasted no more than a few minutes. As the cars surrounding them were closing in, as the two helicopters hovered above, Rit zapped Dorian to forget what had transpired, and Drew zapped Becka's panic away.

_____ **49.**


Sandor Smith was furious but controlled when Drew was brought to him.

"We will now shift strategies," he said. "I wanted to go slowly with you, work you into things gradually, accommodate you as much as possible, hence the swims in the pool, guests for lunch, et cetera. That phase is over." His eyes were inhumanly cold. "It's your turn to listen carefully, for I have something important to say."

Her repaired goggles in place, Drew sat across from him in the same office where they'd been together many times before. She was trying to remain more angry than frightened. She had been returned to the suite, but had not seen Rit or Becka since the escape attempt. She had laid alone on the bed for what seemed like days, her mind a buzzing generator of frightening questions. Would they harm Becka? What would happen to Rit now? How evil are they? Where is Bo? When will this end? Will we ever get away? She tried to stop the questions and the horrible answers that were the possibilities. She tried to make her thoughts go back to a pleasanter time, to the tree near the aquarium where they sat at Lake Michigan and where she felt the first touch of Rit's lips on her eyes. They had seen a rat that night. Drew could picture it slinking by them swiftly and crawling between the chunks of granite that lined the shore. Was it an omen, that rat?

Then her thoughts went to "if onlys". If only they had made it to the lodge in time, to safety like the other campers. If only she had done like Rit and never told a soul about the power, not even Wiley. If only Wiley's need to be the benevolent dictator of the world had not emerged to taint and distort an otherwise wonderful woman. If only Zayre had never come. If only they had made it to France. If only she could know that Becka would be OK.

"From now on, Miss McAllister," Smith continued, "this compound is your home. You will remain here always, except for the occasional business trips we will arrange. Outsiders who know of your power will be eliminated. That includes Rit Avery, Wiley Cavenar, Bo Clemmens, and Judith Brodie. They will die in a bomb explosion, an accident assumedly caused by their own ineptness. We have dossiers documenting the radical, subversive activities of you and your group, which the press will get wind of. There will be a fifth body in the charred rubble which will be identified as yours. We'll be taking an impression of your teeth soon. Your own dentist, Dr. James Furmanian, will make the identification. As far as the world will know, you will be dead."

Drew was dizzy. There was a whirring din, a buzz, in her ears, in the center of her head.

"Your ex-husband, Steven Tremaine, will have a fatal car accident. In fact, that may already have happened. Your daughter will be adopted by Madeline Drury. She will live with Madeline Drury and be raised by her and her husband. Her welfare will be assured as long as you remain alive and cooperative. If you kill yourself, your little girl will be injected with lethal bacteria and die within six months of your suicide, slowly and painfully. If you do not kill yourself, but refuse to cooperate with us, your daughter will suffer. You will be kept informed of her well-being and development by way of home movies which Madeline Drury will make. You will be made as comfortable as possible in your confinement here. We will..."

Drew had never fainted before in her life. When she regained consciousness she was in the center of a thick fog. Nothing had distinct outlines. Nothing she looked at, nothing she thought. She was unresponsive to Smith's attempts to communicate with her. They took her to the infirmary.

## 50.

Steve Tremaine was on his way to the Lake County Clinic where he donated an afternoon a week doing general dentistry. He was driving at a steady 55 mph on the Edens, thinking about his ex-wife and how unusual it was for her to go away like this without keeping in touch. How long can one stay at Disney World, he wondered. That's far too much school for Becka to be missing. Drew's friend, Judith, wasn't any help at all. "In Florida, I believe," she had said. "I don't see much of Drew anymore."

Steve had no idea who any of Drew's other friends were. Her parents had said they were hoping for a visit from Drew while she was in Florida and were surprised that they hadn't yet heard from her.

Steve wondered if Drew was going through some sort of crisis. She'd quit her job. Who knows how she was supporting herself. The child support payments certainly weren't enough. Maybe she hooked up with some rich old man. She seemed different the last couple times he'd talked to her, Steve thought. Not depressed like she sometimes got; no, the opposite, actually, lighter somehow, more confident. He was just letting his mind get into the speculations about what might be going on with her and wondering if Becka was all right in her care when the car began to rumble.

The slight vibrating increased until he felt the steering wheel shaking beneath his hands. "Fucking car," he murmured, applying the brakes. The brake pedal slid fully to the floor but there was no effect; the car did not slow down. He pumped the pedal frantically while desperately trying to keep the car on the road, but the steering, too, was unresponsive. The steering wheel felt loose in his hands, not connecting, not turning the wheels.

The road had a slight decline and he was still going 55 mph, the legal speed limit, when the car crashed into a viaduct, spun nearly 360 degrees sideswiping another car, then came to a smashing halt against the viaduct wall. The steering wheel was wedged into Steve Tremaine's chest cavity and his head hung limply from his broken neck.

## 51.

Drew lay motionless on the narrow white bed in the infirmary. Her eyes were open beneath the goggles, but seeing nothing. The doctors talked about her being in shock, about her having been subjected to more stress than she could tolerate. They talked about malingering, conversion reaction, possible fugue state, catatonia. Her vital signs were within normal limits, but Drew McAllister remained psychologically unresponsive. She did not talk. She barely moved. Her breathing was shallow.

Sandor Smith sent for Rit Avery.

## 52.

Wiley Cavenar received a letter from the Illinois Psychological Association Ethics Committee informing her of the ethical concerns expressed by Fred Greeley and asking her for her side of the story. Wiley was sitting at her kitchen table, writing out her response, when the doorbell rang.

Two men in business suits showed her a paper, a warrant for

her arrest, they said, and waited while she got her coat and her purse. They didn't read her her rights. They didn't allow her a phone call, nor did they answer her questions. They didn't take her to jail. They took her to a windowless room in the basement of an old building south of the Loop and locked the door. Wiley was sure it had to do with Drew.

There was another woman in the room, sitting on the floor, leaning her back against the wall. She was thin and boyish wearing a plaid shirt and jeans.

"Do you know what's going on?" Wiley asked her immediately.

"Who are you?"

"My name is Wiley Cavenar. I'm..."

The woman turned her head away and scowled. "So they got you, too."

"You know me? Who...?"

"Did they tell you anything?"

"Nothing," Wiley said. "What...?"

"Sh-h." The woman stood and walked around the room, examining the bare walls. She went to the door and lay down on the floor, placing her head on the concrete and peering through the crack underneath the door.

"What are you doing?" Wiley asked.

"I want to make sure they can't hear us."

"Who's they?"

"The CIA. Drew's in serious trouble. It looks like we are, too." The woman spoke quietly.

"Drew McAllister? You *do* know her? Are you...?"

"Shit," the woman said. She sat on the floor again, shaking her head.

"Tell me what's going on," Wiley insisted.

The woman shrugged her shoulders. "Why not?" she said looking up at Wiley. "Sit down, you're giving me a sore neck."

Wiley joined her on the floor.

"My name is Bo Clemmens. I'm a friend of Rit Avery and of Drew."

Wiley nodded tersely. "Where is Drew now? Do you know?" She was afraid Bo would say the CIA has her.

"The CIA has her. Rit, too."

Wiley banged her fist on the cement floor. "Damn!" Her eyes were red and wet. "I thought maybe she made it. I kept hoping. I thought maybe she got away, that she'd call me when she could and..."

"I'm afraid your world domination dream has fizzled." Bo

262

smiled sardonically.

The comment did not sink in or possibly Wiley did not hear it at all. She was quiet for a long time and so was Bo.

"Where does Rit Avery fit in?" Wiley asked at last. "Do you know?"

Bo was nodding her head. "Yes," she said. "Unlike you, Rit was trying to protect Drew from being used."

"Unlike me? What are you talking about?"

"What are you talking about?" Bo mimicked contemptuously. Wiley stood. She started to pace. "Where do they have her? Do you know if she's all right? What are they going to do with her?"

Bo looked at Wiley disdainfully. "You're not the only one who wants to use her."

"What is this shit?" Wiley spat. "You think I'm...that I would harm Drew?"

"We know about you, Dr. Cavenar. You can cut the charade. We know all about your plan to use Drew's power for your own grandiose scheme. There's a leak in your organization."

Wiley looked angrily at Bo, then away. "Tell me what you know about what's going on? How did they find Drew? Why was Rit Avery trying to protect her? How did she find out about Drew in the first place?"

"You got a cigarette?" Bo asked.

"No, I don't smoke."

"What good are you," Bo said nastily.

Wiley sighed. "Obviously, we have to clear up your misconceptions about me before we can proceed," she said. "We need to be on the same side." She sat several feet from Bo and leaned back against the cold cement wall. The solidness of it felt good for some reason. "So you've heard I have an organization, and a *grandiose* scheme..."

"I'd call ruling the world rather grandiose."

"...using Drew to take over the world."

"With you as top dog. You might as well admit it, your plan's shot to hell now anyway."

"There's no organization," Wiley said.

"Eleanor Clark says different."

Wiley shook her head. "Did Drew tell you about our research?"

"Yes." Bo looked cooly at Wiley. "Only she didn't know then what your real motivation was."

"To take over the world."

Bo nodded.

Wiley sighed.

Bo looked away.

"*Take over,*" Wiley said, more to herself than Bo. "Poor choice of words." She was looking at Bo now. "*Make changes for the better,* that was my motive. Is that a crime?"

"You're rationalizing, *doctor.* Admit you were in it for the power. You'll feel better, *doctor.*" Bo was sneering.

"Drew and I talked a number of times," Wiley said, "about how a power like hers could be used to create change in the world, real change, beyond..."

"Oh, really, you planned it together, huh? That's funny, Drew never seemed particularly interested in using her power that way." The sarcasm dripped venomously from Bo's angry tongue.

"She was overwhelmed by it. She needed time to get used to it. You can understand that, I imagine. She wanted to play with it. She wasn't yet in a place to plan a systematic, constructive way of..."

"So you did it for her. How nice of you. Behind her back, making yourself the chief Chief."

"Nothing was behind her back. Do you know about the protocol for the experiment and the stuff I wrote about projected uses if the power did turn out to be as it appeared?"

Bo rolled her eyes.

"Listen, will you," Wiley said impatiently. "You're condemning me without sufficient data."

"Oh, save me," Bo moaned. "You supercilious..."

"Listen." Wiley stood again and looked down at Bo, wishing, as she had many times before, that it was *she* who could zap. "Drew's ability to implant beliefs in people has immense implications. I would assume you have enough imagination to realize that. I was working with Drew to explore the power and implement ways to use it. Anyone with the ability she has owes it to the world to use it for... Anyway, I wrote all my ideas out. I discussed most of it with Drew, some of it. She read it. She knows my proposal. She knew the research was the first step. She knew I was planning to get a group of feminists together, people with ideas, historians, economists, activists, theoreticians, philosophers. I had one meeting so far, with a small group. I told them it was an exercise. We brainstormed, that's all, talked about the possibilities. I didn't tell them Paz...Drew, really existed. That would have been the next step if Drew agreed to it. That's when she disappeared."

"You say Drew knew of all that?"

"Yes. Well, she knew about the plan. I discussed most of the possibilities with her, nothing concrete, but..." Wiley's head lowered. "I should have told her about the meeting beforehand."

"Slipped your mind."

"Drew was dealing with so much," Wiley said softly. "The power, itself, and a shitload of personal things—quitting her job, the ending of her relationship with her boyfriend." Wiley paused here. "I'm not sure...how well do you know Drew, her personal...?"

"I know she's just come out as a lesbian, if that's what you mean."

"Yes," Wiley said. "That's a lot to deal with in itself, plus a shattering disappointment by her first woman lover. Her work in the research part of this project was already asking a lot. I chose not to overwhelm her with the other part of it, but she certainly knew about the plan, the possibilities of using the power to...I was about to tell her about the meeting."

"Drew had no idea of your plan. Believe me, she was appalled and crushed. She really had trusted you. She was very upset, to say the least, when she heard about your meeting."

"Because I didn't tell her beforehand? I should have, but I didn't think it would matter that much. She knew I intended to have the meeting. It was all in my notes."

"Your notes?"

"Yes." Wiley moved to the corner and rested her shoulder on the wall. "Early on, before the experiment began, I wrote a section on the research and a section on the proposed plan. Drew read them. I talked about starting with a group of women, brainstorming, and then beginning to formulate specific plans for using Drew's power..."

"If you're telling the truth, and for some reason, you're beginning to persuade me, then it's confusing. It doesn't make sense. Drew didn't seem to know about any *plan*. She said you had idealistic ideas, but never anything about actual steps to implement them."

"It was all in the file I gave her. We went over the hypotheses together, in her living room." Wiley was looking at the blank dirty wall, trying to recall. "I remember that she said it was boring, that I was obsessive-compulsive. No, she said 'repulsive'." Wiley paused. "I left the file with her to read. I remember I had to leave, to meet someone, a friend of mine, Jill Ramsey. Maybe she never did finish reading it. The plan part was at the end. She gave it all back to me and then I just gave her copies of the protocol, the procedure for the study, what she'd need to zap the subjects."

"Maybe she never read it," Bo said, wanting to trust this woman, wanting not to be with an enemy in this small locked room.

"The brat." Wiley laughed. "I bet she didn't. Actually, we never did talk in much detail at all about specific ways she could use the power to wipe out the patriarchy. She never seemed to want to and I never pushed her. I just assumed...so, she believes I was using her?"

Bo nodded. "I'm afraid so. For a while we even considered the possibility that no one was pursuing her, that you had gotten Zayre and Granser to..."

"That I...?"

"Yes. Well, Drew never believed it, but Rit and I thought it was possible."

Wiley's mouth was open. "You know what I thought? The same thing. I thought Rit Avery was behind the whole Zayre/Granser/Brian McAllister business. I thought they worked for her."

"Good God!"

"Brian McAllister told me they did."

Bo snickered.. "Well, why shouldn't he?"

"But then I found out Rit wasn't the one."

"How?"

Wiley rubbed her arms. She felt very cold. "I learned that somebody had called the Secret Service, told them all about Drew's power."

"Who?" Bo asked. The muscles of her narrow jaw were clenched tight.

"Someone who was real scared and conflicted and confused." Wiley paced a few steps. "What a mess. So, what do you think they have in mind for us?"

"I'm afraid to think."

Wiley sat down next to Bo again. "We should have made it public right from the start," she said. She shook her head. "I knew it was risky."

"I wish I had a cigarette," Bo said.

"She shouldn't have let anybody know. Even me, maybe. She should have zapped me to forget."

The door opened and a woman was brought in.

"Judith!" Wiley said.

## 53

Occasionally the fog was penetrated by people with white coats, sometimes by angry voices asking questions, shouting, shouting. The nightmares wouldn't stop. The sorcerer was unrelenting, drilling his bolts of lightning into her head, burning her brain. The smell of her own brain burning made her nauseated again and she vomited out the food they put into her stomach through the tube. The sorcerer came again. More burning. This time it was Becka. The burning jumped from mother to daughter. Drew frantically poured bucket after bucket of water on Becka to stop the burning, but the water wasn't wet. The sorcerer laughed and handed her more buckets with dry water and Becka burned. Then it spread to everyone. Friends from high school, her cousin, Rosemary, Rit, her parents, Kate, thousands of strangers all burning from the lightning the sorcerer pierced her brain with.

"Drew, can you hear me? Listen, sweetie."

The rubbing on her arm felt good. The hand in her hand was strong and gentle. The smell of the burning receded. Drew looked at her. "Rit?"

"Yes, babe, it's me."

Drew squeezed back on the hand that held hers. "Am I alive?"

"You're alive. I'm here with you. Can you feel me here with you?"

"Yes, it's really you?"

"Yes, Drew."

"You're not burning?"

"I'm fine, Drew. You're a bit of a mess yourself. You haven't been eating."

Drew lay silently for a while, looking into Rit's face. She still wore the goggles. "We have to get out of here," she said.

"Yes, Drew, but we have to keep calm so we can plan. You have to hold on, hang in."

"Let's go. Let's leave. Let's go home, Rit. Maybe to the van. I love the van. It has everything."

"Even a john."

"I like that chair by the window, where I always used to sit and pretend to read, but watch you instead."

"You little sneak."

"I love you, Rit." Drew began to cry. "I'm destroying everyone." She sobbed.

"No, Drew. That's not fair. That's bullshit. Remember I told you to hang in. Now, do it. Pull it together."

Drew stopped crying. "Right."

"Good."

"We gotta fight back."

"And keep cool. We have to be able to think clearly."

Drew began to cry again. "They're going to kill everyone...with a bomb, even Judith...Wiley...Bo...and, oh, Rit..." Rit held her as she sobbed. "They're going to kill..." She clung to Rit, crushing Rit's body to her own, clinging desperately. "And they're going to take Becka away from me. Oh no, oh no, oh no." Drew drifted back again, back into the fog and the burning. The sorcerer was relentless.

Rit was taken away.

"You've managed to terrify her half out of her mind," she said to Smith. "It's making her nuts. You'll get nothing out of her that way."

"We'll see," Smith said.

"She thinks you're going to kill me and some of her other friends."

Smith didn't answer.

"Did you tell her that?"

"You're not stupid, Avery," Smith said. "You know we're not about to let civilians walk around out there full of classified information."

Rit felt like making a vegetable out of him, zapping him senseless. "There are alternatives to violence," she said, instead, speaking calmly. "Think, man. You want her to cooperate and you tell her you're going to kill her friends. That's stupid. It's particularly stupid because you have an obvious alternative."

Smith waited, the pulsating vein along his neck reflecting his reaction to her abuse, but not his face.

"She can remove things from people's minds, remember? She can zap us to forget, remove from our memories everything connected with her power and your actions."

Smith's eyes narrowed. He was silent for a while, then smiled coldly. "You just saved your life," he said. "Let's go. We'll go tell her together."

Rit was able to get Drew aware enough to listen. After she heard, after Smith confirmed it and told her that Wiley, Judith, and Bo would be flown here immediately, Drew began to believe it. She sat up in the bed. The sorcerer was fading. Drew suddenly felt very hungry.

Becka was staying with Madeline. That part of the plan had not changed. She was told her mother was ill; later she would be told her mother was dead. Drew was moved back into her suite and Rit was allowed to stay there, too. Wiley, Bo and Judith were to arrive soon for the zappings. Impressions of Drew's teeth were made as arrangements for her "death" proceeded.

Rit tried hard to penetrate Drew's despair.

*I'll be freed soon,* she reminded her. *I will work from the outside to free you. We will overcome!*

*They're going to fake my death,* Drew wrote.

*It doesn't matter. We'll overcome.*

*Steve is probably already dead.*

*We'll overcome.*

*They've taken Becka from me.*

*Not for long.*

*Are you sure?*

*I'm determined.*

They hugged then and some of Rit's strength flowed to Drew.

Drew met with them, one by one, in the room with the one-way mirror. She had been instructed exactly what to say to them. She was to say no more, no less.

Bo came first. Drew zapped her and Bo was taken away.

Wiley was next. The mix of feelings in Drew as she looked at her long-time friend tore her unbearably and she made the zap numbly, but it worked, and Wiley, too, was gone.

When she saw Judith, her tears blurred her own vision, but did not affect the zap.

Rit was the last one. She, too, became immobile, intently looking into Drew's eyes and then she, too, was taken away.

Drew saw them for less than two minutes each. There had been no goodbyes, as there were to be no goodbyes to Becka, who soon would learn that both her parents, unfortunately, were dead.

The next morning, Drew rehearsed the implantation she was to do with the woman who would be brought to her. "You want to tell Mr. Smith everything you know about the Dram-X deal. Everything. After you are finished, you want to forget that you told him, forget the conversation entirely."

"Up until Drew returned from the hospital, there are no gaps?"

"Right," Wiley said. "I've been reconstructing it over and over, Bill, and that's when it begins, one night at her place. We went out for icecream, I remember that, and afterwards we had a long talk, but I have absolutely no idea what we talked about. That seems to be the first gap."

"Whatever it was you talked about might be the key to the amnesia. Have you asked Drew about that conversation?"

"She's gone. That's part of it, too. She's been gone for weeks. She didn't even tell me she was leaving, or at least I can't remember her telling me. Supposedly she went to Disney World with her daughter. It doesn't make sense. Her daughter's supposed to be in school."

"After that conversation, the one at Drew's place, what happened then?"

"I remember that I didn't sleep much that night. I was obsessed with this research project, on hypnotizability. But I have no idea why. It's never been a strong interest of mine, as you know. I've gone to some workshops, have used it on occasion in my practice, but that's all."

"You can't remember what started you on the project?"

"No."

"You had a conversation with Drew one night and from then on you were diligently absorbed with this research project. They may be connected."

"Yes, but how? I have no idea."

"Well, let's get you into trance at this point and see what we can disgorge."

The induction was fairly rapid. Wiley was an average or better hypnotic subject. The age regression was successful. She recalled and discussed with vividness events prior to Drew's return from the hospital, dredging up details she would have thought were totally forgotten.

"Now it's a summer's night in July, last July," the hypnotist said. "You're at the restaurant with Drew, eating icecream. Tell me about it."

"The icecream's delicious. I'm gobbling it up as if I'm starving."

Wiley licked her lips. "But then I don't want to pay for it. *This is awful, I'm not paying for it. I refuse. All right, you take care of it, Drew, if you insist. I'll wait outside.* Then I'm standing under the streetlight reading something. I...I don't know what. I can't make out the words."

"Bring the paper a little closer to the light."

"Yes, that's better. There are words written on it, but I still can't quite...I don't know what it says."

"All right. What happens next?"

"We're walking back to Drew's. We're sitting in the living room, talking."

"Yes."

"We're talking."

"Yes, what are you saying?"

"It's so clear, how Drew looks, her expression, what she's wearing."

"What is she saying right now?"

"Her mouth is moving but I can't make out the words."

They continued the attempts for another ten or fifteen minutes with no success. Then they talked some more, starting with Wiley's associations to hypnosis and hypnosis research. They came up against many gaps in tracing her life for the past few months, most of which seemed to relate to Drew in one way or another.

"So you decided to close your private practice, give up your career here. Sounds like you were planning to leave town."

"Yes, but I don't know why. I've always wanted to live in San Francisco. Maybe I was planning to move there. I withdrew $2500 from my savings account recently. I don't know what I spent it on. It's gone."

"Hm-m."

"There are two days that are a total blank. I was sitting in my kitchen writing a letter to the Ethics Committee when..."

"Why were you writing them?"

"Some subjects in the study filed a complaint against me: Leaving them with post-hypnotic suggestions without their informed consent."

"What were the suggestions?"

"To campaign for the clothing of animals."

The hypnotherapist laughed. "That's cute. Did you do it?"

"No, not to my knowledge."

"Clothing animals. Maybe your loss of memory relates to sexuality in some way." He cocked his head and smiled warmly. "Any associations to that?"

"To sexuality?" Wiley laughed. "Yes, many, but nothing problematical, at least, not that I'm aware of."

271

"Anything connected to Drew?"

Wiley was silent.

"Can you talk about it?" Bill asked after a while. He was a plain man, very soft-spoken with pale skin and a dark trim beard.

Wiley looked at him. They were in Bill's ultra-modern office in New Town. "I'm in love with her," she said, looking away then, out the window. It was raining. "I have been for years. She doesn't know."

Bill got up from his chair and sat on the edge of his desk near to Wiley. "It could be connected with that, Wiley. It's certainly something to think about."

"I think about it."

"I'll bet. Let's get back to the two days of total amnesia, it might provide a clue. You were writing a response to the Ethics Committee and the next thing you remember is entering the front door of your home two days later."

"Right."

"Any clues at all that might indicate where you'd been, how you spent the time—check records, receipts, ticket stubs? Anything like that?"

"Nothing."

They talked a while longer but still with no results. "Well, Wiley, I don't know what to say. It's very odd, atypical for amnesia or fugue state, but, clearly, you're blocking out parts of your recent life for some reason, possibly related to your feelings towards Drew. Maybe you should consider entering therapy to explore it more."

"I think I'll move to San Francisco."

The therapist laughed. "I'd miss you. You're my only real competition at the poker games."

"Come to San Francisco."

"My lover would love it." Bill rose to walk Wiley to the door. "Yes," he added, "Jeremy's convinced we'll end up there eventually."

"Thanks for the time, Bill. I'm not sure what I'll do at this point. I was hoping hypnosis would be the answer."

"It's certainly part of the question. Poker game a week from Friday?"

"Right. I'll see you there," Wiley said, "if I don't forget."

## 56

Becka refused to leave the house, to talk, to do anything. Madeline's tenderness, her cajoling, her sternness, her explanations, her brige offers had no effect.

"I don't believe you," Becka repeated to most everything Madeline said. "I want my mommie." Then she'd lapse back into silence.

The relationship between Becka and Madeline Drury had been developing nicely until the separation of Becka from her mother. Becka quickly grew taciturn and rebellious. Her growing trust in Madeline disappeared. And so, a final meeting was arranged.

"I was lonely for you," Becka said, holding Drew's hand tightly as if to let go even for a second would tear them apart again.

"Me too," Drew said.' "Are you sick, mom? That's what Madeline said, but I thought maybe you made them look at your eyes and so they put you in those handcuff things again."

"I was sick, hon, but I'm...I'm mostly better now. Is Madeline being nice to you?"

"I guess. She give me stuff and she wants to hug me and read to me, but I like it better here with you."

"Can you let her be your friend?"

Becka thought about this. "Yeah, I could," she said, "but...she could come visit us and she can babysit sometimes, but, mom?"

"Yes, Becka."

"I'm gonna stay here now, right?"

Drew fought the tears. "It's OK to let Madeline be your friend."

"OK, mom. Can we go home pretty soon?"

"Wouldn't that be nice," Drew said, swallowing, trying to keep her voice calm despite the lump in her throat. "How's Teddie?"

"He's OK, I guess. Hey, mom?"

"What, hon?"

"Can we get a dog?"

Drew cried.

"What, mom?"

Drew couldn't stop her crying.

"Why are you crying, mom?"

"Listen, Becka," Drew said. "Look at me and listen carefully. This is important."

Their eyes held each other and Drew did what she had to do, what she had no choice about doing.

273

"...and even though you lose someone you love, you know you can keep living and let yourself have a good life. When that happens to you, you can feel the sadness and cry as much as you have to and then go on and make the best of what you cannot change. It's OK to like Madeline; it's OK to let her care about you and..."

Drew had to stop because the pain was choking her, and when Becka's eyes cleared, Drew made herself do the next thing she had to do because Becka had to know and she had to be with her when she learned it.

"Sit here, honey, I have some sad news to tell you."

"What, mom? That we can't have a dog? Is that it?"

"No, my love, it's even sadder."

Drew cried as she spoke and Becka cried in sympathy, crying before she even heard the sad news, before her mother told her that her father had been killed in a car accident. And after she heard, Becka whimpered lightly, sadly, not fully certain what it meant that daddy was dead, gone forever. They talked about it some, but mostly Drew rocked her, cradling her, until they came and took Becka away.

_**57.**_

As Drew sat numbly in her room, a thirty-four year old woman in Detroit was being raped by three angry, taunting men. They left her bleeding in the laundry room of her run-down apartment building where she had come to wash her clothes and her husband's and those of her four children. In Cincinnati, a lesbian mother was sitting in the sterile courtroom listening to the judge say that she was unable to provide a healthy environment in which to raise her daughter. In Boise, an elderly widow was shuffling down the supermarket aisle fighting an internal battle. Hunger finally won and she slipped the can of Chicken o' the Sea tuna into the pocket of her threadbare coat. In Chicago, Judith Brodie was pushing Vic's hand away from her breast. In Little Rock, a thirty-eight year old secretary was taking a letter dictated by her twenty-six year old boss. She had a master's degree in English Literature, 18th Century, he a B.A. In Gary, an angry man, laid off from his job in the mill was striking his pregnant wife in the face and shoulders, and kicking her in the belly. At the meeting of the Senate Foreign Relations Committee, the Secretary of State was saying that the U.S. must reduce vulnerability of its land-based forces and further develop the capability to deter a Soviet attack. In Tallahassee, the father of seven year old Lou Ann was putting his hand down her pink, flowered underpants. In Washington, Rit Avery was in the oval office having a private meeting with the President of the United States. In Buenos Aires, a group of soldiers began firing submachine guns into a crowd of demonstrators. In Washington, a general was advocating the creation of a military strongman in the Pentagon. In Warsaw, martial law was again imposed in an attempt to crush the union. In Los Angeles, a hopeful actress was giving the assistant director a blow job. In Athens, the Premier was demanding that the Greek borders be guaranteed against attack by Turkish forces. In an unincorporated area of Vermont, Becka McAllister was sitting at a table drawing a picture of her father, her mother, herself, and their dog standing in front of a smiling house. At Capitol Hill, a bill was introduced that would relax the air pollution standards. In Thailand, a combined air-ground attack was being launched on the jungle lair of Chang Chi-fu in an attempt to cut off the heroin supply. In Austin, a priest was telling a nervous eighteen year old woman to do penance for her lustful thoughts. On the outskirts of Nairobi, a nine year old girl was having her labia and clitoris removed by a sharp piece of glass.

## 58.

The intercom summoned Drew to another meeting with Sandor Smith. The rehearsal for the next implantation wasn't scheduled until tomorrow, so she was puzzled and apprehensive. They had given her some phonetically spelled out sentences in various languages to memorize. Was this to be a test of her progress? Or maybe they were finally going to allow her the call to Rit she'd been requesting. She felt a little lighter, thinking that, but then the next thought crushed her to numbness. Perhaps Smith was going to inform her that her 'death' had taken place and that Becka had been told and was being comforted by her new mother. The escort tipped open the peephole in her door and, seeing that her goggles were in place, came in and accompanied her to Sandor Smith's office.

Smith sat at his desk and to his right sat a middle-aged man in a tan suit. The man rose when Drew entered and reached his hand out to shake hers as Smith introduced them.

"This is Mr. Clarendon, Miss McAllister. He has something to discuss with you. You're to go with him."

"This way, Miss McAllister," Clarendon said courteously, taking Drew's elbow and leading her from the room.

They walked through the grounds, the same route Drew had taken with Becka and Rit when they wore the artists' coats and thought freedom was near. Clarendon directed her around the Reception Center to the parking lot. The chauffeur standing next to the black "government official" car opened the back door and held it for her. Drew got in followed by Clarendon. The chauffeur remained standing outside the car.

"I'm a special emissary from the Office of the President of the United States," Clarendon began. "Would you like a drink?" He opened a drawer and withdrew two glasses.

Drew declined.

"I've been sent by the President to give you this..." He handed her a sealed envelope, "...and to assist you."

Drew looked at him quizzically. "I should open this?" she asked.

He nodded.

The neatly typed letter on White House stationery informed Drew that she was to meet individually with all personnel at the Vermont compound who definitely or possibly were aware of her presence there and the meaning of it. She was to meet first with Sandor Smith and implant in him the belief that he wished to complete a list of names of all such personnel and arrange for her to meet with each of them. If any were not presently available, they were to be sent for. At the meetings, she was to implant in each person the belief that he or she would be truthful with her and cooperative. She was then to ask them for the names of all people who were aware of her power and/or presence there. She was to write down their names and the means of locating them. She was to tell Clarendon to arrange for meetings with them. Starting with Sandor Smith, she was to implant in each individual with whom she met the belief that he or she no longer would have any memory of her power or the incidents involving her, and that when she left

276

the compound, they would forget she had ever been there. They were each to be zapped to destroy any written or other evidence of her power or presence at the compound. When all the meetings have taken place, the letter continued, she and her daughter would be taken by Mr. Clarendon to the airport for their flight to Chicago. She was to implant the belief in Mr. Clarendon, at that point, that he would forget all that had occurred regarding her, and that he would return to Washington. The letter was signed by the President of the United States and contained a hand-written P.S. *See you soon, cutie. Rit.*

Drew's hand shook as she re-read the letter.

"This may take several days," Clarendon said "I'm having a room checked over now to make sure your meetings will be private. We can begin whenever you're ready."

Drew couldn't smile though her heart was singing. She couldn't speak, though her mind was full of a thousand words. She had no way to express her joy. Her body tingled and shook. Her heart pounded. She could already feel Becka's little body cradled in her arms and picture her reunion with Rit. But all she could do in response to Clarendon's statement was to nod her head, slowly, up and down with her mouth slightly open and her eyes round moons.

The office they used was a comfortable one, more warmly decorated than others she'd seen at the compound. It was in the Reception Center on the second floor. It had two large windows and as Drew waited for Smith to arrive, she watched the breeze lifting dying leaves from the tree branches and carrying them, in whirling patterns, away.

They came, one by one, including Granser, whose name was Samuel Truax, and Brian McAllister whose name was Jeffrey Morton. Several doctors came and many clerical personnel and some of the janitorial staff. The wife of one of Drew's escorts had to be zapped, and the cook from the cafeteria, and Gregory Marshall, the head of the compound, and the artists who were painting the mural, and the guards. Zayre did not come, for he was dead, Drew learned. Anderson had his turn and Madeline Drury and her husband, Lawrence, and the voices on the intercom. They all came, one by one. And no one overheard what went on in the office. No one but Drew knew the exact contents of the implantations, nor of the extra zaps she gave to some of her visitors, most of them, actually.

Sandor Smith would soon begin a quiet sincere campaign for the disbanding of the CIA. Granser would find himself impelled to resign from government service and devote himself to working caringly with autistic children. Rigid office clerks would become humanistic feminists. Medical personnel would devote half their time to non-compensated treatment of the impoverished ill. Madeline Drury would adopt two orphans and raise them well and lovingly. Hardened CIA agents would develop an aversion to violence and force; and some discover that they became tumultuously sick to their stomachs whenever they told a lie.

Drew was still feeling somewhat dazed when, the last implantation completed, she and Becka walked hand in hand, unescorted, through the Reception Center to meet Clarendon for their trip to the airport. The nightmare was over and Drew felt as if she were living a dream. Becka told her mom she was glad they were finally going home, which Drew considered an understatement, and that she missed her friends and couldn't wait for the dog they were going to get. She did not mention her father, but Drew knew that would come.

They rounded the corner that led to the main lobby, and there, standing near the wall, her back to them, in the flesh, real, no longer just a longed-for image in Drew's head, was Rit. She was watching the artists working on the mural. In the painting, a sleek black panther, camouflaged by rock and trees, crouched in readiness to spring towards its unleary prey, while a flock of wild birds flew off in the distance. Drew stopped walking. She let the suitcase slip to the floor.

"Mommie, it's Rit!"

The embrace felt even better than it did the hundreds of times Drew had imagined it. Rit took her arm and her suitcase "Let's go home, woman."

## 59.

If Drew had had any illusions about the benevolence of governments, or of people in general when power was involved, she no longer did. The rose- colored glasses had been replaced by locked steel goggles. The naivete was gone. When she thought about it, as she did much of the time after her return home, very little of what had happened was really surprising. That's the way it is in the patriarchal system, she thought. She knew that. She'd learned it well in the sixties. Vermont had just been the final lesson, leaving her a cynical, angry woman, one not very hopeful about "mankind". She wasn't sure that women, for the most part, were any different. Wiley's betrayal haunted her. Thoughts of Judith and Madeline Drury did not help.

But the scars probably would have healed with time, the bitterness simmering into a fine layer of healthy skepticism, much of the pain and fear and disillusionment forgotten, if it hadn't been for one loose end. Jed Humphreys did not forget. Blind, unzappable Jed Humphreys did not fade away with time. If he had, Drew might have made the "adjustments", resumed her life in Chicago, worked on filmmaking and raised her girl and enjoyed her relationship with Rit and her power, discreetly used, and had an interesting, pleasant, and private life. But Jed Humphreys did not forget.

"It's Wiley again, mom." Becka covered the phone with her hand, the wrong end. "Should I tell her you're still too busy to talk to her?"

Drew was in the round chair. "I'll take it," she said.

She had been avoiding Wiley since her return home, keeping the phone conversations shallow and brief, putting her off when Wiley asked questions and tried to arrange for them to get together. This time, Wiley was so insistent that Drew agreed to meet with her. She would see her tomorrow and get it over with.

When she opened the door for her old friend, surprisingly, Drew's heart opened part way, too. She couldn't help feeling the affection and tenderness which had been for so long a part of their friendship, but she moved away and Wiley did not try to hug her.

"I feel like Alice in Wonderland," Wiley said when they sat down with their coffee. "I'm desperate for answers. I told you about the gaps in my memory. I couldn't wait until you got home, hoping that...but obviously something's wrong with you, or between us. What is it, Drew? I feel like I'm going crazy. Please, if you can, help me with this. Talk to me."

"How can I help?" Drew asked, partly wanting more than anything to relieve this wonderful woman, comfort her, partly despising her.

"Would you tell me where you were? You were gone for over a month. Why? What happened?"

"I was vacationing, in Florida."

"It doesn't make sense," Wiley said. "Why no postcards? No

calls. You didn't even tell me you were leaving. Drew, obviously there's much more to this. These memory gaps, they mostly seem to relate to you. If there's any way you can help...if you know anything that might explain this...these changes..."

It was a cloudy day and Drew switched the table lamp on. The soft light highlighted Wiley's high cheekboned, very serious face.

"Why are you different with me?" Wiley continued. "You've been home for days and I almost had to coerce you to get you to see me. Why? At least, tell me about that."

I could zap her into peace of mind, Drew thought. I could zap her out of my life. Or, I could leave her like this and let her suffer with it. Maybe I should tell her the truth and let her realize I know of the dark side of her character, the power-hungry side, not so different from those pigs in Vermont, then punish her for her betrayal and zap her to forget I can zap. "You betrayed me."

"I what?"

"Listen to me, Wiley, I have some important things to say to you."

Wiley stared into Drew's hard and angry eyes.

"You can remember. Everything. Your memory is restored. You can recall the things that I zapped you to forget, and when we discuss them, you will want to tell the truth. You will want to be completely truthful as we talk tonight."

Drew waited. After a few moments, Wiley moved. She shook her head, her eyes wide.

"Drew, my God, you're all right!" She sat staring and blinking her eyes, her head spinning as the memories poured back. "You got away." She moved to where Drew sat and grabbed her hands, then hugged her, then held her hands again. "How? How did you escape?" She hugged her again. Drew tolerated it stiffly.

"I zapped my way out."

"Yes, of course." Wiley closed her eyes a moment, thinking. "And you zapped me, didn't you, and Judith and Bo? That's why they brought us to Vermont. It was for a zapping, wasn't it? For you to zap us to forget."

"Yes."

"They made you do it."

"They wanted to kill you. It was Rit's idea to zap you instead. You and Bo and Judith."

Wiley nodded her understanding. More rushes of memories and feelings came. "You think I betrayed you, don't you? That's why you're so cold."

"I found out, Wiley." The tone was angry, but there were tears in Drew's eyes. "About your meeting, about how you planned to use me."

Wiley's face was drawn and full of pain. "I didn't betray you, Drew. In no way was I..." She stopped midsentence. For close to a minute, she stared at nothing across the room. "I don't think I did...," she said, finally, her voice hoarse, her expression very pained. "Maybe it was a betrayal of a sort," she said. She looked at Drew. "I had no intention of doing anything without your full knowledge and consent and participation. I wanted you to change the way the world is. Maybe it was betrayal to want that so badly. A denial of your will and your needs. I wanted you to use your power to make things better. I thought you had an obligation to do it and that I had an obligation to convince you to. I suppose I also got off on the prospect of being a part of something so big, so important. Yes, I was loving it." She shook her head. "Maybe it is betrayal."

"You wanted to be the ruler, take over the world, be the emperor."

Wiley thought about that. "No," she said. "I don't think so, Drew. It wasn't that. It was more like an obligation, that's how it felt, like a moral obligation." She looked away again, off into the distance. "I had no right to make that judgment for you, though."

"It was more than that, Wiley. What about the meeting?"

"Yes, I jumped the gun with that. I should have waited until you were ready. No, more than that, I should have been prepared to accept the possibility that you never would be ready, that it was *your* choice."

"Ready for what?"

"To proceed with the plan I outlined, the proposal I wrote. Bo thought maybe you didn't read it. It was in the file with the..."

"You mean that stuff you left with me that night? Your hypotheses?"

Wiley nodded. "Yes, I know you read the hypotheses, but I mean the rest of it, the projections, the plans for how to use your power."

Drew's eyes were softening. "I didn't quite read all of it," she said.

Wiley nodded.

"It was...uh, rather formal." She was smiling now. "But quite professional, I'm sure."

Wiley wanted very badly to take this woman in her arms and hold her and be with her forever. "I talked about the steps to develop a plan, a plan for using your power to begin changing the social/political structure of the world. That we'd begin by having brainstorming meetings and..."

She looked at Drew. "You told me my ideas sounded fine to you."

"I said that?"

"Yes."

"I know you're telling the truth."

"I think I always have with you, Drew."

They talked a while more and Drew filled Wiley in on her adventures with Rit and Bo and about events in Vermont. Wiley was amazed when Drew told her about blinding the government agent and about some of the other details of their captivity. "Just like the movies," she said, shaking her head. "Life imitates art."

"I wonder if it was what you told me about that guy in the movie that gave me the idea to blind Humphreys. It might have been, unconsciously."

"It might have."

Soon Becka came home from school and a little later, Sarah, too, came home. Sarah greeted Wiley warmly and talked about how good it was for Drew to finally have come back from her vacation and for all of them to be together again, then she changed her clothes and went to meet her boyfriend, Larry. Sarah was so preoccupied with him that Drew was sure she and Becka still wouldn't be seeing much of Sarah. Becka was uninhibitedly delighted to see Wiley. She chattered non-stop and wouldn't let Wiley out of her sight until after dinner when she went to do her homework and Drew and Wiley talked some more.

The two of them were clearly very good friends. Drew felt bad that she could have doubted Wiley. Wiley's only badness was wanting so badly to do good, she thought.

Wiley was not being quite so easy on herself. She was feeling guilt for presuming to impose her values on Drew and for not discussing things more fully with her. She wondered if she had been too intent on meeting her own needs.

"You were trying to protect me," Drew protested.

"Yes, but probably also myself," Wiley acknowledged. "I didn't want to risk your getting turned off or scared off by the magnitude of it...the potential of the power. I thought you weren't ready to handle it."

"That sounds familiar."

Wiley smiled. She was wearing a suede vest with turquoise beads and pieces of silver. She picked at the beads as she spoke. "I guess I am slow in letting you in on things," she said, almost shyly. "In all these years, I've never told you that I'm in love with you." She couldn't believe she had said it, and yet, it was the truth and she

282

felt impelled to be totally truthful with Drew.

Drew inhaled suddenly and deeply. "You're in love with me?"

Wiley nodded. "From the start."

"Oh, wow!" Drew flung back her head. "I...I had no idea... I didn't know, I mean, I thought...God, Wiley, I feel awful."

"Why feel awful?"

"Well...about...for you."

Wiley looked sad. "Don't, Drew. It's OK. I didn't tell you because I expected...well, tell me, do you still...is Judith still...?"

"No." They were both silent a moment. "Not Judith..." Drew looked very pained. "I'm in love with Rit," she said slowly.

"Oh," Wiley replied. Her eyes were just slightly red around the edges. "I see." She took several deep breaths. "Well, I guess I should meet her some time. She must be quite a woman."

Drew moved around uncomfortably on her chair.

"And thank her," Wiley continued, "for saving my life."

Drew reached out her arms to her friend. "Oh, I do love you so much, Wiley. You know that." They held each other. "I'm sorry."

Wiley stiffened. "Please, Drew, that I can't bear. Anyway, I'm the one who should be sorry, sorry that I told you. I shouldn't have. It must have been all the confusion and pain, and then being with you again and finally understanding. I just...I got carried away. You gave me no sign. It wasn't fair to you."

They were holding hands, both crying.

"Wiley, you'll still be my friend, won't you? This doesn't mean..."

"Hey," Wiley said, lifting Drew's chin. "I'm not going anywhere. You're a part of my life, all right? I'm part of yours. Nothing's changed about that, Drew." She looked at her. "Has it?"

Drew smiled through tears. "You're a rock."

Wiley laughed. "So, enough of this. By the way, I like your hair that way." She looked around the room. "It must feel good to be back. The ordeal in Vermont sounds like it was awful for you. Do you feel like talking some more about it?"

Drew shook her head. "No." She looked very troubled.

"What is it?"

"Wiley, I can't...we can't just pretend that you didn't say what you did, that you don't feel...it must be very painful for you."

"I'm not pretending, Drew. I know exactly what I feel and I know that your feelings aren't reciprocal. I accept it. I have for years. I'm dealing with it the same as I always have."

"But, Wiley, how hard it must have been for you all these years."

"Sure, it was, but it hasn't stopped my life by any means. I just have a sense that someday it will come to be. I sense it. It's not time yet, that's all."

Drew turned away.

"I'm sorry," Wiley said. "I don't know why I keep saying these things. I have no right to burden you with this."

Drew suddenly remembered the zap. Of course, she thought, she *has* to tell the truth. Guilt ground in her guts. She closed her eyes.

"I didn't want you to know, not yet. You're not ready for me yet. Someday, on your terms, I believe you will be, as someday, on your terms, I believe you'll use your power very well. I don't know why I'm saying this. I can't seem to stop my mouth today." Wiley bit on her knuckle. "So, what about you, Drew? What are your thoughts about where you'll go from here?"

I have to erase the zap, Drew thought. "Actually, I'm not sure," she said. "I've contacted Art Trevor. I'm going to work with him again. Other than that, I don't know." I have to erase the zap.

"There's some unfinished business with the experiment," Wiley said. "Some zaps that need erasing."

"What?"

"Some of the subjects."

"Oh, yes, yeah, we left some stuff hanging, didn't we?" I have to tell her. It isn't fair.

"Worse than I thought," Wiley said. "There was a mistake on the instructions you used. We shouldn't have let those people leave believing giraffes are bright and animals need clothes."

"I wondered about those," Drew said. "I thought it was your perverse sense of humor."

"It turned out not to be very funny."

"Well," Drew said, beginning to giggle, "I'm sure it's given extra meaning to their lives."

Wiley couldn't help joining her. "It's great to have a cause," she said, snickering.

"Something to be dedicated to."

Wiley shook her head. "We have to arrange for you to see them."

"Yeah, we do. I suppose I could drop in on each of them, have a little chat."

"That is the ethical thing to do," Wiley said, still smiling.

"I suppose," Drew responded. "Other than that, I'm not sure, Wiley. I definitely don't want to continue with the experiment."

"Me neither."

"We know enough, anyway, about my power."

"Enough to fill a tome."

"Now, about the other part...about changing the world and all that..."

"Yes?"

"Fuck the world!" Drew's eyes were angry slits.

"Oh."

"Let the pigs rot in their own evil."

"Hm."

"They're beyond redemption."

"Mm."

"The whole value system and structure of society is built on a foundation of competitiveness and force and greed and violence and oppression. To hell with them."

"Who?"

"The pigs."

"Who are they?"

"Men."

"All of them?"

"Yes, to some degree. They're all part of it."

Wiley nodded. "And women?"

Drew shrugged. "I don't know." There was a long silence. "I'm bitter," Drew said.

Wiley nodded. "Yes."

"Maybe I'll get over it. For now, it feels good to feel the hatred. It's very hard to consider trying to do anything good for them. Besides, I'm afraid to try. Somehow they found out. I wish I had zapped Granser to tell me how, when I had the chance. I didn't think of it then. I could still do it. I probably will some day. He's working with autistic kids somewhere." She chuckled. "Anyway, they found out somehow and they probably would again if I started using the power, and then the same thing would happen. Someone, some group of pigs would try to own me, control me, blackmail me."

Wiley knew she should not tell Drew about Judith, but she felt she had to, had to tell the truth.

"I'll not take the risk," Drew said, "even if I do get over the bitterness. And I suppose I will. I know I'm overgeneralizing. I know it's not as bad or hopeless as I'm saying, but I don't feel like being fair and balanced about it."

"No."

"Not now. Fuck 'em."

"Hm."

"I'm doing OK. I'm going to play it by ear."

"That's what you need to do, I guess."

"Right. You know who called me?"

"Who?"

"Judith."

"Oh?"

"She's coming over tomorrow."

"Hm. What do you make of it?"

"Who knows? Unless she tells me voluntarily, I've already decided to zap her to find out what really happened, why she dumped me."

There was a coldness in Drew at that moment that Wiley had never seen before. "Would you do that?"

"Sure, why not?' Drew said offhandedly. "I did it to you. I zapped you to tell the truth today."

Wiley's jaw dropped in disbelief. "You did?" Her eyes filled with tears. She took several long breaths. "So, that's why I told you after all these years of..."

"You see what I've become." Drew's cool detachment had changed to a look of self-contempt. "I'm no different from the rest of them. I'll even zap my friends to get what I want."

Wiley struggled to recover, to understand, accept, forgive, and respond to her friend. "You didn't think I was your friend when you zapped me," she said.

"That's true." Drew thought about it. "Yes, I was justified. And Judith certainly hasn't been much of a friend lately." The cold look was back. "Tomorrow, I'll find out why." Her eyes softened a little then. "Maybe it will work out like it did with us, and she and I can be close again."

"I don't know," Wiley said. "Judith's been having a real difficult time because of...of what happened in Greece."

"You talked with her about it?"

"Yes. If you zap her to remember and to tell the truth, I'm afraid you're not going to like what you hear."

"What do you mean? Tell me."

"She..." Wiley clamped her teeth together. "Drew, you need to give me back my free choice. You said you zapped me to be truthful today. It isn't right. I want you to remove the zap. It's not that I want to lie, but I want to be the one..."

"Of course, oh, of course, Wiley. Yes. Listen, I have something important to say to you." Their eyes locked. "You want to be as truthful with me as you choose to be. You realize it is your choice what to share and what to withhold. You believe as you did before coming here today in regard to telling me the truth."

"Did you do it?" Wiley asked when her eyes cleared.

"Yes. What about Judith?"

"Do you intend to zap her to tell the truth?"

"Yes."

"Is it negotiable?"

"No, I won't change my mind."

"She's been through hell."

"Poor dear."

They were sitting in the living room. Wiley and Drew and Judith had spent many hours talking together in this room. "Because of her own rejection of her attraction to you," Wiley said slowly, "Judith came to believe that you zapped her into loving you. She disowned her own feelings and, in the process, had to see you as a villain."

Wiley told it all, all of Judith's torment and conflicts and thinking that culminated in her call to the Secret Service.

"That piece of shit!"

Drew looked so cold and hard, it frightened Wiley. "She thought it wasn't you, Drew, that the power had made you a different person."

"Psychological doubletalk bullshit." Drew pounded her fist on the coffee table. "That bitch! She caused Becka's father's death, Wiley. And I should be understanding because she was conflicted?" Drew spit the words out scornfully. "Because she was afraid her mommie would reject her for making love with me? Ha! Poor dear. Look what she did! Look what she put us all through, and Becka...No, dammit, she's responsible. I consider her responsible."

Drew was on her feet walking wildly around the room. "Thought it was sick, huh? To love me. Thought it was disgusting." She stomped across the carpet. "Thought I forced her to do it with a zap, huh?" Drew's lip curled in scornful anger as she spoke. "And I thought I was in love with a slime like that."

Wiley could not reach her. Drew's anger continued and grew. She dwelled on it for the rest of the time Wiley was there and for most of the next day. By the time Judith arrived, the frenzy was gone, the hot anger turned icy cold.

"I came to apologize," Judith said.

"For what?"

"For how I behaved, how I treated you after...after we got back from Greece."

"Oh, that. Forget it, Judith. It's no big deal."

"I...I imagine it must have hurt a lot. I know how you felt."

"Oh, it did puzzle me for a while, but that's in the past."

"I wanted to explain."

287

"OK, explain," Drew said casually.

They were in the dining room, sitting at the dining room table. For some reason, that's where Drew wanted them to sit. "What happened in Greece," Judith began, "our being together like that...it was so...I felt happier, more complete and fulfilled than I've ever..."

"You mean because of our fling?"

"Fling?" Judith's lovely face paled. "Well, yes, but, I...I didn't think of it as a fling."

"Oh, you didn't?"

"No, it...it had a very...powerful effect on me. It was wonderful, Drew, you know that." She was fighting tears. "But, then, afterwards, well...to tell the truth, it scared the shit out of me. When I was home, at my parents...anyway, I ended up denying my feelings, pretending that I felt nothing for you, that I wasn't in love with you at all, and..." She ran her hand through her fine, sand-colored hair. "I had managed to wipe it out of my mind, for the most part, until a few days ago. Something strange happened to me, Drew. I had a blackout or something...I don't know, it's strange. There are periods of time I can't account for."

"I wonder if you're having a mental breakdown," Drew said flatly.

Judith bit on her lip. "I don't know... For the past few days, all I could think about was us, how it was, how much I...how much I love you, Drew."

"You're kidding," Drew said with amusement.

Judith looked puzzled and clearly deeply hurt. "No, Drew, of course I'm not kidding. I've stopped fighting it. I know it will be a struggle, but I'm willing to make it. I have to, I'm in love with you. A woman. I guess that means I'm a lesbian and I'm trying to come to terms with that, whatever the cost. I know it's what I really want, who I really am. I've been fighting..."

"Judith, please, this is disgusting. I've almost forgotten all about that repulsive little episode."

"Repulsive?"

"Have you become that perverted, Judith? God, you know it's sick. I'm worried about you."

"Drew, I...I don't understand."

"Obviously. You seem to be a troubled woman, Judith. You probably should see a shrink."

Judith's face twisted with disbelief and pain. She began to cry. "That's...just what my mother would say," she sobbed.

"Good for her. Get help, Judith. You're really fucked up. Maybe

288

Vic can help you. Have you told him?"

"No, Drew, no, of course not. I...I ended the engagement. Two days ago. I told him it's over. I never wanted to marry Vic. I..."

"Too bad," Drew said. "How did he react?"

"He thinks it's temporary, the jitters, like stage fright. He said he'll wait."

"Good boy. Tell him about your sickness. He'll make sure you get help."

"No, Drew. It's not sickness. What's...?"

"I'll tell him then, for you, Judith, to help you. You're not yourself. Something has twisted and perverted you. This has to be stopped."

"Drew, I can't believe this. In Greece..."

"A lot has happened since Greece," Drew said angrily.

"But..."

"If Vic can't get you to go for the cure, I'll call your mother. She'll make sure you get the help you need."

"My mother, oh, no! She'd...oh, no. Oh, God!" Judith stumbled to her feet and toward the door.

"I'll call her soon," Drew said, as Judith ran from the house. "It has to be reported."

## 60.

Drew lay in the round chair where she'd been since Judith's exit. It was three a.m. Her gut churned. Sleep was impossible. There had been no tears, but her eyes were red, and under them were dark rings. She got up again to go to the john, to shit the liquid out of her tumultuous innards, then she stumbled to her bed. Her eyes stayed wide as she lay on her back staring blankly at the ceiling. What's wrong with me? She got up and took a shower, the second one that night, and still she could not rest.

When daylight came, like a zombie, she went through the motions of getting Becka off to school, then again collapsed, this time on Becka's bed. Still, sleep would not come. She took another shower, a long stinging hot one, staying until the water got cool then cold. She was rubbing roughly at her skin with the towel when the phone interrupted the ritual.

"Hello."

"Hi, sunshine, you sound awful. What's the matter?"

"I don't know. I'm...something's wrong with me...I can't sleep...I..."

"How did it go with Judith?"

The cramp tightened in Drew's gut. "I don't want to talk about it."

"Meet me for lunch," Rit said.

"I don't know..."

"One o'clock. At Berghoff's."

"All right." Drew felt better after they hung up. She lay on the couch in the thick blue robe Rit had given her and was immediately asleep, waking in time to dress and arrive only ten minutes late.

"I was vicious to her."

"Less kind than usual, I'd say."

"I keep seeing that raw pain on her face."

"Sweet revenge."

"You know, it really was. It felt good, but afterwards...I don't know...I got sick. Maybe it's just a virus."

"Guiltococcus."

The lines of Drew's jaw hardened. "Why should I feel guilty?" she said defensively. "She deserved it."

"She's a twit."

Drew took another drink of water, her third glass. She hadn't ordered any food, the thought of eating nauseated her. "She said she's in love with me."

Rit laughed. "Too late for that."

"I feel dirty." Drew rubbed at her scrubbed white hands with the napkin.

"That part about telling her mother was an inspiration."

"She was horrified."

"I'll bet."

"She knows I didn't mean it, doesn't she?"

"You're tearing yourself apart, Lady MacBeth. I don't think you have the stomach for this sort of thing."

Drew's eyes teared. "What's happening to me? I used to be a nice person."

"You're a nice person who's been badly fucked over."

"Do you think I'm justified, Rit?"

"That's not for me to say."

Drew banged her glass on the table. "Oh, don't pull that. You didn't leave it up to me when this all started, when Granser visited and you forced me to..."

"That was different."

Drew drank more water. She tried to smoke but the cigarette tasted like rancid manure. "At least it went well with Wiley."

Rit nodded. "They're the hardest ones for me to get a handle on," she said, "the do-gooders."

"Wiley's not a *do-gooder.*"

"Yes she is."

"I think of do-gooders as naive and sappy and ineffectual..."

Rit smiled.

"Wiley's not like that."

"No, she's not sappy."

"I think you're jealous."

Rit laughed. She took a bite of her sandwich. "Sure you can't handle some food?"

"Maybe you feel guilty yourself for misjudging Wiley."

"No," Rit said, chewing. "An honest mistake."

"Was Judith's?"

"What?"

"Was Judith's an honest mistake?"

Rit tilted her head. "You have to make your own judgment of her. To me she's a twit."

Drew's face was drawn and melancholy. "I don't know what to do." Her fingers were tearing the paper napkin to bits. "She tears my heart to shreds, then she tosses what's left of me to the beasts. Wiley would forgive her because she'd label it all, explain it away, as if that means she's no longer culpable. Well, I don't think that way. I can't forgive her. But I still...when I saw her yesterday, despite everything else I was feeling, the hatred, the contempt, somewhere deep down, the love feelings were there." Drew mopped up drops of water from the table with the napkin bits and wadded them together. "I can't stand myself for being so cruel and yet I can't...I hate her for what she did. And you know, she doesn't even know the worst of what she did. My zap freed her conscience and I'm left feeling like the villain. This is ridiculous, I'm sitting here feeling guilty as hell and she called the fucking government on me."

"So you evened out the score somewhat and now you're torturing yourself because what you did wasn't nice."

"It was cruel."

"You were injured and you fought back."

"So you think I'm justified."

"I think you're one of us, you know, homo sapien, with all the

291

baggage that goes with it."

"I could call her and explain."

"You could."

"It wouldn't take away what I did to her."

"No."

"But look what she did to me. It was a thousand times worse."

"Yes."

"I don't feel forgiving. What I did to her only felt good while I was doing it, but it's done and even though I feel guilty for it, I don't forgive her. I don't know if I ever will."

"And so it goes."


# 61.

Drew showed Rit the letter. It contained only one line: *Dear Ms. McAllister: Your file is not closed. Jed Humphreys*

"Bastard," Rit said, throwing it on the table.

Drew paced. "I know he hates me, Rit." She recalled the scene the day she had attempted to restore his vision. "He tried to strangle me right in front of Smith."

"He's probably a very dangerous man."

Drew bit at her lip and paced faster. "I wonder if he'll be able to convince anyone else about me."

"Very unlikely," Rit said. She picked up the envelope. "Mailed from Las Vegas."

Drew went to the window and looked out below at the cars and passing people. "I wonder what he'll do. He'll probably never give up and I'll never have any peace from him."

"I wouldn't put anything past him," Rit said.

"What can we do?"

Rit hesitated momentarily. "We have a number of options," she said, placing her fist on the letter. "We could have him eliminated. Zap the people who could have it done."

Drew looked at her with disbelief. "You can't be serious!"

Rit shrugged. "I don't like the idea."

"No way," Drew said vehemently. "We'd be no better than they are."

"He wouldn't have to die. He could be sent someplace."

"Locked up, you mean."

Rit nodded.

"Other options?"

Rit walked over to where Drew stood and leaned on the windowsill next to her. "We could wait and see what he does. Play it by ear."

Drew shook her head. "I don't like that at all." She crossed her arms. "No, it's much too risky."

"I know."

"What else?"

"We could split."

Two days later, Drew and Rit and Becka disappeared. No one knew where they went. Ten days after that, Wiley, too, was gone. Bo, who had been away visiting her ill grandmother since leaving Vermont, no sooner returned to Chicago than she, too, disappeared. Their friends and family learned that they were travelling somewhere, in South America, it seemed. Jed Humphreys was one of the first to learn of Drew's disappearance. His man had lost them. It had appeared to be a routine excursion when Drew, Rit and Becka got in Drew's car. The man Humphreys had hired followed them to a shopping mall and stayed with their car. The stores closed, the parking lot emptied, but Drew's car remained. Jed Humphreys ordered his man to the airport and had others check the trains and buses, but Drew and Rit were gone.

For some, that might have been enough, the satisfaction of having scared the enemy away, disrupting her life, causing her to be on the run. But for Jed Humphreys it was not nearly enough. He was soon forced to abandon his original hope of convincing his former colleagues of Drew's dangerousness and usefulness. They assumed this "delusion" was connected with whatever psychopathology had brought on his psychosomatic blindness, and discounted his accusations as absurd. He had been retired from government service with full disability benefits; psychiatric treatment was strongly recommended. Jed Humphreys would have no part of that. He knew he was not crazy; he was obsessed with hate and the need for revenge, but he was not insane. No one believed him except Lila, who believed anything Jed Humphreys said.

Lila Murphy had been Humphreys' rehabilitation therapist, teaching him to navigate in his sightless world, and now was his mistress. Humphreys kept her well and treated her well for she knew how to treat him. After his dismissal from the agency, he purchased a flourishing nightclub in Las Vegas. Lila was crazy about him, fascinated by his past exploits, awed by his strength of will and his virility and flattered that such a man needed her.

Humphreys had a devoted woman, people who respected and feared him, wealth and status, but he found no peace. His need to even the score would not let go of him.

"She's a lesbian," he said.

Lila scoffed. "What a waste." She stretched her shapely leg over the edge of the sofa, the satin gown sliding off of it and hanging onto the floor.

Though Humphreys could not see the smooth curves of Lila's body, he often appreciated them tactually. "That might be the key to finding her," he said. "There's an underground, you know, a 'women's community', they call it." He chuckled. "Many of them are fat cows or boney four-eyed bean poles with about as much glamour as a toad."

"Poor things."

"Drew McAllister isn't one of those. You'd be surprised, Lila, some of them are as beautiful as I know you are."

"Maybe I should become a lesbian," she said.

He reached for her and found her breast. She moaned with pleasure. Lila Murphy loved Jed to touch her. Sometimes he was rough, but he was strong enough to be gentle, too. That's how Lila thought of it.

"As a matter of fact, that's exactly what I have in mind," Humphreys said. "I want you to go undercover for me, get involved in their subculture, ask around, find out where these disappearing women are disappearing to."

"What disappearing women?" Lila stretched her arms and let them fall around Jed's neck.

"I told you, darling, pay attention." He cupped her cheeks in his hands. "Since McAllister disappeared three months ago, there's been a rash of other women going off. Not only McAllister's friends, but other ladies of the same type. My contacts had no trouble finding out where they go initially, to Brazil, a resort in Brazil. But the trail ends there. A few return home but the rest disappear."

He was still holding Lila's face. Her mouth was slightly open.

"You're going to do something for me."

"I am?" She moved her tongue over her lips. "Tell me more."

"You're going to infiltrate their organizations, my little spy, and find out where they go. Wherever it is, that's where we'll find McAllister." His jaw tightened. "I'm sure of it."

Lila's hands teased around Humphreys' crotch. "Do you think I'd make a good lesbian?"

He pushed himself into her hands. "You'd make a terrible lesbian, but you're an excellent actress."

"I told you about *The King and I* ."

"Several times. You were the leading lady."

"That was a long time ago."

"You've got it in you."

"Oh, yes, I want it in me."

"Get yourself invited to Brazil."

"I love spy things," Lila said. She sat up and lit a cigarette. "I should have become a spy instead of a rehab therapist."

"I know." Humphreys chuckled condescendingly. "And I know you can do it. We're going on a little trip, you and I, to Chicago. There's a women's bookstore on Halsted Street. That's where I want you to start. There are people who will talk to you if you play it right. You can't be so sexy though, you have to learn to become less of a woman. I want you to get involved with these lezzies. Get yourself invited to Brazil and find out where they go."

Lila pulled him on top of her, unzipped his pants and reached inside.

They flew to Chicago the next day. The day after that, Lila donned a pair of old jeans and a loose sweatshirt. She removed her make-up.

"I look ugly."

"You look as beautiful as ever to me," Humphreys said. The bitter look crossed his face, but only briefly. "I suspect you look like you should for your assignment."

They were friendly in the bookstore; it was no problem to get connected. From the bulletin board on the wall, Lila learned of a discussion group that would take place on Tuesday night. She went and listened and observed as the group of women talked about "Feminism and Classism" and afterwards, she went to a bar with several of them. Lila found the women amusing in their boyish ways and their teasing talk of "political correctness" and their anger at the "patriarchy". She loved excitement, exploits, and was enjoying her assignment, though she became uncomfortable, maybe even slightly repulsed, at the women's expressions of affection for each other. You don't know what you're missing, girls, she thought, recalling last night and how Jed had filled her with his huge prick and brought her to ecstasy.

It was her third trip to the bar that yielded the information she sought.

"I can't believe it," the woman was saying, and Lila overheard. "The timing couldn't be worse. I'm supposed to leave for Brazil in three weeks and that's just when Cora's coming to town."

"What lousy timing."

"Cassie invited me. She just got back herself a week ago. She said it's even better than she thought." The speaker took a drink from her glass of beer. "She's going back and she's gonna stay. Everyone who goes is supposed to invite just one person. Cassie invited me and now I can't go. It's my last chance with Cora."

"I hope it works out for you two. That's too bad, though, about Brazil. What's there, anyway? Is it a new commune or something?"

"Yeah, something like that. A bunch of women starting this new place."

"Those things never work out."

"Maybe not. I probably wouldn't stay, but you get this trip to Brazil, to a beautiful resort in the mountains full of women." She shook her head. "Cora's arriving the very day we're supposed to leave."

"It's all women?"

"Yeah, they even help you finance the trip if you can't afford it. You stay at this retreat, like, and they talk to you about this new women's place, Dega-J, and then if you're interested, you can go there and stay if you like it, you know, live there. They're just starting it. I think Cassie asked me partly because she thinks I'd like it because I get so sick of all the pigs here and partly, I think, because I'm a plumber. She didn't say that directly, but I got that impression."

"They need a plumber at this resort?"

"Well, I don't know. Not at the resort, at the other place, Dega-J. I don't know. Anyway, I'm so pissed. That's the only time Cora can come and I just can't be gone. I can't."

"What a shame."

Lila cornered the woman later. Her name was Elena. She was friendly and so was Lila. Lila played her part well. She had watched the women in the bar closely, and the women at the discussion group. She imitated their mannerisms and was sure Elena considered her one of them. "God, I wish I could get away," Lila said casually during the course of their talk. "My next contract doesn't begin for over a month and I have all this free time and nowhere to go."

"You're on vacation, huh? What do you do?"

"I'm an electrician. My father taught me. That's about the only good thing I ever got from him, but I consider myself lucky. It's hard to get anything worthwhile from men."

"Yeah."

"I'm a pretty good electrician, too. I wish I could go somewhere warm where there are a lot of neat women, though, before I go back to work."

The conversation continued. Lila made up what she thought was a passable history. She had purchased a book at the bookstore which she read aloud as Humphreys listened. "I came out when I was twenty," she said to Elena. She told a moving story, one she had read the night before. "I just really love being with women."

Elena shared some of her life, too, and talked of Cora who had moved away, but might come back to stay. Elena's roommate, Cassie, came after a while and joined them. Lila's friendly, humorous ways and her sincerity and the alcohol they drank brought on a quick friendship. The next night the three of them had dinner together. Lila flirted with Cassie. The night after that Cassie and Lila went out, ending up at the bar. Lila hoped she could get what she wanted without actually having to have sex with her. She told her she had just ended a relationship and was still smarting from it.

A few nights later, at Elena and Cassie's apartment, Lila was hesitant when Cassie invited her to the resort in Brazil. Both roommates insisted she take advantage of it and, in the end, Lila conceded and the plans were made. Lila and Cassie would be leaving for Brazil in two weeks.

"You're an excellent operative," Humphreys said. "My sweet little protege, my lezzie spy. You didn't do anything with any of them, did you?"

Lila giggled. "Are you afraid I'd like it?"

Humphreys ran his finger over her face. "Not in the least," he said.

They met at the airport, six women in all. Humphreys had gotten Lila the passport she needed, using her cover name, Lila Baxter. They were to fly to Viracopos, Brazil, and be met there by someone from the resort. It all went smoothly. Three of the women had been to the resort before, including Cassie, and three had not. The new ones had been invited by the old ones. *Networking*, they called it. They were surprised that Cassie and Lila had only recently met. The others had invited old friends.

They went a hundred miles by bus from Viracopos to the countryside. The resort was, indeed, beautiful, very large with a swimming pool and endless rooms and surrounding grounds. There must have been a hundred women, many from the states, but others from South and Central America, some from Europe and even a few from the mid-east and Africa. For several days, the women got acquainted and relaxed, hiking in the mountains and swimming. Inevitably, some romances began. Lila had no trouble avoiding that. People flirted, but no one pushed, and Cassie seemed satisfied with the friendship she and Lila were developing. On the third day, the old people, those who had been there before, left. There had been a goodbye party the night before. Lila was a little sad to see Cassie go; she had grown fond of her.

The first meeting would take place that afternoon. Lila put her tape recorder in her purse and joined the others, about fifty of them, all newcomers. The meeting started with a short talk by a woman named Spark, followed by a film which showed women living and working in a very lush setting with a grand estate containing several beautiful buildings. There was an extensive sea coast and great expanses of mostly virgin land, much of it "suitable for raising a variety of crops", the narrator said. It might have been an island or a peninsula; that was not clear from the film. "The place is called Dega-J, the narrator said, "a beautiful setting in which to develop a culture of our choosing. You are invited to join us there and become a part of it." Where Dega-J was located was never mentioned, Lila noted.

There were many questions after the film.

"Is there a commitment to stay any particular length of time?"

"No, you may leave whenever you wish," Spark responded.

"So you can come and go."

"Yes, but you have to return by way of here, this resort. You can never go directly to Dega-J."

"Why is that?"

"To protect ourselves."

No one asked *from what*. They all seemed to understand.

"What kind of social structure is there, what kind of rules?" a woman with a heavy Slavic accent asked.

"Whatever you and the others decide on," Spark replied. "So far, there aren't many rules and not much formal stucture, really. It's hard to say exactly how it will evolve. We're just beginning."

"In the movie, there were no males. I assume men aren't allowed?"

"That's right. Men are not invited. The only males are those born there. So far, there is one. Some women who come are pregnant. Others who want to bear children can choose to become pregnant by imported sperm."

*Imported sperm.* Lila had to suppress a giggle.

"Is Dega-J just for lesbians or not? That wasn't clear?" The speaker was a tiny woman with a large husky voice. She sat way in the back of a crowded room.

"No, though most of the first people to come are lesbians and everyone who's invited, we assume, is women-identified."

"What's the purpose of Dega-J?" a woman in front asked. "Is it supposed to be a utopia?"

"It's supposed to be whatever we choose to make it." Spark was sitting on the stool now, in front of the large room. "It's founded on a premise of self-respect and respect for others. You must want to believe and act on that premise in order to choose to live in Dega-J. That's the only requirement, besides being female."

Several women began to speak at once. Spark acknowledged a black woman sitting near Lila. "We saw women doing all kinds of work in the film. Are jobs assigned?"

"No, so far each person does the work she chooses, makes her contribution in whatever way makes sense to her."

"Then some can choose not to work?"

"Like I said, everyone at Dega-J respects everyone else's rights so no one would choose to be parasitic."

There was some snickering. "How can you be so sure?" an Oriental woman asked.

"Everyone chooses to participate," Spark said simply.

Over the murmuring, a clear voice rose. "How is it funded?" The speaker had an accent which Lila could not identify.

"Paz is supporting it financially for now, until it gets going more."

"You've mentioned Paz several times. Who is she, a millionaire lesbian philanthropist?" The speaker laughed and so did many of the other women.

"That is one of the things you cannot learn until you come to Dega-J."

"And if we don't like it there, you'll fly us back home."

"Yes."

"At your expense...at Paz's expense."

"Yes."

"It's not a religious cult, is it?"

"No."

The questions and answers went on for a long time and after the meeting, the discussion continued and it continued over the next two weeks. Each woman was asked to decide, over those two weeks, whether or not she would like to be a part of Dega-J. If she decided yes, she would have up to a month to settle her affairs at home, and return to the Brazilian resort for the flight to Dega-J.

"It's too good to be true," Sharon said to Lila. They were sharing a cabaña on the east cliff. "There must be a catch."

"They've sold me," Lila said. "I'm ready to leave today." She pictured Jed listening to the tapes. She knew he'd be pleased with her. She had little doubt that Drew McAllister was behind Dega-J, little doubt that they had found her.

Jed was diabolically delighted with the information Lila brought to him. Two weeks later, he sent her on her way. Revenge was near and he slept peacefully for the first time since the day the world went dark.

## 62.

It was a private plane that took off from a private airstrip on the Brazilian resort. It was hard to tell what direction they were flying for the plane seemed to turn frequently and the flight was at night so the sun gave no cues. Most of the twenty-six passengers appeared to be uninterested in exactly where they were going. They accepted the need for secrecy, having no trouble believing there were those who would seek to subvert or destroy a functioning community of women.

The flight took eight hours. They were asked to keep the window shades down as they neared their destination. No one objected. Lila was able to sneak two peeks, but all she saw was the sea the first time and an airstrip the second.

A string of electric cars was lined up to take the new arrivals to the settlement, a couple of miles from the airstrip. All of Dega-J was private land, they had been told. Lila rode in the car with Delores, who was from Mexico, Sharon, a Canadian, and one other women. Their driver was Cassie, and the reunion was warm. Lila Murphy was not acting then. Cassie looked very tan and healthy. She practiced Esperanto on the newcomers.

"Do you have to learn it?" Sharon asked. "I've always been awful at languages. They tried to teach me Latin in high school. What a joke."

"If you stay, I think you'll want to learn it," Cassie said, "but wait and see. I'm taking you to the main house. That's where you'll stay the first night. Tomorrow morning, you'll meet Paz and make your final decision about staying here. If you decide to remain at Dega-J, then you can choose where to live. I stay in a tent, now, but two other women and I are building a cabin." She held up her hand. "Look at these callouses. I love it."

Lila couldn't picture herself building anything and her lie to Cassie, about being an electrician, was beginning to worry her. Plug in the cord, turn on the switch. That's what she knew about electricity.

It looked just like the film, sunny and inviting with the bright blue sea frequently visible. The estate had several buildings. Lila's room was in the largest one, on the third floor. She had a choice to room with others or alone. She chose a single. It was a com- fortable, airy room with a small private balcony.

The new arrivals had snacks in the large ballroom and met some of the Dega-Jays. Lila had to admit they were nice people even though they weren't normal, but she kept her distance. As soon as she could, she went to her room and to bed. She was anxious for the meeting tomorrow with Paz. Once she knew what Paz looked like and was sure she was Drew McAllister (Jed had given her a photograph), she would plan just when and how to pour the acid into McAllister's evil green eyes, blinding the vicious shrew who had blinded the man she loved.

After a cafeteria-style breakfast, the new arrivals were asked to go to the alcove meeting room on the main floor. There was an atmosphere at this place that bothered Lila. Actually, she liked it, but it bothered her. It was the people; there was a kind of open- ness about them, a non- pushy friendliness; it made her feel edgy.

In the alcove, Lila spotted a familiar face, a tall woman who looked like she might be part Indian, American Indian. She was leaning on a chair talking with several others. Lila had a photograph of her, too. It was Wiley Cavenar. Lila watched her closely, very excited that her expectations were being fulfilled. After a few minutes, Cavenar moved to the center of the group.

"Hi and welcome. My name is Wiley. I'm one of the coordinators. I'll get to know your names in time, but right now I want to ex- plain our procedure. First, you're going to meet Paz, each of you, individually, and then Paz and I will talk about Dega-J, explain some things to you, and then let you wander around and get a feel for the scene here as you work on your final decision about stay- ing with us or not. Ah, here she is."

A woman had walked into the alcove room. Her hair was curly and dark on the ends, the rest straighter and lighter with auburn highlights. Lila felt it in her body, the sudden fiery sensation in the pit of her stomach, the lump in her throat and speeding up of her heartbeat. It was, without doubt, Drew McAllister.

"This is Paz," Wiley Cavenar said. "She'll begin meeting with each of you now, brief meetings, in that room over there." She pointed to a door off to the side of the alcove. "The order doesn't matter. You'll all have your turn. As soon as someone comes out, the next can go in. Those of you who don't know English will be accompanied by a translator."

Several women moved toward Paz. Lila stayed stationary in her chair. "Where's a john?" she asked the dark-haired woman next to her.

The woman shrugged, obviously not understanding English. Lila turned to another. "Where's the john?"

"I saw one out in the hallway, to the right," the woman said, in accented English.

Lila neither acknowledged the answer nor moved from her seat. She watched the first newcomer go in for her meeting with Paz, a very tall blond. Less than two minutes later, the blond woman exited and the next one went in and soon the next and the next. When Delores had her turn, Lila got up and went toward her. Delores was a chubby, cheerful Mexican woman with whom Lila had talked several times.

"How did it go?"

"Fine. She seems real nice."

"What did she say?"

"Nothing much. Asked me why I came here, to Dega-J, that's about all, what my motives were."

"What's the room like?"

"The room?"

"Where you met with her."

"I don't know, a room." Delores looked at Lila, puzzled. "Why?"

"I'm curious."

"I was only in there a minute. There were some chairs. Paz was in one, sitting there and..."

"Did she get up at all?"

"No."

"Did you sit?"

"Yes."

"Where? Where did you sit?"

"In the other chair. Right across from Paz. Are you nervous, Lila? Don't worry, she's not scarey. I was a little scared myself, but really, she's nice. It was nothing."

302

"What kind of chair, the one you used? An easy chair or..."

"A regular chair, just like these."

"Where in the room is it located, the chair you sat on?"

"God, you *are* nervous. OK, I'll tell you exactly what I remember, exactly what the room's like and what Paz said. Then you can relax, OK?"

After her talk with Delores, Lila went to the john, then joined the remaining women waiting for their turn with Paz.

"You want to go next?' someone asked.

"Yes, thanks." Lila walked toward the door, slowly, seeming only mildly uncertain. She went inside, closed the door and smiled.

Paz was seated in straight-backed chair. She looked very relaxed and happy. "Hello," she said. "You know my name, it's Paz, and you are...?"

"Lila. Lila Baxter, from Chicago."

"Chicago. My old home town. Have a seat, Lila. Are you OK? You look a little..."

"Upset stomach this morning, but I'm fine," Lila said. She sat.

"Lila, I'd like you to listen carefully. I have something important to say to you."

Their eyes held each other's and, as Paz spoke, Lila stared unblinking, listening.

"You have no wish nor do you have the ability to explain to anyone outside of Dega-J where Dega-J is or how they can find it. You have no wish nor the ability to explain to anyone outside of Dega-J the things that you will hear in the meeting today, nor anything that you learn about my special powers or that have to do with my powers. If you ever leave Dega-J, you will have no wish to write of life here nor to speak of it in more than vague and non-specific ways. In a moment, I'm going to ask you a few questions and you want to answer them truthfully and completely."

Paz waited. After a few seconds, Lila blinked. "I have kind of a touchy stómach," she said.

"You might want to visit the health area," Paz replied. "It's in the next building, just south of here. Tell me, Lila, why did you decide to come to Dega-J?"

"Oh, the idea fascinates me," Lila said sincerely, "to live in a community of women and develop our own culture, to be free to create a life style that isn't hemmed in by all the damn rules and all the sex-role things and...and so I came."

"Any other reason?"

"No, well, I like new things. The idea just really appeals to me."

"I'm glad," Paz said. "You'll hear more about it soon. OK, that's

303

all. Enjoy yourself, Lila. I'll see to you later."

Lila stood and moved toward the door. She found the handle, exited and walked down the hall, along the wall, to the john. In the stall, she bent her head down and pulled at her upper eyelid. A small disk fell onto her palm, and then another from her other eye. They were contact lenses, the exact color of her irises, but opaque. She slipped them in a plastic box, then into her purse. Able to see again, Lila Murphy walked back into the alcove room and waited for the meeting to begin.

Wiley Cavenar and Paz sat on chairs, the others around them in a half moon design. Wiley spoke first. She told the story of Paz—the tornado, the amazing discovery, the experimenting and learning about the parameters of the power, the kidnapping, the threatening note from the man Paz had blinded and who she could not help. Lila was the only person in the room who did not feel the rushes of excitement as the story unfolded and the anger at the malevolent CIA agent. Paz picked up the thread then.

"I was so angry that I decided I never wanted to do anything ever for anybody who was not close to me. I wouldn't use my power for others. To hell with them. After that letter, Rit, my lover, and I and my daughter went to the resort in Brazil, Rit's resort. For several weeks, I stewed and thought about life and my power and what to do. I thought about misuse of power and using others and having no respect for others' rights and needs. God, I thought a lot."

Paz took a deep breath and ran her palms over her cotton pants.

"The anger gradually receded," she said softly. "Being with Rit and Becka at that wonderful place helped, I'm sure. I felt like I was healing and being restored. I decided, finally, while sitting by the little waterfall, I'm sure you've all been there, I decided then that I *would* use my power for others, but only those I was sure would not impose their will on anybody else. I decided to begin on a much smaller scale than Wiley wanted, and to deal only with women for a while, for now, at least."

Paz paused waiting for the translators to catch up. She looked around the semi-circle at the many different faces and the many different expressions. They all seemed fascinated, but most were clearly unsure of what to think.

"I don't expect you to believe yet that I have the power we claim I have, not just from our telling you. It's like a fairy tale, isn't it? A kid's fantasy, like magic, science fiction, all of that." People nodded. "I agree. But, nonetheless, it *is* true." She smiled. "Time for the proof." She turned to Wiley who'd been setting up her video camera.

"The miracle of modern technology," Wiley said, "will assist us in convincing you." She finished hooking up the equipment. "We need volunteers to be zapped, the more the better, at least a dozen, especially those of you who feel most skeptical. I'll film the zappings, then replay it. When we're done, you'll be convinced."

A few people immediately offered to be subjects. After watching what happened with them, others volunteered, too. At one point, Lila felt an ugly urge to suggest Paz zap someone to believe she cannot see. She held her tongue but her disgust did not subside. The demonstration took about an hour, then Wiley said they should take a break.

"You need time to digest what you've learned," she said, "and get ready to hear what comes next."

Lila spent the break learning what she had to learn. First, she spoke to a woman she found cutting up potatoes in the cafeteria kitchen. She asked her about life at Dega-J and especially about living arrangements. "Very flexible and individualized," the woman said. She told Lila where she was staying herself, where some of her friends were, and where Wiley and Paz and Rit and the other coordinators stayed. Paz was staying here at the estate main house, Lila learned. She had a room on the second floor and so did Rit.

"Where is Rit now? We haven't met her yet?"

"She's at Sapphic Valley, eight or nine miles away. They're drilling a well there. She'll be back in a few days." The woman diced potatoes rapidly the whole time they spoke.

From the kitchen, Lila went to the second floor. There was a library, johns, several large meeting rooms, lounges, and many bedrooms. The halls were filled. Women came and went, some of them new arrivals who were talking about the demonstration and being amazed and excited. Lila took a seat in one of the comfortable elegant chairs in the carpeted hall along the corridor where the bedrooms were located. She held a book on her lap and watched the people come and go, as she waited for Paz. After twenty minutes, Wiley Cavenar came up the main stairway and headed Lila's way. Lila kept her head bent to the book. Wiley went to the last door and knocked three rapid taps. "Paz," she said, "are you in there?"

"Paz is out by the pond," a passing woman said, "with Trish and Kali."

"Thanks, Nettie." Wiley left.

Paz's room was neat but comfortably lived in. Lila explored it quickly, then left. Directly around the corner from the room was a stairwell. It seemed to be rarely used, Lila noted, probably built as an extra fire exit. She walked the isolated stairs up to the third floor. Her own room was ten feet from the stairwell door. It will be easy, she thought.

The meeting resumed after lunch. Since witnessing what Paz could do, the women in the audience had spoken of little else.

As soon as everyone was settled, someone raised her hand to speak, but Paz cut her off. "Not yet," she said. "I know you have a million questions. You better, but not yet. Wiley has something to read to you now."

Wiley withdrew a sheet of paper from her jeans' pocket. It was ragged on the edges. It contained one typed paragraph with several typos and crossed out words.

"Paz composed this," she began, "at the waterfall she mentioned. It's gone through a few minor revisions."

Lila remembered that waterfall well. She had sat there many times during her stay in Brazil, thinking of Jed.

"Let me read it to you." Wiley held the paper before her, some distance from her eyes.

She'll probably need glasses soon, Drew thought affectionately as she watched her friend.

Wiley cleared her throat. "*You realize,*" she began, her voice steady and clear, "*that you and every other person is inherently and equally valuable and worthwhile. You wish to maximize your own fulfillment in life while respecting and not violating others' rights to search for their fulfillment in their own ways. You do not want to impose your will, your preferences, or your ideas on others. You wish to seek compassionate, empathic resolution of conflict, and true understanding and acceptance of differences among human beings.*"

Wiley stopped, looked at the faces, then read it again, slowly.

"It might not be the zap you would choose," she said, looking around at the women when she finished, "but it's what Paz chose and so it's the one we use."

"I'm open to negotiation about it, though," Paz interjected. "What you heard are basically my ideas, but Wiley had some input and Rit Avery and a few other people. You'll each have your chance, too."

"Now for the final and really most significant aspect of Dega-J," Wiley said. "Possibly you've guessed it already." She looked especially radiant since her move to Dega-J. The Indian features seemed more prominent for some reason. "Every woman who stays at Dega-J," Wiley continued, "believes what I just read to you, believes it all deeply and fully. They believe it partly because maybe they already did, but they fully and deeply believe it and are committed to it, because they've been zapped to."

There was murmuring around the semi-circle. Wiley waited.

"If you have a problem about being zapped to deeply believe those ideas and if you're unable to resolve that problem within the next two days, then you simply choose to leave Dega-J and that's the end of it for you. If, however, you feel comfortable being zapped to believe those things and you want to remain here, then you will meet with Paz and have those beliefs implanted in your belief system. We're open now for questions and discussion."

Lila barely listened though the talk went on for hours. She faded in and out, her mind elsewhere. She had no doubt that Paz's door would be unlocked tonight. First the chloroform, a few seconds over her nose with a saturated cloth, Jed had said. Hold her down until she stops struggling. And then the acid. One drop in each eye.

## 63.

Becka was in bed at ten, her mother at her side, as usual, for their quiet talk time and a story and a goodnight hug and kiss.

"Did you meet some of the new women?"

"A few. They're OK but I wish there were more kids."

"I know. There will be next time, six or seven of them are supposed to come. How are you and Carrie getting along?"

"Fine. Mom, is it OK if I let Alice B be Carrie's dog, too. She loves her so much so I said, well, she can be both our dogs, but can I really do that or does she have to adopt Alice B or something?"

Drew smiled warmly and touched Becka's soft warm cheek. "You can do that," she said. "You both can love Alice B and take care of her. I think it's a fine idea."

Becka pulled her stuffed lamb under the covers with her. "I had another bad dream last night."

"I know. I think you're getting over it, though, hon. They don't seem to be as bad as they used to be."

"Will you zap me not to have a bad dream tonight?"

"Now, what do you think?"

"I know...but I have the right to ask, right? Carrie said everyone gets zapped, even the kids."

"Just the special zap," Paz said, "no others. And not all the children. If they're born here, they don't need the zap. It will be a part of them. They'll learn it just by living here. Then far far in the future, I won't be needed anymore. No more zappings but the ideas will live because they'll be planted so deeply in everyone who grew up here."

"I'll always need you, mom."

Drew kissed her nose. "I love you, twerp. Ready for your story?"

Paz did not go to her own bedroom, next door to Becka's, until well after midnight. There was always much going on at Dega-J, especially when new women came. She was exhausted when she finally climbed the stairs, quietly made her way down the carpeted corridor, peeked in on Becka, then went to her room and collapsed. She slept immediately.

At two a.m., Becka moaned and pulled her knees up to her chin. A man was chasing her with a chain. He wanted to get her and chain her wrists and put things on her eyes so she could not see. He was getting closer. She ran as fast as she could. She could hear the clanging of the chain. He was right behind her.

In the room next to Becka's, a female figure bent over a sleeping one, while Becka's nightmare continued.

He caught her, grabbed her by the neck and Becka awoke with a muffled moan of a scream.

In the next room, the standing figure quietly moved to the door, opened it, left the room and went around the corner.

"Mommie," Becka called. Her heart was pounding.

She pushed the covers off rapidly and slid her bare feet to the floor. She ran next door and to her mother's bed. Drew did not move when Becka crawled in next to her. Her arm was up, partially covering her face.

"Mom?"

Becka's mother did not respond.

"Mom, I had a bad dream. Mom." She touched her silent mother softly on the shoulder.

Drew moved slightly and then came awake. "What is it, hon, another dream?" She took her daughter in her arms. "Do you want to talk about it?"

Becka talked about the chain and how he wanted to do something to her eyes and when she was done she fell asleep in Drew's arms.

On the floor above, Lila was packing her things. "I'm not like

308

you, Jed," she mumbled. "I couldn't do it. I thought I could but I couldn't."

She shuddered. "I don't have what it takes. Sorry, Jed." She shook her head as she packed the t-shirts she had brought and sandles and the tiny tape recorder. I know he'll be pissed, I know it. I really thought I could do it.

There was one other woman who had decided not to stay. They had to wait until the following day to leave. Lila spent the time in her room, her things all packed and ready. They didn't quiz her about her reasons, but accepted her decision easily. The other woman who was leaving, a musician from Seattle, said she couldn't tolerate the idea of having ideas implanted in her head, no matter what the ideas were. She found it morally repugnant. No one attempted to persuade her to see it otherwise. The next morning, the electric car was in front of the main house, the driver waiting to take them to the airstrip.

Lila closed and locked her suitcase and was about to go downstairs when there was a knock at her door.

"Paz...uh, hello. Come in, come in. I decided that I won't be staying, you know, well, I suppose you heard that."

"Yes, I did." They stood facing each other. "Listen carefully, Lila, I have something important to say to you."

Lila had no time to avoid the eyes. They caught her and she stared and listened.

"In a moment, I will ask you some questions. You want to be completely honest with me."

Lila's eyes cleared. "I think I have everything," she said. "I certainly enjoyed my visit. Thank you for, uh, for everything. It's really quite a place here and..."

"We need to protect it, you know, so I have to make sure you're not taking anything with you that might cause us any problems. You don't have any written information about Dega-J, do you, or you didn't tape record anything that went on here, did you?"

Lila swallowed hard. "How did you know?" Her pale face had grown even whiter. "I was very careful."

Paz's soft green eyes became angry and dark. "Know what?"

"About the tape recording, how did you know?"

"I didn't."

"Oh."

Paz clenched her teeth. "You're the first. I was afraid it would happen someday. Why did you do it?"

"He told me to," Lila answered immediately.

"Who?"

"Jed Humphreys."

When the dizziness went away, Paz wiped the drops of sweat from her forehead and cheeks and talked with Lila for a quarter of an hour while the driver waited in the electric car. Lila told Paz everything, of course, and when she left, her memory of what had gone on at Dega-J was very hazy and quite distorted. She could remember a group of women living somewhere in the snowy mountains and how they worshipped the moon and lived an ascetic isolated life. She could remember drinking a brew that made their minds fuzzy and caused strange visions to come. She could remember clearly how she sneaked into Paz's room, who was Drew McAllister, and put one drop of sulphuric acid in each of her eyes, then ran and hid, and how the women thought it was a local hillsman who came and blinded their leader. Beyond that, Lila could not remember much, for not much else happened, she told Jed Humphreys, who believed what she said and was finally satisfied.

---

## 64.

Judith added another wool pants suit to the Salvation Army box. All the furniture was sold, the sublease was signed. There's no turning back now, she thought. Edie Travers, Judith's lover for the past five years, held up a smooth, fine-grained, wooden box.

"This?" she asked.

The box was a gift from Drew, over a dozen years ago. "Yes, that goes with."

Both Judith and Edie were going. When Rit Avery called from Chicago a month and a half ago with the invitation from Drew, Judith could not have imagined she would actually do it, totally uproot herself and move to that mysterious place called Dega-J. At first, she wasn't even going to go to the resort. It had taken a long time for the pain from her last meeting with Drew to diminish and finally stop, and for the longing to taper into occasional mild bouts of melancholy. Why should I stir it up again, Judith thought.

"I thought she'd forgotten all about me by now," she had said to Edie after Rit's first call.

"Apparently not. It seems you two have something that just won't go away. I know it eats at you sometimes, missing her, I mean."

They were in the park near their apartment where they often went together, especially when they needed to talk something over. Judith leaned against a tree. Her sand-colored hair had a few gray strands now and was cut short. Her face was still creamy smooth and even more beautiful with the added years. "It's strange," she said, looking at the flowers surrounding the little fountain. "Yes, you're right, I really do miss her, still, after all this time." She shook her head. "Do you think she feels the same?"

"That Avery woman said so, didn't she?" Edie replied. She was sitting on the grass. She re-tied her running shoes. "Not in so many words, but..."

"I don't know. She didn't say much." Judith looked at her partner. Edie's olive skin contrasted with her own much fairer complexion, and Edie's shiney black hair made Judith's look even lighter. Edie was not pretty, certainly not in the traditional sense. She was a strong, giving, self-confident woman, and that was very attractive to Judith who loved Edie deeply. "I'm not in love with her. You know that, Edie, don't you?"

"Yes, I know."

"I guess I love her, though."

"I know."

"I'm not sure what to do," Judith had said that day in the park. "No word in ten years and suddenly this invitation."

Judith already knew, before the call from Rit, that Drew McAllister was not dead. For a while, after the disappearance, that possibility had wracked her. No one heard from her in over three months, then Marie got a letter. Brazil, Drew had written, she and Becka were living in Brazil. Judith tried to forget her. In many ways, she was feeling very good about her life. She had ended things with Vic which, she knew, was long overdue. She was thinking about women, knowing some day she'd begin acting on the thoughts. She was standing up to her sister, Paula. That really amazed her, how, suddenly, since Greece really, she no longer let Paula push her around. She was even feeling somewhat less intimidated by her mother. There was still a lot to do on that. After her talk with Wiley at the restaurant...Judith couldn't remember most of that conversation for some reason...but after that talk, she had gotten into therapy. The focus was on her relationship with her mother.

Despite the many good developments in Judith's life over the past ten years, there was still an empty feeling, somewhere in the background, a gap that had come when Drew disappeared and would not go away. Long periods would go by without any of Drew's old friends hearing from her, and again, Judith would think, with dread, that maybe she had died. Every so often, over the years, Judith would call Drew's parents in Florida. She's fine, they always told her, still living in Brazil.

Then, ten years after Drew disappeared, a phone call comes from some arrogant-sounding attorney, an offer for an all expense paid trip to a resort in Brazil, "because Drew very much would like to see you," the attorney had said. It didn't make sense, and yet in a way, it did. From the moment Judith hung up the phone, memories of Drew flooded back. Good ones, mostly, and the good feelings that went with them.

She had heard about the resort before and had suspected Drew was there or, possibly, at that other place, the one they called Dega-J. She knew that many women went to Brazil and that most of them ended up moving away for good. Letters came, postmarked Brazil, but the women talked of Dega-J, which may have been in Brazil or maybe not. They were always vague. Judith had been hearing about it for years. The disappearances interested her. She had fantasies of going there herself, but the opportunity had never come. Until now. Some of Judith's friends referred to those who left as deserters; others called them the chosen people. While there were many rumors, reliable information was hard to get. It was all shrouded in mystery. Judith knew one woman who left, a friend she met at a nuclear disarmament meeting. She wrote a few times, but the letters contained very little information. As the years passed, Judith grew more and more convinced that Drew was one of them. She was sure Drew's condemnation of lesbianism at their last encounter was bullshit. It was Drew's anger, Judith realized soon after it happened. She tried to call Drew a week after that meeting, but Drew was gone.

Judith added the wooden box Edie handed her to the almost full leather suitcase. Some people said Dega-J was a religious cult, like Jonestown in Guyana, others that it was a feminist utopia. Judith had doubted both of these possibilities.

At the very least, she had concluded, if I go to Brazil I'll find out more about this whole mystery. Rit Avery had told her Drew would not be in Brazil, but in Dega-J and that, in order to meet with her, Judith would first have to make the two week visit to the resort. Edie had remained neutral while Judith worked on her decision. What finally let her decide to go was when it was agreed that

312

sion. What finally let her decide to go was when it was agreed that Edie could go also.

In Brazil, they had both been completely enthralled by the movies they'd seen and information they'd heard about Dega-J. Edie had absolutely no doubt about moving there. "I can't imagine going back to living in Denver now." Her eyes were glowing. "I can't wait. God, it actually exists! There's really a place like that and we can go there!" Their lives in Denver were comfortable and relatively satisfying. Judith was a vice-president of a small cookware company, Edie a social worker at Rocky Mountain General Hospital. They had a network of friends, a beautiful apartment with a view of the mountains and a growing passion for downhill skiing. But, to Edie, Dega-J was a dream come true.

Judith, too, was convinced that life at Dega-J would probably be as close to nirvana as anyone could hope for, yet she was hesitant. "We could just go for a visit," she had said, "not make a commitment yet."

Edie's face fell. "I suppose that *would* be more sensible," she said. They were sitting near the waterfall at Rit's resort. Edie watched the cascading flow of sparkling water a moment, then turned to face Judith. "But it just seems like a waste of time and money to go back and forth. I'm totally convinced, Judith. I know I want to stay."

Judith nodded, tried to smile but clearly was troubled.

"It's Drew, isn't it?"

"I don't know how I'll react to seeing her."

Edie was silent for awhile. "Well, OK, then. OK, let's not close any doors behind us. We won't quit our jobs. We'll take vacation time and we'll hold onto the apartment. Then, if it doesn't work out at Dega-J, we'll go back to Denver and pick up our lives where we left off."

Judith looked appalled. "Live in patriarchal, homophobic, capitalistic, pig-country America when we have a chance to..."

"Judith!" Edie was laughing.

"I know." Judith laughed too. "But it's true; it would be awful to put up with it when we know we have such a fantastic alternative."

"Unbearable."

"Totally. No, we could never be satistfied at home now." Judith tossed a smooth white stone into the river. "No matter how it turns out with Drew," Judith had concluded, "there must be room for both of us at Dega-J."

Three weeks later, they were in the midst of packing. Judith began going through the camping gear in their box-filled apartment. "I guess we won't need the down-filled sleeping bags."

"No. I already promised them to Elise and Ella. Is that OK? I didn't want to sell them to some stranger."

Judith laughed, then grew quiet. "Edie."

"Hm-m."

"This is it. We're really doing it."

"I know. I'm kind of scared."

"Me too."

Edie sat on one of the stuffed and sealed cardboard boxes. "It's a damn big step we're taking. A big risk. I'm scared, but I can't wait to get there."

"Me too."

This time, they stayed in Brazil for only three days and then boarded the private plane for the flight to Dega-J. There were three other newcomers on the plane and several women who lived on Dega-J and were returning after trips to their home countries.

"This is Tora Stone's idea," one of the Dega-Jays said a short while after the plane took off. She handed Judith and Edie each a sheet of paper. The woman's name was Kara Shara. "Tora is great, but has an irresistible need to summarize things, you know, like data. I think this is a little dry, myself, but look it over if you like."

Judith was eager to read it, hungry for any information on their new home. "Do you know Drew McAllister?" she asked Kara Shara.

"No, I don't think so."

The page was decorated on the margins with an attractive pattern, similar to the Greek meandros design. Judith pushed the memories away and focused on the words.

DEGA-J Statistical Information Sheet

Climate: Temperate, short rainy season
Square miles: 218
Topography: Small mountain range, fertile valleys, forest
Natural resources: Copper, nickle, lumber, salt
Agricultural crops: Rice, soybeans, sugar cane, fruit trees
Industries: Cotton mill, electronics assembly plant, bicycle factory, lumber mill
Population: 48,600 (96% female)*
Religions: Various
Main Language: Esperanto
Ethnic background: Varied

Governmental stucture: Varied

Settlements: 48 villages of various sizes, none over 5,000 inhabitants

Note: Dega-J is not a nation in the traditional sense. All. inhabitants eventually become naturalized citizens of Brazil although Dega-J is not located in Brazil.

*Maximum population goal is 66,000.

Judith and Edie were picked up from the airstrip by a black woman from South Africa who spoke English with a pleasing accent. Her name was Sarana. She said she did not know Drew McAllister. In the red and yellow open air car with a canvas sunshade, she drove the new arrivals through the hilly countryside. The road also took them through several settlements. "This is Pinaka," Sarana said, "one of the newer villages." She stopped at a fountain to talk with someone and Judith and Edie got out of the car, too, and watched the passersby. There were women dressed in every imaginable way, in pantaloons, in gowns, in jeans, in robes, in skirts, in capes, in overalls, in dresses of every style. Some of them were topless, others in formal white suits.

"The people look so different," Edie said when they returned to the car. "From each other, I mean."

"Yes," Sarana responded, "there's tremendous variety here. That's what I like best about Dega-J, the diversity."

At the edge of the village, they drove past some women laying bricks. "Everyone here," Sarana said, "those women there, building the garden wall, the women lounging in the grass up there, the doctors, the clerks, the artists, those who live simply off the land, the technicians, the scientists, the rationalists, the communists, the goddess worshippers, the vegetarians, the entrepreneurs, the entertainers, the mediators, the meditators, the poets, the anarchists, the fruit sellers, the telephone operators— all of them, every one of them, believes deeply, fully, completely in the rights and value of each individual, including herself. That's the gift Paz gives to each person who decides to stay."

"How does she do that?"

"That you'll find out tomorrow when you meet Paz, and then you'll know all you need to know to decide whether to stay or not."

"We've already made a commitment to stay."

"I know, but some people change their minds at the final stage."

Judith felt uneasy, but was distracted by the sights around them. They were passing through another town, a village, Sarana called it, that reminded Judith of a small version of San Diego. "This is Artemesia," Sarana said. "It's one of the villages that has a constitution and body of laws. Some villages have formalized that sort of thing, though most of them haven't."

"Can people move from village to village?"

"Oh, sure." Sarana looked strangely at Edie, then she smiled. "People can do anything they want on Dega-J."

"I don't suppose there's much of a crime problem," Edie said.

Sarana laughed. "I haven't heard that word in a long time." She laughed again as she rounded a curve and brought them once more where they could view the rocky western shore. "We do have our conflicts, though," she said. "We exchange a lot of words, but no blows...ever. There are no weapons on Dega-J, no jails, no police. It's a different world here. They say about Paz that she didn't like the way the world was and so, because she could, she made another world here on Dega-J, one more to her liking."

Sarana's lilting laughter filled the air again. .

By the time they reached the main house, they had seen an impressive variety of architecture, many modern-looking buildings made of concrete, glass and steel, numerous smaller structures of brick or stone, some of straw, others of wood and even some of canvas. There were some wide, paved streets and many narrow roads. From the hilltops, they could see forests, and, of course, the beaches, for Dega-J was an island.

Sarana pulled into the circular drive of the main house. "This is one of the original buildings," she said. "It was here when Paz bought the island. This building and those..." She pointed to four other buildings of similar architectural style which were visible from the main house. "There were those buildings, the dock, the airstrip and some roads when we first started," Sarana said. "We built the rest."

Judith was not listening. She was scanning faces, looking for Drew, afraid to see her and at the same time itching to. A suitcase in each hand, they followed Sarana inside and to their room on the second floor.

"We'll unload your things and put them in the storage room downstairs until you decide where you want to live," Sarana said. "If you want company, come on down to the lounge on the first floor."

They checked out the room and Edie was eager to go out among the women, talk to them and look around. Judith felt exhausted. The sun was beginning to set, the trip had been a long one, and she was afraid to leave the room. "I think I'll stay here," she said.

Edie looked at her. "Are you all right?"

Judith shrugged her shoulders and nodded at the same time. Edie went to her, sat next to her on the large double bed, and put her arms around her. Judith let her head rest on Edie's shoulder.

"It's a little too much, isn't it?"

Judith nodded.

"OK. Let's lie down together."

Edie removed Judith's shoes and then her own. They lay on the bed talking softly, finally dozing. When they awoke it was very dark and quiet. They went downstairs. No one was around. The wall clock said 3:47.

"I suppose that's a.m.," Edie said.

"I'm hungry."

"I think we missed dinner."

They were in the reception area of the main house. When they'd arrived, there had been scores of women. Now, they were alone in the large, elegant foyer.

"Do you think they have room service?"

Judith giggled nervously, then jumped. A woman had suddenly appeared in front of them. Judith's eyes were wide. "I can't believe it," she said.

The woman smiled broadly and approached her open-armed. "Judith Brodie."

They embraced then moved back and looked at each other.

"I thought you moved to Portland," Judith said.

"I did, and then I moved here. You just arrived?"

Judith nodded.

"Welcome! You'll love it."

"This is Edie Travers. Edie, Angie Boyar. We knew each other back in Chicago, God, eight-nine years ago."

Angie got them snacks and they sat in the small lounge area that looked like Judith's fantasy of a room in India. There were small carved wooden tables with ivory inlay and brightly colored carpets. Angie talked at length of her life for the past eight years at Dega-J because Judith and Edie wanted to hear. She lived in what had been the servants' quarters in the Old Section, she told them, where they were now. Before Paz bought the island, it had been a retreat for the Campion family, the previous owners, and their jet set friends.

"As soon as the health building was finished," Angie said, "I started hanging around there, spending less and less time at my store. Now that's where I do most of my work. In the labs. I got

317

fascinated by the machines, and the people there taught me things. I read like mad, too. I do the X-rays now, EEG's too, and EKG's, blood tests. Back in the states I suppose I'd be called a multi-faceted medical technologist. Here I'm called Angie and I like what I do."

She talked for a long time, reminiscing about the early days and some of the conflicts about whether or not to have officers and laws. "A fabulous woman named Rit Avery mediated the discussions. God, I miss her."

"She's the one who invited us here," Judith said.

"You know Rit?" Angie nearly bounced out of her chair. "Oh, how is she? I haven't seen her for...it seems like years. I guess it's been four or five months. How do you know her?"

"She's a friend of a friend, Drew McAllister." Judith had been waiting for a chance to ask the question. "Do you know her?"

"No. Rit knows lots of woman. I had a terrible crush on her when she was here. I still do, actually. It broke my heart when she left. She was with Paz, but they never became soul-partners. The highlight of my life was the little fling I had with her. I still feed off of it. I know it's just a crush, but, God it was fun."

"Why did she leave?"

Angie smiled. "My guess is that Rit doesn't have the tempera-ment for a place like Dega-J. Some people don't. She thrives on the craziness of the other way, I think. But she stayed three years. That's pretty long for her. I know it was because of Paz."

"They were lovers?"

"Were they! I loved to watch them together. Got a lot of vicarious pleasure from it. That's weird, isn't it? She comes for visits a cou-ple times a year. I love her visits. Jessie understands. She's my soul-partner, like I said. You'll have to meet her."

They talked until they could see the tip of the sun and then the whole ball of it and then they parted and Judith and Edie slept again, nestled in each other's arms until someone knocked on their door and asked if they'd like breakfast.

## 65

Wiley watched the snorkler moving slowly among the gray rocks along the shore, the top of her head, her shoulders and two moons of her bare butt floating above the water line. The swimmer was Wiley's soul-partner, the woman with whom she shared the roomy A-frame up the hill, and with whom she shared her life.

Pulling off her mask, the woman emerged dripping from the sea and came to Wiley. She took the towel Wiley offered and rubbed her hair with it bringing out the auburn highlights. She draped the towel over her tanned shoulders.

"See any mermaids?" Wiley asked.

Paz seemed not to hear. She sat down next to Wiley on the smooth rock. "I wonder if she's changed much."

"Judith?"

They spoke in Esperanto.

"Remember how we used to be, Wiley, Judith and I, before the tornado?"

Wiley's eyes scanned the horizon. "I remember," she said.

Paz looked at her soul-partner and the looking drew Wiley's eyes. "You know it's the friendship love that's survived," Paz said, "nothing that threatens what we have."

"I know."

"I could never stop loving Judith."

Wiley nodded. "She'll be here soon. Sarana said she'd drive her over some time late morning. I'm going to be at the office today, run some data, debug the new program."

"How's it looking so far?" Paz asked. Her toes played with the white pebbles on the ground. "Any findings with the new study?"

"I haven't run that yet, but just eyeballing it, it looks like what I expected—the more pre-zap pathology, the more contradictions in the post-zap self-constructs."

"M-m." Clearly Paz's thoughts had wandered. "Why don't you let me think up the title of your next paper?"

"You don't like my titles?"

"Well, *The Effect of the Coefficient of Cerebral Friction on Cognitive Reverberations and Personality Quirking* is a little awesome, wouldn't you say?"

Wiley chuckled. "Listen carefully, Ms. Paz, I have something important to say. *The Effects of Quasi-hypnotically Induced Core Value Beliefs on Personality Development and Cognitive Restruc-*

*turing*. That's the title. It's clear, succinct and highly communicative."

"Do you hear what I hear?"

They both turned. A rider on an amber mare was galloping toward them. It was a young woman, a beautiful, graceful woman with long flying hair, dressed in white pantaloons and a sea green vest. She dismounted and joined them, handing them each a huge fruit, mangos.

"Hi Wiley, your hair's getting grayer every day. It looks great."

"Thanks, twerp, I'm rather proud of it." Wiley ran her fingers through her hair, then adjusted her wire-frame glasses.

"I'm going to the Health Building today. Angie's going to show me around the labs."

"Sounds good," Paz said. "You might be ready to apprentice to one of the medics soon."

The young woman smiled. "Well, today's the day, huh?"

Paz nodded. "Think you'll remember her?"

"I doubt it."

"She'll remember you."

"How come you didn't invite her sooner, Paz? You've always cared for her."

Paz's green eyes narrowed and then quickly softened again as she looked at her daughter. "She made some very bad mistakes," Paz said, "mistakes that brought me a lot of pain. I guess I'm slow in forgiving."

"They must have been very very bad mistakes."

"They were."

"You don't have to tell me about it."

"Maybe someday. She was the first woman I ever loved."

"Yes, you told me that part."

"How is Gemma?" Paz asked.

"OK. We went into the deep west woods yesterday for herbs. We found belladonna."

"Mm-m. Bring her sometime soon for dinner, Becka. She loved the cheese crepes last time. I'll fix them again."

"I worry about her. She's seeming more old lately."

"She is old, but she has a lot of life left, you can be sure of that. You're not babying her, are you?"

Becka laughed. "She wouldn't let me do that. I do acupuncture for her legs. She says I do it almost as well as she now."

"You had the best teacher."

"I know."

Paz's naked body, nearly twice as old as her daughter's, still was very firm and toned. Often Paz could be found at the water and more times than not, far under it, with her scuba gear and underwater camera. On land or sea, a camera of some sort was usually with her. Paz had made six documentaries of Dega-J, each with a different theme, one feature length dramatic work written by a close friend, Maru, from India, and many experimental films. She found time to throw pots as well, having learned the craft from a Peruvian potter. Paz's pieces could be seen in homes and public buildings and communal houses in many of the villages.

Becka rose. She had grown to be a tall woman, an inch taller than her mother. "See you later, Wiley," she said. "Have a good reunion, Paz. I'll see you tonight."

Both women watched her mount up and ride off down the trail until she disappeared in the hills.

"She's talking more about men, lately," Wiley said. "She's gotten active in the debate."

"Yes, she believes there's no reason that we can't love men as well as each other."

"She's curious, too, I think."

"I can understand that."

"She's borrowed every one of my books about sex-roles," Wiley said. "What she read made her angry, but she concluded that it's as if they've been zapped, men that is, zapped to believe a bunch of nonsense that you could cure."

"She's right," Paz said laughing. "If we end up inviting some males, I think it will work out fine."

"I predict many of us, especially the younger ones, will end up bi-sexual."

Paz laughed. "I haven't heard that term in a long time. If they come, I suppose you'll want to study them."

"Of course. As a matter of fact, I've got a design in mind. It has to do with men's reactions to the..."

Paz was staring at the sea, clearly far away. Wiley knew exactly where her soul-partner's thoughts had gone. She had the same expression she'd had a month and a half ago in their living room, July 14th, the tenth anniversary of the tornado. Although it was ten years ago that day that Paz acquired the power to implant thoughts into others' minds, Wiley knew that what she was remembering was not the magic sliver of mirror, but how wonderful the week before had been, how close she and Judith were.

"You're thinking of her again," Wiley had said that evening in their living room.

Paz's expression did not change. "How do you always know?"

she asked.

"Not so difficult for a trained observer," Wiley said, "or even for a chimpanzee. It happens every year on this day."

Paz nodded sadly and didn't speak right away. "You'd think I could forget about her by now," she said at last.

"I don't think you'll every forget about Judith. She's in your blood."

"Yes. Like Rit. Only it's different with Rit."

"I know. It evolved fully and you and Rit remain good friends. With Judith, it's still hanging. There's more to do."

"I miss her, Wiley." Paz touched Wiley's leg. "I love you more than I've ever loved anyone and I can't imagine that changing, and I have so many good friends, but I still miss Judith. It's strange."

Wiley did not reply.

"I don't think I feel the anger anymore."

"No, not anymore."

"Or the guilt."

"I don't think it's that either," Wiley said.

"There's a longing kind of feeling."

"I know."

Paz's gaze went to the window again. "She's probably forgotten all about me by now."

Wiley reached over and lit a candle. The golden light danced on Paz's troubled face.

"She lives in Denver, you know," Paz said.

"You've managed to keep pretty good track of her over the years."

"She's with a lover there."

"Yes."

"I'm sure I'm just a dim memory to her."

"I doubt that, Paz. Have you thought about writing her or calling?"

Wiley had always resisted making such a suggestion before, hoping Paz would come to it herself. The years kept passing. Life was good for them on Dega-J. They were both very content, yet there was that nagging incomplete part in Paz, as if a slice of her was missing.

Paz shook her head. "I've written her a dozen letters."

Wiley was surprised.

"I never mailed them." Paz suddenly sat up straight. "I have to see her in person," she said as if just realizing it. She stared once more out the window into the twilight. "Maybe I'll go to

Denver."

"You said the same thing last year."

"I know."

"And the year before."

"I'm thinking of inviting her here."

Wiley let her breath out. This is what she'd been waiting to hear. The next day, Paz called Rit, and the day after that Rit called Judith Brodie. Now, a month and a half later, Judith was on Dega-J and very soon the reunion would take place.

Paz pulled the towel off of her shoulders and slipped on her cotton pants and t-shirt. "I think I'll go do some editing while I wait for her," she said, picking up her snorkle tube and mask. "How about you? Are you heading home?"

"No." Wiley pulled her soul-partner gently to her and covered her with her arms and kissed her on the side of her face.

Paz kissed back, moving to Wiley's lips, a deep kiss that aroused them both. "M-m, I love you, woman."

"M-m, I'm glad you do, love. I'll be home before sunset. It will go well with Judith, hon. I'm sure it will."


---

## 66.


Drew could feel them coming. She put her pieces of film away in labeled cans and went onto the porch to wait. Sarana hadn't said exactly what time, but Paz sensed it would be very soon. She sat in the well-used rattan chair and looked down the road. In less than ten minutes she saw the car. It took another two minutes before they pulled up in front of her house and in that two minutes, Drew's mind filled with a hundred pictures, memories of her and Judith, quick flashes and snatches. She saw them laughing in the kitchen, going to a movie together, sharing anger about their boyfriends, riding their mopeds, having a meal, sharing dreams, wondering about life and the future, consoling, being there, giving, and then falling in love. The last picture was of their last night in Greece. They had not made love that night, but stayed up nearly until dawn, talking, touching hands, enjoying what they had, being what they had been for many years, very close friends, and perhaps what they could be again.

Drew went down the porch stairs, her eyes fastened on Judith. Judith was out of the car walking toward Drew. She looks the same, Drew thought, having foolishly worried that she might not recognize her. She looks wonderful. Both of Judith's hands were extended.

Drew took them. "Judith."

"Drew."

Tears blurred their eyes and the embrace felt just as they each had hoped it would. They both knew in that instant that it was not a mistake, that this was how it should be, that they belonged together here on Dega-J.

Sarana watched them from the car. They were both talking at once, and interspersing their words with hugs and touches and tears and laughter. Then they walked up the stairs, their arms around each other, and disappeared into the house.

They talked for hours and the more they did, the more the years disappeared. It was on the upstairs balcony, after they had lunched together, that Drew zapped Judith's memory back, part of it, that is, up until their departure from Greece. She knew without a doubt that Judith's guilt about what had followed their return home from Greece would give her no peace, and so she let those memories remain in oblivion where they belonged.

"Oh my God. Drew, I'm...I'm remembering things. Yes, how could I have forgotten? The rapist, the...me being your guinea pig with Wiley and the eclipse and all that." Judith spoke rapidly as the memories poured back. "That tennis player in Greece, the brothers, Nikos and Yiorgios, and, yes, good old Mrs. Pendleton...Oh, Drew, I...I...it's all coming back...but why? What happened that I forgot it all and now I remember everything."

"I zapped you, Jude. I zapped you to forget ten years ago and I just zapped you to remember again."

They stayed on the balcony for a long time. Drew told Judith about the CIA and the pain of their captivity and how they got away. She told only one lie in all she said. "We never did find out how the CIA got on to us," she concluded, "but it doesn't matter now."

Judith was overwhelmed by the story, and cried and held Drew for the pain and terror of it and for Becka and for Steve.

It was late afternoon then and Drew suggested they go outside. "I want to show you my favorite place," she said. "I've been wanting to show it to you for a long time. I know you'll love it, too."

Arm linked in arm, they made their way down the narrow,

twisting path, a bumpy path with pebbles and rocks and overhanging branches, until they came to a stream.

The two women sat side by side on the little bulge near the pampas grass and stared at the clear, sparkling water as it came from around the upward bend and flowed past them into the cool pool where Drew often swam.

"Now it feels complete," Drew said, squeezing Judith's hand. She laughed. "I'm hopelessly sentimental sometimes."

"I know. That's part of what I love about you."

Flower petals came floating their way. Children playing upstream, Drew knew.

"It feels like this is where I belong," Judith said, "though I didn't really know..."

"It's like the circle is finally closed."

First there was one petal and then two, followed by more and more. When the petals reached the pond, they formed a colorful grouping, blues and reds, white, violet, lavender, yellows, many sizes and shapes, coming together on the surface of the clear pond water, overlapping, joining, creating a varied harmonious carpet of color.

They talked of Dega-J while sitting at the pond. Judith's eyes gleamed as she listened. "I'm ready for the zap, *Paz*," she said, when she had learned it all.

Drew smiled. "All right." She turned slightly to face her friend. "Listen carefully, Judith, for I have something very important to say to you." A narrow beam of sunlight filtered over Drew's shoulder and across Judith's cheek. "*You realize that you are inherently valuable and worthwhile. You realize that every other human being is inherently valuable and worthwhile, as well. You wish to maximize your own fulfillment in life while respecting and cherishing others' wishes and rights to search for their fulfillment, in their own ways. You do not want to impose your will, your preferences, or your ideas on others. You get no pleasure in other's pain, nor in besting them. You wish to seek compassionate, empathic resolutions of conflict with others, and true understanding and acceptance of differences among human beings.*"

"I don't feel any different," Judith said when it was over. "Well, wait...maybe a little." She closed her eyes. "There's a certain peacefulness." She looked at the pond with its potpourri of colorful flower petals. "And also the sense that there's so much I want to do, to experience. I feel like I've come home."

That night five women had dinner together, Wiley and Paz and Becka and Judith and Edie, and then they went to the main house for a party being hosted by the women of Carpediem, one of the mountain villages. They danced to drums and flutes and later to electric guitars and then they waltzed.

The floor of the huge ballroom was filled with women of every size and shape, with skin from deep rich black to tawny brown and lighter and lighter to almost white, wearing costumes of every color, pattern and design. They made a vibrant grouping as they came together on the dance floor, interspersing, joining, creating a rich varied harmonious blend, each one adding her uniqueness and helping form the whole.

A few of the publications of
THE NAIAD PRESS, INC.
P.O. Box 10543 • Tallahassee, Florida 32302
*Mail orders welcome. Please include 15% postage.*

WINGED DANCER by Camarin Grae. 228 pp. Erotic Lesbian
adventure story. ISBN 0-930044-88-6   $8.95

PAZ by Camarin Grae. 336 pp. Romantic Lesbian adventurer
with the power to change the world.   ISBN 0-930044-89-4   8.95

SOUL SNATCHER by Camarin Grae. 224 pp. A puzzle, an
adventure, a mystery—exciting Lesbian romance.
ISBN 0-930044-90-8   8.95

THE LOVE OF GOOD WOMEN by Isabel Miller. 224 pp.
Long-awaited new novel by the author of the beloved *Patience
and Sarah*. ISBN 0-930044-81-9   8.95

THE HOUSE AT PELHAM FALLS by Brenda Weathers. 240
pp. Suspenseful Lesbian ghost story.   ISBN 0-930044-79-7   7.95

HOME IN YOUR HANDS by Lee Lynch. 240 pp. More stories
from the author of *Old Dyke Tales*.   ISBN 0-930044-80-0   7.95

EACH HAND A MAP by Anita Skeen. 112 pp. Real-life poems
that touch us all. ISBN 0-930044-82-7   6.95

SURPLUS by Sylvia Stevenson. 342 pp. A classic early
Lesbian novel. ISBN 0-930044-78-9   7.95

PEMBROKE PARK by Michelle Martin. 256 pp. Derring-do
and daring romance in Regency England.
ISBN 0-930044-77-0   7.95

THE LONG TRAIL by Penny Hayes. 248 pp. Vivid adventures
of two women in love in the old west.   ISBN 0-930044-76-2   8.95

HORIZON OF THE HEART by Shelley Smith. 192 pp.
Sizzling romance in summertime New England.
ISBN 0-930044-75-4   7.95

AN EMERGENCE OF GREEN by Katherine V. Forrest. 288
pp. Powerful novel of sexual discovery.   ISBN 0-930044-69-X   8.95

THE LESBIAN PERIODICALS INDEX edited by Claire
Potter. 432 pp. Author and subject index.
ISBN 0-930044-74-6   29.95

DESERT OF THE HEART by Jane Rule. 224 pp. A classic;
basis for the movie *Desert Hearts*.   ISBN 0-930044-73-8   7.95

SPRING FORWARD/FALL BACK by Sheila Ortiz Taylor.
288 pp. Literary novel of timeless love.   ISBN 0-930044-70-3   7.95

FOR KEEPS by Elisabeth Nonas. 144 pp. Contemporary novel
about losing and finding love.   ISBN 0-930044-71-1   7.95

TORCHLIGHT TO VALHALLA by Gale Wilhelm. 128 pp.
Classic novel by a great Lesbian writer.   ISBN 0-930044-68-1   7.95

LESBIAN NUNS: BREAKING SILENCE edited by Rosemary
Curb and Nancy Manahan. 432 pp. Unprecedented auto-
biographies of religious life.   ISBN 0-930044-62-2   9.95

TO THE CLEVELAND STATION by Carol Anne Douglas.
192 pp. Interracial Lesbian love story. ISBN 0-930044-27-4   6.95

THE NESTING PLACE by Sarah Aldridge. 224 pp. Historical
novel, a three-woman triangle. ISBN 0-930044-26-6   7.95

THIS IS NOT FOR YOU by Jane Rule. 284 pp. A letter to a
beloved is also an intricate novel. ISBN 0-930044-25-8   7.95

FAULTLINE by Sheila Ortiz Taylor. 140 pp. Warm, funny,
literate story of a startling family. ISBN 0-930044-24-X   6.95

THE LESBIAN IN LITERATURE by Barbara Grier. 3d ed.
Foreword by Maida Tilchen. 240 pp. A comprehensive
bibliography. Literary ratings; rare photographs.
ISBN 0-930044-23-1   7.95

ANNA'S COUNTRY by Elizabeth Lang. 208 pp. A woman
finds her Lesbian identity. ISBN 0-930044-19-3   6.95

PRISM by Valerie Taylor. 158 pp. A love affair between two
women in their sixties. ISBN 0-930044-18-5   6.95

BLACK LESBIANS: AN ANNOTATED BIBLIOGRAPHY
compiled by J.R. Roberts. Foreword by Barbara Smith. 112
pp. Award winning bibliography. ISBN 0-930044-21-5   5.95

THE MARQUISE AND THE NOVICE by Victoria Ramstetter.
108 pp. A Lesbian Gothic novel. ISBN 0-930044-16-9   4.95

LABIAFLOWERS by Tee A. Corinne. 40 pp. Drawings by the
noted artist/photographer. ISBN 0-930044-20-7   3.95

OUTLANDER by Jane Rule. 207 pp. Short stories and essays
by one of our finest writers. ISBN 0-930044-17-7   6.95

SAPPHISTRY: THE BOOK OF LESBIAN SEXUALITY by
Pat Califia. 2d edition, revised. 195 pp. ISBN 0-930044-47-9   7.95

ALL TRUE LOVERS by Sarah Aldridge. 292 pp. Romantic
novel set in the 1930s and 1940s. ISBN 0-930044-10-X   7.95

A WOMAN APPEARED TO ME by Renee Vivien. 65 pp. A
classic; translation by Jeannette H. Foster.
ISBN 0-930044-06-1   5.00

CYTHEREA'S BREATH by Sarah Aldridge. 240 pp. Women
first entering medicine and the law: a novel.
ISBN 0-930044-02-9   6.95

TOTTIE by Sarah Aldridge. 181 pp. Lesbian romance in the
turmoil of the sixties. ISBN 0-930044-01-0   6.95

THE LATECOMER by Sarah Aldridge. 107 pp. A delicate love
story set in days gone by. ISBN 0-930044-00-2   5.00

ODD GIRL OUT by Ann Bannon     ISBN 0-930044-83-5   5.95
I AM A WOMAN by Ann Bannon.     ISBN 0-930044-84-3   5.95
WOMEN IN THE SHADOWS by Ann Bannon.
ISBN 0-930044-85-1   5.95
JOURNEY TO A WOMAN by Ann Bannon.
ISBN 0-930044-86-X   5.95
BEEBO BRINKER by Ann Bannon     ISBN 0-930044-87-8   5.95

Legendary novels written in the fifties and sixties,
set in the gay mecca of Greenwich Village.

## VOLUTE BOOKS

| | | |
|---|---|---|
| JOURNEY TO FULFILLMENT | Early classics by Valerie | 3.95 |
| A WORLD WITHOUT MEN | Taylor: The Erika Frohmann | 3.95 |
| RETURN TO LESBOS | series. | 3.95 |

These are just a few of the many Naiad Press titles—we are the oldest and largest lesbian/feminist publishing company in the world. Please request a complete catalog. We offer personal service; we encourage and welcome direct mail orders from individuals who have limited access to bookstores carrying our publications.